D0811154

Tynnwyd o Stoc
Withdrawn from stock

I've travelled the world twice over,
Met the famous: saints and sinners,
Poets and artists, kings and queens,
Old stars and hopeful beginners,
I've been where no-one's been before,
Learned secrets from writers and cooks
All with one library ticket
To the wonderful world of books.

© JANICE JAMES.

THE STONY PLACES

Rob Craigallan had built an empire from the wealth of wheat. By 1900 he was one of the richest men in America. But who would inherit the wheatfields, the mills and ship-yards? Who could play the stockmarket and move through the Washington intrigues with Rob's nerve and skill? Rob had always chosen power first and love second, but now the bitter fruit of that hard choice reaches out to stain his children's lives. A brilliant and moving sequel to *A Sower went Forth*.

*Books by Tessa Barclay in the
Ulverscroft Large Print Series:*

**A SOWER WENT FORTH
THE STONY PLACES**

TESSA BARCLAY

THE STONY PLACES

Complete and Unabridged

ULVERSCROFT
Leicester

First Large Print Edition
published June 1984
by arrangement with
W. H. Allen & Co. Ltd.
London

Copyright © 1981 by Tessa Barclay

British Library CIP Data

Barclay, Tessa
    The stony places.—Large print ed.
(Ulverscroft Large Print Series: general fiction)
I. Title
823'.914 [F]   PR6052.A

ISBN 0-7089-1137-4

GWASANAETH LLYFRGELL CLWYD
RHIF
DOSBARTH
CLASS NUMBER
RS F
1392
UL
CLWYD LIBRARY SERVICE

Published by
F. A. Thorpe (Publishing) Ltd.
Anstey, Leicestershire

Printed and Bound in Great Britain by
T. J. Press (Padstow) Ltd., Padstow, Cornwall

1

THE news had come by telegraph, since the telephone was not yet installed at Craigallan Castle. In fact, there was some doubt whether Mr. Craigallan was going to allow this new-fangled invention into his new home, on the grounds that it didn't fit in with the sixteenth-century ambience he was creating. Soames the butler hoped the embargo wouldn't hold. He came from the household of an Ohio millionaire, where every latest convenience of 1894 was installed, including the telephone, gas lighting, and an Acme Brilliant Hard Coal Heater in the servants' hall.

Soames was comforting himself with a cup of piping hot coffee and a piece of Nellie's pumpkin pie. He had been summoned from them by the telegraph boy. "Can't understand why he's given us such short notice," he groaned as he subsided into his chair and picked up his fork again. "The house won't be comfortable to live in for another month, you know, Nellie."

The black woman shrugged as she brought a cup of fresh coffee to replace the one that had gone cold. "Mr. Rob, he always move fast when he makes a decision," she remarked.

"Yes, but what's the point, Nellie? Why not wait a few more weeks so we can get everything spandy for him? And warm." The butler stretched out his feet towards the glowing cook-range that took up one side of the kitchen. "Great old stone place like this," he mourned, "it's never going to be warm until we've had the steam-heat going for at least a month."

Nellie made no reply. It seemed to her pointless to question Rob Craigallan's decisions. He was coming tomorrow: so said the message from the Waldorf Astoria in Manhattan: "Arriving Wednesday. Prepare as many rooms as possible, at least two beds."

The original plan had been to have the house-warming at Christmas, when the unmade gardens would be hidden in snow and the house itself, with its sixteenth-century air, would look good for Christmas parties. Nellie understood that Rob had intended to stay on throughout spring to supervise the planting of the grounds, travelling now and then to New York City or to Chicago as business required.

Nellie had come from Rob's house at Brown Bridge on the Great Plains to keep an eye on the setting up of Craigallan Castle. The newly-hired butler might think he was in charge, but Nellie knew that Rob's trust lay with her. Old acquaintance bound them together; she had known the millionaire wheat tycoon since he was a farm boy at the Van Huten farm in New York State. She didn't know why her employer was coming so soon, but expected him to bring his daughter, Ellie-Rose.

2

"If you want to tell me what you need, I'll send a boy with the grocery order," Soames said, picking up his pencil. He had some tact; he had guessed that Nellie, born on a plantation before the Civil War, could neither read nor write.

"Well, we better have three or four dozen eggs, Willie, and two pounds o' fresh butter to see us over the weekend, and we're low on coffee. We got plenty sugar and tea—Mis' Ellie-Rose likes tea if she home in the afternoon. I reckon we better have four pounds o' shortenin', and a good piece o' Swiss cheese—Mister Rob enjoys that. You chose a butcher yet, Willie?"

"Not yet. Haven't had time."

"You better take me to the shops, then. I'll take a look and see what's good. I think a nice veal fillet in breadcrumbs would just be easy to serve, makes no difference what time he arrives tomorrow. An' I can do a *crème brulée*. That's easy on the stomach after a man's been shiftin' hisself over them bad roads from Manhattan."

Willie was still apt to be surprised at the range of Nellie's cooking ability. So far he knew little about her and would have been surprised to learn how well she had been schooled at the Van Huten farm all those years ago.

The butler had gathered there was no Mrs. Craigallan coming to live in the Castle. He knew a Mrs. Craigallan existed, for he had seen her photograph in the society magazines. For some reason, Mr. and Mrs. Craigallan kept separate establishments.

At first Soames had been a little perturbed about this. But discreet inquiries among the bellboys at the Waldorf Astoria had unearthed the information that though Mr. Craigallan had lady friends whom he visited in other parts of Manhattan, there was no mistress in residence anywhere.

At Craigallan Castle, once the place was straight and the workmen had gone, events would follow a tranquil routine. There would be small parties from time to time for Miss Ellie-Rose Craigallan, the young lady, and business dinners for the master. Big occasions at Christmas and New Year and perhaps Fourth of July, although he gathered Miss Craigallan preferred Long Island in summer. He had asked pointblank, at his interview with Mr. Craigallan, how many there would be in the family. The reassuring answer had been, "Myself and my daughter only, as a rule. My son Cornelius has apartments of his own in New York and Chicago."

The butler was finishing the shopping list when he heard the bell clanging at the front door.

He forestalled the chambermaid, Kitty, and went to answer it. A plump, pretty woman in her early forties surged in, bringing with her the scent of gardenia perfume and fresh air trapped in the folds of her sable wrap.

"Pay the cabbie," she commanded, "and have my trunk brought in. What's your name?"

Soames had recognised her at once from photographs in the newspapers. This was Mrs. Craigallan, Luisa, the wife whom he had expected to stay in her own circles in New York and Albany.

"I'm Soames, madam, the butler," he said, bowing.

"Very well. See to the cab and then come to me in the drawing-room." She walked, without need of directions, into the room beyond the new Tiffany glass doors. She had been here before, he understood. With an inward groan he went to deal with the cabbie and the luggage.

Luisa threw off her wrap over the back of a leather Chesterfield. There was no fire in the great stone hearth but she would have it lit as soon as Soames reported to her. She surveyed the room. Really, it still needed a great deal done to it. Why Rob had to be so stubborn and refuse her help she didn't know! Her brother Julius was an expert on the decorating and furnishing of houses, had even been able to make a career out of it—why couldn't Rob avail himself of his talents?

She paced to the windows and looked out on the terrace. Stone urns and benches graced it. Beyond that a wilderness of mud stretched to a clump of trees which surrounded, as she knew, a small lake. In winter it would be possible to have skating parties. That would be fun. Luisa knew she looked her best muffled in silks and furs, rosy from the cold, gliding with unexpected grace on the glittering surface of the ice.

On the whole Luisa approved of Craigallan Castle. Her daughter Ellie-Rose kept laughing about it, saying it was vulgar, but Luisa could see

5

nothing worse in the Castle than in some of the houses recently put up by other rich men: Andrew Carnegie's Italian Classic edifice, for instance, or that Castle of Chenonceau that had been put up on Fifth Avenue.

Luisa's arrival at the Castle was part of a plan laid a long time ago. Earlier in the year she had offered her services to her estranged husband as housekeeper and hostess of his new home but had been tersely rebuffed.

Her plan was quite simple—to move in now, on her return from her summer vacation, and be in residence when Rob arrived a few weeks later to supervise preparations for the housewarming. She was, after all, his legal wife.

The butler came into the drawing-room after a discreet tap on the Tiffany doors. "Your luggage is indoors, ma'am," he announced.

"Yes, well . . . Soames, did you say your name was? The next thing is to light the fire so that I can be comfortable—"

"If you'll excuse me, ma'am, there hasn't been a fire—"

"I'm not interested in what there hasn't been," she interrupted on a sharp note. Just as well to put him in his place at the outset. "I'm telling you what I want now. Light the fire, and then show me which rooms are ready upstairs. While I choose a bedroom you can have a light meal made ready. I suppose the dining-room is furnished?"

"No, ma'am. And as to rooms upstairs—"

"Don't bother to describe them. Just show me."

She waited, tapping her foot, while he put a light to the kindling that was set ready in the fireplace. The flame licked and caught, smoke crept round the sides of the billets of wood. Then the smoke, instead of rising and disappearing up the chimney, billowed out into the room.

In a moment Luisa was coughing and choking in exaggerated reaction. "Good God, can't you even light a fire, Soames?"

"It's what I was trying to tell you, ma'am. There hasn't been a fire lit in this fireplace yet—the chimney hasn't had time to draw."

"I can see I've a lot to do here before the place is liveable," Luisa said, waving a hand in front of her face. "Very well, while it clears, show me the bedrooms."

"Very good, ma'am." Soames had decided it was useless to argue or explain. She was determined to take charge, and as far as he could see he was powerless to prevent her. He led the way.

On the first floor a gallery led round the flag-stoned hall on two sides. Oaken doors with arched tops opened off it. Ellie-Rose had said they suggested the discomfort of monastic cells, but Luisa found them rather impressive. Soames opened the first two then walked on. Luisa halted and looked in at the opening of the first room. She saw a capacious bedroom, furnished so far with only the basis of the eventual decor—rose pink carpet, dark oak furniture, a reproduction four-

7

poster bed without the hangings, curtains not yet up at the windows. The next room was the same except the carpet was blue.

"Which of these rooms is my husband going to occupy?"

"Neither of those, Mrs. Craigallan. I thought . . . er . . ."

"Show me his room."

He led her along the passage leading off the gallery. The door he opened showed a room much larger than the others, with windows on two sides. More had been done to finish the decorations here. The bed was made, curtains hung at the windows, toilet articles were laid out on the dressing table.

Luisa was impressed. Rob had never allowed her upstairs on the occasions when she had dropped in on him while the house was under construction, but now that she saw the accommodation she was stricken with envy. Years ago she had left her husband, refusing to travel with him out to the Plains to start again after the old Van Huten lands were lost to them. Her later attempt at a reconciliation had come to nothing through her own clumsiness and bad timing. Since then, as Rob became richer and richer, she had wanted very much to be mistress of his household if not of his heart; she knew he would never really like her, that he perhaps never had liked her even when he first married her, but she felt she could be a social asset to him now that he had a place in New York society.

8

She longed for the courage to say to the butler, "Have my trunk brought up and put in this room." But discretion was the better part of valour. If Rob found her in possession of this room when he arrived, he was quite capable of throwing her out bodily, in front of the servants. She wanted to stay in Craigallan Castle, so it was better to choose a room other than the master bedroom.

"Which room is my daughter to have?"

"This way, ma'am." The butler led her back to the gallery and to the passage off the other end. Here a bedroom was partly-prepared but likely to be even more luxurious than Rob's, and Luisa felt a pang of jealousy that Ellie-Rose held so firm a place in Rob's heart. When Ellie-Rose moved into Craigallan Castle, she would live in circumstances of comfort and ease such as Luisa herself had never yet known.

"I'll use this room," she announced. "Have the bed made up."

"But, Mrs. Craigallan—"

"Have my trunk brought up. I want to change out of my travelling dress."

Defeated, Soames withdrew. He summoned one of the gardeners indoors and, after making the man take off his boots so that no mud should stain the new flagstones of the hall, ordered him to take up the trunk. Then he sent Kitty to unpack for the master's wife.

Nellie had already been alerted that a lady had

9

arrived, with her luggage; Soames's description left her in little doubt it was Luisa.

"What you done?" she cried. "You ain't let her move into the house?"

"What else could I do?" Soames protested. "She's Mrs. Craigallan, isn't she?"

"You wait till Mister Rob get here. He'll have the hide off'n you!"

"It's not my fault. It's not my *place* to prevent Mr. Craigallan's wife from coming into her husband's house." Soames threw himself onto a chair. "If you want her to leave, you go and tell her."

"Yes, an' I will," Nellie said. She took off her apron, patted her thick black hair, straightened the front of her bodice, and marched out of the kitchen, to the consternation of the butler.

Kitty was laying garments out on the bed for Luisa to choose a gown, before the rest were hung in the closet. She looked up in surprise as the cook walked in, without even troubling to give more than a token knock. Nellie jerked her head at her. Kitty, astounded, looked for orders to Luisa. "Get on with your work, girl," Luisa said.

"You go out in the passage, Kitty," Nellie said. "Go on, git!"

Once more Kitty looked at the master's wife. But this time she received a shrug. Bewildered, the chambermaid went out.

"You're taking a great deal on yourself, Nellie," Luisa said with annoyance. "I didn't send for you!"

10

"No, and Mister Rob didn't send for *you*. Mis' Luisa, what you think you doin' here?"

"I'm joining my husband in his new home."

"You pokin' in where you ain't wanted. If Mr. Rob had been here when you arrived, you'd have gone out a'most as quick as you come in." Nellie narrowed her black eyes. "But you knew he wasn't here, didn't you?"

"It's none of your business what I knew—"

"Listen, Mis' Luisa, we known each other a long time. It's no use trying to faze me. You thought you'd slip in here and get you'self rock-steady before Mister Rob came. But you made a mistake. Mister Rob, he comin' tomorrow. We got orders to get some rooms ready. So ef'n you got sense, you'll have your things put back in that trunk and you take you'self off, quick's grease in a skillet."

"He's coming tomorrow?" Luisa was taken aback. She'd expected to have longer to make herself part of the establishment, to have done useful things to the house, to have supervised some of the cleaning and readying, so that she would have some claim on Rob. Even if in the end she failed to make herself a permanent resident her stay would do something to establish a myth in New York society, that she and Rob were on good terms.

She wanted very much to be the hostess of Craigallan Castle. She was tired of shifting from place to place, making her home with relatives. Luisa hoped, by being very good and helpful, to inveigle herself into Rob's good books. She didn't expect to

11

live with him as his wife; all that was over—and she regretted that, too, the more she saw Rob out and about in New York. He had worn well, better than she had herself. At forty-two he was still upright, slender and vigorous, with a head of thick russet-coloured hair untouched by grey. He'd resisted the fashion which ordained that men over thirty must become portly. He was still clean-shaven although he'd let his sideboards grow as a slight concession to fashion.

She had seen other women turn as he walked by. She had heard them speak of him. "So attractive! A really goodlooking man!" Some went so far as to call him "fascinating". When she recalled that she could have been at his side now, enjoying the prestige of such a husband, Luisa could have kicked herself. Thirteen years before she had made a wrong decision, refusing to face the prospect of poverty and hardship out on the wheat-belt where Rob hoped to make a new life. Thirteen years ago she'd preferred to go and live with Mama. It was the worst mistake she'd ever made in a life which, in general, had been cosy enough. From time to time she dreamed of putting it all right again, and this visit to Craigallan Castle was her latest ploy.

But Nellie's words gave her a shock. She'd hoped to have a week or two to get a grip on the household. Of course she knew that her arrival here couldn't be kept secret from Rob, that eventually he would have come from New York to find out what the devil she was up to. But she'd intended to make

12

him feel some small gratitude, and perhaps let her stay on a while. Why not? The place was big enough. They need hardly see each other, even if Rob were to take up residence.

"He's coming tomorrow?" she said. "I understood he wasn't moving in until late fall?"

"That's what he always said, but we got word he coming tomorrow. Listen, Mis' Luisa, the las' thing you want is for him to be put in a bad temper the minute he set foot in the door. Why don' you pack and go, while half your things is still in the trunk?"

Luisa was uncertain. She didn't want to face Rob so soon. Yet if she packed up and scuttled away, how was it going to look to the servants? How would she ever gain any control over them when in the end she came back to be mistress of the household?

And she was tired. Travelling exhausted her these days. She wasn't as young as she used to be, after all. Although Rob made her a handsome allowance, it wasn't like travelling with her own retinue, with her own husband to handle the tiresome details. From time to time Luisa had had a lover to take care of such matters, but at the moment she was alone. Perhaps it was for this reason she'd felt so drawn to the idea of settling into Craigallan Castle.

She made up her mind. "Send the girl back to finish my unpacking," she said. "I'm not moving from this place tonight—I've travelled enough for one day."

"You makin' a big mistake," warned Nellie. But

13

she knew that tone of old, that self-pitying, stubborn note in Luisa's voice. She had been in the old Van Huten household from the time that Luisa was a little girl, spoiled and indulged; she knew Luisa wouldn't budge from her decision to stay.

She went out. What should she do now? Send a message to the Waldorf, telling Mr. Rob what had happened?

The only problem was that Nellie couldn't read or write. She'd have to ask Soames to check the telegram when they sent it from Carmansville. She put this to the butler as they hurried out to attend to the ordering of supplies, even more important now that Mrs. Craigallan had arrived so unexpectedly.

Soames shook his head. "I'm not sending any message," he said, "and I'm not taking part in sending one."

"But Mister Rob ought to be tole—"

"Look, Nellie, you know this pair from way back. But I'm a stranger. I don't want to get the reputation of poking my nose into my employer's private affairs. After all, Nellie, he'll be here tomorrow. What's so important about letting him know twenty-four hours ahead?"

She hesitated.

"You can meet him at the door," Soames continued, pressing his advantage as he saw her uncertainty. "You seem to be an old acquaintance of his so you can talk to him in a way I couldn't. Come on, Nellie, make it easy on us. We don't want to

14

start off by sending urgent messages to the master about his wife!"

She understood his unwillingness. He had given up a good place with Mr. Hanna, didn't want to jeopardise his post here. "All right," she said, but not with any conviction that it was the best thing to do.

Luisa didn't concern herself with the opinions of the servants. So long as she had a good meal served to her in her room, and had a good fire to sit by in the evening, she was happy enough. She had a novel to read for entertainment. She went to bed late, slept well, rose to find a squall of rain drenching the late morning, and sent for breakfast in bed.

Thus Nellie was occupied when the carriage bringing Rob Craigallan swept up the rain-soaked drive. The wet gravel gave out less sound than on a dry day. The gardeners had taken refuge in a half-built summerhouse, the grooms were getting the stables ready for the horses that would occupy them when the master bought them, no one was about to see the carriage come in. Even Soames, generally very alert, was on his knees in the library at the back of the house, making a trial of the new chimney with a few sheets of newspaper and some twigs.

He was summoned by the peal of the front door bell. Instantly alarmed, he leapt up. He was about to dash to the kitchen for Nellie, but the bell clanged again. He dared not delay. He hurried into

15

the hall, pulling on his coat. His hands were dirty from dealing with the burnt paper. He tried to keep them out of sight as he opened the door.

"Come on, Soames, where the devil have you been?" Rob said, stepping in. "What're you thinking of, keeping us outside on a wet day like this!"

"Sorry sir, we were expecting you closer to lunchtime—"

"This is close to lunchtime," Rob said, with impatience. He'd never lost his farmer's habit of early rising, and to him ten-thirty was well into the day. "We'll keep that front door unlocked from now on," he added. "No need for a key now we're going to be staying here."

"Yes, sir. Er . . . Mr. Craigallan—"

"Come in, come in," his employer said to someone still on the threshold. "Don't stand there hovering in the damp."

To the butler's astonishment, a boy walked in.

He looked about eleven years old, neatly dressed in short jacket, knickerbockers, a soft-collared shirt and loose scarf-tie, topped with a tweed cap. One look at him was enough to establish that he was some relation to the master—the same russet hair, the same pale clear skin, even something of the same features. The eyes were different, however, a rich dark brown, not Craigallan's grey.

"This is Gregor. Gregor, this is Soames, the butler. If you want anything, ring for Soames and he'll fetch it."

16

"Yes, sir," the boy said in a baffled voice.

"You'll find some cases and a valise in the carriage," Rob went on to the butler. "The coachman will help you bring them in. Are the grooms here yet?"

"Yes, Mr. Craigallan, they—"

"Well, tell them to put the carriage away and see to the horses. They're pretty tired—it's a rotten climb up the Heights in this weather."

"Yes, sir. Mr. Craigallan—"

"We'll have some coffee and cake in the drawing-room as soon as you've seen to the luggage. The drawing-room is furnished?"

"Yes, sir. But I must just tell you, sir—"

"Later, later. It's a dreary day, and a dreary welcome to your new home, Gregor. You'd like some cake, wouldn't you?"

"Yes, sir," the boy said, but not as if he cared one way or the other.

"Look lively then, Soames. Come on, Gregor, I'll show you the upstairs rooms and you can choose which one you want."

"Mr. Craigallan!" cried Soames in desperation.

"Will you get on with your job and stop bleating?" Rob said, turning a cold glance on him. The man's hovering manner annoyed him. He'd wanted to bring Gregor into the house with something of a flourish of trumpets, but the bad weather, the dismal appearance of the grounds as they drove up, the need to ring for admittance as if the place were locked against them, and now the butler's unwelcoming attitude—all these had spoiled the arrival.

Eager to please the boy, Rob hurried to the staircase and led the way up. He opened the same doors on the first floor that Soames had opened for Luisa's surveyal. "Have whichever you please," he urged. "You can see the drive from this one, and from the window of the one next door you can just glimpse the paddock."

"I'll take this one, thank you, Mr. Craigallan," Gregor said.

"Sure? Well, all right, try it, and if you want to change after a day or so, that's all right. Twenty-eight bedrooms, boy—you can sleep in a different one every night for four weeks once we've got the place fitted up." Rob laughed, with more enthusiasm than the idea really merited, but he wanted to inject some jollity into the occasion.

The boy smiled obediently. He walked into the bedroom, went to the window, ascertained that indeed you could see the end of the drive from there, opened a door in the wall to see a big clothes closet, opened another to find a bathroom. This house must be almost as big as the Waldorf Astoria Hotel, he told himself, and almost as well supplied with bathrooms if every bedroom had one.

Watching him, Rob sighed a little. He'd felt it was urgent to move out of the hotel. It was all right for himself and for Ellie-Rose, but for an eleven-year-old it was an unnatural environment. Even though Craigallan Castle was unfinished, he'd felt

18

it would be more suitable for Gregor. It might even be fun for the youngster, helping to choose the equipment and the horses.

Soon Ellie-Rose would be here. However much she might tease about the place, telling him it was grandiose, she wouldn't let him down when it came to making it into a home. It needed a woman's touch, he told himself. At the moment it was cold and unfriendly, but once Ellie-Rose had got to work on it, set vases of flowers in the right places, and all that kind of thing . . . then it would have a different atmosphere.

And Gregor—Rob was sure there wasn't a boy in the world who wouldn't get fun out of being let loose in the new stables.

He stole a glance at the lad. He was standing by the door that opened on to the bathroom, absently, his gaze on the carpet. As far as it was possible to guess from his expression, his thoughts were miles from Craigallan Castle.

But who could tell? In the few days that Gregor had been in his charge, Rob had learnt very little about him. He was quiet, self-contained, almost distant. Always polite, always obedient, but there was nothing forthcoming about him. Rod had heard one of the maids at the Waldorf describing him to another as "old-fashioned". But it wasn't quite that. Rob knew what the term usually meant—a child shy and over-dependent on adults. Gregor wasn't like that. He was quite independent. He simply seemed to be very much a person, not

19

unformed as most children are, but complete, in command of his character.

"Come on, boy," Rob said with cheerfulness. "Come and take a look at the rest of the place. I'll show you where I'll be sleeping."

He led the way along the gallery, into the corridor and to the spacious room he'd set aside for himself. "When Ellie-Rose gets here she'll be in a room like this, off the other side of the gallery," he explained. "Come on, I'll show you."

He wouldn't have admitted it for the world, but he was trying to impress the child. He took him back to the gallery, chatting rather loudly to still the echoes he caused. They were approaching the room intended for Ellie-Rose when its door flew open.

Luisa had heard the sound of their approach, and her heart had come into her throat on recognition of Rob's voice. She was angry with herself; she should have been up and dressed when he arrived. Rumpled and with her hair in a mess, she was at a disadvantage. The time had long gone by when Luisa looked her best without the aid of hairpads, tortoise-shell combs, curling tongs, and a little rice powder on her too-pink cheeks.

She stood in the doorway, barefoot and clutching her peignoir across her rounded bosom. She was hunting in her mind for some phrase of greeting that would disarm her husband.

He had stopped dead at sight of her. She saw the spark of anger flare in his grey eyes, and felt a thrill of alarm.

20

Behind him appeared a child, a boy in neat but inexpensive clothing. She had never seen him before. One glance at his face told her he was Rob's child; the resemblance was too great to be otherwise.

All her good intentions vanished at sight of him. Her unpredictable temper surged up within her.

"And who the hell is *that*?" she cried. Which was not how she'd intended to begin her plea to be allowed to stay at Craigallan Castle.

2

THE shrill tone acted on Rob like a dash of cold water. He jerked his head at the boy. "Go downstairs, Gregor. Soames will bring you the cake and coffee in the drawing-room—that's through that arch with the glass doors."

"Yes, sir," Gregor said, obediently turning.

Rob moved forward, pushing Luisa into the bedroom. The door closed behind them.

"Now," he said, "what are you doing here, Luisa?"

"I'd have thought that was obvious. I'm staying here."

"That's not what I mean. Why are you here?"

"Well," she flared, "I thought it was time you and I sorted out our differences and lived together like decent people. I thought we'd make a new start at Craigallan Castle. I didn't know you were bringing your little by-blow here!"

"Luisa—"

"When does his mama arrive? You're a sneaky one, Rob—you always let on you'd lost touch with her after she ran away from Brown Bridge."

"Sit down." He shoved her urgently on to the only chair as yet available in the room. "God, you look a mess," he said, knowing it would hurt her and put her off balance. "You eat too much, Luisa. You'll soon be like a pork barrel."

She went red, drew her peignoir's lace up to her throat, and tried to smooth back her tangled hair. "I wasn't expecting you so early," she said.

"So early? It's a quarter before eleven. When did you get here?"

"Yesterday. Your man told me you were expected today. But not about the boy."

"He didn't know. No one knows as yet, except Ellie-Rose—"

"You've involved Ellie-Rose in your sneaky affairs—?"

"Luisa, don't talk nonsense. If you look back you'll remember that Ellie-Rose lived at Brown Bridge with me and—"

"And your mistress!" she flashed.

"With Morag, yes. Ellie-Rose was fond of her. Morag was more of a mother to that girl than you ever were, Luisa, and you know it."

"Oh, it suited her to act the part, I've no doubt! She was always a sly one—"

To her surprise, Rob laughed. It was a bark of unamused laughter. "Sly? That's the last word in the world to use about Morag McGarth. She was always too honest, too open. If she'd been sly, she wouldn't have given up her post in Boston to come and help me start all over again on the Plains. If she'd been sly, she'd have outstayed you when you turned up at Brown Bridge, Luisa. And she wouldn't have brought up that kid single-handed, without a cent of money from me, for all these years."

Luisa peered up at him. His face was strained, anxious. "Where is she, then?" she demanded. "Morag?"

"She's gone to a sanatorium in the Rockies."

"A sanatorium?" Luisa drew away from him, as if he might carry with him the taint of Morag McGarth's disease. "What is it, her lungs?"

He nodded. "I just found her a couple of weeks ago—after all these years, Luisa. And she was so ill the doctor said her one chance was to go to the mountains—"

"So she cadged some money from you and left her little bastard on your hands—"

"Be quiet," he said in a tone that warned her she had gone too far. "I don't expect you to believe this, because it's so totally unlike the way you'd have behaved, but she didn't even get in touch with me until she thought she might be dying, and needed to make some provision for the boy. It was Gregor who actually sent for me. Morag was too ill to do it."

"So he sent for his great big rich daddy—"

"He doesn't know, Luisa. He's got no idea he's my son."

For once, Luisa was stricken to silence. She stared at Rob. "How does he account for the fact that you've taken him under your wing, then?" she asked after a moment.

"He's too stunned to think about it as yet. He and

his mother were very close. He hasn't got used to the idea of living apart from her."

"Oh, a mama's boy—"

"No, quite the reverse. He was the man of the house. He looked after her. If you could have seen it, Luisa . . ." His voice trailed off. He'd been about to say, "Even you, prejudiced though you are, would have been touched." But he knew she would not. She would never forgive Morag McGarth for having loved Rob in a way that was totally different from the feeling she herself had once had for him. That generous, undemanding love was beyond Luisa's understanding.

Rob was always conscious that he had never given enough return for Morag's love. He had always taken, never given—until now, when he was prepared to spend all the money in the world, hire the best doctors, pay for treatment in an exclusive sanatorium, if only Morag's life could be saved. Guilt was harrying him now, because he had taken her son from her—the only thing left to her from their love of long ago.

She had had no choice but to confide Gregor to his care. There was no one else. Rob guessed what anguish it had been to hand the boy over to him—a man who was almost a stranger to Gregor. After thinking it over, Rob had decided to keep the truth from him; Morag had let him think his father had died years ago and that she was a widow. The two had been so close that it would be a shock to the boy, Rob guessed, to learn that she had lied to him in this one respect.

He had brought Gregor to the suite at the Waldorf Astoria as a makeshift measure while he thought what next to do. His daughter Ellie-Rose seemed to take Gregor in her stride; she remembered him as a baby, no doubt, from the time of her own childhood at Brown Bridge.

When Rob was forced out of the farm in New York State he had decided to make a fresh start out on the wheatlands, but Luisa was determined not to go with him. Instead she wanted to take their daughter and live in Boston. Rob had managed to make a financial arrangement whereby he got custody of Ellie-Rose; he had been prepared to start again with only Nellie, the cook, who had volunteered to go with him. Out of the blue Morag had arrived, having heard about his predicament. She had lived with him at the derelict farm at Brown Bridge, helping him to make a home for Ellie-Rose. There, after a year or two. Gregor was born.

But once Rob turned the farm into a success, Luisa had arrived expecting to take up residence. She had created a great scene, had thrown a pot of scalding coffee over Morag and her baby—the scars of which Gregor still bore, although the burn mark had ended as a fold of skin just below his left temple which helped to give him a strangely quizzical expression.

"He's your half-brother," Rob had explained to

Ellie-Rose when Gregor was in bed at the hotel that first evening. "Morag's child."

"I know, Papa. You don't have to go into long explanations."

"He's my responsibility from now on, Ellie-Rose. I'm going to take him to Craigallan Castle."

"Poor kid," Ellie-Rose said with the sarcasm of a sophisticated twenty-year-old. "He'll fade away in that mausoleum."

"Ellie-Rose! It's going to be a show-place when I get it the way I want it."

"Yes, a show-place—like a museum."

"Well, when are you going to come and help me make it liveable?"

"Give me two or three weeks, Papa. I've got engagements I ought not to break."

What would she say if she arrived and found her mother in residence? There was no great affection between the two; Luisa had abandoned Ellie-Rose for the life of Boston, and Ellie-Rose merely tolerated her mother's occasional attempts at friendship now that she was grown-up and a social asset to Luisa.

He stood staring down at Luisa now. He felt he had to get rid of her. She would be such an obstacle in getting the new household going peacefully; she would be so antagonistic to Gregor. "You're to pack up and go," he said. "I want you out of the house by nightfall."

"I'm not going! This is my home—the house my husband has built for me."

"It was never intended for you, Luisa, and well you know it. Every time you've come here trying to wriggle yourself into it, I've made it perfectly clear I don't want you here."

"Of course, Ellie-Rose is to play hostess, isn't she?" The note of jealousy of her own daughter was naked in her voice. "But it's kind of a peculiar-looking household, isn't it? One middle-aged man, married but with no wife. One young unmarried girl. And one eleven-year-old boy from nowhere."

"You know I don't give a damn how it looks to other people—"

"That's certainly true." She had to give him that. When she had arrived at Brown Bridge and, as she liked to think, scared Morag out of the farmhouse, the neighbours had been scandalised that one Mrs. Craigallan should move out and another should immediately move in. For his part, Rob hadn't turned a hair. He had gone about his business in Brown Bridge and St. Joseph, unperturbed by stares and frowns. He ignored their disapproval—just as he had ignored Luisa even though she was living in the same house with him.

She tried another tack. "If you don't care for yourself, think of Ellie-Rose," she appealed. "Twenty years old and still not married! And d'you know why?"

"Because she hasn't met anyone good enough."

"Rubbish! Do you think she wouldn't have married Beech Troughton if she could have got him? But you can bet," Luisa said with a malicious

28

smothered grin, "his family stamped on *that*. Even if you were leading a model life, you wouldn't be good enough for the Troughtons—"

"The Craigallans go back a lot further than the Troughtons—"

"So you say—but that was in Scotland. The Troughtons go way back, here in America, and they're not about to let their darling son and heir marry a girl from a nothing family. And let me tell you, Rob—" she nodded with emphasis—"even less fussy parents are going to get a bit pursed up if they visit here and find only you and your by-blow for Ellie-Rose's family."

"Ellie-Rose isn't going to want to marry a man who gives a hoot about things like that—"

"That's what you think! Ellie-Rose enjoys having a position in society. See how she reacts when she issues invitations and gets them turned down because folk don't like the circumstances here."

"But your character, on the other hand, is without stain?" he inquired on an ironic note.

"Whatever I've done, I've been discreet about it. What offends the leaders of New York society is lack of discretion. And having Gregor here is indiscreet—at least, it's going to cause raised eyebrows if I don't appear on the scene. They'll put two and two together and take it that I refuse to come because I'm affronted by his presence."

Rob frowned at her. She was perfectly capable of putting that story about, just to spite him. Not that he cared whether New York society visited or not—but perhaps it would make a difference to Ellie-Rose. She was young, after all. It could happen that some young blade would be frightened off by the gossip and Ellie-Rose would get her heart broken.

He walked to the window and stared out. The colours of fall had been washed out of the trees by the rain; the last few leaves were being wrenched away in the gale. The outlook was drear. His pleasure in his new house was done away with by Luisa's presence. He did not want her there.

But maybe it was better to have her where he could keep an eye on her, rather than let her gossip among her cronies in New York. Julius's talents as decorator gave him entree to many great families so it would be easy for him to spread whatever story Luisa chose to tell. And it was useless to think Luisa would stay her hand because it would harm her daughter. Luisa had no real love for Ellie-Rose. True, she would like her to make a good marriage, but only for the prestige it would bring.

He glanced back at her over his shoulder. "If I let you stay, you'll behave yourself?"

"You won't have anything to complain of," she said, hiding her glee at the defeat signalled by the question. "Any little romances I may have, I'll be the soul of discretion. And I'll be a perfect hostess—"

"I wasn't thinking about that," he cut in. He swung about. "I was thinking about Gregor."

"Oh, yes, Gregor." The little come-by-chance.

30

He seemed to be very important in Rob's view of things. She must tread carefully here, and always remember to use the child to her own advantage no matter how much his mere existence angered her.

"Oh yes, Gregor," he mimicked. "I can tell by the way you say it that you've got it in for him already, Luisa. Well, that's one of the conditions if you stay at the Castle. You've got to be good to Gregor."

"I'm not the kind of person to be unkind to a child, Rob—"

"Hah!" The disbelieving contempt would have provoked her to angry words if she hadn't been so intent on settling the main topic—that she could stay on as mistress of the household. She held her tongue, and her husband went on: "I've no illusions about you, Luisa, just as I suppose you've none about me. I daresay we deserve each other. But let's be clear about this. I want you to stay away from Gregor—"

"Oh, don't be absurd."

"I mean as a general rule. Of course at meals you'd unavoidably be thrown together, but I don't want you getting him alone to tell him things I don't want him told—"

"About his dear mama, you mean."

Rob's brows came together. "It isn't going to work," he said. "You're bound for mischief, I can hear it in your voice. Clear out, Luisa, and do what you like about blackening my reputation in New York."

31

"No, no, Rob! I promise, I promise! I won't talk to Gregor more than I have to. I won't even let him know I knew Morag, if you'd rather I didn't." She was scared. She'd nearly thrown everything away because of her too-ready tongue. After all, what did it matter about Morag? She was off somewhere, coughing her lungs out, dying, probably. Morag was no threat to her any more, Morag with her thin face and great dark eyes. Nor was the boy a threat. Quite clearly, Rob wanted to do his duty by him for Morag's sake, but she believed him when he said he hadn't been in touch with Morag until recently. There could be no bond between son and father, there could be no question of the child superseding her own children where Rob's money was concerned.

He hesitated now. "I think . . . if he's going to see you by day . . . it might be a help to him to hear you knew his mother. But don't labour it, Luisa. Morag was employed in your father's house when she was a girl—that's enough for him to know."

"Very well. I knew his mother way back. And his father? Who, according to Morag, was his father?"

"His father was drowned at sea, when he was a baby—that's what she let him believe."

"Hm. I suppose his name was supposed to be McGarth?"

"That's right."

"Are we supposed to have known him too?"

He shook his head. "Let's not make it too complicated."

32

"All right, we knew Morag at Van Huten's Farm but not her husband. What was he—deck-hand, sea-captain, what? How did she come to meet him, according to her fairytale?"

"He's not going to talk to you about his mother, Luisa, so don't rack your brains over it. You'll find him a quiet child. Just let him be, that's all I ask. Occupy yourself helping Ellie-Rose with the furniture and the decorations—"

"Helping? Surely, Rob, as your wife, I should have the say—"

"No. Let's be clear about this. You can stay, you can live almost any kind of life you like. But you're not to start acting monarch of all you survey. Ellie-Rose has better taste than either of us so I want her to be in charge of getting the place in order."

She let it go. By and by, she could have it out with Ellie-Rose herself. One thing was certain; when the house was finished and opened to guests, Luisa must come forward as hostess. It would look very odd indeed if her daughter were to take precedence in public—Ellie-Rose herself wouldn't want it. If she just bided her time, Luisa felt confident she would end up in full control at Craig-allan Castle.

As for the boy, she would ignore him as far as possible. That seemed to be what Rob wanted, and it would suit her very well.

The subject of their conversation was at that moment sitting in the drawing-room, with a tray of cake and coffee he didn't want, being fussed over by

33

Nellie the cook. As soon as Soames had come into her kitchen and announced Gregor's arrival Nellie shrieked with surprise and delight. Without pausing to explain herself in any way, she fetched a newly baked devil's food cake from the larder, cut a huge wedge, put coffee and cream on a tray, and hurried into the drawing-room with it.

"So you're Gregor," she said as she set it before him. "Chile, I knew you when you was just a little mite in your mama's arms."

Gregor drew back in surprise. Ever since Mama had been taken so ill and told him to send for Mr. Craigallan, his world had been all askew. Instead of being left in the care of the neighbours at home on Long Island, he was confided to Mr. Craigallan. The hotel to which Mr. Craigallan took him was very fine, finer than any of the hotels round Oyster Bay; he had tried to settle there because, apparently, that was where Mr. Craigallan lived. He had even tried to make friends with the pretty young lady, Miss Ellie-Rose, who lived in the family suite at the hotel and who had visited Mother at Oyster Bay. But Ellie-Rose had little to say to him, although Mr. Craigallan had apparently expected her to like him.

As far as Gregor could gather, Ellie-Rose had known Mama when Gregor was a baby. Now here was this strange black lady, claiming to be an old friend too. Warily Gregor eyed her, hiding his bewilderment.

"How do you do," he said, holding out his hand.

34

Nellie laughed, patting him on the shoulder. "Why, you don' need to talk polite to me, Mister Gregor. My name's Nellie, I'm Mister Rob's cook. Been with him a long, long time."

"But not here," Gregor said, making conversation politely. "This is a new house, Mr. Craigallan said."

For the first time, Nellie was on her guard. Mr. Craigallan, the boy called him, not Papa. "No, I was with Mr. Rob at his farm at Brown Bridge," she said. "And before that, at Van Huten's. But never mind about me. How's your dear mama? I declare it's years since these old eyes saw her."

"She's . . . rather ill," Gregor said. "In a special nursing home. That's why I'm here, with Mr. Craigallan."

Nellie heard the misery hidden behind the polite, informative tone. Years of living in other people's houses had attuned her to subtle nuances in words and gestures. She was too sensitive to force his confidence, and too sensible to blunder on without knowing what Morag had said about the boy's parentage.

"She'll be better soon, I 'xpect," she said gently. "And meanwhile you'll be happy here, Mr. Gregor. Your mama would want you to be happy."

"I think it may take some time. Dr. McAllister told me. And Mother said I mustn't expect to see her for quite a while because she doesn't want me to visit."

"But you kin write to her," Nellie suggested,

"and tell her all about the Castle. I declare, I never thought I'd ever come to be living in a castle."

"No," agreed Gregor. "It's very big, isn't it?"

"Big and beautiful. You chose a bedroom?"

"There was another lady upstairs," Gregor said, recalling her and looking expectantly at Nellie for an explanation.

"That was Mis' Luisa," she said. "Mrs. Craigallan. She be leaving today, I reckon."

But she was wrong. Shortly afterwards Rob came into the drawing-room to check that Gregor was being looked after, and found them in quiet tête-à-tête. "Hello, Nellie. That was kind of a surprise upstairs."

"She arrived yesterday, Mr. Rob. We didn't know what to do." She generously shared blame with Soames, not attempting to explain that it was the butler who had been afraid to act.

"You should have let me know, Nellie."

She shrugged. He would remember by and by that she couldn't write, couldn't send a telegram, or an express message.

"You want I should send Kitty up to pack for her?"

Rob shook his head. "She's staying."

"But, Mr. Rob—!" Her expressive glance flicked to Gregor.

"Gregor's staying too. We'll be quite a family party," Rob said, and she heard the anxiety behind the sardonic words.

36

3

ELLIE-ROSE learned that her mother had moved into Craigallan Castle the following day, when business brought Rob back to New York for a few hours. "That must be interesting," she said drily.

"Everything is under control," her father said. "But I want you to get there as soon as you can, Ellie-Rose, before she gets delusions of grandeur and starts ordering suits of armour and Tudor chests."

"And Gregor?"

"He's all right. He's putting the books on the shelves in the library, when he's not lying on the floor reading them."

"What does Mama say to him?"

"Very little, thank God. And that's how I want it to stay."

When Ellie-Rose reached the Castle a little over two weeks later, she found a strange atmosphere.

At meals, the three adults and Gregor were together. Conversation was about domestic generalities—whether Rob was going into town, whether Luisa could have the carriage in the afternoon, whether a pony should be bought for Gregor's exclusive use. When they left the table they went their separate ways. Rob had asked Nellie to keep an eye out for Gregor but she had no problems to report. The boy occupied himself, Luisa left him alone.

"But he's got to be educated, Papa," Ellie-Rose pointed out. "He's got his school books with him from Oyster Bay and he seems to study each day besides delving into your library—but that's not enough."

"He'll go to school. But not yet. He still hasn't gotten over the separation from his mother."

Ellie-Rose had the feeling that Gregor would get over that better in school. She guessed he was unhappy, having now and then come across him sitting in a window seat, hands clasped round his knees, eyes staring unseeing at the view outside. But he seemed to withdraw from any expression of concern or sympathy.

"I get the impression he's a very clever boy," Ellie-Rose ventured. "You ought to be careful what school you send him to. Not one of those idiot military academies where the sons of the Four Hundred go."

"I'll ask Cornelius," Rob said. "He's in touch with the clever world."

Cornelius, Rob's eldest child, spent most of his time at the headquarters of Craigallan Agricultural Products in Chicago. There he worked on plant biology, a branch of science he seemed to be inventing himself but which was proving of enormous importance. As the tide of pioneers moved further and further westwards the Great

Plains, once the inexhaustible source of wheat for the United States, began to be plagued with pests, diseases and crop failures.

Cut off from most of society by total deafness, Cornelius Craigallan had turned inward, to his own resources. While he was still a boy he had solved a problem of seed damage for his father, and from that had grown an interest in the wheat plant.

Scarcely anyone else in America was doing research on wheat; it had always been there, always would be. "Daily bread"—it was a truism, a fact of life, a quotation from the Bible. But only by finding out more about it would the American farmers be able to grow it in the wildly differing climates and soils they found as they opened up the country in the final long move westwards.

Summoned from his laboratory by his father's letter, Cornelius came to Craigallan Castle. Ellie-Rose hugged him in welcome; there had always been a special relationship between them ever since she, the quickest and the first, learned how to communicate with Cornelius by using sign language.

It was the same now. Flying fingers, quick touches to make him watch her lips when something was beyond her silent vocabulary, occasional laughing pantomime—all this in the first few moments of his arrival.

Gregor watched in hidden amazement. "Can't he speak?" he asked Nellie.

"If'n he could hear, he could speak, Mister

Gregor. Nothing wrong with his voice, 'cept he don't know how to use it. He went to special school in Boston, learned how to make some kind of words, but it ain't easy, Mister Gregor, to speak words you've never heard."

"Ye-es," Gregor agreed, grasping the problem at once. Immediately he began to learn how to talk to Cornelius, always facing him fully when he addressed him and taking pains to master the finger language.

Luisa watched it all and was jealous. She had never learned how to talk to Cornelius. Though he was her own son, her first-born, he was almost a stranger to her. As a small child he had scared her with his tantrums and his strange cries. When Rob put him into the care of Dr. Alexander Graham Bell, she was aghast—her halfwit son was being brought out into the open, to shame her before her friends.

The sign language disgusted her. She thought it savage. She refused to learn it. Throughout his boyhood she'd been happy to leave the care of him to others, and even now, when he was grown into a very handsome young man with a reputation as a scientist, she tried to have little to do with him.

Yet she felt lonely and excluded when the others were in a conversation with Cornelius. They would talk and laugh, half-saying things in words and half-pantomiming or signing. It went by too quick for her, she couldn't make out the bits they didn't vocalise. She watched Gregor arguing with her son, taking his sleeve and shaking his head to emphasise his point; and Cornelius taking the boy's hand, rapidly showing him the words he needed in sign language to carry on the discussion.

"What right has he?" she found herself asking. "What right has he to be close to my son?" Closer, she meant, than she herself had ever been.

Luisa had never been able to hide her emotions successfully. Her feelings spilled out in an ugly little scene.

Cornelius and Gregor had been out for a walk in the grounds. Gregor had shown Cornelius a plant he had found growing by the lake, whose name he didn't know. An argument had developed over its identification, they had brought back a specimen to identify in a botany book in Rob's library.

They trudged into the hall, bringing with them several ounces of Carmansville winter mud. Hearing them clattering across the flagstones, with Gregor declaring he could find an illustration to prove him right, Luisa came out of the drawing-room.

"What on earth are you up to?" she cried.

"What?" Gregor said, pausing and turning.

"You're treading mud all over everywhere! Where were you brought up, in a stye?"

Gregor was taken aback. "I'm sorry," he said.

"Sorry isn't going to clean up that mess, though, is it?"

"Mama," Cornelius put in in his croaking voice, "the maid can mop it." His words were always only a sketch of what another man would have said, and the sound angered Luisa the more, to think that her own son should make these moronic noises while Gregor spoke so well.

"That stone is imported from France," she told Gregor with accusation. "It wasn't meant to be clumped over in muddy boots! Take those boots off," Luisa ordered.

"What?"

"Your boots—take them off. Carry them into the kitchen to be cleaned, and then go upstairs and put on some house shoes."

"Mama," Cornelius put in with ironic surprise, "you want me to take my boots off too?"

"Don't be silly, Neil. You have a right to do what you like in this house," Luisa said. "*He* hasn't."

Gregor stared at her, then without another word bent, untied his boots, and took them off. When he raised his head, his cheeks were red, but not from the exertion.

Cornelius gave his grunting laugh, bent, and began to untie his laces.

"Cornelius!"

He didn't hear his mother's call. Almost stamping her foot in irritation at him, Luisa walked forward and tapped him on the shoulder. The slight impetus was enough to make him lose his balance. He went over on to the flagstones, dropping the jar containing the water plant he had brought in for identification. The jar smashed, muddy water went all over the hall floor.

"Oh!" raged Luisa, "you great fool!" And to Gregor, "Now see what you've done!"

Rob was working in what he called his office and Luisa called his study, further down the hall. He heard the crash, left his desk, and put his head round his door. "What's going on?" he demanded.

Gregor was attempting to pick up the pieces of broken glass as Cornelius got to his feet again. Cornelius, turned away from the study door, was unaware that Rob had come out or spoken. "Why did you push me, Mama?" he asked Luisa.

"Good God, I didn't do it on purpose! I just wanted you to stop acting the fool—"

"What on earth is the matter?" Rob asked, coming to join them.

"Mama doesn't want us bringing mud indoors," Cornelius said.

"What's that about, Luisa? You suddenly grown houseproud like an old-fashioned Dutch house-wife?"

"That's not the point—"

"What is, then? What's that?" Rob nodded at the pieces of broken glass, the strands of weed spread across the floor.

"Just *look* at the mess!" Luisa cried. "Go on, pick it up, every scrap."

Gregor was trying to do just that. At Mrs. Craig-allan's angry urging, he moved forward on his knees to pick up a shining scrap of glass, and in doing so knelt on a shard he hadn't seen.

The sharp sliver went through the knee of his

knickerbocker, into the flesh. He gave a cry of pain and scrambled back. Cornelius, guessing what had happened although he couldn't hear the cry, helped him up and picked the piece of glass out of the tweed. At once a speck of blood oozed out where the glass had pierced. "A cut," Cornelius said, fetching out his handkerchief.

By now the various sounds had brought the butler to the hall. "Take Mr. Gregor upstairs and bathe his knee," Rob commanded.

"That stupid child!" exclaimed Luisa in fury. "It's all his fault!"

Gregor limped towards the stairs.

"Just look at him!" Luisa railed. "Making a drama of a little cut—"

"Might be glass in it," Cornelius said, raising his voice as he sometimes did without knowing it, and thus over-riding her exclamations. "Better have doctor, Papa?"

"I think you're right. Soames, send for a doctor."

"Oh, that's right, make a hero out of him! He's always right and I'm always wrong." Luisa turned and flounced back into the drawing-room.

Cornelius took his father's arm and went with him into the office. "Gregor has to go," he said. "She can't stand him."

"But it's too soon, Neil."

"She hates him. Really hates him."

This sad judgement in Cornelius's half-voiced speech struck home to him in a way that Rob found unbearable. It was true—Luisa hated Gregor.

44

"We must settle on a school, then. What about that one in Bangor, where your friend from Husson College is a teacher?"

"I wrote to him. He says they could take him in for the next semester. But that's not till after Christmas."

"He's got to stay here until after Christmas, then."

"Better not, Papa."

"But we can't send him anywhere before that. Good lord, Neil, he's got to have Christmas with us, surely!"

Cornelius shook his head. "Do you think he'd have fun? Deluding yourself, Papa. Mama has shown him he's only here on sufferance—"

"That's not true—"

"It is as far as Mama is concerned, and you know it. Papa, let him come to me."

"To you?"

"Sure, why not? He can have a good Christmas in New York. I'll take him to shows, stores—different from here, I know, no big outdoor place, no pony to ride."

Rob was unwilling. To allow Luisa to put Gregor out of the house was to admit failure. But Cornelius pointed out that their first concern should be for Gregor. "Parted from his mother. Enough troubles without Mama picking on him. And she will, Papa. Now she's let feelings get away from her, she won't be so careful any more."

Rob sighed. His son had no illusions about Luisa;

45

bitter experience had taught him that his mother could be very hurtful. And Rob knew Cornelius was right, Luisa was allowing the barriers to come down. Soon she'd forget the promise she'd made about not making life hard for Gregor. There was no knowing where it might end. And Rob didn't want the boy hurt.

Later he went into Gregor's room. He was sitting reading, a bandage round his injured knee. "What did the doctor say?" Rob asked.

"It's nothing, he picked out a little splinter and everything's fine. Didn't even need a stitch."

"That's good." Rob hesitated. "Gregor, how would you like to go and stay with Neil for a while?"

"Could I?" Gregor said, with something like eagerness.

"Would you like to? It would just be over Christmas. Then you'll be going to school—Neil has a friend at Petersfield School in Bangor, it's highly recommended. What do you say?"

"What does Mother say?" Gregor asked.

"I'll write to her. She'll agree, I'm sure, Greg. It's really whether you want to."

"I'd like to go to school soon," Gregor said in a polite, neutral tone that masked his eagerness. He longed to get away from Craigallan Castle, from its hidden currents and its formidable grandeurs.

If he could choose, he'd go to the town where his mother was now living, and stay near her. But he knew that wasn't possible; grown-ups had control of you, you had to do as they said. But if he couldn't go to his mother the next best thing was to get away from Mrs. Craigallan. Her veiled hostility, her wish to put him in his place, make him know he was a charity child . . . he knew she was his enemy and he couldn't understand why. Until he knew how to deal with her, it was better to be out of her path.

Ellie-Rose felt guilty when Cornelius told her he was taking Gregor to New York. They talked almost silently, using their hands; that way Cornelius could be quicker, more exact. Somehow, Ellie-Rose had failed Gregor; she hadn't taken enough interest in him.

Gregor was Morag's son—Morag, that surrogate mother who had helped Ellie-Rose through her early teens at Brown Bridge: the passion for her school teacher, the despair at not getting the part in the school play, the occasional tantrums when Papa was too busy to pay attention to her. And the loneliness of the Plains in winter, the sense of being nobody, nothing, in that great expanse of unending snow, where a man could be lost in a blizzard just by stepping out to feed the chickens . . . Morag and she had made taffy, constructed toy theatres, learned new card games from the *Ladies' Compendium of Leisure*, sewed new clothes both for themselves and for Ellie-Rose's dolls.

To Ellie-Rose, Morag had been Mommy. Far off in Boston, there had been another lady, Mama, who sent birthday and Christmas presents and received duty letters in reply. Mama kept promising to visit, or to have Ellie-Rose to stay, but nothing ever came of it until the day she walked in, bringing Cornelius.

And then suddenly Morag was gone, and Mama was the lady of the house at Brown Bridge—sulky, capricious, one day showering Ellie-Rose and Cornelius with little presents, the next lecturing them for being spoiled, thoughtless, and selfish.

That had not been a happy period. Papa had been different after Mama came. The house was different, the neighbours were different. Ellie-Rose had learned from the other school children at Brown Bridge that their parents thought the Craig-allan household "shocking". She realised that Morag, so much beloved, wasn't Mommy, was no relation to her. Her mother was Luisa. But everybody knew that you ought to love your own mother best. Why then did she feel nothing for Luisa except uneasiness, wariness?

At the time, that period of her life seemed to go on for ever. But it could only have been a matter of months before Luisa got bored with the whole thing. Although she was Rob's legal wife, the neighbours refused to accept her somehow. Rob almost ignored her though she stubbornly stayed on in the farmhouse. There were no new acquaintances, no cosy coffee parties, no picnics with other families. In the end she packed up and left, scarcely bothering to bestow a farewell kiss on Ellie-Rose and Cornelius.

Ellie-Rose's childhood seemed to go with her. It

was time to think of finishing-school. That would have happened anyway, for the daughter of a man as rich and influential as Rob Craigallan couldn't finish her education in some hick public school. But somehow Luisa's short stay in the house at Brown Bridge seemed to signal the end of one life and the beginning of another; the end of girlhood and the beginning of womanhood.

Years had gone by before Ellie-Rose saw Morag again, and then it had been by the merest luck—*bad* luck, as Ellie-Rose had thought. She had gone to Oyster Bay on Long Island for a weekend with Beecher Troughton, trying to persuade herself she was in love with him. When she saw Morag there in her little modiste's shop, she had recognised her at once, and Morag had recognised her. The mere fact that she had seen her with Beech spoiled the adventure. She had gone home, and the affair with Beech was over.

But then she found she was expecting his baby. She realised now she'd been a fool to think he would marry her because of that; men of good family like Beecher Troughton don't embark on illicit affairs with girls they intend to marry. There had seemed no one to turn to. And then Ellie-Rose had thought of Morag.

Why Morag? Well, because Morag had stayed somewhere in her unconscious all those years, the epitome of undemanding friendship, kindness, comfort. Morag would know what to do about the baby.

Looking back now, Ellie-Rose understood that what she had needed above all was for someone to undertake to tell her father. Rob idolised Ellie-Rose in an unthinking, complacent way. And for her part Ellie-Rose adored her father. She'd never seen a man, a young man, to come up to him in her estimation. Perhaps that was why she'd thrown herself into silly love affairs instead of looking for a husband like most girls. She couldn't bear the thought of confessing to him that she was going to have a baby, she, unmarried, well-brought-up, respectable. He would be unbelieving, disappointed, shocked.

So perhaps that was what she wanted of Morag. Whatever her reason for making the visit to Oyster Bay that misty day in the fall, it had ended with Ellie-Rose having a hysterical attack which now seemed incredible to her own recollection. She, the clever, clear-thinking Ellie-Rose, had actually tried to drown herself off the jetty at Oyster Bay!

Morag had jumped in to keep her afloat until the boatmen could pull them aboard. It was because of Ellie-Rose's foolishness that Morag's sickness had flared up so dangerously. Ellie-Rose had worked that out for herself, and she knew it was because of this that Gregor was cool towards her. He blamed her. He never came out and said anything like an accusation—no, he was too self-contained, too controlled to burst out with it. But she saw it flicker in his eyes sometimes when he looked at her: "You nearly killed my mother!"

If Gregor had been a different kind of boy, Ellie-Rose would have lavished friendship on him, trying to make up for what she'd done. She *wanted* to love him. There was a lot she liked when she looked at him. He was a handsome lad, and the scar at his temple gave his features a strangely inquiring appearance—one eyebrow a little lifted in ironic survey. He was quick and intelligent, able to hold his own in conversation on almost every subject except the rich society in which the Craigallans lived.

And he was Morag's son, her father's son, her half-brother though he didn't know it. She *ought* to love him. Yet she knew she'd neglected him.

She had lost her baby. At first, to her own bewilderment, she had grieved over that. She couldn't understand herself. It was a baby she'd never wanted, never intended. But afterwards, when the shock to her physique had brought on a miscarriage, she was saddened beyond any expectation. She still hadn't got over it, though two months had gone by.

She had told Beecher Troughton that he had nothing to worry about any more. She had taken up her round of social engagements yet had been quite happy to curtail them when Papa asked her to move into Craigallan Castle and help look after Gregor.

But she hadn't looked after him.

"Do you think Mama has been unkind to him in other ways, Neil?" she asked now. "From what you tell me, she really picked on him. Maybe she's been doing that all along, without our realising. Maybe that's why Gregor has seemed so . . . subdued."

Cornelius shook his head. "I think she'd had it all bottled up. That's why so rotten when it came pouring out. If you could have seen her, Ellie!"

"She can't bear it that he's Morag's son."

"You remember her, do you, Ellie? For me she's just a faint memory."

"I saw her recently. I came on her by chance, then went back to talk to her. I wanted . . . advice, perhaps. Comfort."

"Over Beecher Troughton?"

Ellie-Rose shrugged and looked down. "That was a foolishness, Neil. I'm over that now."

Cornelius could have told her that Beecher Troughton was not going to propose. What he couldn't understand was why his sister should be so unhappy about it. Beech wasn't good enough for her. She'd have found the life of daughter-in-law to the rigid Troughtons quite against the grain.

"You want to marry a man with more to him than Beech," he said. "You need someone who'll give you something to do besides looking after his house and bringing up his children."

She laughed. She took his hands and knocked them gently together, an old trick when she disagreed with what his fingers were saying. "I'll have to get married some day, Neil," she said, for him to lip-read. "I'll be an old maid soon."

"You?" he croaked. "Never!"

They sat for a moment, busy with their own

52

thoughts. Ellie-Rose was thinking about her brother. Would he ever marry? What woman would be able to come to terms with his deafness, with that strange speech? And, before that, how could Cornelius get to know women? He tended to stay away from social gatherings, immersed in his plant research. She must do more for Cornelius. And with that came the thought, which she voiced: "I must do more for Gregor, Neil. I've promised Papa that I'll get the Castle decked out, but I'll come to New York whenever I can."

"You could help choose his clothes. He's got to have a new outfit to take to Petersfield—sports gear, which I can buy, and ordinary clothes, which you could supervise."

She was pleased at the thought. It was helpful, practical. She imagined herself writing to Morag at the sanatorium: "Gregor is off to school in Bangor, Maine, a very good school which Cornelius recommends, and I've seen to his clothes . . ." She wanted to get close to Morag again, but had needed some way of making the approach. She felt in her heart she ought to begin by begging her forgiveness for the selfishness, the thoughtlessness, that had brought this crisis of illness on Morag—but she couldn't bring herself to do that in a letter. By and by, when the doctors allowed visitors, she would make the trip to Pike's Peak and put into words what she couldn't set down on paper.

Luisa didn't trouble herself to appear for Gregor's leave-taking. She went out to spend the afternoon and evening in New York, so Gregor had to leave a message of thanks for her hospitality. He thought Mr. Craigallan suppressed a grim smile at his words, but all the same he promised to pass the message on. "Serve her right," Rob was thinking. "It'll show her the boy's got manners, even if she hasn't."

She was pleased to get Gregor out of the house. She wasn't sorry either, to have Cornelius go. She was never easy when he was around—if any of her friends had happened to drop in, she'd have found herself apologising for him.

Once he was gone she found that Ellie-Rose and her father tended to be away all day quite often. At first Luisa was delighted; she felt it gave her scope at the Castle to carry out her decorative schemes. But to her fury she found Rob had left instructions that nothing was to be bought for the Castle unless he had given his permission. The craftsmen and suppliers he had engaged would do no work unless he personally issued orders.

What enraged her was that no such embargo existed about Ellie-Rose. Whatever Ellie-Rose said was to be done, was done. But her daughter wasn't always there, so the work could come to a standstill. It meant the place wouldn't be open for its Christmas house-warming after all. And Luisa had already issued verbal invitations to many of her friends.

She went storming to New York to tell Rob what a mess everything was in. "Mud everywhere, they haven't got the gravel properly down on the paths yet so you can't step outside without putting on boots! The conservatory isn't anywhere near finished so there's not a plant or a flower to be had for the house unless I order from the florist—and there isn't a decent florist nearer than Fort George, and heaven forbid I should ever order anything from a backwoods village like that!"

"Luisa, you can live with chrysanthemums from Fort George for a month or two, for God's sake! So long as the house itself is comfortable—"

"But that's just the point! Nothing's being done! When Ellie-Rose isn't there, everybody stands back and says, 'No, Mrs. Craigallan, we've got to wait for the young lady's say-so.'"

"Ellie-Rose has other things to do just at present, Luisa—"

"Either Ellie-Rose is in charge of the furnishing of Craigallan Castle, or she isn't!"

"Just at the moment she's busy with Gregor . . ."

"Oh, Gregor—of course, I should have known it! It's because of that brat that everything has to go into a decline! And for heaven's sake, why has he got to go to an expensive private school like Petersfield—"

"It's not so expensive, Luisa—"

"It is, too, expensive! Millicent Bloodworth's boy went there and she told me it cost a *fortune*—"

"She was exaggerating to impress you," Rob interrupted, with a faint smile. But Luisa was quite right; Petersfield was very expensive. He had a feeling he was trying to assuage his guilt towards Morag by sending her boy to a school like that. But it would be justified, he was sure of it. The more he got to know Gregor the more he was astonished by the boy's brains.

Rob would call on him at Cornelius's apartment off Sixth Avenue and find the two had been up and about early, walking round Gansevoort Market or fishing off one of the piers. They bicycled in Central Park in the evening too. Almost all the time they seemed to be engaged on some project— Gregor could talk with Cornelius about botany with some confidence, could take interest in his work although the New York apartment had none of the scientific equipment that crowded the laboratory in Chicago.

So even though Rob would gladly have paid the fees at Petersfield if Gregor had been a dolt, he had the satisfaction of knowing that the boy would do well there. It was a secret regret to him that he couldn't acknowledge him as his son; "my son, doing so well at Petersfield . . ." But that couldn't be. The scandal would be too much.

"In any case, Luisa," he defended himself now, "you didn't come to reproach me for spending money on Gregor. It was about the house . . ."

"What I don't understand is why there should be all this money poured out for Gregor's education, but when I want a little to buy a painting or a vase, I can't have it—"

"My dear, you can have anything you like so long

56

as you buy it out of your allowance—"

"But it's wrong to expect me to pay for things for the Castle out of my allowance—"

"I don't expect you to. I thought it was perfectly clear. The furnishing and decoration of Craigallan Castle will be paid for by me—"

"But you've given Ellie-Rose discretion to buy what she likes on your behalf—"

"Quite so. I trust her judgement."

"But not mine!" Luisa was scarlet with indignation. "Is that any way to treat me in front of the household staff? They all know Ellie-Rose takes precedence! It's making my position untenable."

He didn't reply, as he might have done, that he was delighted to hear it. Nothing would have pleased him more than if Luisa had packed up and left. But he knew her too well to expect that. For the moment she was set on being mistress of Craigallan Castle; she wanted the glory of the housewarming ball, the prestige of receiving guests in that pseudo-baronial ballroom. For a time at least he would have to put up with her. By and by she might get bored again, or fall in love and be tempted away.

"Luisa, you insisted on staying when I made it clear I didn't want you there. I always intended to give Ellie-Rose control of the place."

"But she isn't doing enough, Rob. The house won't be ready until well into the spring if things go on as they are."

"I don't really care, Luisa."

"Well, please yourself, but you'll lose the servants. It's no fun, you know, living in the middle of a mess, continually cleaning up for months on end."

"Don't be a fool. With this depression dragging on, no servant's going to walk out on a good job."

Rob wasn't greatly concerned about whether or not the servants stayed. But he could see Luisa was going to go on and on raising problems. She wanted the house ready for entertaining—and in a way there was logic on her side. The place had cost a fortune to build; it was perhaps rather absurd not to get it properly in use. But he was damned if he was going to give Luisa a free hand, as she obviously wanted.

"I'll see if I can get Ellie-Rose to make more headway—"

"Look here, Rob, if you won't give me control of the work, why don't you hire someone who knows what he's about? Ellie-Rose no doubt has taste and all that kind of thing, but she's got no more idea than I have of where to go to find what she wants, nor what sort of price she ought to pay."

He felt Luisa's narrowed gaze upon him. What did she want now? "What do you suggest?"

"Let Julius take it on." And, as Rob was about to object strongly, "Now, wait a minute, Rob. I know you have all kinds of a grudge against Julius, I know it was his fault you lost the farm at Van Huten's, but he's really made a name for himself as a decorator of houses. All the best people go to him—"

"I don't want my house tarted up by your brother, Luisa!" The mere idea annoyed him. "I wanted the place to look as if it belongs to us."

"And so it will. Ellie-Rose has got sketches and bits of silk and velvet for colour schemes—let her give all that to Julius as a basis to start with. And she can check what he does day by day if she wants to."

"Ellie-Rose would rather do it her own way—"

"Perhaps she would, but how long is it going to take? Come on, Rob. Ellie-Rose gets on well enough with her Uncle Julius."

Rob didn't give in at once, for it didn't do to let Luisa think she'd had an easy victory. By and by he agreed Julius could be approached, if Ellie-Rose was in favour. Ellie-Rose was to be the final arbiter in anything Julius put forward.

But even Julius couldn't get Craigallan Castle ready for a Christmas ball. The earliest would be the end of January; Rob complained that the weather would be at its worst and guests would have an uncomfortable drive out to Carmansville.

But Luisa was determined. She'd got a guest list more or less drawn up already. "We *must* have it before the end of January," she insisted. "I have the opportunity to invite Major McKinley if we can fit it in by then. After that he'll be back in Ohio."

To Rob that was no inducement. He had a poor opinion of the former Governor of Ohio. In the first place, he had a pest of a wife who kept falling sick at the most inconvenient moments for her husband's social and political activities; and he, softhearted fool that he was, would leap up from a fundraising banquet to hurry to Ida's side. For another, a couple of years ago the man had been made bankrupt. It was acknowledged that McKinley himself had not been spendthrift. If anything, the reason was worse; he had kindly signed notes on behalf of a friend of his, an Ohio manufacturer called Walker. It genuinely seemed that the Major had never checked to see how much he was into on Walker's behalf, until the man's business went broke. His debts were then found to be about a hundred and thirty thousand dollars, for most of which his friend McKinley was liable.

Rob was one of a number of rich Republicans who had subscribed to a fund to pay Walker's debts so that McKinley shouldn't be publicly embarrassed. Everyone agreed that it only showed what a noble heart he had, to have trusted his friend. Rob couldn't help feeling it showed him to be an idiot—but it was harmful to the Republican Party to have one of their front runners in a fix like that, so he had donated money to clear the debt. Not that Rob was a very devoted Republican—but he didn't mind investing a little money in hopes of future favours.

It was funny how the women seemed to dote on McKinley. Rob couldn't see the attraction. The man was rather short, portly, grey-haired, and a bit of a bore. Yet most women, and even some girls, thought him wonderful. If Luisa could get McKinley to their house-warming, that would undoubtedly make it a big success socially.

"Are you going to invite his wife?" he inquired.

"Of course. She'll accept, but she may not be able to come if her health is poor. But the Major will come if they've jointly accepted."

"Huh," Rob said. "If you really think it's important, go ahead."

"Of course it's important! McKinley is the future President of the United States."

Rob shrugged and let it go. He couldn't really believe that McKinley would make it to the White House. He was too lacking in that final touch of steel. Woolly, verbose . . . Rob thought his chances poor.

All the same, Hanna thought he'd get there. And Hanna was quite a different barrel of oil. Hanna was a man after Rob's own heart, a self-made oil millionaire. And if Mark Alonzo Hanna really believed in McKinley for President, perhaps it wouldn't be a bad thing to have him as a guest to Craigallan Castle.

61

4

THE Craigallan Ball was talked of long after it took place. There had been a keen curiosity beforehand to see what the interior of the Castle was like: many a New Yorker had made the drive out to Carmansville on a Sunday afternoon to gaze at the exterior and marvel—either with naive acceptance or ironic disapproval—at its similarity to an ancient fortress.

There was also some interest among the rich to see what Julius Van Huten had done with the decorations. He was now well-established as a man of taste, whose work could change a dull apartment into an Arabian wonderland, a Louis Seize palace, or a Bavarian cottage. It was known that he had had a free hand with money, the antique dealers of New York had been buzzing around him like bees around a honeypot—so the place must be a veritable museum of fine pieces.

Julius had done his bit to enhance the interest in the ball. It was to his credit if his work was seen and approved. The *haut ton* had muttered that they would refuse the invitation when it came, for who after all was Rob Craigallan? An upstart, only arrived in the United States twenty or so years ago, son of who-knows-whom in Scotland, famous for rather sharp work on Wall Street and on the Board of Trade in Chicago with that odious character, Sam Yarwood.

Their view changed when it began to appear that they might not even be invited. As the leaders of society met for tea or bridge, they chatted—and put out feelers. Mrs. Astor hadn't received an invitation. Neither had the Vanderbilts. The Hamiltons had heard nothing.

Then it became known that Governor McKinley of Ohio and his wife would attend. That in itself was an attraction, for he was popular even with Democrats. President Cleveland was disliked because of the depression that had gripped the country throughout his tenure of office and it was whispered that McKinley, already nominated by the Republicans, might be the man to step into Cleveland's shoes in '96. What with the need to know what Craigallan Castle looked like inside and the possibility of meeting the future President, the ladies of the Four Hundred began to be very anxious to hear from Mrs. Craigallan.

Their invitations arrived at last—specially engraved, different from the design sent to the more ordinary mortals. Flattered, and by now desperate not to be left out, the leaders of society accepted en masse.

Julius knew that most of the guests wanted to see the Castle so he didn't mask its interior with swathes of silk or canopies of flowers for the ball. The ballroom was a study in grey stone and white— camellias, gardenias, stephanotis, frangipani, mahonia, and bauhinia. The perfume was almost overpowering as the evening wore on: the Craigallan ball lived in memory as the evening when ladies had to be escorted outdoors for fear of fainting due to the scent of the flowers.

Those who wished were taken on a tour of inspection at the supper interval, when the orchestra played operatic selections, and the hungry helped themselves to cream of artichoke soup, whitebait, clams, *timbales de veau, cotelotte d'agneau*, asparagus in cold wine mayonnaise, plovers with watercress, venison *à l'ecossaise*, peaches, strawberries, hothouse grapes, maraschino sorbet, lemon ice-cream, a selection of ten cheeses, and fine wines to match each dish.

The sightseers were pleased with what they were shown, they were swept through room after elegant room until their feet were tired in their dancing slippers. Back in the supper room, no sooner were they seated with their choice of food and wine when the *pièce de résistance* of the evening was provided. A band of Scottish pipers, in what the reporter for the *Journal* later described as "kilties", marched in playing a wild tune, filling the room with a skirl of sound that took the breath away—and, remarked that wit Harry Lehr, the appetite too. Others in "kilties" appeared, to dance a reel and a sword dance in the ballroom. What made it all the more remarkable to the guests was that these lightfooted, elegant dancers were men—fierce-looking men at that, with beards and moustaches.

Then on came a pretty girl in a long white gown and a tartan sash, to sing meltingly beautiful songs in an unknown language—Gaelic, so Mr. Craigallan said, the language of his youth. He also claimed that the tune the pipers had played on marching in was the "March of the Men of Glen Bairach", where he was born. No one could argue with him. For those who liked to be impressed by such things, his reputation was enhanced.

Rob's final gesture was to have his wild Highlanders invite the young lady guests to join them in reels and schottisches. A Scottish fiddler in tartan trews stepped forward and began to play. The men in "kilties" moved about among the audience, taking the prettiest girls by the hand, urging them out to the floor. At first they drew back, frightened or pretending to be so. But the irresistible lilt of the fiddle tempted them, and also the wish to shock their elders.

Within five minutes the ballroom floor was full of silk-clad beauties being coaxed through the complexities of a reel. The Highlanders said little, simply danced the steps and pushed their partners. When they swung them, the girls felt a little drunk—either with vertigo or excitement. The men were so big and brawny, their hands were so rough—and yet they danced as lightly as thistledown. It was entrancing.

Rob set a fashion that night. He was the first millionaire to make an asset out of his "foreignness". He didn't try to be a more elegant New

Yorker than Mrs. Astor; instead he used what was dramatic from his past.

"You've certainly pulled it off, pal," Sam Yarwood said to him round the side of his cigar as the waltzes resumed in the ballroom. "They'll be talking about this right into the summer."

Rob accepted a glass of Pommery from the supper-table waiter. "It didn't matter so much to me," he said, "but Luisa kept on about how I was harming Ellie-Rose's chances by the way I lived. So I wanted to push the boat out this time, get her properly launched."

"She's launched, all right," Sam grinned. "Seen her with McKinley's protégé?"

"No, who?"

"Congressman Gracebridge."

Rob remembered the name. McKinley's personal secretary had provided a list of people whom the Governor would like invited, and among those names had been Curtis Gracebridge. Rob couldn't remember that man at all, though he must have been presented by name as he came into the ballroom.

"What's he like?" he asked, moving towards the arch between the supper room and the ballroom, to look for Ellie-Rose.

"Oh, tall, dark, thirty-ish. I guess you could say he's handsome. That's him, Rob—just turning by the doorway."

Rob's eye found him. The man was turning Ellie-Rose in the sway of the Lehar waltz, gazing down to speak to her with a smile. One glance was enough to tell him the young man was deeply smitten.

"Congressman, eh? Republican?"

"Well, McKinley sure wouldn't ask you to invite any Democrats on his account!"

"Of course. Who does he represent—an Ohio district?"

"No, Nebraska, I think."

"Is that so?" Rob was interested. Brown Bridge in Kansas, his big wheat farm, stretched towards the Nebraska border and during the recent years of depression he had bought farms in that state as the farmers went into bankruptcy. It wouldn't be a bad thing to have a friend who was member of Congress for a part of Nebraska, even if it wasn't the region where Rob had property.

"He's a bright boy. McKinley's interested in him, he's likely to go far—specially if the Major really makes it to the White House."

"Think he will, Sam?"

"Well, Cleveland sure as hell won't stop him! The Democrats have lost control of the Senate, and they'll lose the White House next time around."

"Hmm," Rob said. "But McKinley? The man's an idealistic idiot, Sam."

"I dunno if you're right there, Rob. He's got strong views about some things, but they're not all impractical. He knows money is the basis of society—"

"But he's in favour of this damned silver currency—"

"Yeah, yeah, but only because silver is a big American resource. You know the big plank in his platform is that Americans should use American products, and not import things from elsewhere."

"Okay then—he wants us to use silver, which is American, as against gold, which has to be imported."

"He'll come around on that," Sam said, tapping out the ash of his cigar into an onyx ashtray. "There isn't enough gold in the Klondike to finance the kind of business that's growing here in the States. The rest of the world won't accept silver. Before McKinley gets to the White House, he'll give up his silver-dollar. I'll take a bet on it."

The waltz drew to its flowing conclusion. Rob said, "I think I'll have a word or two with Congressman Gracebridge. He might be useful."

McKinley was enjoying the Craigallan ball. More important, his wife Ida was enjoying it. She had had no headache, no fainting spell. Ellie-Rose had made it her business to hover over her at first, to depute a maidservant to keep an eye on the Governor's wife and bring her anything she wanted the moment she wanted it. She had visited the area where Mrs. McKinley was holding court several times to make sure all was well. As a result, she had been described as "sweetly kind" by Ida McKinley, and introduced to William's young protégé, Congressman Gracebridge.

Now as Curtis Gracebridge conducted her to a chair, Ellie-Rose's father came into view. "Papa,"

Ellie-Rose said, subsiding onto the chair and wielding her fan," are you enjoying yourself as much as I am?"

"Not bad, not bad," Rob said. He looked at Curtis. "We met when you arrived, of course. Gracebridge?"

"That's right, sir. I must say, you sure know how to give a party!"

"Having a good time?"

"I was having a swell time from the outset," Curtis said, "but now I've been allowed the honour of a dance with Miss Craigallan, I'm voting this the best night of the year."

"That's rash, isn't it?" Ellie-Rose laughed. "The year's got another eleven months to go."

"Nothing will surpass tonight, ma'am. This is the night I met you."

Ellie-Rose fluttered her fan and raised her eyebrows. "You're the member for Nebraska?" she inquired. "Not one of those romantic Southern states?"

"Us Nebraskans can be as romantic as anybody," Curtis said, acknowledging the teasing thrust.

"How long are you staying in New York, Congressman?" Rob asked.

"Only another couple of days. I have to be in Washington for a debate on a new roadbuilding grant for the Great Plains."

"You going to speak? I'd be interested to know your view. I'm a Plainsman myself, you know."

"Of course, Mr. Craigallan. Everybody knows

about your spread in Kansas. I hear you've got some property in my own state?"

"That's right, in the south of Nebraska—"

"That's not in my constituency, I represent Central Nebraska. But of course I'm interested in what you intend doing with the land. We had a lot of farms foreclosed in the past three years, Mr. Craigallan. Some of the banks took them over in payment of outstanding debts but they haven't been able to get anyone to take them on and get them going."

"You and I must have a talk about it—"

"Please, Papa," Ellie-Rose broke in. "We're not here to talk politics, not tonight!"

"Sorry, Ellie. You're right. Perhaps I might drop in on you some time, when I'm in Washington."

"You come to Washington often, Mr. Craigallan?"

"Only when there's something happening that interests me. Just at the moment I'm worried about what the Department of Agriculture intends to do about—"

"Papa!" warned Ellie-Rose, tapping him on the sleeve with her fan. "No more politics!"

Rob laughed and gave in. The orchestra struck up a polka, and he went in search of Luisa. It was time he showed himself a good, loving husband by dancing with her.

Luisa was looking like the cat that licked the cream. The evening had succeeded beyond her wildest dreams. "Isn't it marvellous?" she said as she bounced round the room in his arms, the diamonds on her bosom sparkling at each step. "Who'd have thought it would take off like this?"

He didn't say that he had thought it would. Luisa liked to think she knew more about society than he did. He said: "Governor McKinley seems happy enough."

"Oh yes, he's been *ever* so charming. He's danced almost every dance. And I gather from his secretary that he only does that if Mrs. McKinley is absolutely feeling at home."

"Seen the young fellow Ellie-Rose just danced with? Gracebridge—Yarwood tells me he's a pal of McKinley's."

"Mmm," Luisa said, panting a little. "He's got no money, though. I asked Vera Tolworth."

Rob didn't pursue it. To him, money wasn't important. In a son-in-law, it would be nice, but Rob had money enough to see that Ellie-Rose was well provided for all her life. What he wanted for her was prestige, a place in the world. He hadn't at all approved of Peter Sumikiss, her first swain, and had been glad when she got rid of him. Beecher Troughton had seemed a better prospect but for some reason nothing had come of that. Now, Rob was already assessing Curtis Gracebridge. Rob hoped Ellie-Rose would encourage him. He could be useful; a Representative for Nebraska would be interested in farming affairs in Congress, and though, strictly speaking, Rob was no longer a farmer, he still wanted to see that his property did

71

well, that he got a good price for the wheat raised by managers on his land.

The ball flowed on to its conclusion. The last guests took their leave in the early hours of a bitingly cold January morning. Their hosts sat for a few minutes, yawning and drooping, amid the remains of the refreshments, the disarranged gilt chairs, the little crowds of empty wine glasses.

"I think it was a success," Luisa said, looking around for congratulations.

"It went well," Rob agreed.

"I thought it was fun," Ellie-Rose said. "I never expected I would enjoy it, you know. I thought I'd be too nervous."

"Everybody seemed to like the place," Julius put in, to remind them of his role in the affair. "I got a lot of compliments."

"There's bound to be a rush of orders for Scottish baronial halls now," joked Ellie-Rose. "I hope you have a supplier who can provide wall-hangings and claymores, Uncle Julius!"

"You can laugh. But two people asked me if I could do something the same for them."

"There's no accounting for tastes! There were even girls who got a thrill out of those hairy Highlanders of yours, Papa."

"I expected them to."

Ellie-Rose smiled at him. "It was a master stroke," she said. "Mrs. McKinley told me she found it 'most educational'."

Rob met her eye. They broke into laughter. Luisa

and Julius looked at them in mystification.

"I don't know what's so funny about that!" cried Luisa. "Mrs. McKinley's approval is worth having, let me tell you! If she likes you, her husband is bound to like you too. And in view of what they say about his election, that's not to be laughed at."

"Then I'll tell you something that will make you very happy, Mama," Ellie-Rose remarked. "I received the final accolade. Mrs. McKinley told me she was going to crochet me a pair of bedroom slippers."

Luisa was truly delighted at the news. It was well-known that Mrs. McKinley occupied her time by sitting with a companion, crocheting or embroidering. To have a pair of slippers by Mrs. McKinley was like being given an order of merit. Luisa couldn't understand why Ellie-Rose and her father went off into peals of laughter when she expressed her pleasure.

A few days later Rob went to Bangor to deliver Gregor to his new school. The boy shook hands with his new headmaster with his usual politeness, was shown his room, bade Mr. Craigallan goodbye, and seemed quite resigned to his new surroundings.

"You'll find he'll settle in a day or two," Mr. Posner, the headmaster, told Rob. "He's quiet at the moment, I know, because he feels a bit at a loss—"

"No, he's always quiet," Rob said. "I'm sure he'll be all right."

"You're his . . . er . . . guardian?" Posner said,

73

examining the enrolment papers on his desk. He was accustomed to euphemisms of this kind.

"That's so," Rob said with equanimity. "His father was a first mate on board the *Rossignol*, lost off Chesapeake in '84. His mother is from the old country—that's how I happen to know the family."

This was said with so much matter-of-factness that Mr. Posner was tempted to believe it. "I have the mother's signature on the papers," he said, tapping them. "She's not well?"

"In a sanatorium in Colorado. I'm going there when I leave Bangor, to tell her how her boy has settled in at the school."

"A sanatorium, eh? Something serious?"

"Damaged lungs. She's very sick but the doctor at the clinic writes that she's improving. But so far Gregor isn't allowed to visit. He writes to her regularly, and I hope you'll have photographs taken if the opportunity occurs, so he can send her one. They're very devoted."

"I quite understand. Perhaps if she makes a good recovery, we'll have the pleasure of seeing her here quite soon."

"I hope so." Rob deposited a sum of money to be doled out to Gregor as pocket money, told Posner how to get in touch with him by telephone in an emergency, and took his leave. His thoughts dwelt with Gregor as the train took him south towards Washington. The next holiday long enough for Gregor to leave Bangor would be Easter, at the end of March. Before that was Lincoln's Birthday and

74

Washington's Birthday, for each of which he would have one day's break. Rob must try to get to Bangor on both those occasions, to take the boy out for a treat.

When he told Posner he was going to see Morag, that was quite true. But he was going via Washington, for he wanted to look up Curtis Gracebridge. Luisa had had a letter of thanks for having invited him to the ball, but Ellie-Rose too had had a letter, exquisitely polite and very circumspect, but breathing admiration in every line. It had closed with expressions of friendship and the hope that he might see her father in Washington in the near future.

Rob decided to drop in on him. Luisa had not been very impressed by his interest in Ellie-Rose, because she regarded him as a half-savage backwoodsman from a hick town, but Rob could see virtues in him. He was able, intelligent, and likely to do well if McKinley was elected. Besides, he was haunted by Luisa's words that Ellie-Rose was heading towards spinsterhood. It was true that most girls of Ellie's age were either married or engaged. It was time to act the part of a concerned father and do some matchmaking.

For his part, Curtis Gracebridge had done a little research on Rob Craigallan. He learned that the man was very rich and likely to become richer. He had made money on the Board of Trade in Chicago by dealing first in wheat futures and then in other commodities. In partnership with the wily Sam

Yarwood, he seemed to make few mistakes. Whether the commodities market was bullish or bearish, Rob Craigallan traded to advantage.

From that he had gone on to building grain silos. As the prairies were brought into cultivation and the seed grain improved, the yields grew greater and greater. But the price went down and down, so that farmers were happy to sell at any level to get the harvest out of their barns. Rob Craigallan rented out storage, or bought the crop and stored it on his own behalf. He seemed unperturbed when the glut grew so extreme that some farmers burned their wheat; he just kept his silos in good order, waiting for the day when disease, bad weather, or some other event brought on a demand for the grain he had in storage. And already it was paying off. He was selling bread-wheat abroad, to Europe and to areas of Africa where white settlers made a market for the grain they couldn't themselves grow in tropical terrain.

But that wasn't the only source of Craigallan's money. He had invested in flour-milling, in agricultural machinery, and in land itself. So far it wasn't entirely clear what he intended to do with the farms he had bought up. Some said he had new crops in mind, that his son Cornelius was a research botanist who gave him good advice, that he was friendly with George Washington Carver and C. G. Pringle, both experts in plant improvement.

Mark Hanna, McKinley's adviser, had been a source of information about Rob Craigallan. "What d'you want to know for?" he inquired when Grace-bridge sought him out before heading back to Washington.

"I . . . er . . . thought his daughter was a very charming young lady."

"Did, did you? She's an eyeful, all right." Hanna looked thoughtful. "She'd be an asset to any man with a career to make. Got money, for one thing—money's always handy."

"I wasn't thinking about that, Mr. Hanna—"

"Then you should, boy, you should. Doesn't do to be too altruistic when you're in politics."

Curtis was pleased when Mr. Craigallan himself turned up in Washington, invited him to dinner, and spent a long evening talking agricultural politics with him.

It could only mean Craigallan approved of him. He didn't put it into words, yet Curtis got the impression that if he were to show up at Craigallan Castle he would be welcome. It was very flattering. As they shook hands on parting, Curtis had the feeling he was being told to make a move on his own behalf. He had made it clear he had no money and had seen Mr. Craigallan wave the information away as unimportant. So it could only mean that Mr. Craigallan liked him for himself.

Rob for his part began the four-day journey to Colorado the next day, satisfied with what he had done. The young man was very attracted to Ellie-Rose, that was plain enough. It remained to be seen if Ellie-Rose liked him. But that was up to Ellie-

77

Rose—Rob had done all he felt suitable in the circumstances.

He had written to the director of the Estival Clinic, Dr. Luce, to ask if Morag was fit enough yet to receive visitors. The reply was that she had improved, that he could visit, but he must not tire her.

The clinic he found to be a strange place, a collection of cabins spread out over a large enclosure of lawns and shrubs. The main building, which housed the offices and treatment rooms, was in the centre, and had two storeys with a balcony running all round. Although it was the first week in February, people were lying on chaises longues on the balcony, protected by windbreaks of striped canvas and well wrapped in blankets.

To the west Pike's Peak raised snow-capped shoulders to the egg-shell blue sky. Pine trees held up their green-black fingers. A cold sunlight gilded the stones and buildings close at hand, and glittered on the snows. A thermometer mounted on the wall of the main building showed the temperature to be two degrees below freezing, yet the air didn't feel unbearably cold.

Dr. Luce chatted with Rob politely. There was little to say yet about Mrs. McGarth. She had arrived in a very exhausted condition after the journey from Long Island, and had only just begun to make headway. "At least we can say she's not continuing to decline," he remarked, showing a mouthful of excellent teeth in an optimistic smile.

"The disease has a stronghold, however, in the middle and lower lobe on the right. Only time will tell if we have prevented the spread to the upper lobe."

Rob gathered there was no chance of a cure. As far as was known, there *was* no cure. "Medical research may one day triumph over this dread disease," Dr. Luce said solemnly, "but not in my lifetime, I fear. All we can do is arrest it, and prevent its increase. And I may say that in Mrs. McGarth's case, I have hopes of stabilising her condition."

Visitors weren't encouraged until after the lunch hour. Rob had lunch with Dr. Luce and his two chief assistants, and then was shown to Morag's cabin. Its windows were wide open to the clear mountain air, and indeed as he approached he realised she was sitting on a glass-protected veranda. His heart contracted at the sight. She was like some rare orchid in a glasshouse.

He had been told to sit across the table from her, and not to kiss her in greeting or leavetaking. She held out her hand and he took it. He was surprised to find it warm and strong, though thin.

"How are you, Morag?" he asked, pressing her fingers.

She made no reply. But her great dark eyes, shining with tears, were fixed on him in a smile of welcome.

5

AT first Rob talked too much, too brightly. He told her Gregor had settled at school, that he had had a short letter saying he liked it, the teachers were good, he thought he'd do well in mathematics, he was learning ice-hockey but thought he might not be quick enough for any of the teams.

When he ran out of news items, Morag nodded and spoke for the first time. "He writes to me. I think he's going to be happy enough. He wrote to me during his stay at your house, Rob. He said . . . he said he met Mrs. Craigallan."

"Yes." Although he tried to make it sound matter-of-fact, it came out grim.

"Did she treat him badly?" Morag asked. He could see the remembrance of things past in her eyes, the picture of that awful day ten years ago when Luisa threw the scalding coffee over the baby.

"She didn't dare," Rob said. "But she'll never like the boy. He'll have to stay away at boarding school most of the time."

"And the vacations?"

"I haven't thought that through yet. He longs to come here, of course."

She shook her head. "The doctors say no. He keeps asking when he can visit—but it seems young

80

folk are more apt to catch the infection than older folk. They say, just wait and see how things are in the summer." She said it without self-pity, though the intensity of her wish to see her son made her pale cheeks even paler.

"They tell me you're doing fine."

"Oh yes. No further inroads since I arrived here."

"Are you comfortable? Is there anything you need?"

"Nothing, Rob." Except to see Gregor—but she would never say that. "You're so kind to me, paying for all this."

Kind! He felt his throat thicken, his eyes fill with unaccustomed tears. Kind—when she had brought up their son alone, staying out of his way for fear of what his wife might do. Ten years of struggle, of poor health, when she could have been in comfort except for that selfish bitch Luisa. For the thousandth time he heard that cry within himself—why had he not married Morag years ago, when they first set out from New York to find work, in the year of their arrival in America?

The answer was simple. Then, he hadn't loved her enough. He had wanted other things more: first a good job, then the chance to improve himself, and after that the control of a farm, of land and wheat—wheat, the golden harvest. He had gained all he wanted: he controlled vast silos full of wheat, manipulated the Board of Trade dealings in commodities so that he never lost money, had reached the point where he was a friend of the men in power. And now he realised that they had not the value of Morag's love. If he had married her and gone on with her in a simple way of life, he might still have done well in money terms because he was quickwitted and energetic; or he might have stayed poor all his life. But he would have been happy in a way he had not experienced except in the few years when Morag had lived with him at Brown Bridge.

"How is Ellie-Rose?" Morag asked, changing the subject as she saw how distressed he was.

"Oh, she's fine. Had a whale of a time organising the ball we gave."

"Yes, she wrote to me about it. She—"

"Ellie-Rose writes to you?"

"Oh, yes, it began when she wrote to say Gregor was off to stay with Cornelius in New York. She kept me up to date on what she'd done for him—his clothes and all that."

"Well," Rob murmured, taken aback, "I didn't know that."

Morag gave a little laugh. "There's a lot you don't know about Ellie-Rose, Rob."

"Such as what?"

"Well . . . she hasn't been happy."

"You mean over Beech Troughton?" He saw her start of surprise and suddenly wondered if there was more to that affair than he had learned. Perhaps Ellie-Rose had been genuinely in love with the fellow. It was possible: Beech was handsome, dashing, a leader of fashion. He'd have thought him a little too empty for Ellie-Rose but then . . . what father ever thought a man good enough for his daughter?

"She must have known nothing was going to come of that flirtation," he went on. "His parents were bound and determined he was going to marry Kitty Highclare and everybody knew it. I think Ellie-Rose just wanted to throw a scare into them."

Morag made no reply to that. For a moment she had thought, from his words, that Ellie-Rose must have told him the whole story. Oh, if only she would! If only father and daughter could come really close! She had seen loneliness and despair in the girl when she came to see her at Oyster Bay, and the wildness that had led her to throw herself off the jetty came from being without a friend, feeling lost and without hope.

It was so strange. These two loved each other. Why was it that the father didn't reach out to learn more about Ellie-Rose's problems? Why was it that the daughter couldn't be open and frank with Rob? It was because they had built up images of each other that they couldn't bear to shatter. Truth had been left out though, as they worked on the picture they had of each other.

But Morag couldn't betray Ellie-Rose's confidence. She said: "Ellie-Rose takes after you, but she has something of Luisa in her too, don't forget. She's stubborn, self-willed, and no more inclined than the rest of us to take advice."

"What makes you say that? You been trying to give Ellie-Rose advice? What about?"

"No, of course not," she said. "I've replied to her letters, of course. She gives me information about Gregor, mostly."

"She hasn't told you about her new swain?"

"No, who?"

"I suppose it's too soon for her to think of him in that way. He only showed up on the horizon at our house-warming. He couldn't take his eyes off her. The Honourable Curtis Gracebridge."

"Honourable? He's in office?"

"Congressman for one of the Nebraska constituencies. A decent fellow. I dropped in on him on my way here."

"Oh, you did?" Morag said, raising her eyebrows and studying him. "To give your approval?"

"No, to see what kind of a man he was in his own surroundings. You can't go much on how a man makes out at a ball—all done up in a stiff collar and dance slippers, makes you feel like a turtle on its back. He's not bad, Morag. Got character. McKinley thinks a lot of him." And more importantly, though he didn't say this, McKinley's shrewd campaign manager thought a lot of him.

"Governor McKinley?" Morag exclaimed. "Oh, he's such a good man! If he's a friend of Major McKinley's, I think he must have a lot to recommend him."

Rob laughed. "Why is it that you women all go for McKinley? You only have to mention him, and they start telling you what a fine man he is."

"Well, he handled that miners' strike in Ohio so well, Rob. Most people would have had the militia firing at the marchers and there would have been a bloodbath—but from what I read, the Governor prevented anything of that kind."

"Huh! You should hear what the manufacturers and mine-owners say! They think he was too soft."

"It's not soft to have regard for human life! You can always rebuild a bridge that's been burned down, but you can't rekindle life in a corpse. And those men had wives and children—what would they have done if the Governor had let the Ohio Militia mow them down?"

"Well, well, let's not talk politics," he replied. "I only mentioned McKinley to let you know the kind of fellow who's taken a shine to Ellie-Rose."

"And how does she feel about him?"

"I don't suppose she's given him a thought since she filed away his thank-you letter for the ball. But he'll be around."

"You mean you gave him permission to be around!"

"Not at all. I dropped in on him for purely business reasons."

"Rob—"

"What?"

She'd been going to say, don't encourage him to pay court to Ellie-Rose just so that you can use him in your business affairs. But she bit back the words. She couldn't really believe that Rob would force

85

Ellie-Rose to allow attentions from a man she didn't like. But she couldn't help knowing that it would be to Rob's advantage to have a Congressman in the family.

Visitors were allowed at the clinic on only two days, Wednesday and, for those who could not take time off from their employment, Sundays. Rob spent the intervening three days in Colorado Springs, which he found very dull. He amused himself by going for sleigh rides round the mountain, and thought it might not be a bad thing to invest some money here. As the population increased, there would be a need for vacation centres, and people from the industrial towns might be very willing to spend money in a place like Colorado Springs.

He asked permission to have a photograph taken of Morag, to give to Gregor when he got back. The photographer made a great to-do of sighting through his apparatus, saying that the glass verandah where Morag stood reflected back side-lights he couldn't blot out. But in the end the photograph was taken.

Rob went to collect it before he left for the train. The man said: "Shall I put it into a black-edged mount?"

"Black-edged?" For a moment Rob was at a loss, then fury seized him. "God damn you, she isn't going to die!" He lurched at the photographer, who drew back in alarm.

Only a friend, eh? Acted more like a lover,

seemed to him. Well, it didn't do to cross rich folks. "Sorry, I'm sure," he said. "Only, being as she's at Dr. Luce's place—I mean, they's bad, them that goes there, not many walks out on their own two legs."

"Mrs. McGarth will be fit and well in a few months," Rob said, getting control of himself. "Please mount the photograph in a regular frame."

The last thing he wanted was to present Gregor with a memorial photograph. He took it out when he was on his way back to New York, and studied the face that looked back at him. Framed in a fur-trimmed hood, it was thin and too drawn. Her eyes looked huge. And yet there was urgent life in the sparkle of their glance, in the curve of her lips. She wasn't going to die. She would fight her way back to health . . . if for no other reason, then because Gregor still needed her.

Rob was wrong when he'd told Morag that Ellie-Rose had given no thought to Curtis Gracebridge. She'd had a letter from him, telling her he'd had the pleasure of a visit from her father, and what an honour it was, and so forth. Alarm bells rang in Ellie-Rose's mind. What did it mean? Was her father matchmaking for her?

She brought back Curtis before her mind's eye. Tall and rather impressive—perhaps, she told herself, more impressive in appearance than in personality. But he was pleasant, not thick-witted. He was, as her friends were apt to say, "husband-material".

Ellie-Rose was wondering what to do with her life. All her friends were settling down. While there was no urgency for her to do so too, it made her think about the alternatives. If she didn't get married, what would fill her world, take up her energies? She could devote herself to good works, of course; one or two much-admired ladies did that. But that argued a highmindedness she knew she didn't possess. Ellie-Rose liked admiration, affection, having fun—she didn't want to become a saint.

There were one or two careers open to women of good family. One could take up the arts in some form—but though she could paint and draw a little, and play the piano adequately, she had no real talent. One could follow Miss Nightingale into nursing, an honoured calling—but Ellie-Rose's slight acquaintance with illness had taught her that she wasn't the stuff of which nurses are made.

If she didn't take up any of the openings that were available, she could just settle down to being unmarried but enjoying life. This was a difficult undertaking for a woman. Men could do it and be well-thought-of—rich bachelors were always in demand at parties and dinners, no matter how middle-aged and eccentric. But no one loved an eccentric old lady, despite her riches; and if one decided to be a demi-rep . . . well, that was all right if your looks held out, but what happened when the double chins began to form? Ellie-Rose shuddered away from the thought and went back to thinking of herself as she was now, not as she might be thirty years hence.

She suffered from the doubts that plagued the daughters of rich men. She didn't know for sure whether the young men pursued her because she was pretty or because she was going to inherit money. For a year or two, it wouldn't matter. She was attractive enough not to care. But when she reached, say twenty-five, twenty-eight, and still hadn't married—could she be sure then that her looks were a chief interest? Or would it be her money that took precedence then? One thing you could say about Curtis Gracebridge—he was really taken with her. She had seen it in his eyes the night of the ball. There was no way of knowing if he would have been equally as taken if she had been a poor relation, and it was unfair to ask the question. All that mattered was that, among the men she had recently met, Curtis had seemed the most captivated.

And there was one more point. When he bowed over her hand in leave-taking, he had pressed it strongly. He was unaware of the fervour in that handclasp. Even through the obligatory kid gloves, she had felt its physical insistence. Something whispered to her that Curtis would be sexually exciting. And she had just enough experience of physical love to know it was important to find a partner who could please her.

She couldn't afford any more near-disasters like her affair with Beecher Troughton. Yet she knew she had a physical side to her nature that would always torment her while she remained technically "single". What was it St. Paul had said: Better to marry than to burn. He had been speaking to men, but it was equally true of women, perhaps.

Now Papa had been to see Curtis. Despite herself, Ellie-Rose allotted importance to that. She needed her father's approval. If and when she married, it would have to be someone who would measure up to what he expected of her. She knew she was never going to land one of the scions of the Four Hundred families—nor did she particularly want to. But her husband would have to be someone of weight and merit. And Curtis wasn't a bad candidate.

She thought it over for a week or two before replying to his letter. When she did, she remarked that Easter was approaching, that the Easter Parade in Central Park was always fun to see, that there was a performance of the Messiah at the new Carnegie Hall if he was interested in music, and finally, if he planned to be in New York for any part of the Easter break, she was sure her father would be delighted to see him at Craigallan Castle.

She gave him credit for not rushing into a reply. A week went past, and then the telephone, recently brought out to the Castle by special contract with the Eddison Bell Telephone Company, rang in the hall. Soames answered it, then came to announce that a Mr. Gracebridge wished to speak to Miss Craigallan if it was convenient.

90

"Miss Craigallan? I'm calling to thank you for your wonderful letter. Did you mean it when you said you and your father would welcome me at the Castle?"

"Certainly, Mr. Gracebridge. Papa spoke quite warmly of you after his visit to Washington."

It amused her to let him think she was acting as an obedient daughter, doing as Papa would have wished, inviting a young man he had vetted and approved of. She would show him different once he was here. But she was quite looking forward to seeing him again.

"It so happens," he said, "that my fellow-Congressmen have asked me to go to New York to see ex-Senator Platt. I wonder if I could call, during my stay in the city?"

"That would be delightful."

"What day would be suitable, Miss Craigallan?"

"Let me just consult Mama and Papa. Will you hold on?" She put the receiver down and went in search of her father. As for consulting Luisa, that had only been said for appearances' sake.

"Papa, your friend Curtis Gracebridge is on the telephone asking if he can come to dine while he's in New York. He's asking for a date—what's your diary like?"

"Ellie-Rose," Rob said, getting up, "let me speak to the poor devil. The least we can do is offer to put him up. I bet he's come to New York to help persuade Tom Platt over McKinley's campaign."

"I think so," she said, but he was already going

out the door of his office. She heard him on the phone, expressing pleasure at hearing from Curtis, heartily inviting him to stay. "Sure, sure—well, even a couple of days—it's no trouble, my friend, you know we've got over twenty bedrooms here. Very well, then. A week next Saturday. That will be fine. Then you can go with us to watch the Easter Parade."

He came back from the conversation smiling to himself. Ellie-Rose knew that pleased look on the quiet features. Plans were going as he wanted them to.

Well, all right, she said to herself. I'll be nice to him. But it's not going to be a walk-over, and they'll soon find that out, the both of them.

But perhaps it was at that moment she subconsciously decided to accept Curtis in the end.

The weather continued very cold, with frozen snow making the roads dangerous. At the clinic at Estival, the scenery was magnificent, but it made the patients draw back from their ever-open windows in something like fear at so much cold beauty.

Morag had had letters, from Rob and from Ellie-Rose. From Gregor she hadn't yet had a word, although usually the mail brought a letter from him twice a week. She had sent him an Easter present, a book from a mail-order firm. She would have preferred to make him something with her needle, but understood that nowadays he couldn't wear home-made clothes; his fine new school expected the pupils to do them credit in tailor-mades. Besides, she wouldn't have had time to get anything ready. She seemed to have insufficient strength for sewing, seemed to spend long hours in sleeping or in a kind of waking dream on her chaise longue on the verandah.

She lay there now, watching the spring day come to its close. In the mountains, shadows fell early, closing in on the clinic to make it seem even more cut off from the active world. She loved to watch the sky change colour as the sun slipped behind the peaks, to see the last remains of light tipping the bushes with greyish silver.

Her eye was caught by a movement among the shrubs. She half sat up. There it was again. Some animal? Deer sometimes came down from the mountain when the weather was hard, to graze on the gardens where householders were trying to raise plants despite the frost.

But no, this wasn't a deer. A small dark shape was moving from shadow to shadow, purposefully. A thief? Her hand came out from under the comforters, reaching for the bell that always stood at her side on the table. But even as she picked it up and it gave an incipient tinkle of sound, she paused.

The figure was too small to be a robber. Could it be one of the Indian children? Sometimes driven by curiosity, they would come to the fence surrounding the grounds and peer in between the slats. But their mothers always swooped on them and bore them off. The clinic was a place of ill omen to them; their medicine men had told them it belonged to the sufferers of the "long sickness".

She lay staring at the gathering shadows. Someone was there, standing in the shelter of a young dogwood. She sat up, pulling her thick shawl round her shoulders. "Who's there?" she called.

No reply.

"Someone's there," she called. "What do you want?"

The figure detached itself from the shadows and walked into full view on a stretch of lawn that lay between Morag's chalet and the bushes.

"It's me, Mother."

She gave a gasp and lay back. Gregor started to run forward in alarm. She threw up a hand. "No, Gregor! Don't come near!"

"But you're upset—"

"Stay there, Gregor!"

She was given strength by the upsurge of anxious terror. Gregor must not come close. Dr. Luce had explained to her that no one was sure how tuberculosis passed from one to another. Certainly young people seemed more susceptible than others. At all costs, Morag wanted to keep Gregor at what she thought of as a safe distance.

He stood obediently in the open, about ten yards from her verandah. He was clad in a thick loden jacket, knickerbockers and thick woollen stockings, heavy boots. His head was covered by a cap with ear-flaps, like a lumberman's.

He had planned for the journey, had put on the

outfit they wore when Mr. Dempster took them out on geological expeditions. He was ostensibly going "home" to Craigallan Castle for Easter. But all through the Good Friday service in the school chapel he had been putting the finishing touches to his plan to visit his mother.

He understood very well that she was too ill to be disturbed. "I didn't mean you to see me, Mother," he said in a subdued voice. "I just wanted to find out how you really were, to get a glimpse of you . . ."

"I'm fine," she said, her throat thick with tears.

"It seems . . . a nice place," he said.

"How did you get here?" she asked.

"On the train. I hitched a ride on a sled from the town."

"And how were you proposing to get back?"

He gave a little shrug of impatience at this unnecessary question. "I found a store-shed on the other side of the grounds," he said. "I was going to spend the night in there and then get a ride back in the morning."

"In this cold?"

"It's quite a warm store-shed, Mother."

Morag gave a little laugh. "Just because I have to live in an ice-house, there's no need for you to do the same. You must go and tell Dr. Luce that you are here, and he'll give you a bed in the main house. Gregor? Do you understand?"

"I don't want anyone to know I'm here," he said.

"They told me I wasn't to see you until the summer."

"Do you imagine you won't have been missed? Come, Gregor, you're not a baby. Mr. and Mrs. Craigallan must be wondering what on earth has happened to you. Weren't you supposed to arrive at the Castle last Saturday?"

That was true. The journey had taken him four days. By now there must be a hue and cry out for him. He had thought of that and discounted it: he knew that he could make the trip out to Colorado and back so as to report for class on Monday morning, and thus be exempt from any charge of playing hooky.

As to what the people at the Castle thought, he didn't care. They might suppose he'd run away from school because he didn't like it. Nothing could be further from the fact. He enjoyed school, loved the feeling of being stretched mentally, of learning new skills physically, and although he had not made any close friends he was on good terms with most of his classmates.

But he had to see his mother. People fobbed him off with generalities when he asked how she was. He needed to see for himself.

He stared at her now in the gathering darkness. Her face was a white blur. If only he could have reached the clinic earlier, when the daylight was better!

"Do you have electric light in your cabin,

Mother?" he inquired. "If so, could you switch it on so I could see you?"

"I'm not supposed to get up and walk about. Someone will be here soon to wheel me indoors, and then the light will be switched on." She was forcing herself to be very cool and practical, although every instinct urged her to get up, run to him, and hug him close. To have come so far, against orders and in this icy weather, only to find he couldn't see her—it was too cruel. And she too, she longed to see him, to find out whether he was fit and happy, to look for changes in his face that were signs of his growing up. It was six months since they had parted; in six months a boy could do a lot of growing-up.

She heard footsteps on the path from the next chalet, fifty yards away. "That's Nurse Beloff," she said. "Don't run off, Gregor—" for he had made a dart for cover. "I'm going to tell her you're here and ask her to take you to the office."

"No, Mother, they'll send me back to New York—"

"You don't really imagine I can let you lurk about in the dark?" she scolded. "Come along now, be sensible. I must tell Nurse Beloff and she'll take charge of you."

He had turned to run. She raised her voice in the tone of calm command that had always been the final stage of any argument over discipline. "Gregor, stand still. I'll tell Nurse Beloff that you're there, but I'll also ask her to put on the light."

He paused. If the nurse did that, he would be able to get sight of his mother. And besides, she was right. It would only worry her if she thought he was bedded down in a shed for the night. He would have to turn himself in.

"All right," he said, sighing.

Nurse Beloff was at first shocked and then amused when she heard of his escapade. "All right, then, Mrs. McGarth, I'll wheel you in the cabin and put on all the lights so he can get a good look. But then he's got to come to the office. We can't have folks running around loose in the clinic. There's sick people here, we don't want them alarmed."

Gregor stood by the dogwood tree and saw the cabin spring to light. He saw a buxom woman in starched white apron and thick serge dress turn back the covers of a hospital cot, and help Morag into it. She plumped up her pillows, administered some liquid from a medicine glass, then stood aside.

He saw his mother reclining on the pillows, her dark hair held back by a small lace cap. A thick, soft shawl was folded round her shoulders. Above the dark wool her face was pale and clear in the overhead light.

She lay for a moment, allowing him to see her. Then she spoke to Nurse Beloff, who helped her into a more upright position. Looking out towards the lawn, she raised her hand in a little wave.

Then the nurse lowered her back among the pillows, switched off all the lights save a bedside lamp. She came out to the veranda and down the steps, stepping heavily and with purpose.

"Come on, then, young man," she said. She put a thick hand on his shoulder as if she was afraid he might escape.

But he had no thought of that now. He walked beside her in the darkness, his head turned away, ashamed in case she should guess he was crying.

6

THE non-arrival of Gregor effectively ruined Curtis Gracebridge's visit to Craigallan Castle. He had had a difficult trip by train from Washington, the locomotive having to be dug out of snow at Trenton. Luisa fussed over him when he showed up, insisting he must have hot rum punch at once.

Ellie-Rose observed it all with dispassionate amusement. She understood her mother's wish to make a good impression but all at once for her it had become academic. Now that Curtis was almost here, it seemed impossible; she couldn't really be going to accept him as an acknowledged suitor? What was he to her? Nothing, merely a handsome, well-set-up young man who had shown he was smitten at the house-warming ball.

Yet when he was shown in, bringing the cold fresh air of outdoors with him and looking so vigorous and eager, she was suddenly pleased with him. He was a *man*—tall and strong and utterly male. When she offered him her hand in welcome, he took it. His was cold from the long drive in the unheated carriage but she felt the latent warmth of the blood beating through it.

She looked up. She met his eyes, to find they were drinking her in with something like hunger. The

100

look was quickly masked. But she thought: "He wants me, he really wants me." The realisation flared in a sudden rush of colour to her cheeks. He smiled, so did she. Good manners glossed over the moment. But it had been there and they both knew it. If she wanted to draw back she must do it at once, by allowing a coldness to show in her manner.

She found she didn't want to do that. She found she wanted to please Curtis Gracebridge. She let her hand stay in his longer than was strictly necessary. It was a commitment, understood by both of them.

The meal, so meticulously planned, was doomed: the broiled butter-ball duck, plain roast beef and greens, followed by blueberry pie chosen carefully by Rob was ruined. Gregor was expected by five o'clock, an hour which Luisa liked to grace with "five o'clock tea" after the current fashion among the Four Hundred. When he didn't appear, Rob made inquiries about the rail line from Bangor. He was told there were delays, but that the trains were running. The carriage had been sent into New York to collect him; he telephoned the station to have a message sent out to the coachman—he was to wait.

But six o'clock came, seven o'clock—no Gregor. Rob sent a wire to Petersfield School inquiring about the delay. The reply came almost instantly: "Gregor left, morning train as arranged, should have reached you four o'clock."

"That boy!" Luisa exclaimed. "Wouldn't you know he'd do something silly?"

"Such as what?" Rob inquired, turning an angry glance at her.

"He's got lost. Probably wandering round New York at this moment."

"Use your head, Luisa. Gregor knows New York at least enough to find his way to Cornelius's place if he was lost."

"But Cornelius is in Chicago—"

"All the same, Gregor would go there if he was in doubt."

"What do you think has happened, then, Papa?" Ellie-Rose inquired, a little apprehensive.

"He's gone somewhere on his own," Rob said.

"But where—?" Then understanding came. "He's gone to see his mother!"

"That woman!" cried Luisa.

Curtis was an unwilling witness to all this. He was puzzled. Mr. Craigallan had been very concerned at first, much more so than his wife. That was odd, you'd think it would be the other way about, that the woman would be anxious about a child. Then there was the way Mrs. Craigallan expressed herself: "That boy!" and then, "That woman!" There was enmity, dislike, in her tone. But after Mr. Craigallan concluded that Gregor had gone to see his mother, his anxiety seemed to be over.

"Are you going to send after him, Papa?" Ellie-Rose asked.

"No, why should I?"

"But Papa—a twelve-year-old boy—!"

102

"This twelve-year-old happens to be Gregor McGarth. He'll be all right. I understand something now that puzzled me before. The headmaster told me that though he doled out his allowance every week, Gregor never hurried out to spend it like the other boys. I reckon he's been saving up the train fare."

"Huh," Luisa said. "Secretive and deceitful—he takes after his mother—"

"Luisa, be so kind as to hold your tongue," Rob cut in.

Curtis was shocked. His father never spoke to his mother in that tone of voice. And who was this mysterious boy that had run off?

"Well, let's go in to dinner," Rob suggested. "Now we know Gregor's not going to show up, we may as well forget it."

"I still think you should send a telegram to Dr. Luce, telling him Gregor's likely to arrive—"

"I'll do no such thing, Ellie-Rose. If I do that, Luce will lock all the gates and alert all the staff, and Gregor will never get near her."

"But, Papa—he's not *supposed* to get near her."

"That's what the doctors say. But I reckon it'll do more for Morag to see him than any amount of sick-nursing by experts."

At dinner the subject was studiously avoided. When the ladies left them, Curtis and Rob had a good talk about politics; there was much to be discussed, because the campaign to put McKinley into the Presidency must soon get under way, and it was necessary to know who could be relied upon and who could not.

"You won't get old Tom Platt to come out for the Major without promising him something substantial," Rob suggested. "He's always felt he didn't get his due rewards from the Republican Party. But if you could swing it, it would be worth it. He could bring the whole of New York State with him."

Curtis refused to admit he'd been sent to sweet-talk Platt. One of the things for which McKinley valued this young Congressman was his discretion. Curtis knew he was intelligent and persuasive, looking for approval only from his constituents in Nebraska. He had a feeling he was heading for big things but he was in no hurry—he had another thirty years or more of politics ahead of him.

All the same, if McKinley got into the White House, Curtis felt sure there would be some minor office for him. When, by and by, another President came in, that would probably mean Curtis would have to go. But with Presidential service behind him he could more or less count on being elected to the Senate, and from there, great goals were possible.

There were two or three things to be accomplished to ensure McKinley's success. They had to find a good running mate for him, to fill the Vice-Presidency—a sinecure, of course, but it had to be someone the voters would like. And they had to swing one or two difficult Republicans behind

McKinley; some of the older men had candidates of their own whom they wanted the party to back, and one of these was Thomas C. Platt. It might be possible to persuade Platt to give up his own candidate, but only for some substantial reward. Curtis had heard a rumour that Platt wanted to be given the Treasury if McKinley got in. It was laughable. McKinley would no sooner give Platt the country's money than he would let a drunkard loose in a brewery.

Curtis had been looking forward to a quiet, pleasurable weekend with Ellie-Rose's family before he plunged into his discussions with Platt. But an undercurrent now seemed to be spoiling the calm surface of Craigallan Castle. The anxiety about the boy, Gregor McGarth, didn't entirely disappear. Mrs. Craigallan's good humour seemed to be gone. She did her best to be polite and attentive, but there was a pout to her lips and a whiplash to some of her words.

Strange how different people were when you got to know them in their own homes. He'd have said Mrs. Craigallan was a jolly, easy-going lady. But there was little jollity in the snap of her dark eyes when she turned them on her husband, nor did she seem gentle in the way she spoke to him.

For his part, Mr. Craigallan seemed to ignore her flares of ill-temper. After one little sparring match, Curtis had turned away in embarrassment to find Ellie-Rose watching him with sympathetic amusement. "You mustn't mind Mama and Papa," she murmured, "they never actually come to blows."

"It's . . . I guess I'm not . . . My parents get on a lot better," he blurted.

"I'm happy to hear it. Perhaps it would be a kindness to tell you that *my* parents have spent a great deal of their married life apart. You could say they agreed to differ a long time ago."

"Apart?" Curtis repeated. "You mean you were brought up by your mother without your father being around?"

"Quite the reverse. I was brought up by my father—out on the Great Plains until I was seventeen." She hesitated. "The lady you've heard mentioned—Gregor's mother—she took care of me out there for a few years."

"Oh, I see. She was the housekeeper."

"Yes," Ellie-Rose agreed, and knew he missed the dryness in her tone.

"Do I gather she's sick?"

"She's in a clinic in Colorado. She asked my father to look after Gregor."

"Ah, now I understand," Curtis said. The good employer feeling a responsibility for an old servant and her family. Of course. His opinion of Rob rose even further. He admired him already as a successful man, a leader of commerce and agriculture. Now he found him to be a philanthropist too.

But that didn't account for Mrs. Craigallan's almost unveiled animosity. It was only when he was driving to New York at mid-morning on Monday, en route to see Tom Platt, that the real reason came to him. He almost blushed at his own naivety.

Time and again Luisa had almost said it in so many words while he was there. The boy was Craigallan's natural son. That accounted for the anger he'd heard whenever Gregor's name was spoken by her.

He had already written to Luisa thanking her for her hospitality. Now, if he wished, he could do nothing more, and let the acquaintance drift on a leisurely tide. On the other hand, he could write again to Ellie-Rose, speaking with warmth of the pleasure of seeing her and asking for another chance to be in her company. If he did that, it would be establishing the beginnings of a serious courtship.

He hesitated. She attracted him tremendously. But there were stresses in that family he found a little alarming.

While he was still hesitating he received a polite little note from Ellie-Rose. She wrote to tell him, in case he had been in any way worried, that Gregor had turned up at school on the Monday of the spring term, safe and sound.

He seemed to hear her voice as he read the words, that voice with its warm, rising tone and its irresistible vivacity. Her picture rose before his mind's eye; grey-blue eyes glowing, head thrown back in a characteristic gesture that showed her lovely throat. He sat down at once to reply, warmly, with muted ardour. He was declaring himself a suitor.

He wasn't vain. He knew he wasn't the only man

seeking the hand of Ellie-Rose Craigallan. One thing gave him hope—he felt that her father rather favoured him. But already he knew enough of Ellie-Rose to be aware she would make her own choice. If she found someone whom she could deeply love, Curtis Gracebridge would stand no chance at all, no matter how much Rob supported his claims.

He weighed up his assets and his liabilities. He was on the verge of a good political career, or at least so all the auguries seemed to promise. He was passably attractive, and about the right age for Ellie-Rose. He would give her a position in society as the wife of a Congressman and perhaps, in the future, of a Senator.

But would Ellie-Rose ultimately find him dull? The idea haunted him. The more he thought he might be unsuccessful, the more he became obsessed with the need to win her. But it would have to be a long courtship, made more difficult by the distance that separated them.

He wrote to her regularly, with growing frequency. It was known of Governor McKinley that he wrote to his beloved Ida every single day when he was parted from her by political duties. Curtis had never understood the necessity until now, as his need of Ellie-Rose grew.

For her part, Ellie-Rose answered his correspondence when the mood took her. She was far from committing herself to Curtis Gracebridge. Yet as the summer came, she began to compare him with the other men who were in earnest about marrying her, and she began to see that Curtis was quite a catch.

He was certainly goodlooking. It was true he often sat back in baffled silence when the talk turned on the theatre or musical events of New York. His career was divided between Capitol Hill and Nebraska, leaving him no chance to read up on the arts. But then that gave Ellie-Rose the opportunity to take him to a concert, or show him a painting, and receive his admiration for her sensibilities.

She began to think it might be fun to take Curtis in hand, to fill the gaps in his education and make him a really brilliant man. She knew she would be an asset to him as a hostess; she could bring all kinds of people to his house, and besides would have the money to finance entertainment on a grand scale.

Her father didn't press her. He took it for granted, of course, that she would marry. That was the accepted career for a woman; though Ellie-Rose might sometimes mutter about "doing something with her life", they both knew she had no vocation to anything outside marriage.

Yet she hesitated still. When summer was in full swing, she decided to go and talk to Morag about it. Morag was an independent witness; from her she might get an unbiased opinion. She arranged to make the trip to Colorado with Gregor, who was now officially allowed to visit his mother.

It was now late August. Morag had made a

marked improvement. The weather had made all the difference to her. Spring had passed into summer, the snows had melted little by little; she had watched with pleasure as the shrubs lost their helmets of white snow and put on instead bright green. Now the sun shone every day; the air was light and dry—like wine, everyone said, but though it was a cliché, it was true. It invigorated, recharged, soothed. The scents of summer drifted through the ever-open windows—dogwood, pine, sagebrush from the plateau, and from the alpine meadows arnica, lily and the earthy smell of marigolds.

She would walk into the grounds to watch the mountain bluebirds flicker in and out of their nestholes in aspen or beech. She could hear the juncos calling as they darted to their nests among the cinquefoil out on the mountain slopes; she loved the juncos, for they came to be fed in the hard weather, their russet and grey gleaming against the snow yet almost invisible now the grass had come through. She would stand listening to the drilling of some woodpecker at work among the timber. The deer didn't come to the garden now; food was plentiful among the mountain dells.

Each day Morag was able to go a few steps further on her walks. Her aim was to go through the gate in the fence and out to the alpine meadows, where the expanse of wild flowers swayed and glowed in the soft summer wind. So far she hadn't reached it, had been warned not to try to do too much, but each day it was nearer, scarcely another hundred paces.

When Dr. Luce told her Ellie-Rose was coming for a stay in the town and bringing Gregor with her, Morag's heart lurched with longing. This time he would be allowed to be near her. They would stroll together in the grounds. Visiting hours were strictly adhered to but if he stayed two weeks, she would see him four times. Four times! She put her hands to her mouth to still its trembling. Only a few months ago, that would have seemed an impossible dream.

On her first visit Ellie-Rose had enough tact to leave mother and son alone. She went for a chat with the medical staff, to hear how Morag's health was improving.

"She has done well—much better than we expected," Dr. Luce confessed. "When she was brought here last October I think we all agreed her chances were very slim. But now, I think it's safe to predict, she will be able to go back almost to normal life in about a year. Barring any setbacks, that is."

"Normal life? She could go back to her home in Oyster Bay?"

"Oh, absolutely not," the doctor said, shocked. "No, no, indeed. Mrs. McGarth must always dwell in a climate where her lungs are not taxed, and she must breathe only the purest air. That is essential. No, when we say 'normal life' we mean of course that she can have a home of her own, take up some activity of a gentle nature—needlework, which interests her, would be quite suitable. She must

111

naturally have an attendant, someone who will look after her in the occasional fevers, but they will not be serious so long as she goes carefully. With this regimen, and in good pure air, Mrs. McGarth can be well and happy."

He went on to give her a dissertation on what he meant by "pure air". Sea air, though healthy, had too much salt and ozone for chest sufferers. The prairies were too hot and dust-laden. The south—Florida, Alabama—too humid. In fact, he averred, the only really pure air was here, around the clinic at Estival in Colorado.

"I hope it will be possible for Mrs. McGarth to live near here. The climate agrees with her and she would be within my reach if she needed treatment."

Both he and Ellie-Rose knew that all the bills were paid by Rob Craigallan, that it rested with him whether Morag could move out to a house in the area.

On their next visit, it was Morag who took the initiative. She sent Gregor out to watch the hummingbird who had taken up residence in the yellow-pines further up the slope. When he had gone, she talked for a time of the beauty of the wildlife, then let the conversation drop naturally.

Ellie-Rose leaned forward in her basketwork chair. "Morag, I wanted to see you face to face so as to tell you how sorry I am for what happened last year. It's my fault you got so sick."

Morag shook her head. "It would have happened

some time, my dear. I'd been going downhill for a long time."

"But I brought it all to a crisis. When I think back on how silly and headstrong I was—"

"That's all in the past, Ellie-Rose."

"But when you've been through a thing like that—tried, even half-heartedly, to do away with yourself, you begin to think things through. I did that later, Morag, and realised I'd been a fool."

"Well . . . I certainly think no wise girl would have got herself tied up with Beecher Troughton," Morag agreed with some dryness.

"You speak as if you knew him!"

"I knew all I needed to. I read about him in the society columns—escorting Kitty Highclare to the Opera Ball, seen with her at a polo contest, squiring her to a gallery opening . . . With a family like the Troughtons, his wife is picked out when he's still in babygowns."

"I suppose I should have seen it that way. I just thought I could take him away from her. And he seemed to offer something I wanted."

"Experience?"

Ellie-Rose looked away. It was not easy to talk about sexual matters, even with someone like Morag, who made no judgements. "I could have written a letter to say I was sorry, but I wanted to tell you in person. I've wanted to make it up to you, Morag, but I don't really know how. I've done a bit to look after Gregor, as far as I could."

"I appreciate that. It was very kind of you to come here so that he could visit."

"I . . . I had an ulterior motive."

"Yes?" Morag seemed surprised.

"I want to ask your advice."

"Go on."

"It's . . . you see, Papa would like me to accept Curtis Gracebridge. I've mentioned him to you in my letters."

"Yes, I remember." Morag had noticed how the references to him increased, and yet there was no great surge of affection in the way he was mentioned. "And how do you feel about it?"

"I'm beginning to think I should take him."

"Why?"

"Well, he's . . . more real than some of the others. More solid. He's a *man*."

"That's certainly an asset," Morag agreed, smiling openly.

"No, but Morag, I do know that marriage isn't just sharing a breakfast table and giving parties. A man and a woman have got to . . . got to . . ."

"Share a bed," Morag supplied.

"Yes. I'm not some little innocent going into it all thinking no further than the orange blossom and white tulle. After all, I was Beech's mistress."

"Is that what you were?"

"That's what people would say. And he wasn't the first, Morag. So I know I've got to get something more than just the title of Mrs. Gracebridge.

And I think, in that respect, I wouldn't be disappointed."

"And yet you don't love him."

Ellie-Rose paused. "What makes you say that?"

"You're too realistic about it all. If you loved him, you wouldn't be sitting here working out what you would get out of the marriage. You'd be longing to be in his arms."

"I . . . I'm quite attracted to the idea of being in his arms. I think he'd make me happy."

"And would you make him happy?"

"Yes, I would." It was said with conviction.

"He loves you, then. There's no doubt of that?"

"None at all."

"What do you want me to say, Ellie-Rose. What is it you're asking?"

"I think I'm asking . . . would it be fair to accept him? If I did, I'd do my best to be a good wife. I'd be a wonderful hostess, and I'd bring him money and all sorts of opportunities that he doesn't enjoy now. I'd be good for his career. I think we would be good lovers. Is all that enough?"

"Enough, without actually loving him. That's what you mean?"

"Yes, Morag. What do you think?"

Morag's answer was prevented by the entrance of Gregor, reporting with enthusiasm that he'd seen the hummingbird, a little jewel on wings sparkling under the outflung bough of the yellow-pine. Ellie-Rose cast a mute glance of entreaty at Morag, who nodded as if to say, I'll think about it.

They had no opportunity for private talk until the day of leavetaking. Fall colours were beginning to creep in among the trees of the clinic's gardens, though the mountain fir still stood darkly green on the upper slopes. It was time to go back to New York.

Ellie-Rose went away to stroll among the plants while mother and son said goodbye for this time. It was Gregor himself who summoned her, walking past with a set, quiet expression. "Mama would like to say *au revoir*," he told her.

Ellie-Rose went into the chalet. Morag was sitting with her head bent.

"Are you all right?" Ellie-Rose asked with anxiety, for there was so much desolation in her drooping attitude that she was taken aback. Morag was usually so courageous.

"I'm fine. It takes it out of me, having to part with him. We're very close, you know. But . . . the time would have come when he had to grow away from me and it's better, really. I know it is."

"Gregor will never grow away from you," Ellie-Rose said.

"Well, not completely. I hope not. Ellie-Rose, about what we were saying?"

"Yes, about Curtis."

"What would you like to hear me say?"

"I guess . . . that you think I could be happy with him."

"You want to marry him?"

"Well, he wants it very much, Morag. And so do

116

my mother and father. I think my mother used to dream of seeing me marry into one of the Four Hundred, but she realises now that it won't happen. She thinks Curtis is the next best thing."

"Yes. That's what he is, I suppose. The next best thing to a man you genuinely love."

"I might learn to love him, Morag."

Morag laughed. "Love isn't something you have to *learn*, my dear! It's a natural instinct, and though you can become fond of someone you can't love him in the way you hope for—that's on a different plane."

"What you're saying," Ellie-Rose ventured, frowning, "is that you think I ought not to accept Curtis."

"I think you should wait. What's the hurry, after all? You're still very young. You can still fall in love."

"I don't think so, Morag. I'm not the falling-in-love type."

"But you can't say that!" the older woman cried, jumping up to take her hands. "We're all the falling-in-love type, Ellie-Rose. It's just a question of meeting the right one."

"But I might wait for ever—"

"Is that what it's all about, really? You're running out of patience?"

"Not quite. That makes me seem thoughtless—and I've thought about this a lot. I wanted your opinion on whether you thought I could make a go of it with Curtis."

"Oh, I think you could make a go of it. That's not quite the same thing as being happy."

"But who is happy, Morag? I'm not—are you?"

"Sometimes. But you're young—you could be happy almost all the time if you met the right man."

Ellie-Rose shrugged. "I haven't that much faith," she said. "The more I think about it, the more I think I'm a fool for marking time when Curtis wants me so much."

"So you're going to say yes to him?"

"I think so."

"What was the point of asking my opinion, then?" Morag asked gently. "Was it just to bring your own decision to the surface of your mind?"

"I suppose so. Do you think I'm wrong, then, Morag?"

Morag pressed her hands. "I hope you'll be very happy, dear Ellie-Rose," she said.

But as she watched her walk with Gregor towards the main building where the carriage waited, she sighed deeply. Ellie-Rose was making a big mistake.

7

THE Craigallan-Gracebridge wedding provided New York with another of its opulent free spectacles. It took place on a bright spring day at St. Thomas's Church before a very large congregation of friends and well-wishers, but was cheered to the echo outside by the crowds that had gathered simply to gloat over the showy event.

Any attempt by Curtis to keep the thing simple was washed away early in the preparations. Luisa, with Julius' help, had organised a lavish and unusual wedding. Julius determined that he would set a trend. No more rows of bridesmaids in semi-crinoline gowns of blue or rose or gold. No more brides in a tight-waisted gown of satin from Poiret. He would choose a theme, and make a set-piece round it.

Ellie-Rose resisted several of his suggestions—she wouldn't agree to the classical nymph idea, threw cold water on his Roman goddess notion, and was generally impossible to deal with. Finally he got her to accept the medieval theme. She would wear a long, slender gown with a square neckline, loose sleeves, and a pointed train behind. Her eight bridesmaids would have voluminous skirts of russet silk over which they would wear over-dresses of

119

patterned brocade. All would have the steeple head-dress, the hennin, draped with floating tulle, white for the bride and filmy grey for the bridesmaids.

Ellie-Rose rebelled about the headdress and was allowed to replace it with a Juliet cap and veil. The bridesmaids were too over-awed and delighted to protest. So the womenfolk of the Craigallan-Gracebridge wedding went to church like an episode from The Canterbury Tales of Chaucer, and caused a sensation.

Naturally Julius didn't expect the men to get themselves up in doublet and hose. They turned up in morning dress.

The reception was held, of course, at Craigallan Castle. The spring weather was kind, the sun beamed down upon them, and all the catering on which Luisa had lavished so much thought was a triumphant success. Open-air spits provided roasted meats; Italian wines were served; iced cakes, specially sculpted, gleamed on the long tables. All the foods of a medieval hunting party were available; quail, pheasant, venison, hare. Pasties in the shape of crowns, or birds and beasts. A boar's head. An ox tongue. Any kind of game fish—trout, salmon, black bass. There was oyster pie and clam chowder. Ornamental dishes, the triumph of the chef's art—a pyramid of wild goose liver in jelly, redwing starlings boned and in plumage, peaches *à la tour d'or* . . . And of course champagne, flowing from a fountain specially erected on the terrace. It never got flat—four perspiring waiters poured in fresh demijohns from the cellars.

The newly-weds had a short honeymoon in Richmond before Curtis had to be back in Washington for a debate. They were to stay in a house lent to them by a fellow-Congressman of Curtis's. But the journey by train from New York was long, so that their first night was spent in New York.

Rob had taken it for granted they would use the Craigallan suite at the Waldorf. He was surprised when Ellie-Rose resisted the idea with emphatic dislike. He couldn't know that to spend the night with Curtis there would remind her too forcibly of her affair with Beech Troughton—that episode, long buried in her past, which still had the power to hurt. Beech was nothing to her now, but she couldn't forget how much she had hoped from their relationship, and how she had lost his child. Sometimes it had seemed to her that it all happened to someone else—but sometimes it was all too sharply clear now that her new life with Curtis was about to begin.

There was a problem from which she'd been shying away. Curtis knew nothing of her past experience with men. He would expect his bride to be a virgin—naturally, that was always the way of things with "decent" girls. She hadn't been able to bring herself to a confession of her past. It had no real importance, except in the physical fact that the consummation of her marriage would not be her

121

first time with a man. But it would be important to Curtis, she knew that.

Without exactly knowing that she was doing it, she made sure the bridegroom got more than his share of the champagne that flowed so freely. He wasn't exactly drunk, but he was certainly very merry when they slipped away to embark on their wedding trip.

They had a suite awaiting them in the pretty little Ansonia Hotel. Rob had arranged for roses, champagne, delicate food. After the drive from Craigallan Castle it was only natural to want to bathe and change and refresh themselves with a little wine. When at last they went to bed, Ellie-Rose was sure her new husband was too overcome with it all to be quite sure what was happening.

She had resigned herself to a disappointing wedding night. She had thought it over and decided it was better to have a less than fervent bridegroom so as to avoid the hurtful question that he might ask were he sober. She underestimated Curtis.

Never a hard drinker, he'd nevertheless had to learn how to keep his head clear. He wasn't by any means drunk. And if he had been, the emotional excitement of having Ellie-Rose to himself would have sobered him.

Ellie-Rose was made growingly aware that this was to be a wonderful experience. Gratitude that her grim stoicism wouldn't be needed made her ardent in her response. They gave themselves to each other with total commitment, young and strong and passionate, delighting in their physical compatibility. Then they slept, for after all champagne brings on a delightful drowsiness.

In the morning Curtis woke first. He lay for a time watching his wife, her face turned towards him with lashes resting on her cheekbones, her dark blonde hair in pretty disarray. He remembered the love-making of the night before. He knew what he knew. He found it didn't make the slightest difference to his feelings for Ellie-Rose—if anything it increased his love, for it meant she had been let down by some other man, someone who'd treated her badly. How could anyone do that to his wonderful, beloved Ellie-Rose?

Gently he touched her cheek with his finger. She woke, the long dark lashes unveiled her eyes so that she was looking into his. He smiled. There was something so protective and strong in the smile that she understood he had found out her secret. A tremor touched her mouth. But next moment he had stilled it with his kisses.

As he made love to her in the soft morning light, she realised it was nothing to be worried about. Curtis knew, and had accepted. They would never talk about it but it would never be an issue between them.

She was suddenly boundlessly happy. She had chosen a good man. She must try to make him a good wife.

He would be very busy outside the Congress in the next twelve months, for the campaign to elect

McKinley was beginning to gather momentum. This was election year. In the fall the matter would be decided one way or the other—a second term for Cleveland, or a new start with McKinley. And as the Major had confidence in the young Congressman from Nebraska, much of the bargaining for support for him was done by Curtis.

Curtis had to admit to himself that his father-in-law's money was an enormous help to him. He never needed to stop and wonder if he could afford to give a party to wellwishers, never needed to consider the cost of travelling about the country on McKinley's behalf. Ellie-Rose's settlement was generous, besides which Rob insisted on making an allowance to Curtis. "It's only fair," he pointed out. "My daughter's got used to living in a certain way, and though she could curtail her expense, there's no reason why she should. Don't be proud about this, Curtis. I look on it as an investment. When you're a big name in politics I can bask in your reflected glory."

Curtis understood very well what was implied. He would get a continual financial support in expectation of favours to come. Well, that was only what you expected in politics; Curtis was no idealist, never had been—and if he had, working to get McKinley elected would have withered his ideals once and for all. You got nowhere in politics without spending money, making deals. Curtis knew he would never do anything to harm his country or his party, but if in serving them he could serve his friends and relations too, that seemed to him to be only good sense.

He and his father-in-law had a good understanding. Luckily, their interest ran more or less together. Rob made much of his money from wheat, from the land, and the supply to farmers of goods and services they needed. Curtis was a farmers' representative. When he stood up in the House to speak, his aims seldom ran counter to Rob's.

While Luisa was throwing herself into the preparations for her daughter's marriage, Morag McGarth had been preparing herself for a new start. Dr. Luce had agreed during the winter that when the fine weather came she could leave the clinic and live in the outside world again, so long as she obeyed his rules. "She'll have a servant, of course?" he said to Rob. "Even if she went to one of the guesthouses which specialise in invalid care, she'd need a maid to be with her in the night hours—"

"I'm having a little house built for her," Rob intervened. The thought of Morag living in a house full of strangers was too painful to contemplate. She must have a place of her own, where she could pursue her quest for good health without being ruled by petty regulations and the inconvenience of others' restrictions.

"Indeed. Well, we don't disapprove of that," said the doctor. He was fond of this use of the royal "we", indicating that he and his colleagues had held a conference over the matter. "Her family will come to live with her?"

"She has no family. I thought you were aware of that."

"Well, we . . . have had conversations with Mrs. McGarth that seem to imply her being alone except for the boy, Gregor. But that might just have been her way of stating a temporary position. People do have relatives who can be summoned up on occasions like this—to share a house."

"No," Rob said. "Mrs. McGarth has no one. That's why I've undertaken the upkeep of her son, and paid for her treatment."

"You are no relative, though, as we understand it."

"No. Just a close friend."

"Quite so. However, that doesn't solve the problem of whom we could call upon to live with Mrs. McGarth when she leaves the clinic. For we are certain she couldn't manage on her own."

"I have it in hand," Rob said.

When he got to Craigallan Castle, the preparations for Ellie-Rose's wedding were still at that time in full swing. Rob found Nellie in the kitchen quietly busy over the making of tiny sandwiches for Mrs. Craigallan's five o'clock tea party.

"Nellie, can you leave that for a moment and come for a quiet word somewhere?"

"I got to get this finished, Mr. Rob. Mis' Luisa, she'll be wanting tea served to the ladies quite soon.

They in a planning session about the flower decorations—"

"Leave it to one of the others," Rob said, gesturing at the three or four other servants who were pottering about the huge kitchen. With a flick of his finger he called a young girl in a black serge gown and snowy apron. "Here, you—take on this job. Come on, Nellie—where can we go?"

"We can go in the still room, Mr. Rob, if you really mean it." Nellie cast an anxious glance backward as she followed her employer into the big cool room where sherbets, jellies and creams were put to set. She knew what Rob did not—that he had handed on the task of making sandwiches to a chambermaid, who was quite unskilled at such matters, and who resented the command.

"Now, Nellie," he said, staring down at her worried black face, "I want to ask you to do something for me."

"Of course, Mr. Rob. Anything you want."

"Wait till you hear what this is before you jump so fast to agree," he warned. "I want you to go a long way from home."

"From home?" She studied him. "You mean here, this here castle?"

"Yes, Nellie."

She smiled. "I tole you once before, Mr. Rob—I ain't had no real home since the soldiers set fire to the plantation in sixty-three."

"You wouldn't mind moving on?"

"Where I going to?" She was hoping he was

127

going to ask her to go with Miss Ellie-Rose when she married. Ellie-Rose had always been a favourite with the black cook.

"Colorado."

"Colorado?" she echoed. "You mean, to Mis' Morag?"

"That's it. She's being allowed to leave the sanatorium. There'll be a little house—it's not ready yet, but I'll see to it that it's comfortable, got all the things you'd need. Point is, Nellie, she can't go out of the sanatorium unless she's going to be well looked after."

"I ain't no skilled nurse, Mr. Rob," Nellie said dubiously.

"I know that. I don't think that would be necessary. As far as I understand it, all she has to do is get plenty of rest, undertake no strenuous physical tasks, and eat well. If she should get sick you call Dr. Luce—the house is the other side of Colorado Springs from his clinic but within reach for emergencies."

"I could sure see she eats well," Nellie said.

"Of course you'd have help in the house. I'd leave it to you to hire some young farm boy with strong shoulders for chopping the firewood and chores like that. But I have to be honest with you, Nellie. The winters there are very cold, and the whole region kind of shuts down from about September to April. Of course there's things going on in the town but not much—it's not a place where you'll get much entertainment except church socials and that sort of thing, until the spring thaw."

"I don' exactly move in a social whirl here at the Castle, Mr. Rob."

"No, but New York is only an hour's drive. On your day off you can go in, see friends, buy a few things. There's not much in Colorado Springs until the vacation visitors arrive in late spring. What I'm saying, Nellie, is that you and Morag would be thrown on one another for company and amusement."

Nellie smiled. "Mis' Morag and me allus got on well, if you remember . . ."

"I know that. But you're older now, Nellie." He paused. "How old are you?"

"That ain't the kind o' question you should ask a lady!" She was laughing. "But since you and me's ole friends, I'll tell you I ain't gonna see fifty again."

Rob considered the point. Morag was ten years junior to Nellie, and it was years since they had seen each other. Would it work, to throw them together with almost no other resource? But who else was there to ask? He couldn't confide Morag to a stranger. It had to be someone she knew, and Nellie was the only person he could turn to.

"I'd pay you well," he said, using his best tactic.

Nellie sighed. "That's kind of you, Mr. Rob. But you know if'n I go, it won' be for the money."

Her quiet rebuke silenced him. He stood fidgeting, not knowing what else to say. For her part, Nellie was thinking of her own future.

She was less and less in favour with Luisa. Unable to read, she could make nothing of the lists and menus her employer was continually thrusting at her; she had to ask one of the kitchenmaids to read them to her. She could learn no new dishes except by demonstration. When Luisa sent the latest issue of *Harper*'s to the kitchen with instructions to try the dish described on the cookery page, Nellie was dependent on young Rose to decipher it for her—and since Rose was a poor scholar and certainly knew no French, the finer details of haute cuisine eluded her.

Luisa wanted to hire a French chef. Rob wouldn't let her. For great events, they had professional caterers, for less elaborate entertaining he insisted that Nellie's skills were enough. But as their load of entertaining increased with the coming of Ellie-Rose's wedding, Nellie found it harder and harder to cope. She had plenty of kitchen hands to do the basic chores, the preparation of vegetables, the stirring of pots—but in the end the responsibility was hers, and she was beginning to acknowledge that the household was outstripping her abilities.

To go to Colorado would be an escape from a situation that would soon become untenable. Colorado . . . She knew nothing about it. But Mis' Morag would be there. Their friendship went a long way back, to the time when Rob and Morag had arrived at the Van Huten farm all those years ago looking for work. She had always been fond of Morag.

"I'd sure like to see Miss Ellie-Rose married," she murmured, as an approach to saying she would go.

"That would fit in fine! The house is being finished now, I'm having furniture and things shipped out. If you get there about the end of April and put everything in order, then Morag can move in with you at the beginning of May. The weather's good just then—and that gives her all the summer to settle in and get strength."

"You want I should travel the end of April?" It was only six weeks away. She would have to readjust her thoughts to fit this new programme; first the wedding, then the trip to a new home and a new career. Instead of being cook in a big household, a position she'd worked her way up to over a long time, she'd be companion to a sick lady.

It scared her a little. She knew invalids could be difficult and clinging. Look at poor Governor McKinley's wife, always calling him to her side, insisting on attention . . . But she had a feeling her days in the Craigallan household were numbered anyhow, and it would be better to go than be fired.

"That will be suitable, Mr. Rob," she concluded. "You want I should tell Mis' Luisa, or will you?"

He frowned. If he told Luisa Nellie was going, she'd want to know where, and how he came into it. He didn't want to tell her he was providing a home for Morag; he could just imagine the tirade it would call forth. "It would be better if you gave notice," he said. "If she asks where you're going, just say you've got a job in a country town."

Luisa didn't even ask. She was delighted. She at once went to the best agency in New York to inquire for a French chef, and installed M. Dugarel within two weeks. Nellie was reduced to assistant cook, a role she filled until the wedding reception was over. Luisa would have been surprised to see how well M. Dugarel and Nellie got on together; he had a deep appreciation of her abilities and was, moreover, about as French as the gumbo of New Orleans, in which city he was born.

Nellie sat on the bride's side of the church during the wedding service and wept a few tears to see her little girl become a wife. Still, Mr. Curtis seemed a good man, a friend of Governor McKinley, intended for great things or so everyone seemed to think. Nellie could leave for Colorado content that at least one of Mr. Rob's children was settling down to happiness. If only poor Mr. Cornelius could get married—but what girl was going to look twice at a man who could hardly speak, handsome and clever though he was?

Rob took Nellie out to Colorado with her quite extensive baggage. In a freight car attached to the train where the final items for Morag's home— books, one of the new Gem Graphophones, a Burdick Cabinet sewing machine, a fine bronze gilt clock for the parlour, wine glasses, crystal flower vases, folding chairs for sitting in the garden, a

132

hammock for sleeping in the afternoon, as well as the few belongings kept in store from Morag's former home in Oyster Bay.

Dr. Luce was a little taken aback when he was introduced to Nellie. He hadn't expected the proposed companion-nurse for Mrs. McGarth to be a black woman. He thought that niggers had little sense and certainly no education, but because Mr. Craigallan insisted he set about explaining the medical background to her in unnecessary detail, and providing her with a detailed list of instructions, which she knew Rob would have to read out to her later.

"She sounds poorly, Mr. Rob," Nellie said. "You sure she fit to leave this place?" They were making their way to the cabin to see Morag.

"Dr. Luce wouldn't let her go if he didn't think it was right. Don't worry too much, Nellie. Morag's got a lot of sense. She doesn't want to have a relapse. You can be sure Dr. Luce has read the same lecture to her a dozen times, so she'll do all she can to keep herself well."

He himself had seen Morag at the beginning of April, when Gregor had come for a visit. Even since then she seemed to have improved; she had gained a little weight, her colour was good, her eyes had sparkle. She greeted Nellie with a warmth that had its roots in their old friendship, and her gratitude for the other woman's kindness in coming out to Colorado. "I'll try not to be a nuisance, Nellie," she promised. "But I must say two things to you. One is that if we obey Dr. Luce's orders, the house is going to have fresh air rushing through it practically all the time, even in winter. Do you think you'll be able to put up with the draughts?"

"Reckon I can wear another flannel petticoat," Nellie said, grinning suddenly.

"And . . . you must think about this, Nellie . . . this sickness of mine is in a stage they call 'quiescent'. That means I'm not infectious. But it can flare up again, so Dr. Luce tells me. You do understand that you might catch it if you're with me then?"

"I'm too old and tough to catch anything, Mis' Morag. I lived through a lot o' things—I ain't goin' to die of a coughin' sickness, no ma'am."

The following day Rob drove Morag to her new home. The house was different from any other Morag had ever seen—lying along the surface of the land like a quiet grey cat, the stone still unrelieved by creeper or vine. It was light and airy, open and uncluttered.

There was a garden, as yet in a rough state. Shade trees would give an arbour for Morag to rest out of doors during the hot months, and would give shelter from the worst of the mountain winds in winter. There would be snow, of course, but there would be sun too, sun glinting back off the cloak of whiteness, making it possible to be out doors on many days. Rob had had huge windows put in, easy to open but well-carpentered so that when closed they kept out the gales.

"Thank you, Rob," she said, taking his hand. "This is beautiful."

"Well, there's no need to cry about it," he said, seeing the tears on her lashes. "It's supposed to make you happy."

"And it does! You mustn't mind me—I cry at the least thing these days. But once I'm settled in I'll be different, I'll be as bright as a linnet, you'll see!"

"I hope so, Morag," he said. "Now, I'll leave you to do what you like with the place. I shan't be back for a while, I'm afraid. This is going to be a busy summer, with the election campaign getting into full swing—"

"But you're not involved in politics, Rob?"

"Huh," he grunted. "Every man who's interested in making money is interested in politics! Especially this year. There's this foolish 'silver campaign' to deal with."

Morag had read in the newspapers about the silver campaign but didn't really understand it—in common with most citizens. It seemed that McKinley's opponent in the election, William Jennings Bryan, was firmly in favour of having the American currency based on silver. McKinley himself had been in favour of a silver standard, and was still suspected by the rich men of the eastern seaboard of wishing to see silver replace gold as the metal of currency.

As far as Morag could gather, moneyed interests everywhere were in a frenzy of fear. If Bryan were elected, they seemed to think their fortunes would vanish overnight. They were determined to prevent that, and funds had poured into McKinley's election coffers. Yet there was a sense of unease, for McKinley had not really taken a stand for gold.

He still hesitated. He felt he would win the White House without turning his back on the silver interest, which he had befriended ever since his young days as a Congressman. His political instincts, generally good, had told him that the issue in this election would be the matter of the tariff law—whether or not to let goods into the United States without having to pay high duty.

For once McKinley was wrong. Moreover, he compounded the error by refusing to listen to his faithful advisers. He was campaigning in Ohio, where he was a little cut off from the unrest among the Eastern magnates.

Rob was cynical about the question of whether the currency should be based on a gold or silver standard. As far as he was concerned, he would make money no matter in what colour—he had commodities as his base of action, not gold or silver. But that shrewd businessman Sam Yarwood had travelled round with a group of campaigning Republicans and wrote that the matter was crucial. "Been pretty well over the country, in twenty-four states, more than ten thousand miles with the McKinley bandwagon," he wrote, "and the people at meetings are simply crazy on the money question. Hard times, farm failures, the falling price of wheat—farmers think it could all be cured if the government came out for silver instead of gold, but the manufacturers are dead against it. They'll back off from supporting McKinley if he don't come out and say he's for gold, mark my words."

That seemed unlikely. The tycoons would surely never back Bryan, the Democratic candidate! Yet they might switch to supporting another Republican rather than McKinley. There was time to do that, to back a Republican outsider. If they did that, the split Republican vote might let in the Democrat.

Rob was in New York on a fine June day when Sam Yarwood had just come back from his trip. They were in the Wall Street office of their brokers, Vinnison, Charle and Co.

A hubbub in the street outside drew their attention. They went to the window of their third floor office and looked down. Below them, odd to see in the narrow sunshine of Wall Street's canyon, were about two hundred top hats, bobbing in procession along the road, stopping the traffic and causing the horses to shy in alarm.

"What the hell?" Rob wondered.

"C'mon, let's see," Sam cried, and ran out.

When they reached street level they found the crowd on the pavement laughing and cheering, some with irony and some with genuine enthusiasm. Serried ranks of Wall Street brokers were marching towards Trinity Church. Some carried placards, hastily lettered in Indian ink and attached to broomstick handles: "Gold or

Disaster!" "Speak out, McKinley!" "Wall Street Backs Gold!"

"Wa'al," grunted Sam. "Did you ever think you'd live to see the day Wall Street went on the march?"

"It's not funny, Sam! Look at them." They were a sight to see, perspiring in their stiff collars, foulard cravats, and frock coats. Moreover, they ought to have been in the Stock Exchange making money. It was true it was near the hour when business finished, but even so most stockbrokers stayed in their offices until it was time to go to the club for a quiet drink.

Rob edged his way out of the crowd and round the nearest corner, where he hailed a cab and was taken to the Waldorf. In his suite he put through a call to Canton Ohio on the recently installed long distance exchange. "Curtis? Curtis, is that you? Listen, boy, all hell broke loose on Wall Street this afternoon. A march. I said, a march! The business-men—no, I witnessed it myself. Listen, Curtis, you've got to make the Major come to his senses. He *must* come out for the gold standard."

"Mr. Craigallan, we've been trying—Both Mr. Lodge and Mr. Kohlsaat have urged him—I don't know what more we can do."

"Write the speech for him, dammit!" Rob said.

"That's hardly possible, Father-in-law—"

"Listen, Curtis, I don't really give a damn who gets in. But you're my son-in-law and it makes a difference to you. So I'm telling you. I saw the

138

writing on the wall this afternoon. Tell McKinley—it's gold or nothing."

Afterwards several men were to claim credit for inserting the word "gold" into the speech that McKinley was about to deliver. He rose in front of his fellow-Republicans in Ohio to give the outline of his political programme, what were known as the "planks" of his platform. He came to the topic of silver; his audience listened tensely.

He took hold of the front of his frock coat and gazed out at the convention. His short, stout figure was given importance by his gaze, eager and penetrating as it ranged the hall. Though he was not a spellbinder like his rival, Bryan, he held the audience in the palm of his hand.

He continued: "The existing gold standard must be maintained . . ."

The rest of the sentence was lost in the hubbub. Pro-silver Republicans cried in protest: "Traitor! Silver for America!" Pro-gold supporters shouted them down: "The standard for ever! Speak up, McKinley!"

Later, when the speech was published in full, those shrewd enough to analyse it saw that McKinley had tried to ride both horses; he wanted to be accepted as a "bi-metallist", a man who thought both silver and gold should be used as a guarantee of currency. But the Eastern newspapers swept all that aside; they took it as accepted that McKinley had come out for gold, and thus shaken hands with the manufacturers, financiers and entre-preneurs of the East Coast. The New York *Tribune* was loud in its praise.

It was never quite certain who had persuaded him to make the changes to that platform speech. Henry Cabot Lodge claimed credit, so did Herman Kohlsaat.

The one man who knew the truth was that wily, round-faced campaign manager, Mark A. Hanna. He had carried the final speech around in his breast pocket for days, patting it slyly when people asked if the candidate had settled his mind on the subject. He let each man think it contained what he wanted it to contain.

There was no doubt that the speech received last minute amendment, while McKinley was with the small group in whom he placed his trust. And something can be guessed from the fact that, when President McKinley formed his administration, he asked The Honourable Curtis Gracebridge to accept the post of personal aide.

8

ELLIE-ROSE hadn't yet established herself as a Washington hostess. There had only been time to settle into their charming little house and have a few dinner parties before Curtis was swept into the current of campaign work for McKinley. Left alone while he went out to stump the country, she busied herself making their home a delight.

She brought Uncle Julius to Washington to re-decorate the house. Although her father might scoff at him, Julius had ability and was quick to pick up every new trend. He wanted to produce a sort of southern-colonial mansion in miniature. Ellie-Rose held him in check when he threatened to go too far, but in the end she had a house that was delightfully cool and airy in Washington's humid, mosquito-ridden summer.

She had always thought the entertaining in New York rather vulgar—showy for the sake of show, to demonstrate wealth and power rather than give pleasure to the guests. For Washington she decided to evolve a new style: elegant yet warm and welcoming, dignified but natural. She understood she would have to lay on dinners for Curtis's fellow-politicians, dinners from which she would be absent so that they could talk business. These she made easy-going and rich, with plenty of good wine and spirits, hearty steaks for the main course, homey pies and ice-cream for dessert.

When she had the wives and daughters too, she chose a lighter style. She decided to model some of her entertainments after the style of a Viennese coffee-party, with rich cream cakes such as *Sachertorte* and the Black Forest cherry gateau. She knew it was important to win the hearts of the wives; if they looked forward to a party at the Gracebridges' they would encourage their husbands to accept her invitations.

But she had scarcely begun to be known for these innocent, waltz-dancing evenings when there came the shock of Curtis's appointment.

It was unexpected even to Curtis. He had hoped to be rewarded, but not so highly. "I just can't . . . say what I feel about it, Ellie," he stammered when he showed her the letter. "I tried to be useful to him, but so did a thousand others. I never expected this."

"Darling, you under-estimate yourself," she told him, smiling at him over the breakfast table. And to tell the truth, she had a feeling that she too had under-estimated him.

She had expected Curtis to do well, but she had thought it would be a long process. Subconsciously she had laid plans to help him reach the heights over a period of some six or ten years. She had thought he would be given some lesser promotion by the President, and would rise during the four years of his tenure. If McKinley were voted in for a second term—but that was unlikely, she had thought—then there would be eight years of probable advancement. By then Curtis would probably be a senator.

Further than that she had not allowed herself to speculate. If she thought he might one day make a fine governor for the State of Nebraska, she kept it to herself. Certainly he couldn't hope to have much of a following until he was into his forties; the American voters were wary of young men.

So she had looked ahead with the feeling that her husband would reach prominence when he left the thirties behind.

Yet now here he was, in the inner circle of the President-Elect of the United States . . .

Her quick mind took it in at once. Now there would be no question of her invitations being refused. Everyone in Washington would want to be friends with a man who had the ear of the President. People would throng her soirées, her garden parties, would queue up for a place at her dinner table.

The appointment had its disadvantages too, she quite understood. Lobbyists would want to be friends with Curtis. Some of them were not very attractive people—she had had experience of those already but not in the number that would batter at their doors from now on. For the first time, Ellie-Rose felt a little reluctant. Politics could be a dirty, boring business.

Ellie-Rose didn't take politics as seriously as the other people she met in Washington. Some of her father's scepticism had rubbed off on her. She had never worn a McKinley campaign brooch, throughout all the months of the electioneering. She refused to idolise the Major, as the other ladies insisted on doing. She thought him a cautious, pedestrian man, and his apparent adoration of his wife was a puzzle.

Ida McKinley bored Ellie-Rose to distraction. She thought her the worst-dressed woman in public life. As a girl, Ida had been very beautiful with her dark thick hair and blue eyes; she had been told that blue became her, and still wore it, often in shades that were too harsh for her wan skin. She was always clad in intricately detailed gowns, embroidered, ribboned, lace-trimmed, edged with swansdown or soft fur, and for the evenings elaborately jewelled. She was never seen informally; whenever she appeared she was fully decked, her hair freshly dressed and her brooches, bracelets and trinkets much in evidence.

Her conversation was dull. She knew little of public affairs or world events, seemed to have no taste in music above the trivial. She loved the theatre but her love for it was indiscriminate; once when the conversation turned to *Peer Gynt*, by the alarming Mr. Ibsen, Mrs. McKinley remarked that she had liked it because the music was so sweet.

Worse yet was the embarrassment brought on by her ill-health. She suffered from a variety of ailments, thought by gossips to be largely mental. In company she would sometimes sit with a fixed expression while the talk flowed around and past her; at such times, any words addressed to her went unheard. Those close to the McKinleys said that sometimes she would have what seemed to be a little seizure, of the kind called *petit mal*, during which she would make a small, distressed sound and lose consciousness completely for a moment.

Ellie-Rose had not as yet witnessed those attacks. All she knew so far was that to be seated next to Mrs. McKinley at one of the many public dinners of the election campaign was a penance, for there was no conversation beyond inanities. The best that could be hoped for was that she would fall silent, so that those on either side could keep up a conversation of their own. But even that was so odd, so awkward.

Curtis was asked to go to Canton, Ohio, the McKinleys' home town, to help the preparations for the move to Washington. This would take until Inauguration Day in March. Ellie-Rose accompanied him, for Curtis declared he couldn't bear any more separation.

It wasn't affection that Ellie-Rose lacked. It was intellectual companionship. Understandably, the President-Elect was immersed in choosing his cabinet, so that around him there circled, like moths round not a mere flame but a bonfire, all the men who had hopes of office. The talk was almost entirely of who would get what post.

Ellie-Rose soon became acquainted with all the applicants, if not in person, then by reputation through unending discussion of their merits or lack of them. The other wives took a great interest in all these minutiae—but then, they were much more partisan than Ellie-Rose had ever been. She saw now that she should have got to know Curtis better in his Washington setting before deciding to be his wife; if she had realised how achingly tiresome it became, she might have refused him. Perhaps only the daughter of a Washington family was a suitable wife for a politician . . .

She wrote to Morag: "You can't imagine how endlessly the intrigues go on. Every man is examined and re-examined, and not only for his own abilities but for what his friends may bring also. It's important not to offend certain persons though it's known they are stupid, ill-informed or biased. It certainly is not the least like democracy; if the populace knew the things that are being done in their name, they would be surprised."

Morag sighed as she read it. This wasn't the letter of a happy bride of less than a year. It was mostly about politics, which Ellie-Rose clearly despised. Yet politics was her husband's career, which she must further as much as she could in her duty as head of his household. There was almost nothing about Curtis himself as a man, only as the agent of the President-Elect's wishes. Curtis seemed to hurry around Canton, and from there to Washington or New York, with special letters and personal

146

messages from McKinley or his close advisers. Although Ellie-Rose had gone to Canton on purpose to be with him, she saw him less than she hoped, and was clearly bored and lonely.

Yet there was no need as yet to be anxious. Soon would come Inauguration Day, and the splendour of that event must make up for the months of dullness in the provincial atmosphere of Canton. Although Morag felt it wouldn't be to her own liking, she sensed that Ellie-Rose might enjoy the prestige of being in the President's immediate circle.

One day after the New Year celebrations—muted in Canton because the Major needed quiet in which to work—Ellie-Rose was asked to call at the McKinley residence for tea. This wasn't an entirely unusual invitation, but the reason surprised her.

"Dear Mrs. Gracebridge," Mrs. McKinley began after the ladies had settled with their tea cups, "you perhaps are aware that as First Lady I shall have to be present at many special events."

"Yes, indeed, ma'am," Ellie-Rose replied, wondering what was coming next.

"I have to collect a wardrobe for my life in the White House. Mrs. Hobart and I have been talking—" Mrs. Hobart was the wife of the Vice-President—"and we feel that though the dresses I have had made here in Canton are very attractive, they are not quite up to the standard of Washington."

You never spoke a truer word, Ellie-Rose agreed

inwardly. Aloud she said, "Mrs. McKinley, your choice in clothes is so individual that you will set your mark upon upon Washington fashion, believe me."

Mrs. McKinley and Mrs. Hobart took that to be a compliment. "Nevertheless," went on Mrs. McKinley, "I need clothes that are beyond the capabilities of the dressmakers here. Mrs. Hobart and I have been discussing a trip to Chicago to choose my White House wardrobe. My dear Mrs. Gracebridge, would you be so kind as to come with us and give us the benefit of your opinion?"

Despite herself, Ellie-Rose was flattered. To be invited to go with the First Lady to choose her clothes . . . ! Later, when they were en route for Chicago, she was less flattered to find that the President's mother, Nancy Alison McKinley, was in charge of the party, that Mrs. McKinley's cousin was married to an official of Marshall Field the department store, and that there could be little hope of taking the First Lady anywhere else to look at dress designs; her clothes would be made by Marshall Field's head designer and that was that.

Nor was Ellie-Rose prepared for being badgered by the Press. They demanded to know what kind of clothes Mrs. McKinley was choosing. She was even offered money if she would divulge the design of the gown the President's wife would wear at the Inaugural Ball. It was less fun than she had imagined it would be, to be cooped up in the house in Chicago while Mrs. McKinley was closeted with

148

the dressmaker, being fitted for an endless succession of blue gowns.

Yet Ellie-Rose began to feel pity for the poor fragile little lady round whom all this fuss was revolving. She was so determined to play her part, to be a credit to her "precious", that it called out admiration. Wrong-headed she might be, selfish and demanding on many inconvenient occasions, but she had a strange, stubborn courage.

At last, on March 1st, the party of the President-Elect set out from Canton for Washington, a band of more than fifty persons with McKinley and his wife in a landau drawn by four white horses.

The Pennsylvania Railroad Company had provided a luxurious private train of seven Pullman cars, draped with flags. From the platform of the train the Major made a speech of farewell to his fellow townsmen. "I reluctantly take leave of my friends and neighbours," he ended, "cherishing in my heart the sweetest memories and the tenderest thoughts of my old home—my home now and, I trust, my home hereafter, so long as I live."

His voice broke. Good heavens, thought Ellie-Rose, he means it. She glanced about her. All the McKinley entourage were moved. The townspeople crowded on the depot were in tears.

Ellie-Rose couldn't understand it. She was glad to be leaving Canton, and would have thought the President of the United States would be even happier. She murmured to Curtis: "He'll never come back here. Once he's lived in the White House he'll find it suffocating here."

Curtis shook his head. "He'll come back. Only death itself would keep him from retiring to Canton once he leaves office."

The reception committee at the Washington depot next morning had clearly been advised that Mrs. McKinley was fond of violets. They sported violets in the buttonholes of their light overcoats or tight-fitting Prince Alberts. They doffed their top hats as the McKinleys alighted.

Later, at the Ebbit House Hotel where the presidential party was staying, Ellie-Rose was buttonholed by the President's mother, soon to be known to the whole country as Mother McKinley. "Mrs. Gracebridge, I've had my eyes on you these last few months, in Canton and all thereabouts, and I've come to the conclusion you're a young woman I can trust."

"Thank you, ma'am," Ellie-Rose said with demure attention. This little eighty-seven year old was quaint and yet authoritative. Ellie-Rose had heard her remark that she wished her dear William had preferred the church to politics.

"You've got to know my daughter-in-law a little, I presume."

"I've had the pleasure of her company on many occasions, ma'am."

"Well, let's not make a secret of it, child. Poor Ida is an invalid and is never going to be any better, no matter how much William hopes for a miracle."

"Medical science . . ."

"Stuff and nonsense," Mother McKinley interrupted. "She's got a deep-seated nervous deficiency—the Lord has seen fit to chastise her in that way and there's nothing to be done. But she's going to be First Lady, and we must all do what we can to prevent embarrassments in public. Mrs. Hobart has already shown that she will always be at hand. Now it so happens that Ida's taken a fancy to you—she doesn't often take to other women, so it's an added blessing in this situation. Can I depend on you, Mrs. Gracebridge, to help my daughter-in-law through the many fatigues of her role?"

Ellie-Rose could hardly have said no even if she had wished to. But although Canton and its inhabitants had bored her, she had come away with some fondness for the McKinleys. She might think them unsophisticated, unfashionable and over-decorous, but she was unwilling to see them look foolish in public.

"I'll do whatever I can, Mrs. McKinley," she promised.

During the inaugural parade Ellie-Rose was certain the President's wife had lost consciousness. But flanked by her husband and a stout, stalwart minister of state, she remained upright in her place. But in the evening, at the Inaugural Ball, worse yet was to happen when Mrs. McKinley, tottering under the weight of her ridiculously ornate blue and silver gown, came close to collapse. Only Ellie-

151

Rose's quick support prevented her from falling, and creating a scene that would have been a great embarrassment to the new President. As the President was leaving the ball, after his wife had safely retired to her White House apartments, he beckoned Ellie-Rose to him with a nod of his head.

"My dear Mrs. Gracebridge," he said, taking one of her hands in both of his, "this evening you have put me in your debt, and I shall always be aware of that."

With a little bow, he moved on. Ellie-Rose stood where she was. "What did he say to you?" asked the onlookers. "What did the President say?"

"Oh, it was just goodnight," she murmured.

But she knew she had been given a promise of personal friendship by the President of the United States.

McKinley's administration had the usual honeymoon period, troubled by the need to know what to do about foreign affairs. Henry Cabot Lodge and Theodore Roosevelt talked to the President about their pet project, which was to annexe Hawaii. Roosevelt urged on the President a plan for command of the seas, a leading role in world commerce, and enhanced prestige.

Teddy Roosevelt was a persuasive talker—bumptious, ebullient, but intelligent. Quite suddenly the President decided he would support the first at least of Roosevelt's aims. He endorsed a treaty sent to the Senate and embodying American control of the islands. The Japanese were greatly alarmed; they even sent warships to the area. But Roosevelt insisted to his President that there was nothing to fear in that respect; he had a low opinion of the Japanese Navy, and as Assistant Secretary to the Navy he presumably had grounds for his opinion. But those around the President were worried. Roosevelt was generally thought of as "pushy", pugnacious, and altogether too fond of his own ideas. It was to be hoped that McKinley wasn't falling under his influence.

What had to be remembered was that, once the United States accepted the principle of annexing Hawaii, there was little to be argued against intervening in Cuba. Cuba had what was called a Patriotic Army, supposedly fighting for liberation against the Spanish. Rob Craigallan shared an opinion with many others when he said the Patriotic Army was nothing but a bunch of bandits, but nevertheless they were more popular with the American public than Spain. Few newspapers had a good word to say for Spain. Hotheads like Roosevelt and Captain Alfred Mahan were open in crying for American take-over. They badgered and speechified throughout the first year of McKinley's office, but without bringing any actual change.

Ellie-Rose would have taken a greater interest in it all except for the fact that just after Christmas she found she was expecting a baby. She didn't settle down well to pregnancy; perhaps memories of that first child, lost after she nearly drowned at Oyster Bay, returned to haunt her; perhaps the strain of

Washington life made it difficult to come to terms with expectant motherhood.

Curtis was all concern and consideration. He insisted she stay in bed late in the mornings, warned the staff to lighten her role as hostess as much as possible. But he couldn't be with her all the time. As the Presidential load became greater, Curtis was needed constantly at the Presidential offices. He and George Cortelyou, one of the junior Presidential secretaries, bore the brunt of the detailed work, the keeping of appointments, the seeking out of contacts or behind-the-scenes workers, the recording of visits and planning of programmes. Neither of them had any influence on the course of policy, but it was they who ensured that the policy could be discussed and, once decided upon, set in motion.

The rainy Washington winter was still holding sway over the capital as Ellie-Rose at last began to feel better. She and Curtis went to an evening party at the home of Comptroller Dawes, where for once the talk was not of Hawaii or Cuba but about the setting to music of Mr. Longfellow's famous poem, Hiawatha.

"You look so much better," Curtis said as he handed her indoors late that night. "You really enjoyed this evening, didn't you?"

"Yes, darling, I did," she agreed, "and all the more because there were no pro-Roosevelt people there to talk about war."

"There won't be a war," he assured her, going

upstairs with his arm around her and his cheek against her hair.

They slept in each other's arms, secure and happy. It was the night of the 15th February.

Next morning Curtis was wakened by the black butler, Compton, shaking him by the shoulder. "Mr. Gracebridge, Mr. Gracebridge, wake up, please, sir, Mr. Gracebridge."

Curtis pulled himself up out of the warm bedclothes, to frown at the black face bending anxiously over him. "What the dickens is the matter?" he asked in a loud whisper. "Don't make such a fuss, you'll waken Mrs. Gracebridge."

"Mr. Gracebridge, sir, you wanted on the telephone. Mr. Cortelyou says will you come to the telephone at once, sir."

Grumbling, Curtis got out of bed. Ellie-Rose roused and stretched out an arm towards him, then finding his place empty opened her eyes.

"Curtis? What time is it?" she queried drowsily.

"Damned if I know," Curtis said, allowing himself to be helped into his dressing gown by Compton.

She half sat up, looking at the two men in dressing gowns. The butler looked alarmed. "Is anything wrong, Compton?"

"I'm wanted on the telephone, is all," Curtis said. "Come on, Compton." To Ellie-Rose he said as he hurried out, "Go back to sleep again, darling."

But she could not. She sat up after the door closed

behind him, took a bed-jacket from the table next to the bed, and draped it over her shoulders.

She had only turned one page of Mr. Kipling's new novel, *Captains Courageous* when Curtis came back into the room. He was already taking off his dressing gown preparatory to getting dressed.

"What is it, Curtis?" Ellie-Rose cried, springing out of bed to run to him. "You're not going out at this hour? It's not six o'clock yet."

"The battleship *Maine* was sunk yesterday in Havana Harbour," he said sombrely, and disappeared into his dressing-room.

She sank down on the settle at the foot of the bed. The *Maine*? On a courtesy visit to Cuba. Surely the Spanish had not been so mad as to attack her?

Thoughts tumbling wildly in her head, she hurried down to see that hot coffee and muffins were ready for her husband when he emerged ready to leave. He stayed only to gulp down some of the scalding liquid then was gone. Ellie-Rose had already sent for a cab for him. In a moment he was gone, having said hardly one more word since he gave her the terrible news.

She knew it meant war. However the sinking of the ship had come about, she felt it in her bones that Teddy Roosevelt and his supporters would find some pretext for naval retaliation. If there had been American lives lost—and that seemed implicit in the way Curtis had reacted—it was almost inevitable that there would be a cry for revenge.

She went slowly upstairs, the hem of her soft

crepe-de-chine nightdress catching on the edges of the treads, and returned to bed. But it was useless to think of sleep. She rose and ran her bath, then dressed without her maid. When she went downstairs she found the household was already in action, although it was an hour ahead of their usual time. Compton immediately ordered breakfast to be brought to her. "Somethin' bad happened, Mis' Gracebridge?" he inquired.

She saw no reason to keep it a secret. All the world would know soon enough. She was depressed and apprehensive. Somehow her coming baby seemed threatened by the thought of war.

At eight o'clock her father rang long distance from New York. "Is Curtis there?" he inquired.

"He's at the White House, Papa."

"Any idea what's going to be done?"

"Not yet."

She heard him hesitate, clear his throat. "Well, it's been hanging fire a long while, Ellie. It's got to come some time, and I think now is the time."

She had no need to ask what he meant.

Around noon Curtis returned briefly. "The President was roused at 3 a.m. with the news," he reported. "The ship was blown up—"

"Blown up? You mean the Spanish garrison opened up on her?"

"No, the guns certainly didn't fire. We're sure of that. But an awful lot of officials are claiming a bomb was planted."

"How many men were killed, Curtis?"

157

He drew in a breath. "So far as we've heard up till now, two hundred and sixty."

"Oh, my God . . . does it mean war?"

He straightened, put a comforting arm about her. "Joe Bailey asked for a declaration of war in the House this morning."

"Oh, no!"

"It's all right. The Speaker told him he was out of order since we had no way as yet of knowing what caused the loss of the *Maine*. I hear there was a roar of disagreement, but good sense prevailed. Don't worry, Ellie—the United States isn't going to rush into battle without knowing if it has good reason."

"I hope you're right, Curtis." She couldn't help remembering Teddy Roosevelt's voice, quick and high-pitched with vehemence, as he talked about "those damned grandees lording it in Havana". He longed for an excuse to throw them out of Cuba; perhaps now he had it, in the sinking of an American battleship.

"Papa telephoned," she said as she accompanied her husband to the door again. "He wanted to know how things stood. What shall I tell him when he telephones again?"

Curtis stood with his hat in his hand, hesitating as Compton opened the door for him. He understood that his father-in-law wanted to have as much inside information as it was possible for him to give, because the possibility of war was already unsettling the grain market. In a war, feedstuffs become important; moreover, Rob had investments in Cuba itself.

For seven weeks President McKinley held the "war party" in check. He himself had served in the Civil War and had no wish to see bodies piled up again. He told his cabinet members, "There must be no war because the country is not *ready* for war."

An investigation was carried out in Havana, in which no evidence was found that anything underhanded had brought the disaster about. Captain Sigsbee of the *Maine* insisted that the explosion had been an accident, some fault that had brought about a fire in the powder magazine.

But the number of Americans willing to wait grew less as spring brought the leaves out on Washington's shade trees. The Hearst press, never cautious, threw good sense to the winds. "Remember the *Maine* and to hell with Spain!" was its slogan. Emotion began to run high against the President for cowardice. Effigies of McKinley were burned in Virginia and Pennsylvania. His portrait was torn down from public offices, placards were defaced on walls. Finally Teddy Roosevelt brought matters to a climax at the annual Gridiron Dinner in New York, a fundraising event.

"We *will* have this war for the freedom of Cuba," he cried, shaking his fist under Mark Hanna's plump chin, "in spite of the timidity of the commercial interests served by such as you!"

Uproar followed. Rob, who was among the guests, knew that the United States was undoubtedly going to war with Spain; McKinley might be reluctant but it would be forced upon him by bravos like Roosevelt. Next morning he went to collect his colleague Sam Yarwood and they drove to Wall Street, to buy and sell so as to make the best profit out of the forthcoming hostilities.

As wars go, the war between Spain and the United States was short and inexpensive. It began in April and ended in December, which was perhaps bad for the United States because it gave rise to the idea that wars ought to be over by Christmas. By a treaty signed in Paris, Spain ceded Cuba to the American government.

President McKinley could have no idea that by these two acts—the acceptance of Hawaii and of Cuba—he had signed his own death warrant.

In the eyes of the revolutionaries not yet taken seriously by the government, McKinley branded himself as a tyrant, an oppressor. He became a target.

His days were numbered.

9

CURTIS had had to remain in Washington with the President all through the steamy summer of the "war" against Spain. But Ellie-Rose's baby was expected in July. Curtis insisted it was unfair and unwise to have her cooped up in the capital, especially as he was so often at the White House for forty-eight hours at a stretch, with scarcely time even to telephone home.

So she went to Craigallan Castle in May, and from there to Saratoga Springs as the heat increased. The baby, a girl, was born at the summer home her father had rented there, under the care of a wellknown doctor and a staff of resident nurses he had hired.

Rob was delighted with his granddaughter, Luisa less so. She didn't want to be a grandmother; it put an end to her pretence that she was still herself a girl, which she had kept up despite the evidence of two grown children.

Curtis hurried to Saratoga Springs for a flying visit. He couldn't stay, he was needed at his White House office. When he returned to Washington Ellie-Rose allowed herself the luxury of a little weep. She found she was rather apt to break into tears at almost nothing, since she had become pregnant. It was to be hoped, she said to herself as

161

she dried her eyes, that she wasn't going to turn into one of those sentimental, drooping women who framed elegant little verses about children and kittens for a central place on their knick-knack tables, to prove how "sensitive" they were.

But she was kept quite busy. The getting to know her baby, the routine of feeding, cuddling, displaying her to friends, occupied most of the daylight hours. Naturally she didn't have any of the distasteful chores such as changing diapers or mopping up dribbles—that was what nurses were hired to do. For Ellie, new motherhood consisted of sitting up in bed, clad in a variety of very beautiful lingerie jackets of silk, chiffon or lace, to receive her former school friends. Most of them were young matrons now, further along the road of maternity; they would lord it over her a little, warning her of the anxieties she could expect over teething or thrush, comparing notes with each other about the derelictions of nursery nurses, sighing that men simply didn't know what it was all about.

Among her visitors were first Cornelius, and then Gregor. Cornelius was shy and delighted, letting the baby take hold of a finger as he stared in wonder at the tiny fist. "She's not like you," he remarked as he straightened from the cradle brought in by the nurse.

"Do you think she's like Curtis?"

He considered, then shook his head. "Like Papa."

Ellie-Rose threw her hands up, but secretly she

162

was pleased. At forty-six Rob Craigallan was still a very handsome man, tall, slim, his russet hair just beginning to have tints of silver here and there. When she was with him, among strangers, Ellie-Rose knew that other women wondered who they were, whether this fine-looking man had a young mistress, and it always gave her a faint, wicked thrill. There was a friendship between them that was different from the usual father-daughter relationship; she called him Papa, but she didn't feel daughterly towards him—she felt she was his comrade, his fellow-voyager. If her precious little baby had to take after a male member of the two families, she preferred she should take after Papa. That implied she would have good looks, and if she took after her grandfather in character, she would have spirit and determination too.

When Gregor came, he was embarrassed. There was always an awkwardness in his dealings with Ellie-Rose. Now here she was in this flower-filled room at Saratoga Springs, whither he had come on a duty visit at Mr. Craigallan's command. She seemed different—softer, gentler. Her face when she held Gina for him to admire was like a madonna by Giorgione.

He dutifully expressed delight in the baby and sat down to make conversation. He had no idea what you talked to new mothers about, except their babes, and about those he was ignorant.

Ellie-Rose guessed his perplexity. "Are you going to spend your vacation in Colorado?" she inquired.

"Not all of it, not this year," he replied. "Mr. Craig is taking me to Chicago in August."

Ellie-Rose liked Gregor's private nickname for her father. "What's the Chicago trip for?" she inquired. "To visit with Cornelius?"

"Oh, yes, that too. But the chief reason is to show me The Pit."

The Pit was the Chicago grain market, the place where dealers in commodities bid for the new harvests or sold grain in the silo. Why on earth should her father take Gregor there? She had seen The Pit, and found it at first dull when nothing happened for over an hour, and then frightening when a sudden surge of business brought all the dealers out in a panic rush of action.

"Whose idea was that?" she asked, frowning a little.

"I don't know. It just kind of came up. We were talking about those two new silos Mr. Craig is having built at Minneapolis, and I think I said it didn't seem possible there could be any need for *more* storage, and he—"

"I didn't know Papa talked about things like that with you?" she put in, half questioning.

Gregor smiled. "What else?" he countered. "That's Mr. Craig's chief interest in life, after all—business, chiefly the wheat business. It's only natural he should talk about it."

"You find that pretty dull, I imagine."

"Dull? Not a bit!" He shook his head, clearly surprised at such a thought. "It's fascinating. In the geography class at school, Mr. Wallace drones on about the new American territories applying for state-hood and their boundaries and stuff like that, but when I talk to Mr. Craig I see those lands—I understand how they came to be opened up and used, I hear from him how the railroad came and took their produce to market . . . It's strange how it all fits together, you know. And it reaches out so far. It's not just growing the wheat—men have been doing that from time immemorial. It's getting it to market, selling it, making sure it gets where it ought to go at the right price, having enough in store for a shortfall . . ."

He fell silent. It occurred to him that a new young mother probably wasn't interested in all this dull stuff about the marketing of grain.

Ellie-Rose bent her head and watched her finger trace the embroidery on the edge of the bedsheet. All this was something of a revelation to her. Her father often talked business with her, although not so often these days when she was absorbed in Washington life and marriage. Sometimes, she knew, he discussed specific problems with Cornelius—wheat deterioration under storage conditions, things like that. But she had to accept that Rob didn't find it easy to hold long conversations with Cornelius. He could speak distinctly enough for Cornelius to lip-read when they were directly face to face, or use the finger language—but that wasn't the most convenient method to discuss the movements of the grain

165

market, the buying of an office block in Wall Street, or the construction of silos. Perhaps, if he and Cornelius lived all the time in the same house, their communication would have been easier. She had to admit it was Cornelius's choice to have his own dwelling places in New York and Chicago.

"How long will you be staying in Chicago?"

"That's Mr. Craig's decision. He says he wants to show me the ropes."

"What for? Is he thinking of offering you a job in the business?"

Gregor shrugged. So far, that hadn't come up. If it did, he wasn't sure how he would react.

Ellie-Rose studied him with eyes that saw him afresh. He was sixteen-going-on-seventeen, tall, rather too thin—outgrowing his strength as so many boys did at that age. But there was nothing gawky about him. He sat on his chair by the bedside without any suggestion of sprawl; he was contained, at ease. His holiday clothes—light coloured trousers, dark blazer, striped blue-and-white cambric shirt with a stiff collar and plain blue tie— looked as if they rested easily upon him. There was none of the too-often-seen tendency to ease his neck against the stiff collar with a nervous finger. His fingers, in fact, were laced idly behind his head, and yet he wasn't lolling, there was no sense of impoliteness in the attitude.

The scar on his temple still showed ever so slightly, drawing up the skin so that his features seemed to express wry interest in the world. She

166

could see the faint down on his chin; he would soon begin to shave, would experiment with moustaches and sideburns like the other young men. No, he wouldn't—somehow she knew he would have more sense than to make himself look ridiculous in those vain attempts at maturity.

"What do you think you might do with yourself, Greg?" she asked. "After school, I mean."

Here it came again. He sighed. Why did adults feel they had to take an interest in one's plans? He had no intention of sharing his with anyone. They were simple. He intended to get as good an education as he could, find a job, and have his mother in a home they would share.

"I'm not looking that far, Ellie," he said.

"What do you enjoy at school? What are you good at?"

"Well . . . maths, and economics . . . I'm not much good at science. Cornelius and I fool around together in the vacations, and it's always fun, but when you do things in the lab at school they get so downright dreary . . . One thing I'm beginning to do pretty well at is languages. Never did that at the school in Oyster Bay, but French came pretty easy and now I'm taking Spanish."

He stopped, hoping he'd said enough to satisfy. He didn't really want to discuss his academic prowess. The truth was, he was an outstanding scholar, although there were some things he did less well than others. The reports sent from Petersfield School to Rob and then on to his mother were

167

always glowing. Except for that one occasion when he'd run away to see her, his conduct was noted as excellent, he had leadership qualities, he took part in leisure activities such as music and theatricals with enthusiasm although showing no special talent, he played good hockey and polo, swam well, was a member of the champion rowing team. His masters had nothing to complain of him in him except that he liked to go off on his own more often than the other students—but when he did so, it wasn't for the purpose of getting drunk or chasing the girls. They couldn't exactly fault him but he puzzled them.

When Rob came in next day to pay his morning visit to his grand-daughter, Ellie-Rose asked him to stay and have coffee. Pleased, he folded himself on to the handsome little armchair at the bedside.

"You're looking so well, honey," he said with fondness, watching her as she took the milk drink from the nurse after she had poured coffee for him.

"I'm fine, Papa. To tell the truth, I'm beginning to be bored with having to stay in bed. I don't feel *ill*."

"Well, you aren't ill. But you do have to be careful. Everybody says this is a ticklish period, this few weeks after the baby's here."

She shrugged. "Some of my friends have been telling me I'll feel terribly depressed—things like that. It's a lot of nonsense."

"I hope so. I wouldn't want to see you unhappy, even if it was just one of the normal after-effects."

"Oh, I'm having something like a holiday, really. Hordes of visitors." She paused, sipped her warm milk. "Gregor came yesterday."

"Yes, so he told me."

"Oh, you saw him yesterday?"

"Took him out to dinner. You get a really fine meal at the hotel in the season, you know, Ellie. When you're up and about, you and I will have to go there—make an outing for you."

"That would be lovely," she replied, from an automatic need to keep the conversation going.

So he took Gregor out as a dinner companion? In other days, she would have said it was Papa giving Gregor a treat. But now she'd just talked to Gregor, and she sensed that her father knew you didn't give "treats" to a boy like Gregor. He didn't have to be jollied or kept amused. If Rob had taken Gregor out to dinner, it was because he enjoyed his company across the dinner table.

"I was asking Greg what he intended to do when he finishes school."

"You did? What d'you think of my plan, then?"

"Plan? What plan?"

Rob stared at her over his coffee cup. "He didn't tell you?"

"Tell me what?"

"I've entered him for Harvard."

"What?" The glass in her hand tilted, warm milk spilled down the front of her exquisite cape of ivory guipure and the Chinese-silk gown underneath.

"Oh, heavens, Ellie, what a mess! Here, let

169

me—" He took the half empty glass from her, offered the napkin that had come with his coffee. She dabbed at herself while he rang for the nurse. It took some moments to repair the damage. Rob was asked to go outside for a moment while the damp garments were exchanged for yet another set of pretty things.

All this gave Ellie-Rose a moment to come to terms with herself. Why should it startle her so much to hear of Rob's plan? There was no doubt Gregor was clever; naturally he ought to go to university.

Yet somehow it took her by surprise. In her own mind she'd been thinking of Gregor starting out in life for himself pretty soon. She understood that her father wanted to give the boy a good education, and wouldn't have dreamed of protesting—as her mother did—that Petersfield was much too costly.

All the same, she'd expected that to be the sum total of her father's involvement. Having given the boy a good education, he'd send him away to do the best he could—and without any fears that he would fail.

She realised as all this ran through her mind that she'd been writing Gregor off as a poor relation. Her father would do his duty by him, but no more.

Now it came home to her that Gregor was her father's son, regarded by him as such. He intended to do as much for Gregor as he had done for Cornelius.

Well, it was only right . . .

When Rob came in again, he found Ellie-Rose sitting up against fresh pillows and wearing a shell-pink sleeved stole of pleated voile. She looked angelic. Yet there was a specially alert tilt to her head.

"Papa, Greg didn't say anything about Harvard," she began. "Perhaps he'd rather not go?"

"Oh, stuff and nonsense. That's a very bright boy, Ellie. He understands the advantages of a Harvard degree."

"But . . . Papa . . . how will you explain your generosity?"

Rob sighed. "That's the problem, to some extent. He says he's had enough from me already, wants to get a job and start paying me back. Never heard such rubbish."

"Surely it's a rather admirable outlook?"

"Yeah, I'm not saying it isn't very noble. But nobility doesn't get you far in this life, Ellie. And that boy has brains. I want them used properly. If he's going to be an asset in the business."

"Ah," she said.

"What d'you mean, 'ah'?"

"You're going to offer him a job too?"

"Sure thing. I don't want to lose him to a competitor."

"You're trying to give him too much. He won't be able to hold up under the load of gratitude you're laying on him. Let him be, Papa. If he wants to go to university, let him work his way through, like other men do."

Her father folded his arms and leaned back. "Cornelius had money spent on his education," he said. "As much as I could afford at the time, and more. I went without so that he could have special tuition at the school for the deaf. And you, Ellie-Rose. You went off to finishing school, had special tutors for music and art . . . Why should Gregor have less?"

"Because . . . because you aren't going to be able to explain it to him."

"I'll manage," he said sardonically, as if to say, Are you telling me I can't handle it?

"Mama won't like it."

"That won't bother me."

"Papa—do you really think you're being wise in . . . sort of . . . grooming Gregor for great things?"

"I certainly do. Because he is headed for great things."

"What do you mean? Are you going to—I mean, what are you planning to do?"

He hesitated, then seemed to make up his mind. "I wasn't going to talk about this to anyone, not for a long time yet. But since you've raised it . . . I'm going to put Greg in at the head of one of the subsidiaries as soon as he leaves Harvard. If he performs as well as I think he will, the sky's the limit for him."

"You're going to give him precedence over Cornelius?" she demanded, a catch in her voice.

"I don't say that, Ellie. But Neil . . . well, you

172

know his limitations as well as I do. Some things he just can't do. He can't run a big office because he can't control a board meeting. He can't deal on the Board of Trade because he wouldn't be able to hear the dealers calling. He—"

"None of those things are vital, Papa. He can hire men to do all that."

"That means he's got to trust someone else. That's not the way to keep control, Ellie—"

"Neil can handle anything if you just do as much for him as you're planning to do for Greg—"

"What, send him to Harvard? Neil doesn't want to go back to school, Ellie—"

"I don't mean that!" she flashed. "Of course Neil is past all that stage. But you never brought him forward the way you're planning to do for Greg. You never gave Neilie one of the subsidiary firms to run—"

"Because he preferred research! You know as well as I do that he wanted to work in a lab, on his own terms." Rob drew up short. Why was he defending his actions to his own daughter? "There's no point in going over Neil's career. He took the path he wanted, and I'm happy to let him go along with it. But I need someone I can depend on in the business, Ellie. It's growing all the time—you've no idea of the ramifications these days, as overseas trade expands—"

"Someone you can depend on! It sounds more to me as if you're bringing him in as the heir-apparent!"

He got to his feet, tall and angry. "You mind your own business, Ellie," he said in a low voice. "Give your mind to bringing up your baby and helping your husband—that's your part. Leave me to make what decisions I think best for Craigallan Agricultural Products."

"If you really think I'll stand still for pushing Cornelius to one side—"

"He's not being pushed aside. He chose to stand aside a long time ago."

"And all for the benefit of an *outsider*—"

"Gregor's my son—"

"Not in any legal sense! It's going to look mighty strange to the rest of the world if you take up your illegitimate son at the expense of your legal heir—"

"Hold your tongue, Ellie!"

"I will not! I won't have you slighting Neilie like this!"

Rob went to the door. "You're upset," he said coldly. "It's part of this business of being a new mother, I reckon. Lie down and take a nap, Ellie. When you wake up you'll think better of telling me how to run my affairs."

He stalked out, leaving his daughter to bury her face in her pillow in a flood of silly tears.

He had no doubt she had worked herself into a state because of post-natal nerves. And to some extent he was right. Yet Ellie-Rose was genuinely hurt on Cornelius's behalf, and also on her own. Somehow it seemed to her that if Cornelius was thought unfit to be the next head of Craigallan

174

Agricultural Products, she herself ought to be the natural alternative. For the moment she didn't consider the fact that she was a married woman with a husband career-bound at Washington; she simply let herself feel that since she had shared so many of her father's hopes and plans in the past she ought to be his successor if Cornelius were ruled out.

But she dried her eyes and got control of herself. If she wanted to be any help to Cornelius, she mustn't be silly about it.

When she and her father met again later that day, the topic wasn't resumed. In the tenor of the Saratoga household their relationship was entirely normal. But Ellie-Rose was watchful. Rob and Gregor went to Chicago as planned to watch the dealing for the August wheat; they came back, with Gregor ebullient about the scene.

"It's like a madhouse! I never saw anything like it! When we talk about the Stock Exchange in economics class, you get the impression that it's all so carefully considered and rational—but what I saw at the Board of Trade was more like comic opera!"

She learned that Rob had given him a small sum of money to dabble in the dealing. Gregor had come out even, with no help from anyone—after one near-disaster he had sent down instructions to recoup so that his money ended up safe.

"The best way of learning," Rob said. "You can listen to other men talking of their activities, but there's nothing like seeing your money trickling down the drain to make you catch on."

Ellie-Rose looked at her father. He was pouring himself a whisky from the crystal decanter, but seemed to feel her glance, for he paused and looked up.

"Is there some particular reason for Greg to learn about The Pit?" she inquired.

"There could be," he replied.

Ellie-Rose's mother was with them. It was the pre-dinner time, when they gathered in the drawing-room before dispersing to dress. Ellie-Rose was up and about the house now, making use of an extensive wardrobe of housegowns and teagowns. In a day or two she would be allowed out, to take the air in the carriage or even stroll in Saratoga's elegant main street.

"Papa was saying you might be going on to Harvard, Greg," Ellie-Rose went on.

Luisa, drowsing over a magazine, sat up.

"It's been suggested," the boy replied, flushing.

"Harvard?" Luisa put in. "It's the first I've heard—"

"There's no need to enter into a discussion of it now," Rob said in a hard tone. "Aren't you going to go up and dress, Luisa? I thought you were going to the opera?"

"Oh, the opera. It's a bore. *Aida*, you know, and all those terrible moth-eaten animals being led across the stage—but Mrs. Hammersley is counting on me to make up the party in her box so of course I have to go."

She rose as she spoke, throwing her magazine carelessly on the sofa where it splayed out, spoiling the pages. "It's a pity you can't come too, Ellie-Rose."

"The last thing she wants is to watch a fat old gentleman clutching a blacked-up fat old lady and telling her he'd give up the throne of Egypt for her," Rob said, rolling his eyes in droll imitation of operatic style. "It might upset her."

It was said humorously, yet Ellie-Rose took it as a quip about her flood of tears the other morning. She was hurt.

Later she left her father and Gregor in deep discussion. She tapped on the door of her mother's boudoir.

"Come in, Pansy—I've decided on the cream—" She broke off as Ellie-Rose came in. She had expected her maid, Pansy, with a lace stole to complete her outfit.

Luisa's addiction to rich food had made her look stout and matronly despite the young colours she insisted on wearing. Whereas Morag contented herself with widow's black and grey and the muted shades that were thought suitable for ladies after thirty, Luisa insisted on the rich emerald, peacock blue, magenta and yellow that the clever German dye-makers had brought into being.

"Mama, don't you think that shade is a little 'difficult' for someone with such a pink

177

complexion?" Ellie-Rose ventured as she watched her mother dressing.

Luisa shook her head, surveying herself in the boudoir mirror. She was wearing a gown of gauze and taffeta with much draping across the bodice and insets in the skirt, all in a very rich plum colour. She seemed unaware that the high colour of her cheeks was emphasised by it so that she looked flushed as if she had drunk too much. To make matters worse, her hair was dressed with a row of bangs across the forehead which would undoubtedly cling there when she became hot as the evening wore on.

"I'm not in favour of this fashion that's coming in for drab colours," she remarked. "It'll end up by making us all look like somebody's governess."

"Better that than look like somebody's national flag."

"Nonsense. You've never seen a flag this colour," Luisa said with complacency, and gathered up her gloves. Like many plump women, she had small hands and feet, and liked to emphasise both by wearing gloves and shoes a size too small. Getting her evening gloves on was a long and difficult process; once on, they could only be got off by slitting them with nail scissors. It was said of many leaders of fashion that they never wore a pair of gloves twice, but the reason was not that they refused to have them cleaned; it was more likely that they had to be cut off at the end of their use.

"I wish I hadn't ordered *boeuf en daube* for dinner tonight," she added as she put perfume on her palms and wrists. "It always makes me sleepy—too bad if I doze off in the middle of the death scene!"

"Mama, you hadn't heard about sending Gregor to Harvard?"

"No, not a word," Luisa said, suddenly looking up with the perfume bottle in one hand and the stopper in the other. "I rather think I wasn't supposed to hear, either."

"Papa hasn't talked to you about it?"

Luisa gave a half smile, but said nothing. They both understood that Rob seldom discussed anything with Luisa, and about Gregor, never.

"The idea of sending him to Harvard is to get him ready for going into C.A.P.," she said.

Ellie-Rose knew she was making a mistake, but she was urged on by a variety of impulses. She wanted to punish her father for some slight she felt she had suffered. She wanted to strike a blow on behalf of Cornelius. She wanted to assert her own importance. She wanted to make the point that Gregor was not of the family—that he was a poor relation with no real claim.

"Huh?" Luisa heard what she said, but didn't quite see its importance. "Well, I suppose the brat has got to have a job—"

"But he's going in at the top, Mama. It isn't just a *job*."

"What then? I don't understand, Ellie-Rose."

Now was the moment when she should draw

back. "Papa's planning to make Gregor his heir," she said.

As soon as the words were uttered she wished them unsaid. Her mother whirled, stiff skirts flurrying on the carpet, making a whispering sound. "His heir!"

"I . . . that may be just my imagination, Mama—"

"By God, we'll soon find out!"

She swept out and down the stairs. As luck would have it, Gregor was just about to come up, to get ready for dinner. He was halfway up the staircase. He looked up at the step on the landing to see Mr. Craig's wife blocking his way, looming there like a great plum-coloured thunder cloud. The thought brought a faint curve to his lips and Luisa, seeing it, felt hate rising within her. Who did he think he was, to sneer at her?

"Well," she said, "so you're going to Harvard, eh?"

"I beg your pardon?"

"Petersfield's not enough, you have to go to the best university in the country—"

"It's not decided yet, ma'am—"

"No, and never will be, if I have anything to do with it! Haven't you and that leech of a mother got enough out of this family yet?"

Gregor went pale. His hand on the banister tightened convulsively.

"My mother has nothing to do with this," he said. "Please leave her out of it."

"That's hardly possible, is it?" Luisa challenged.

180

"You only have a place here because Mr. Craigallan has silly notions of honour—"

"I've told Mr. Craig that I don't expect any more—"

"Oh, sure, sure! But that's not what your mother says, is it? You can bet she holds him to the contract!"

"Mama," Ellie-Rose put in anxiously, touching her on the shoulder, hoping to warn her what she was doing.

"What—what contract?" Gregor asked.

"The one that insists on the full pound of flesh—"

"I've never seen any contract, ma'am."

"Oh, it's not in writing! A man of honour doesn't have to sign his name in ink to feel obligations to his bastard."

"What?" It was a gasp.

"Oh, come on, don't pretend she hasn't told you. Your precious 'Mr. Craig' is your father."

There was a silence. The boy stood looking up at her. Luisa felt every nerve tingle with dislike. She went down the staircase until she was on the step just above him, so that their faces were on a level. She stared into his eyes.

"Never looked in the mirror?" she sneered. "Never seen the resemblance? Everybody else has, I assure you."

From the landing, Ellie-Rose saw Gregor go utterly still. It was difficult to tell whether he was surprised. He and Luisa were locked in a gaze of complete concentration.

"Your mother said your father died at sea," Luisa said. "Unoriginal—she probably got it out of a musical drama. But it was better than admitting she was a whore."

Gregor's hand came up from the banister. For one awful moment Ellie-Rose thought he was going to hit Luisa in the face. But the hand closed on the shoulder above the exaggerated folds of the plum-coloured sleeve. The fingers dug into the plump flesh. He exerted some strength, and Ellie-Rose saw her mother sway, teetering on the tread of the stair.

One more centimetre, and he would have sent her toppling. Luisa's mouth opened in a soundless cry of panic. Across her face raced terror, behind it visions of broken bones.

Then as suddenly as his first movement, Gregor took his hand away. He turned round, jostling Luisa as he did so, but in negligence, not with purpose. He took the stairs in two great leaps of his long legs, reached the hall door, flung it open with a crash, and was gone.

10

TRAVELLING expenses were no problem. Gregor had his month's allowance, and an extra fifty dollars that Mr. Craig had insisted on his taking as vacation money. His clothes weren't of the most suitable for a long train trip; in particular, it was cold at nights. At Topeka he left the depot while the train took on water and fresh supplies of coal, to buy a donkey jacket. Huddled in this, he slept well enough in his corner.

Signs of fall were already beginning to show among the trees as they climbed upwards into the foothills of the Rockies. The pines on the ridge of the range hiding the Arkansas River were still a dark green cloak, but on Pike's Peak there was a lacy sprinkling of snow already.

"Goin' to be an early winter," the ticket man said at Denver as he changed to the spur line for the Springs. "Seen the deer edgin' down already into the valley."

The Pueblo coach set him down on the far side of Colorado Springs at the crossroads. Mists were curling round the tree tops, unusual in this dry region. Gregor pulled his topcoat around him against the dampness and trudged up the road. Ever since that blinding moment of anger on the stairs of the house in Saratoga Springs, he had been going over and over everything he knew about his life, almost obsessively. He was tired; he hadn't slept properly in four days, and all his muscles felt cramped from being tucked up in a train seat. He was hungry and thirsty.

The road opened out from between its rocky banks to a fertile valley, sheltered and small. A stream ran fast down the incline, bordered with mertensia and the fading blooms of the summer's wood lilies.

As Gregor opened the gate of his mother's garden, the door of the house opened. Nellie was standing in the opening. "Afternoon, Mister Gregor," she said, and stood aside to let him in. She didn't seem in the least surprised to see him, unkempt and without luggage.

Morag was sitting by an open window in the big living-room, with a piece of needlework in her hands. She set it by, got up, and put an arm around him. "You look worn out," she said, kissing him gently on the cheek. "Nellie's got some soup ready and she'll whip up an omelette."

He sank into the armchair to which she was directing him. "You were expecting me?" he said in wonder.

For answer she picked up a piece of paper lying on the table beside her workbox. It was a wire.

He read: "Gregor probably on his way to you. Some troubles here but don't be alarmed. Let me know when he arrives. Next move rests with him. Keep me informed. Love Rob."

184

Gregor crumpled it and threw it back on the table. "Keeping tabs on me, is he?"

"He didn't want me to be taken by surprise if you turned up unexpectedly," she said in a gentle tone.

"No . . . I should have thought of that—it might have been a bit of a shock. I should have sent a wire myself." He was vexed. For once in his life he'd been too taken up with his own affairs to think of her.

"Did you take the coach?"

"From the Springs—yes."

"We thought you would, although of course there was the chance you might hire a carriage—"

"The coach was just leaving when I got off the train."

By talking about the commonplace details of his journey she was taking the drama out of his arrival. He sensed it, and for a moment was angry with her. But he was too tired to make an issue of it now, and next moment Nellie came in with a tray. The aroma of the soup was irresistible; an enormous gnawing hunger seized him. He drew a chair up to the table where she placed the tray and fell to, spooning up the thick broth and eating chunks of new-baked bread.

Just as his spoon was scraping emptily in the soup plate, Nellie reappeared with a four-egg omelette. "It's got ham in it," she said, putting it down with one hand while she twitched the soup plate away with the other. "If you want another, just holler and I'll set the pan on the stove again."

185

But his hunger was appeased by it, and the meal was rounded off by two cups of Nellie's rich, dark coffee. While he'd been eating Morag had taken up her needlework again and sat sewing, glancing at him from time to time as she asked about the food on the train and at the depots, commented on the new jacket he'd bought, and otherwise making small talk. He made scant reply—he was too busy eating. Somehow he felt as if the ground had been cut from under his feet by the fact that he'd needed a meal—he'd rehearsed what he was going to say when he walked in, all the way from Saratoga. And now the timing would be all wrong.

"Well," his mother said as he finished the second cup of coffee, "your visit was supposed to be next week?"

"I just made up my mind to come," he said. "I couldn't stay *there* any more."

"Why not?"

"Not in the same house with *her*."

"Who?" She hesitated. "Luisa?"

"She's never liked me," he said grimly. "Now I know why."

"Why, Gregor?"

"Because she resents me—and who can blame her? Her husband's little left-hander."

He heard her draw in a breath, but it wasn't in surprise—it was pain. "I'm sorry," he said at once. "This is awful for you."

"No. I suppose I've been aware it had to come,

ever since I had to ask your father to take care of you when I fell ill."

A silence dropped between them like a curtain. From the huge open window came the call of a grosbeak flying into the woods.

"Why didn't you tell me?" he asked at last. "Why did you let me think my father died when I was a baby?"

She inserted the needle into the linen, drew it through, and looked at the stitch. Then she turned her dark eyes on him. "Gregor, have you thought about what it's like to be the mother of an illegitimate child in our world? You were a tiny baby, badly injured. I had to get work so I could pay for your treatment to save you. What do you think my chances would have been if I'd said I had no husband, never had had?"

"No . . . yes . . . I understand that. You had to lie to others. But why did you lie to *me*?"

There was the hurt, there was the ache that had been edging into his consciousness. He had thought they knew each other perfectly; no secrets from each other, complete honesty. But it wasn't so, never had been.

"Let me try to explain it to you," she said, pushing away her needlework. "At first we lived in New York and you were a baby in arms and didn't need to know anything about your father or anything else; you were in a hospital some of the time."

"Because of this?" His hand went up to touch the scar at his temple.

"Yes, and because the burns you'd experienced made you very sick. You kept catching infections. Oh, for a couple of years, Gregor, it was often touch and go. And then you were better, and I had you at home all the time, and we'd had so much trouble, so much separation, the only thing I wanted was for us to be together and happy. To other people I had to keep up this story of being widowed—no one had any reason to doubt it. I suppose I looked respectable enough . . ."

"Oh, Mother!" he said, with a little exclamation that was half a laugh and half a sob.

"In the end we settled on Long Island, because the air there was thought to be more healthful—ozone is supposed to be good for chest complaints." She smiled and shook her head a little. "Not that it seemed to do me much good, but then I had to work to make a living—I dare say it's good for you if you can spend all your time strolling by the shore."

"Mother, I always told you you worked too hard—"

"I'm not reminding you of all that to get your pity, Gregor. I'm just trying to explain to you how things were. Everyone believed I was a widow. While you were little, it seemed right to let you believe that too. A secret is a heavy burden for a five or six year old—you might have blurted it out: 'My father's not really dead.' And that might have made life awfully hard for you, Greg. Even people as kind as our neighbours at Oyster Bay might have turned away from us. Certainly the other children might

188

have called you names. Children can be cruel sometimes."

"But later," he insisted. "When he came to see you—"

She seemed to shrink. "I ought to have explained. I know it. But I was worried—not about you, about Ellie-Rose. She . . . was very unhappy. I wanted Rob to be thinking about her, not accepting you as his son and being bothered with all that. You see, if I'd told you Rob was your father, then you'd have wanted to see him, talk to him, get to know him . . . And that wasn't the time."

Gregor remembered Ellie-Rose's visit. He had been eleven years old then. The drama of that night would never leave him—the sudden rush of running feet as she went out of their house, his mother flying after her in the cold night air without a coat or shawl, his own cry of rebuke as he came down-stairs to stop her. And then the floundering about in the dark as they tried to get the two women out of the water—his mother supporting Ellie-Rose, who had nearly drowned.

Everyone had politely agreed that Ellie-Rose missed her footing and fell in. But he had thought then that she tried to drown herself. She had almost killed his mother. But Mother had been so sick he couldn't think about anything else.

"Then, you know, Gregor," she went on in a bemused voice, "I thought I was going to die. I really thought so. I sent for Rob to confide you to his care, to look after you when I was gone."

"Mother!"

"When you think you're dying, you put first things first. All I could think of was that someone must look after you. And Rob was the person who had to do it. I didn't stop to think whether you knew he was your real father—that thought never crossed my mind. All I knew was that he was strong, that he would be there when I'd left you, that you'd be safe. I didn't realise then that I was going to survive."

"Don't talk like this!" he cried, springing up so that his chair fell over. He took her hands and knelt beside her. "Don't talk about dying—"

She turned her hands in his so that he released them and instead took his in hers, holding them firmly. "Son, I don't want to die. I've enjoyed the extra years your father has given me, here in this sheltered place. I've loved having you come to see me, watching you grow . . . And the price I had to pay for that was to let you be a sort of pensioner of the Craigallans."

"But you should have told me then—"

"When? At what point? At first I could only write to you, you weren't allowed to visit. I thought of putting it all into a letter, true enough. But Rob told me now difficult things were between him and his wife. Luisa would only keep quiet if you were not acknowledged."

"She hates me," he said.

"Perhaps she does. Luisa's always one to feel things strongly."

190

"Why did he ever marry her?" Gregor blurted. "You can see he doesn't love her!"

"Oh, that's too difficult to explain. We were all young then, and she wanted him—"

"You knew her then?" he asked in surprise.

"Oh yes. Rob and I worked on the Van Huten's farm. Luisa's father owned it—a very rich man, highly respected. You have to understand Gregor . . ."

"What?"

"People don't always marry for quite the right reasons. Even Ellie-Rose . . ."

"Ye-es," he agreed. It was bewildering. Even Ellie-Rose, so clever and pretty and rich, who could have had anyone—she had married Curtis because he seemed to offer prospects of moving in Presidential circles.

For a little while he was quiet, thinking of what his mother had told him. Then he pulled his hands free, got up, and moved away. "I don't understand," he said, colouring up. "You say, he married Luisa. But . . . you knew him . . . it must have gone on even then. Yet after all—I'm the *youngest* of his children."

She made no reply. He insisted: "Were you carrying on with him after he was a married man?"

"You see?" she said very quietly. "You ask me why I didn't tell you all about it, and then you speak to me in a tone that's like the Day of Judgement. You can be shocked like everyone else, son, and all the more so because it's your mother who's being shown up as a scarlet woman."

"But I don't . . . It seems so unlike you . . . I can't have been so wrong?" he pleaded.

"No. You're quite right. Rob and I separated after he got married to Luisa. For a long time we didn't see each other. I won't go into all the ins and outs of it, but in the end I heard that he and Luisa had split up. It sounded like a permanent break—Luisa had gone to live in Boston and your father had gone out to the Great Plains to make a new start. You can just imagine, now you know Luisa, how little the life out there would appeal to her. I never thought she'd want to be with him again, ever. So I went out there to join him."

"He asked you to do that?"

"Oh, *no*, Gregor! He didn't even know where I was! I was the one who sought him out. And so there we were, miles away from anywhere at Brown Bridge, trying to bring the Lafleche Farm back to productivity. And everyone thought I was Mrs. Craigallan, and it seemed too much trouble to correct them. I began to think I was Mrs. Craigallan. The years went by—four years, Gregor. And then you were born."

"Then why did it all break up?"

"Because Rob was making so much money," she said simply. "He discovered he had this talent for dealing on the grain market, and one thing led to another. Luisa heard about it, and she came, and . . . and . . . Well, that was the end. And after that I never saw Rob again until sheer chance

192

brought Ellie-Rose in my path. I had read about him in the newspapers, of course, and about Ellie-Rose and the parties she went to—all that kind of thing. I can't tell you what happened—it would be betraying Ellie-Rose's confidence. But on her account I went to see your father, and then he came to Oyster Bay to see you. He had a right."

"What right? Letting you go, putting up with Luisa instead—"

"That's not how it was. I left him, I didn't give him the chance to argue a case. I . . . I was too exhausted to argue, I just wanted to get away. I've thought since, that I was wrong. But that was the choice I made, and I lived with it. When he came to see us, he had a right. And later, when I got so sick, I thought he had the duty, too, to take you into his life."

"Well, I've walked out now," Gregor said in a hard voice. "I won't ever go back, either. Not after the names that woman called you."

"Luisa? Oh, Gregor . . ." There was genuine amusement in her response. "You don't want to pay any heed to Luisa. She hits out—she's like a—" She broke off. "Remember when you used to help Dick Twyler haul his lobster pots? You'd poke a lobster and it would extend a big claw—snap, snap . . ." She made miming movements with her hand.

Despite himself, Gregor laughed. Then he said soberly, "Luisa used words, not lobster claws."

"When I was a little girl I used to sing a little

rhyme: 'Sticks and stones will hurt my bones but names will never hurt me'."

"You were wrong," he said. "Words stay in your memory after a bruise from a stone has faded."

"Only if you dwell on them. Son, Luisa is the kind who hits out when she feels threatened or thinks she's being put upon. You still haven't explained how she came to flare out at you."

"Ah . . . well . . . I don't really know. I think it was about Harvard."

"Harvard?"

"Mr. Craig's talking about sending me to Harvard."

"Oh, Gregor." It was a gasp of pleasure. "Oh, but that would be grand, wouldn't it? I didn't know about that. It hasn't been mentioned to me so far."

"It's a recent idea. Somehow it seemed to come up in conversation . . . I don't recall the beginnings of it. Then we were all in the parlour, chatting, and I think someone mentioned it. But I don't remember that she paid much heed. Then about half an hour later she came charging down the stairs shouting at me."

Morag shook her head. "She never seems to learn," she murmured.

"Mother—I almost threw her down the stairs."

"Gregor!"

"I swear I wanted to. All at once I just wanted to pay her out for all the things she's said and done, always getting at me—and then to top it all, she said these things about you. I could have killed her."

Morag shivered. The early twilight of the mountains was falling, helped by the rain clouds coming in from Pike's Peak. She got up, went to the window, and struggled to close it to keep out a flurry of rainy air. Gregor came to take her place, pulled the folding door almost closed, then pulled over it the louvred screen that allowed a limited amount of fresh air to come into the room.

Gregor lit the lamp. The room sprang into relief, comforting in its familiarity. In the few years she had been here, his mother had made it like home, as much part of his background as the little house at Oyster Bay. She sat down in her chair so that the light touched little strands of silver in the thick dark hair. She had silver at the temples; on her it didn't seem ageing, only becoming.

She looked up at him. "Gregor, I'm not going to tell you you must do penance for getting angry. Anger isn't always a bad thing. I think there is such a thing as righteous anger, and you had reason to feel it against Luisa. But you've got to forget all that. It doesn't matter what a foolish woman says. It doesn't, truly. Time goes by and you're busy over something else, and the memory comes back, hardly stirring a single fast pulse-beat."

"I don't think I'm like that, Mother. I don't forget an insult easily." He thought of the fights behind the sports pavilion at Petersfield to settle scores; he had had his share of those, and of contests to prove himself the better academically after some affront from a fellow pupil. He had never let any insult lie. Sooner or later he had paid off the offender.

"At least, if you can't forgive and forget, rise above it. You have to see Luisa from time to time—"

"No!" he broke in, with quick determination. "I'm never going to live under the same roof as that woman, even for a single day. That's why I'm here. I couldn't stay in Saratoga Springs after the way she spoke. And I'm not going back."

"Well . . ." She thought: Enough is enough for the moment. The first crisis has passed. "You were coming here anyhow, for a stay. We'll just say your visit's been advanced a week, that's all. It's so nice to have you here, Gregor. The rain's been a bit limiting, I haven't been able to go out for my usual walks. Maybe you'll feel like sitting with me and winding up that terrible talking machine—it needs a young arm!"

She picked up a new cylinder that Rob had brought for the Graphophone, a song by the great Russian bass Chaliapin. There was another of choruses from Floradora. Somehow they began to talk about those, and plans for tomorrow. About an hour later Nellie brought in the evening meal. Almost immediately afterwards Gregor began to fall asleep in his chair; the long journey, the food, the warmth of the room were beginning to overwhelm him.

When he had gone to bed, yawning and rubbing his eyes, Morag wrote a brief note. To Nellie she said, "Go to the farm, will you, and ask Fuller's boy to ride down to the telegraph office with this? It's urgent—Mister Rob will be waiting to hear the news."

She had written: "Gregor arrived today. All well for the present. More news later."

Next morning dawned clear and cloudless. Underfoot there was moisture, and dew sparkled on the grasses, but the promise was for a fine day.

"Let's go out!" Morag exclaimed as they ate breakfast. "I'm dying to get out in the open after four days cooped up." She let him think it was the weather that had kept her indoors, but it had been anxiety after receiving Rob's wire. She had stayed at home for fear there was news other than his safe arrival at the door.

The day was typical early September weather—warm, golden, with a cool breeze to refresh the walker. Morag put on her walking boots and a good costume of skirt and jacket in linen. Over it she pulled a thick knitted cardigan, bulky and un-feminine but easy to carry if she got too hot. She tied her hair back in a blue cotton kerchief.

"You look as if you were about to run off with the raggle-taggle gipsies-o!" Gregor laughed when he saw her. He himself had found more comfortable clothes in the closet in the room always regarded as his bedroom and in which he had left many of his belongings on previous visits. He was in flannel shirt and cord breeches tucked into logger's boots.

Taking his mother's arm through his, he led her

197

out of the garden and along the bank of the stream, up towards the trees where the white-crowned sparrows darted in and out. This was a favourite walk, up through the wood and out onto a bank of scree which gave place to soft turf. In spring the alpine flowers crowded the dell, gleaming and flickering in the wind from the peak. He had watched her pick spring flowers there for the parlour, during the Easter vacations.

Now the autumn flowers were blooming—marigolds, daisies, mountain rue, and four o'clocks. They walked through them, startling the bees from their work. Then they came to the pine forests, cool and dark on their slopes, extending for yards, clothing the mountains with green like a loden cape.

They talked at first about the things they saw—the blacktail doe leaping away at their advance, the outline that might have been a white-tailed ptarmigan against a grey rock.

Then Morag began to sound a little short of breath. They sat on a big rock by a stream to rest. Gregor launched a twig on the waters and surveyed its bumpy journey down the rapids to wreck on a boulder.

"I sent a telegram to Saratoga Springs after you'd gone to bed," Morag said. "I didn't want your father to be worried."

Gregor flinched. Yesterday, in the first flood of information, he had heard Mr. Craig referred to as "your father" but it had gone past in the need to say what had to be said. Today was another day, and it shocked him to hear the words; it made them part of the routine of life.

"I doubt if he would worry overmuch," he said, aware he sounded foolishly resentful.

"Of course he worried. He wasn't sure you'd actually come to me. I wanted him to know it was all right."

"It's anything *but* all right!" he cried. "It's time to sort it all out and start again. I want it understood, Mother. We're not going to be under any more obligation to him."

"We're not?"

"No, I'm old enough to leave school now. I'm going to get a job, and then you can come and live with me."

"Where are you going to find this job?"

"Oh, heavens above, after all that fancy education I've had, there'll be something I can do. I'm good at figures, I can speak passable French and Spanish, I ought to be able to get a job in an office."

"In Saratoga Springs?"

"No, of course not," he said, irritated that she could be so limited in outlook. "I'd stand the best chance in New York or Chicago, I suppose. I could ask Cornelius if he's got any ideas. Cornelius has a lot of friends in research establishments—they must need people like me to do correspondence and so on."

"You want me to come and live with you in New York or Chicago?"

"Yes, as soon as I can get fixed up with a place. Of course it won't be fancy but we can be together, and we won't owe anything to anyone."

"But we do owe something—"

"I'll pay all that back!" he said fiercely. "We won't be beholden! There's money to be made in the big towns."

She reached forward and touched his sleeve. "Gregor," she said in a quiet, matter-of-fact tone, "I can't leave here. If you move me to one of the big towns, you'll kill me."

"Mother—"

"No, listen, you have to face it. I'll go with you if you want me to—you're my son and the thing I want most in the world is to be a help to you. I'll keep house and cook for you—but we must face the fact that my health will begin to deteriorate at once."

"But you've been so well this past year—"

"Because I live here in this pure, clean air." She straightened and stared out towards the valley below. "This is a beautiful place, Gregor. I live here because your father made it possible. You talk about owing him nothing, but I owe him my life. If I stay on here, Dr. Luce says I can have several good years—the disease will remain dormant and I can be quite active. But if I go into a smoky area, a damp area, an area clogged with industrial fumes, I'll go downhill at once. I know this is so. I made a trip to Topeka in the spring, if you remember—to have some tests done with the X-ray machinery. I felt much less well while I was there. By the end of the week I felt I couldn't breathe, and my cough had come back."

She knew her son was looking at her, but she didn't turn to meet his gaze. She didn't want to see his stricken expression. For many months now she had been very fit and Gregor had taken it for granted she would continue to improve until at last she could move into town. Until now she had never come out into the open with the complete truth.

After a long silence he said: "I see. It's no good thinking I can set the balance straight. We're always going to owe your survival to him."

"But why not, Gregor? If things had only gone a little different, I should have been Mrs. Craigallan."

"But you're not, are you? And he's got no legal claim with us—only the fact that he's got the money that pays for all this." His hand made a little gesture taking in the bright mountain view.

"It's not the money, Gregor. You're being unfair to us all when you say that. The important thing is that he's your father."

"But that doesn't give him any rights over me!"

She thought for a while. Then she said in a cool tone: "I'd be more convinced by all your protestations if I didn't have the feeling they were based on a pretence."

"A pretence? Oh, I see what you mean—you pretended all this time that my father was dead—"

"I don't mean that at all, Gregor, and I think you

201

know it. I mean the pretence you've been keeping up to yourself."

"I?"

"You're too intelligent not to have suspected the truth. Are you saying that in the last few years you've never looked in the mirror and said: 'I'm like him to look at'? You've never asked yourself 'Why should he bother so much about me?' I think you knew, son. You just wouldn't let yourself admit it."

Gregor sprang to his feet and walked away. He stood, feet parted, hands on hips, as if surveying the landscape. Morag sat with her hands folded in her lap, waiting. After a few minutes he came back.

"You have a way of making me feel like a kid caught with his hand in the cookie jar," he said on a rueful note, and flung himself down at her side again.

"So you had guessed?"

"No. I . . . sometimes thought of it. But I wouldn't think of it. I wouldn't let myself. I don't know how to explain it."

"Oh, I understand," she said, with a kindly, almost teasing glance. "It was like when you were small, and had realised there was no such person as Father Christmas—but you didn't want to say so because it would spoil things for the other kids, and even for me when it came to hanging up stockings. Better to go on with the fairy tale."

"Something like that," he admitted. "Just a sort of shadow somewhere behind me, the kind you turn suddenly but never quite catch." He shook his head. "I never thought I looked like him, though. That was one of the things I said to myself: It can't be so, I don't look in the least like him."

"But you do, Greg! Your hair's like his only darker, and you've got Rob's eyes."

She didn't add that in other ways, also, he was like Rob—the same quick, eager mind, the intelligence that drank in knowledge and saw how to use it, the vigour of attitude towards life. It was important not to let Gregor throw away his chances out of some quixotic feeling about insults from Luisa. Morag didn't care what Luisa said; Luisa's power to hurt her was all in the past, and she discounted that now.

"Now that it's out in the open, my dear lad," she began again, in the tone of affectionate reason he knew so well, "you must be sensible. You want to do well in life, I'm sure, and I want to see you do well. Your father has a right to help you towards that. You can't hold it against him that he did nothing for us over a long period—that was my fault. Nor can you blame him because his legal wife is childish and resentful. You must look to the future, prepare yourself to be the kind of man we all want to see."

He shook his head, unusually stubborn in the face of her arguments. "I'm never going to put myself in the position of having to listen to Luisa Craigallan's jeers."

"That isn't too difficult," she pointed out. "You'll be at school, and then you'll be at college.

You only have to explain your feelings to your father to ensure you're not around when Luisa's at the Castle."

He couldn't give up easily the dream that he would earn money and take her away to some home they could share. But as they talked he began to see it was childish; the real facts were different. His mother had to stay in the mountains—all the fancy education would be wasted, all the brains that he knew he had would be rusting away. His recent trip to Chicago—that one glimpse of The Pit in action—had stirred something in him. He couldn't stay here and be a farmhand or a hotel clerk; he knew it would make Morag unhappy if he gave up all that Rob was offering for the sake of living near her in Colorado.

He didn't come right out and admit she had won, but as they returned from their walk it was becoming accepted that he would return to Petersfield school when the new semester began. From there on, matters would have to be arranged between himself and Rob. But Morag understood that Gregor would listen to what his father had to say without a prior resolve to reject it.

In the afternoon Gregor strolled across the valley to talk to the local farmer, Fuller, an old friend. Morag sat down to write to Rob. First she wrote a simple telegraphic message: All well, letter follows. Then in the letter she sent a brief account of what had happened. Both of these she sent off next day,

204

when Gregor hired the stanhope from the Fullers to take her into Colorado Springs.

Rob received the letter with thankfulness. For a long time now Gregor had been growing important in his life, but only when it seemed he had lost him did it come home to him how much he valued his youngest child.

He had heard the commotion from his room where he was changing for dinner. The rented house in Saratoga was of wood, where every sound travelled. He had pulled on his dinner jacket and hurried out, recognising in the outcry Luisa's voice, raised in a shriek of invective. When he got to the landing, all he was in time to witness was Gregor's back going out of the door, and the heavy swing and clash as it closed behind him.

"What the hell's going on?" he demanded.

"He—he—tried to kill me," Luisa panted. She was leaning against the wall of the stairs, looking indeed very frightened and unusually pale.

Rob glanced at his daughter for further enlightenment. She shook her head, to let him know her mother had never been in much danger. At that moment the servants, realising that the drama was over and they could now appear without putting the family in an embarrassing situation, appeared in the hall. Soames helped his mistress back up to her boudoir, where she collapsed with a moan of terror on her chaise longue. He gave way to Pansy, who applied smelling salts and then, when Luisa was half-sitting up with her stays undone, brandy.

Rob had meanwhile taken Ellie-Rose into her bedroom. "What did she mean, tried to kill her?"

"It was just that he took hold of her. He was angry, Papa. He had a right to be."

"What happened?"

"She . . . she said things about Morag."

Rob clasped his hands behind his back and stared down at her. "And what brought that on?"

Ellie-Rose was aghast at what she had done. She had seen her mother angry and enraged over small things but she'd never before seen the virago unleashed.

"It was about Harvard . . . she and I were talking . . ."

"Ellie-Rose," he said with a sternness she'd never heard before, "I thought you got the message—I didn't want that talked about."

She knew she ought to make a clean breast of it, but she was terribly reluctant to increase his displeasure. It was so unusual for her to be in his bad graces. And now, when she was a new mother, and her husband miles away in Washington . . . she couldn't bear it if Papa was angry with her, it would be too much.

The unaccustomed tears welled up in her eyes again. She said: "I didn't mean it to go the way it did. Mama just seemed to lose control. She told Gregor that he's your son."

She and Rob were gazing at each other. He saw the tears well over the rims of her eyes and spill down on her cheeks. Any other time he would have

206

leapt to her side, to comfort and soothe her, assure her that he would make everything right, no matter what was troubling her.

But this time he stood staring at her, his hands behind his back. She saw his mouth assume a grim line.

"Papa?" she faltered.

He drew a deep breath and let it out again. "I suppose it had to come some time," he muttered. "But not this way . . ."

"He looked so—desperate!"

He paused, then said, "He'll be all right."

"If he does anything silly, it'll be my fault—"

"Gregor won't do anything silly. He may get drunk, or pick a fight with someone, but he'll be all right."

He waited up, but Gregor didn't come home. First thing in the morning he went down to the depot to inquire, learning without surprise that Gregor had taken a ticket to Saratoga Springs. He sent a telegram to Morag to warn her the boy was on his way.

When at last he got Morag's letter, he was greatly relieved despite the assurances he'd given Ellie-Rose. He knew he would be all right physically; a boy going on seventeen, tall and strong and nobody's fool, doesn't come to much harm. But it was his mental state he'd been worried about, his emotional reaction to Luisa's outburst.

Luisa insisted she'd only told him the truth. She refused to repeat the form of words, and Rob was too fastidious to ask Ellie-Rose to report them. He guessed they weren't the kind of thing a lady would say.

So he was unsurprised when Morag said in her letter that though her son was willing to go back to Petersfield and continue with his education, he utterly refused to meet Luisa again. "And I think it best if you can arrange matters so that they don't run across each other," she wrote. "I fear there would be fireworks."

As the new semester at Petersfield approached, Rob wrote suggesting that Gregor should come to New York as usual to be fitted out with new clothes. He'd already been outgrowing the suits he came home in when school broke up.

"Luisa will remain in Saratoga Springs with Ellie-Rose for the moment," he wrote. "Ellie-Rose goes back to Washington to rejoin Curtis when the capital's climate is cooler, and at that time I've arranged for Luisa to take a trip to Egypt with her mother. With luck the trip should take them all winter."

He went to his Waldorf suite to await Gregor. He had sent Soames to meet him at the station and bring him to Manhattan. To Rob's eyes he looked taller, more filled out, and had a good tan from days walking in the woods and on the slopes with his mother.

When Soames had shown him in and withdrawn, they stood looking at each other.

"Well, son?" Rob asked, and waited.

There was a pause during which Rob held his breath. Then Gregor said, "Well, Father?"

The tension relaxed. "Sit down," Rob said. "We have to talk."

"There's not much to say," Gregor remarked. "Mother and I have been through it all. I've come to terms with it."

"But there are things to be said," Rob insisted. "I only went along with the idea about keeping it a secret because that's the way things were when I first found you again. I suppose I intended to tell you some time, but not for a few years yet, when my plans began to work out."

"Plans?"

"Yes, Gregor. That's what we have to talk about. I told you before all this trouble blew up that I wanted you to go to Harvard, and you were resisting the idea."

"Because I felt I owed you enough already—"

"But that's not an issue now, when you realise that the boot's on the other foot—*I* owe *you*."

"I don't entirely go along with that—"

"It's my duty as your father to do the best I can for you, Greg. And the best I can do means something big. It means putting you in at the head of my business so that you can take over when I'm gone."

Gregor's lips parted in a gasp of disbelief. "Me?"

"Yes, you."

"But . . . what about Cornelius?"

Rob shook his head. "Cornelius is a great guy.

He's struggled against his handicap and made something of his life. But if you asked him I know he'd agree he's not the man to head up Craigallan Agricultural. He hasn't the drive, the ambition—even if he could hear what the hell the opposition were saying about us."

"But it doesn't seem right—he's your heir—"

"I'll leave him well provided for, don't doubt it. Ellie-Rose too—there's a trust for her children, money's no problem. It's handling the business, Greg—that's the issue. I've got land in four states of the union, storage silos in the United States and Canada, flour mills, freight facilities, grain ships, shares in estates and plantations here and overseas. It's big, really big. It would overwhelm Cornelius. But you, Gregor—you could handle it if you trained for it. It could be yours when I'm gone."

Gregor sat silent, letting the words sink in. Then he realised that by holding his hand, he had been given the perfect weapon with which to repay Luisa Craigallan. He could accept all the ambitions his father wished to lay upon him, and when he had taken his place in the Craigallan empire he would show Luisa that her own son was rejected.

It was the perfect revenge.

11

ELLIE-ROSE returned to her home in Washington in the fall. She walked into the house, finding it strange—smaller than she remembered it, and less pretty. But after all, it was three years since she first decorated it with help from Uncle Julius; it was time to do it up again, to freshen it and make it a suitable setting for the beautiful little girl she was bringing home with her.

During the two months since her birth, it had somehow been decided—by Ellie-Rose's quiet insistence—that the baby would be called Georgina, in honour of Admiral George Dewey, victor of the Battle of Manila. Almost inevitably, nurses and servants had begun to shorten the name to Georgie, but Ellie-Rose had guided them to the pet name Gina. Already she was Gina, and although Curtis argued for Violet, his mother's name, that was only added as a second name: Georgina Violet Craigallan Gracebridge.

The physical happiness that came with their first night together did away with much of Ellie-Rose's sense of having been neglected. She was back with her husband in their home to which he could hurry whenever his day ended at the White House. He had seldom been able to get to Saratoga Springs because of political crises but now they would make up for that.

For Curtis, everything was as it used to be. He would come in as dusk fell, and find Ellie-Rose beautiful and welcoming, her lovely dark blonde hair piled on top of her head and smelling as it always did of roses, her throat encircled by the high lace collar of the present fashion, her pretty figure back to perfection in its tight-waisted gown of fine wool. It would be an interval of pure delight while he helped her to unfasten these stiff garments, unpin her hair, and climb with him on the high, cushiony bed. They had no inhibitions about making love in the daytime; other wives, Ellie-Rose gathered, considered it sinful to have anything to do with their husbands except at night and with the lights out, but such notions never played any part in her marriage.

Afterwards they would bath and dress, and then the baby would be brought in for them to admire and play with before going down to dinner, or out for the evening. Sometimes the functions would keep them very late, and they would be too weary when they got home for anything but sleep. But often the wine and the rhythms of the dancing they had enjoyed would unleash a flood of physical passion, and they would come together without restraint, forceful and strong, young and ardent, perfect lovers.

And yet . . .

Something had changed. The separation of four

212

months had made a gulf between them. Ellie-Rose was aware of it even if Curtis was not. They might make love with all the old delight but afterwards there wasn't the same closeness. When they were first married, they had lain in each other's arms, talking a little, dozing and waking to kiss and talk again—little secrets, personal confidences, endearments only used at such moments of intimacy.

They still lay in each other's arms till sleep came. But there were fewer little secrets, less drowsy conversation.

"It's because all he ever talks about in his waking hours is politics," Ellie-Rose told herself with a little moue of resignation, and then was brought up short by the disloyalty of the thought. It wasn't true that Curtis talked only of politics.

But it was only natural that he should be obsessed with the goings on of the Washington roundabout. Everybody in the capital was the same. Mrs. Henry Cabot Lodge had said to her, when she first arrived, "So you've set out on the career of being a Washington wife, my dear. You'll find it fascinating—so long as you enjoy talking politics."

She hadn't added, because it didn't occur to her, "But God help you if you ever begin to find them boring." But it occurred to Ellie-Rose now, after her absence.

She wasn't foolish enough to think that the business of running the government was un-important. What began to irritate her was the assumption among Curtis's friends that the only way to run the government was the Republican way, the way the present leaders of the Republican party approved of.

For instance, this matter of the "war" with Spain. Everybody was now in a state of great jubilation at the way Spain had been laid low—"By golly, we showed those damn grandees!" was the general tone. Yet Ellie-Rose remembered very well how shocked Curtis had been at Teddy Roosevelt's outbursts at the outset. Because she had been away and had not seen the gradual change to the view, she was startled to find Roosevelt was now one of the heroes of the hour. He had taken part in the war, resigning his post as Assistant Secretary to the Navy in order to raise a regiment that became known as Roosevelt's Rough Riders. Now he was Governor of New York State, a figure of adventure and admiration.

Curtis envied him. Yet a year ago, Curtis had called Roosevelt a jingoist and had written him off as a political buffoon; "he'll be sorry for his wild outbursts," he predicted. Now Curtis was echoing some of the things Roosevelt said, and was sorry he himself had not left Washington for a commission in the services.

Ellie-Rose didn't dislike Teddy. He amused and surprised her. Some of the things he said were funny though cruel. "That man," he once remarked to her, speaking of the President, "has no more backbone than a chocolate eclair!" She had laughed, although at the time she knew Curtis would have disapproved entirely. It seemed to her so true: McKinley *was* like a chocolate eclair, plump, filled with creamy sweetness, coated on the outside with rich trappings, and yet somehow insubstantial.

Now, if Teddy Roosevelt were to say that again within Curtis's hearing, he might protest, but he might also privately agree. Curtis was tending to go along with the prevalent views of the Republican big-wheels: that the United States should take over all Spain's overseas possessions and run them, instead of handing them over to the inhabitants. At the beginning of the war there had been much talk of helping the Cuban Patriotic Army, of giving independence to the Filipinos. Little was heard of that now. Even McKinley himself seemed to be in favour of American imperialism.

Although Ellie-Rose still felt a fondness for the President, her respect for him dwindled after she returned to Washington. While she was away she had listened to her father and his friends, and they were cool in their assessment of McKinley. Good he might be in the church-going sense, loyal to his friends and without resentment to his enemies; but he was not as open and frank as she used to believe. When the pressure of public opinion came to bear upon him, he would hesitate and refuse a decision until it was too late to stand up against the pressure. Then he would go along with it, bowing to what he called "the democratic impulse" but forced into it rather than observing it.

"And then you see," Rob had pointed out, "before too long some confidant of his will come out with the news that, all along, that's what he intended to do. You don't know whether to believe it or not—is he really as clever as a wagonload of monkeys, or is it just that the monkeys scramble all over him till he's one of them?"

That argued a great subtlety of mind. And as Ellie-Rose watched and listened to McKinley in the Washington round, she couldn't believe his was a subtle intellect. She began to think he ruled by instinct. And on the whole, the instinct seemed to have a bias towards self-preservation. He did what the big-wheels and the Press urged him to do. He had gone to war because it was what everybody wanted—and in the event he had been proved right, if to gain the Spanish possessions was his aim.

But now the United States had them. What on earth were they going to do with them? Ellie-Rose had a feeling the President had no idea.

To Curtis she couldn't voice such notions. That added to the distance that seemed to be growing between them. It troubled her, but she consoled herself with the thought that all the same they were a very happy pair. Not like some Washington couples, only held together by the united ambition to make a career, finding in politics the justification for a marriage that had never been more than a base from which to build influence and power.

Since her mother was wintering with Grand-mama in Egypt, Ellie-Rose was called on to go to Craigallan Castle on several occasions to play hostess at a grand dinner. She found this very agreeable—the break from the Washington routine, the chance to play a starring role in front of a very elite audience. In Washington there were of course grand dinners, but at those Ellie-Rose had to be just one of many Washington wives, pretty and elegant, willing to listen to the usual Washington gossip. At the Castle, there was gossip too, but it was different gossip—about finance, about the ideas of entre-preneurs untrammelled by any need to pay lip service to party ideals, about how to exploit the territories now under United States care. Ellie-Rose had no doubt that when she led the wives away so that the men could enjoy their brandy and cigars, the talk was even franker about how money could be made.

The precedent was set that she could leave Washington to travel from time to time: Curtis was safe in the care of the servants during her absences. There was a growing restlessness in her. At first she thought it was one of the after-effects of childbirth. Other young matrons were fond of confiding to her how they had felt different afterwards—a variety of symptoms were trotted out for discussion—"nerves", headaches, anxiety, disinclination for "that sort of thing", fatigue, ennui.

Ellie-Rose lost her tendency to burst into tears over very little. The feeling of being responsible for everyone, from little Gina to her brother Cornelius, waned. Yet she was continually finding that her life was unsatisfying. She tried to lose herself in motherhood, as other women did, but for her it wasn't enough. Or at least, being the mother of Curtis's child wasn't enough.

It shocked her when that thought first formed in her mind. She had nothing to complain of in Curtis. She was often very proud of him for the way he was singled out for praise by the President. He was making a good career, and it promised to be even better if—as seemed likely—McKinley was elected to a second term. In four years Curtis had made himself one of the Major's Indispensables, as they were called. In another four—who could tell?

But she groaned inwardly when the re-election campaign began to gather momentum. This time Curtis was even more closely involved in the pre-planning. He travelled—to visit the bosses of the Republican party in other states, to make deals set up by Mark Hanna, to bargain and come back with offers to the inner circle of the White House.

Roosevelt, too, did his part for the Republicans. He made a grand tour to immense acclaim wherever he went—honour guards of Rough Riders, western rodeos, exhibitions of sharpshooters—all very manly and adventurous. Hanna was furious.

"What the hell's he playing at?" he snarled to the Indispensables. "It's more like a circus than a speechifying tour!"

Curtis was sent to talk to the Governor of New

York State, an office Roosevelt had won without difficulty on his return from the war. He returned to the White House with gloomy news. "He didn't come out with it, but I've no doubt in my mind what he wants."

"What?" Vice-President Hobart asked.

Curtis looked at him, colouring with embarrassment. "The Vice-Presidential nomination."

"What!"

Curtis looked at the startled faces of the Republican leaders. "I'm sure that's what he wants."

"But he's quoted here, a couple of days ago—" Hanna shook the newspaper he was holding—"as saying he's enjoyed being Governor of New York and wants to be Governor again."

"That's a fallback position," Curtis said.

At the convention in Philadelphia in June, the worst fears of the old brigade were realised: after the unanimous adoption of McKinley as the Republican candidate for the Presidency, Theodore Roosevelt was nominated and accepted with cheers as the Vice-Presidential candidate.

There could be no doubt the two men would take office. No American President with a victorious war behind him could possibly lose an election, so Roosevelt would come in on the coat-tails of McKinley. "It's ironic," Curtis said. "I don't think there's another man in the Republican party that the Major dislikes more than Roosevelt."

Ellie-Rose had no sympathy with him. She felt

that if he had spoken out, the situation could have been saved. But once again McKinley had preferred to wait and see what the public wanted, and then went along with that—even though in this case it was a man he privately detested.

She still saw Mrs. McKinley during the frequent social events at the White House, but was not as much in favour as before, because she was away from home so much. She liked to travel to New York to stay with her father, or to visit Cornelius. She even managed a trip to Colorado so that Morag could see Gina, now a healthy little toddler. On this occasion she put up at the best of Colorado Springs' hotels, and though Gina was taken to visit Morag's house, she was kept out in the garden so as not to risk any infection. Morag didn't kiss the child or even take her in her arms, although Ellie-Rose could see from her expression how much she longed to.

The two women sat in the shady porch while Gina pottered about making a bed for her doll out of the petals of mariposa lilies. "Tell me all the news," Morag said, looking eagerly at Ellie-Rose. "What does Curtis think about the nomination?"

"Of Roosevelt? He's worried about how it will work out. I wrote you that he had warned the Major about Roosevelt's ambitions—"

"Will he have to work with Mr. Roosevelt?"

"Not directly. Never mind about that. What do you hear from Gregor?"

"Oh, he loves it," Morag burst out. "You can tell

from the way he's thrown himself into every kind of activity—debating society, theatricals, linguists' circle—all sorts of things."

Gregor was a freshman at Harvard now. Ellie-Rose had seen him at Craigallan Castle at Easter, looking subtly different, no longer a schoolboy. He had never been like most schoolboys, she felt, but with Petersfield behind him he seemed to have walked forward into a young maturity, rather impressive. Later she had gone at his invitation to a performance of *The Importance of Being Earnest* in the production of which he played a small part behind the scenes. She had been interested to see that he didn't get himself up in the odd rig-outs of the other undergraduates, but was still himself—quiet, quick, and privately amused at the antics of his fellow students.

"Does he talk about girl friends?" she asked.

"Oh, sisters and friends of his friends. No one in particular. Why? Have you had any hints?" Morag asked with eagerness.

"No, not about Gregor. But—what do you think, Morag?—Cornelius has a sweetheart."

"Cornelius?"

Ellie-Rose nodded.

"Somebody he met on a visit to the Bells?"

"No, it isn't anyone connected with the teaching of the deaf—though that's quite a likely source of girl friends, I suppose. He's going to Beinn Breagh in July as usual, I suppose. I wonder if he'll take her there?"

Most years Cornelius spent some time with the man to whom he owed such powers of speech as he had—Alexander Graham Bell. The great man had bought an estate in Nova Scotia five years ago, to which he invited friends of a scientific bent. Cornelius would come back with tales of trying to fly a huge tetrahedral kite, or sitting out in the dusk attempting to measure the sound level of bats in flight on an electrical dial. Dr. Bell's interest in mechanics and in speech-training, had led to the invention of that instrument already beginning to seem essential in modern living, the telephone.

Morag was intrigued at the notion that Cornelius might take this girl to Beinn Breagh. She knew how highly he esteemed the privilege of being allowed to visit there.

Cornelius came to see Morag rarely. His first visit, she felt sure, had been out of a sense of duty—for without Morag he would never have learned to communicate with others. It was thanks to her that, as a very small child, he had been taken by his father to Boston to consult the great Dr. Bell. Later, when it became necessary for him to live with a relative in Boston so as to receive tuition from the teachers at the Bell Institute, Morag had gone to work as housekeeper in the house where he lived. She it was who had worked with him, practised with him, played with him.

Then family crises had taken her from his life. He only learned years later that she had gone to live at Brown Bridge. He understood now, as an adult,

222

that she had gone to live with his father as his wife, but at the time all that was unknown to him, and when he met her again it was only briefly, scarcely more than a jolting glimpse before she disappeared again.

When Rob made himself responsible for Morag's medical treatment and upkeep, he saw no reason to make the fact a topic of family conversation. It was Ellie-Rose who gave away the secret. She mentioned she was going to Colorado to see Morag. The first name struck a chord in his memory. "Morag" . . . the first Christian name he had ever learned to utter. He remembered his struggles to say it, and the delight on her face when at last it came out so as to be recognisable.

Ellie-Rose said that Morag was living in the mountains, trying to recover from a serious lung sickness. He felt it his duty to go with Ellie-Rose to see her. He understood at last that the dear friend, the comforter of those young years had been his father's mistress, that Gregor was her son by his father. But he felt he must pay the visit—he owed her that for all she had done for him.

To his eyes she looked almost the same. Thinner, and her eyes seemed larger in her pale face. But essentially it was the same Morag who had kept house for Aunt Remegen and who had always been ready to sit with him, encourage him to puff the piece of cotton away with the surge of breath as he said "Ha! Ha!" in his efforts to learn to sound aspirates.

He was shattered at the wave of emotion that overcame him when he saw her. She understood after the first glance, and talked with Ellie-Rose to let him recover. He found it difficult to be with her. He made the trip about once in each year because his conscience told him he must keep in touch with her, and wrote duty letters at Christmas or in thanks for a birthday present—she remembered his birthday, and that of Ellie-Rose, as well as her own son's.

But there wasn't the easy closeness between them that had arisen between Morag and Ellie-Rose. She knew she had his goodwill, but she didn't have his confidence. But then, few had Cornelius's confidence—Ellie-Rose perhaps, probably no one else.

Now Ellie-Rose was saying he had found a sweetheart. Could it be so? Could Cornelius—withdrawn, shy, clever—have found a girl he could communicate with?

"What's she like?" she asked. "Where did he meet her?"

"Oh, she's a strange little creature," Ellie-Rose said, out of the confidence of her own good looks. "Not a bit pretty, really, but very vivid and mercurial. Her name's Stephanie Jouvard—"

"A Frenchwoman?" Morag put in, surprised.

"No, actually not. Her parents are second generation American. But Uncle Julius met her in Paris—"

"How does Julius come into it?"

"He introduced her to the family. That last trip

when he and Mama went to Europe . . ."

It had become an accepted thing that Luisa spent much of the year travelling. It was assumed that her health was poor, that she couldn't stand the winters of New York but had to go to the sun from fall to spring.

The truth was that Rob had faced Luisa with an ultimatum. He would continue to support her as was his legal obligation, and would see that she had funds for a luxurious life style, on condition that she stayed away from Craigallan Castle as much as possible.

"It's your own fault, Luisa," he pointed out in a cold tone when they first discussed it. "You knew the conditions—you were to keep your mouth shut about Gregor and do your best to get on with him. Well, you've just thrown that condition to the winds."

Luisa went red with indignation. "Are you telling me that you prefer this . . . this bastard child, over your own wife?"

He met her angry gaze.

"Yes," he said simply.

Against that even Luisa couldn't fight. She agreed to the first trip abroad, to Egypt, and went with her mother to look at the Pyramids. Travelling itself didn't please Luisa; she was too fond of comfort. The crossing on a luxury steamer was like being in a moving hotel, however, and once in the various capitals of Europe en route to Egypt she found life charming.

225

Europe, she found, was full of princes and barons and dukes. Society was well-ordered; service in the big hotels was superb, everyone knew their place. The women were elegant and witty, or dowdy and over-educated, but it was the men who charmed Luisa. They bowed over her hand, rushed to open doors for her, sent servants running at her merest whim. They made the men of New York seem ill-bred. Indeed, when she got home after her trip she found New York vulgar and even provincial.

Luisa made a token appearance at Craigallan Castle, played hostess at one or two dances and dinners, then removed for the summer to Saratoga Springs, where Rob had now bought a house. It was tacitly agreed that this was her home in America; she could do what she liked with it, invite whom she pleased. Rob would call on her there at some time during the hot weather, for appearances sake, but otherwise wouldn't trouble himself about her.

When fall came around again, she took herself off to Europe—not only without complaint, but with positive alacrity. Dorothea didn't go with her this time, but instead Julius tacked himself on to her caravan. Europe was where all the painters were, all the antiques, all the real leaders of taste.

In one of their visits to Paris they had met the Jouvards, who were making something of a pilgrimage back to the land of their forebears. Luisa gathered there were counts or dukes in their family, executed during the French Revolution. Their daughter, Stephanie, had been living in Paris with

226

relatives; she was devoted to art, wanted to be a painter, but that, Mr. Jouvard said with a very Gallic shrug, "isn't a thing you can really let your daughter do, now is it?"

Julius took to the girl. She was about twenty-one or two, pretty in a way. But what interested Julius was her talent. He could see in her work something of promise. Her aim was to be a portrait painter, but meanwhile she had studied in some of the great *ateliers* so that her technique was excellent; she could paint landscapes in the classic manner, her sense of colour was outstanding.

Julius needed to be alongside every nuance in the changing art world. When a rich woman wanted him to decorate her house or apartment, she might ask him to buy paintings as well. He needed someone who could paint in the style of the new masters, to produce artwork for women who merely wanted wall decorations.

When he put his idea to Stephanie, she accepted it philosophically. Like most art students, she had learned that recognition didn't come at once. She wouldn't be the only painter who kept his hand in by painting "in the style of" of while working at other times towards a private goal.

Besides it gave her the opportunity to live in New York. Her parents were insisting she come home from Paris: "You've played around abroad quite long enough," her father remarked. They wanted her to settle down with them in New Jersey, meet a nice young man, and get married.

Nothing was further from Stephanie's wishes. Although living with an aunt and uncle in Paris, she had had a lot of freedom. She had become part of the student set. She had had relationships which made it impossible for her to go back to New Jersey and settle down to domestic bliss with a lawyer or a doctor, which seemed to be her mother's hope.

She knew she had to come back to the United States. Her mother was determined on that. Mary Jouvard had seen enough to alarm her in her daughter's way of life in Paris. But if she agreed to return while nevertheless showing she had opportunities offered her in New York—that was a splendid compromise. And her parents would be quite satisfied with the arrangement; they had got to know Mrs. Craigallan, wife of the agricultural magnate, and her brother Julius Van Huten. Julius was clearly a man to be respected; he had friends among the very best people in New York. His own name was a very old one in America.

So they all travelled back together on the American Line's flagship, *New York*. Mr. and Mrs. Jouvard couldn't help being impressed by the attention Mrs. Craigallan received from the stewards and officers.

Luisa had made her usual stay at Craigallan Castle on her return. There were some guests Rob wanted to invite, as usual; Luisa presided over these events. She included the Jouvards in the guest list, at the suggestion of her brother. There would be some very influential people at the dinner and here was a good opportunity to introduce Stephanie and her work to those who might very likely buy.

Cornelius was at the Castle at the time; he generally came to stay for a few days when his mother returned from her travels, feeling it was only right for the family to gather at such a time. That was how he met Stephanie.

Nothing might have come of it, for Cornelius had been introduced to dozens of young women in the course of his mother's entertaining. Generally he bowed and looked attentive. At the dinner table Luisa would arrange for him to sit with people he knew and who knew him, so that his deafness and his inability to make himself understood in speech wasn't a problem.

On this occasion Stephanie Jouvard happened to be the occupant of the next seat opposite Willis Martin, an old friend of the family's. Always alert and interested in people because they might make good subjects for a portrait, she quickly understood that the young man sitting next to Mrs. Willis Martin had a speech difficulty. His eyes were as alert as her own, fixed on the face of the lady across from him as she spoke. When he replied, she could just catch the strange, slow delivery.

When both her dinner neighbours were busy taking their first mouthfuls of *quennelles de veau*, Stephanie looked up and caught Cornelius's eye.

"Are you completely deaf?" she asked, shaping the words clearly but not voicing them.

He coloured, and for a moment she thought he

was going to be affronted. But next moment he half-smiled, nodded, and said in his flat voice: "A'most."

"You manage very well," she told him.

"Thank you."

There for the moment the conversation had to rest. She couldn't think of anything else to say, and moreover her neighbour claimed her. But some time later, when the gentlemen joined the ladies in the drawingroom, Stephanie beckoned Cornelius to join her on a window seat.

Surprised, he did so. He was unaccustomed to young ladies showing an interest in him once they realised he couldn't converse much in the normal way. It had long ago ceased to hurt him when they looked embarrassed and smiled too brightly at him.

He sat down at Stephanie's side. Soames brought coffee, in the fine little china cups that Luisa adored. They gave their attention to that for a moment. Then Stephanie looked at him and said: "Must I look directly at you when I speak?"

"Please," he said. "Otherwise I can't make out what you're saying, unless you can speak with your fingers."

"No, I know nothing of that. It's very interesting. You have to do that?"

"Often—when words won't come out, or people don't understand."

"All your family can use sign language?"

"Not Mama," he said.

Stephanie suddenly understood why this deaf

230

and dumb son had never been mentioned before in her acquaintanceship with Luisa. Luisa was ashamed of him.

She frowned. "Have you always been deaf?"

He nodded.

"Oh, how awful," she said, without artifice.

When strangers expressed sympathy, as they sometimes did, Cornelius never knew how to respond. He knew he had a severe handicap, but it was so much part of his being that he hardly thought about it. It limited his circle of friends to some extent, but it seldom seemed much of a hindrance. Because his father was extremely rich, Cornelius was cushioned from some of the worst effects. No one laughed at him and shouted "Dummie!" at him—he was the son of Rob Craigallan of Craigallan Agricultural.

Only when it came to making friends with a young woman did it suddenly rear up, like a great iron barrier between them. Cornelius had seen girls he longed to get to know among Ellie's circle of acquaintance. He had seen girls with Gregor, sisters of fellow-students. But to have to go through all the primary stages—the shock and alarm when they first heard his monotonous delivery, the impulse of pity when they learned the reason, their embarrassment when conversation became difficult—it made him unwilling to embark on relationships with girls.

The only women with whom he could talk without effort were Ellie-Rose, one or two of the stenographists at his laboratory in Chicago, and the women folk in the circle of the Bell entourage. There were either members of Dr. Bell's family, who had been brought up to think of deafness as natural, or teachers who had come to know Dr. Bell through his work.

He seldom sat *tête à tête* with a vivacious young lady, and almost never at her request. He couldn't quite understand it.

He said now, "I don't know what it is to be able to hear. So in a way I don't think it's so awful."

"No, I suppose it would be worse if you had had your hearing and then lost it." She sighed, expressive green-grey eyes going dark at the thought. "You know, I suddenly realise how unkind it is, the way we laugh at deafness."

Cornelius shrugged.

"Doesn't it make you angry?" she insisted.

"I don't enjoy it."

"No." She hesitated. "I'll never laugh at that again."

To her surprise, he grinned. "Yes, you will. Some of the jokes are very funny."

"Oh! You mean *you* laugh at them?"

"At cartoons."

"At what?"

He made a squiggle in the air, indicating a drawing.

"Oh, cartoons. Yes, I see." She fell silent, thinking of some of the cruel quips she'd seen in cartoons—elderly men holding a hearing horn to one ear, that kind of thing.

Cornelius felt he ought to make some contribution to the conversation. "Mama says you an artist?"

"Yes, trying to be. I want to be a portraitist."

"A what?"

"Portraits." She flicked a hand at her own face.

"Yes. Have you had an exhibition?"

"A what?" She couldn't catch it.

"A show."

"Not yet," she said, with such a moue of regret that he laughed. Her face was very expressive, mobile and alight all the time she talked. She had rather an olive complexion and dark hair, worn up on top of her head in the current fashion with two carnations holding the curls in place. She dressed well, though less richly than some of the girls he knew; her dinner gown was stiff corded silk in a soft green which picked up the green in her eyes. She wore no jewellery except a single strand of pearls round her throat.

Luisa, glancing about the room to see that all her guests were at ease, saw them sitting close together in the window seat, apparently deep in talk. Charming little creature, she thought, so kind-hearted to put up with Cornelius . . . It was far from Luisa's understanding that they could actually be enjoying themselves.

"Do you have a career?" Stephanie asked.

"I'm a plant biologist."

233

"What?"

He said it again, but the phrase was so un-expected and his diction so poor that she couldn't fathom it. He produced a little notepad from the inside pocket of his dinner jacket and wrote it out for her with a gold pencil.

"A plant biologist? What on earth is that?"

"My father deals in crops. Crops," he repeated, as she looked puzzled at the sound, and mimed growing plants by putting his hand out, palm level, and raising it quickly.

She giggled. "Crops. They come up fast, don't they?"

He too laughed. And later, when he remembered it, realised it was the first time anyone except Ellie-Rose had made fun of his attempts at communication.

Before she left with her parents she had written down on his notepad the address of the studio Julius had found for her near Gramercy Park. "Come and look at my work," she said.

As she went out, a footman held out an umbrella to shield her from the rain before she got into the carriage. A point of the umbrella knocked the carnations in her hair. One fell, unnoticed, on the flagged hall.

Farewells were being said, promises made to see each other again soon, to come to tea or make a theatre visit. No one saw Cornelius stoop and pick up the pink carnation to slip in the pocket of his jacket.

The household retired shortly afterwards. Upstairs in his room, Cornelius took the flower out of his pocket. Already it was beginning to look crumpled and drooping. He stared at it, at the pink frill of its petals already turning transparent with decay.

Idiotic, he thought. Romantically scooping up the flower she dropped. He'd never seen *Carmen*, since opera could mean nothing to him, but he understood there was a scene in that where the hero warbled about a flower his beloved had given him. But that was opera.

In real life, people didn't cherish flowers because they'd been worn by a pretty girl. Stephanie was a nice girl, but she wasn't going to take any more trouble over him. She'd done her duty tonight, spending most of the evening with him after dinner, but as to expecting him to turn up at her studio— that was nonsense.

He dropped the flower in the waste basket. "Idiotic," he said aloud, to emphasise the point.

But ten days later, when he still hadn't paid the visit to her studio, he received a note reproaching him. "I know you're probably very busy with important things to do with plants," she wrote, "but I've bought a cake, every day for over a week, hoping you'd be here for tea. Please come because I've already fed eight cakes to the landlady's cat, and that's bad for it."

He could scarcely believe it. She really wanted to see him. He sent a note by return: "The landlady's cat had better not expect cake tomorrow."

When he had sent a servant to deliver it, he sat with his hands clasped, head bent. Almost no one except Ellie-Rose ever made jokes with him. He doubted if his mother even knew he had a sense of humour.

Yet, in a short evening's conversation, Stephanie Jouvard had divined that. He had met someone with whom he might actually laugh.

It was the one of two completely natural sounds that Cornelius could make—laughter, and weeping. He hadn't wept since he was a child. He had seldom laughed.

But things might be different now.

12

STEPHANIE JOUVARD'S initial interest in Cornelius was easy enough to understand. After being introduced she had smiled at him and he had smiled back, bowing politely and, as far as she could tell, repeating her name in a murmur. Then he had stood back while other people were brought to her.

He was an extremely handsome man, tall, of a rather pale complexion, with dark thick hair and grey-blue eyes, somewhere in his late twenties. Like his father before him, Cornelius had started looking about twenty when he was seventeen and would continue to look about twenty-plus well into his thirties. He had a certain withdrawn air, rather intriguing.

When she first noticed it, she thought it was because he found the gathering boring, as she did. The bourgeoisie in all their splendour always roused her sense of the absurd. She thought he might be a fellow spirit.

Then she learned that he was deaf, and almost dumb. That roused her compassion. She was always quick to feel for the underdog. Besides, he handled it so well—without embarrassment, without self-pity.

Then she guessed, from the things he said, that

his mother was ashamed of him. That roused her more strongly to his side, for during her acquaintance with Luisa she had learned to dislike her quite a lot. Luisa in Paris epitomised all that made Stephanie ashamed of Americans abroad—the display of wealth, the expectation of servility because one had so much money, the laziness that took it for granted that everyone else would learn English.

She had let herself be taken by her parents to this grand dinner at Craigallan Castle, ready to laugh secretly at the pretentious grandeur of the place, the overdone medieval setting. She soon forgot her surroundings in her interest in Cornelius. She devoted most of her evening to him.

Perhaps there was a little ostentation in her act—a desire to show to Luisa Craigallan that she wasn't the kind of girl who avoided a man because he had been born with a handicap, a desire to prove to all and sundry that she was sensitive and altruistic.

But her invitation to her studio was genuine. She wanted him to see her work. She had found him quick, intelligent—and fun.

Then there was the matter of his work. He was a scientist. She had the usual artist's contempt for people who worked only with their heads, but from what she could gather, Cornelius's work was directed towards helping farmers. The seeds he was helping to protect from blight, pest and other attacks would be sown by peasants in poor countries, not only in the rich United States.

Not that the United States were so rich. During her stay in Paris Stephanie had heard much discussion of the wrongs done by capitalists to the workers, and of the strikes put down so harshly in America. The Pullman strike, the coalminers strike—and now the farmers of the Great Plains and the Midwest were protesting, crying out that they were ground between the millstones of poor prices for their crops and mortgage payments they couldn't meet. Thousands were leaving the land, their farms forfeited to the big banks.

It seemed to Stephanie that the work Cornelius was doing would help the lot of these poor farmers. He would make it possible for them to grow better crops, produce greater yields. Her grasp of economics was so poor that she didn't realise the sting in the tail of it—that the more grain was produced on a falling market, the more the price would fall.

Cornelius knew this, but that was not his concern. That was an immediate problem, and he was working long-term, looking forward to the time when farming would be rationalised, with farmers as managers on big estates such as Papa owned. Cornelius respected his father's judgement.

When he arrived at Stephanie's studio, there were other visitors. This hadn't been her intention, but he had chosen a day when Julius had sent prospective buyers. She had tea brought in, and gave Cornelius a secret smile when she passed him a piece of cake.

The prospective buyers—two ladies and the husband of one of them—chatted quite knowledgeably about painting, chose two of her offerings, and left—though the ladies were clearly a little unwilling to leave her alone with a man, it seemed so unladylike and she was clearly a lady, though an artist.

But she detained him, on purpose to show him the work she hadn't displayed to the buyers; portraits, strong, rather harsh in style, very revealing of the sitter according to Stephanie's view of him.

"What do you think?" she asked.

Cornelius was staring at the canvases, so that he didn't know she was speaking. She touched his arm, and he turned. "Do you like them?"

She saw him hesitate. Then he said, in his colourless voice: "I don't understand them."

That surprised her. Most people said politely: "Oh, yes, they're very good." Or, impolitely: "Why do you give people green faces?"

After a moment he went on: "You are not patient. Don't suffer fools gladly."

"Can you tell that by what you see here?"

He looked embarrassed. "I'm not an art expert. You would do better to ask my Uncle Julius."

She knew Julius's opinion—she had an excellent technique, a good eye, and might become a vogue if her way of attacking instead of complimenting her sitters became a talking point.

But she didn't want to become a vogue. She

240

wanted to be told she had genius. Not by Cornelius, evidently . . . Yet she respected him for taking the time to work out what he really saw in her work.

A thought came to her. "May I paint you?" she asked.

He was looking at her, but the question was so unusual that he didn't grasp the outlines her lips were forming. "What did you say?"

"Your portrait—may I paint it?"

"Me?"

"Yes, you. Why not?"

"Why me?"

Because, she could have said, there's something there—something deep and valuable, behind that guarded look. For once she would paint a portrait, and there would be no attack—only an exploration of another human being by way of the set of the head, the lines on the face, the expression of the eyes.

He didn't take her seriously, and for the time she let it drop. She accepted his invitation to dinner on an evening early in the following week, and a picnic the following Wednesday. Then, at her suggestion, he took her to see the laboratory at the headquarters of Craigallan Agricultural Products in Chicago.

Cornelius spent quite a lot of the journey teaching Stephanie the sign language to which he had to resort when he couldn't make himself understood in speech. She was a quick pupil; her artist's eye grasped at once the significance of some of the set phrase-gestures. At first Cornelius had been unwilling to act as teacher, for it seemed to emphasise his greatest problem, the one that might keep him from developing their friendship into something deeper.

Other men could "romance" a girl, flatter her, whisper, as the phrase goes, sweet nothings. Cornelius didn't have that option. It had kept him from growing close to most women except those within the Alexander Graham Bell circle, where sign language was almost a second tongue.

He had solved the problem of physical need early in his life. He had gone to Sam Yarwood, his father's wily yet open-hearted friend, and asked for an introduction to one of the high-class houses of pleasure to which he had entry. The girls of the Everleigh Club saw him from time to time and liked him—he was never rowdy, like some of their clients, and if he didn't talk much well, what the hell, there was too much talk as a rule. The Everleighs, two upper-class girls from Kentucky, would have been shocked at the use of the word brothel; they were running a genteel place of refreshment for tired businessmen.

But friendships with girls on the Levee were not the kind of thing you thought of in relationship to respectable women. There were two entirely separate races—one you made use of and paid, the other you respected and paid court to. It was in the latter essential that Cornelius was at a loss. He could think of complimentary things to say, but it was very difficult to say them—and he had the feeling any fine speech would sound absurd in his flat, toneless voice.

He had an apartment in Chicago not far from the offices of Craigallan Agricultural. Stephanie, naturally, stayed at an hotel. It was absolutely essential that they should be known to have separate accommodations; it was bohemian enough in Stephanie that she had asked to make this trip with him, an unmarried man and not a relation.

Next day he showed her round the laboratories. Most of it was beyond her; the earnest young men peering down microscopes, the rows of plants in the special planthouse, the office where statistics were compiled. But she was enthralled by the drawing room where careful note was taken of every phase of development in the experiments, the photographic room with its row of special cameras. She spent nearly two hours examining the work, talking with the artists and photographers.

Cornelius couldn't know it, but this visit increased her regard for him enormously. He was head of the Research Department; all this was under his control. True, he held that post because he was the son of the owner—but she had seen the way the assistants deferred to him. There was genuine respect there.

She saw him for the first time in his own environment—not shy and reserved in the social round, but in command of an important department in a huge business. The scientists who worked in direct contact with him had taken the trouble to learn sign language so as to be able to converse easily; she watched the way their hands flickered, the quick understanding nods and the touch of a finger to emphasise or contradict.

She wanted to be important to him. At first it had been a sort of humanitarian instinct that made her single him out but now it was different. She had seen that he had power; and power—though she didn't understand this—has an aphrodisiac quality.

Without knowing why she did it, she asked to see his apartment—coaxed him into giving her dinner there. "But it's hardly proper, Stephanie," he objected.

"Oh, all that idea of behaviour is so stuffy," she said. "In Paris, I spent evenings with a man friend without having to bother about propriety."

"We could have dinner at your hotel—"

"That's a bit overpowering, don't you think? We can't talk there so easily, either—people would stare." She meant at her attempts to use sign language.

That was the argument that convinced him. He got his secretary to telephone his manservant to prepare dinner, and drove her to his apartment when their day at the laboratories was over.

The servant, Larry, had never had a young lady alone as a dinner guest except Miss Ellie-Rose. He was intrigued, pleased, and determined to do all he could to further the romance, if romance it was. Wine, delicate food, candles . . . he provided the surroundings. When dinner was over he asked if his master would need him again that evening. "If not, sir, I should like to visit my sister."

Cornelius was taken aback. It was Stephanie who replied. "I can't think of anything we're likely to need, thank you," she said.

"No, miss? Thank you, miss. Mr. Craigallan?"

"All right then," Cornelius said, bemused. It was as if Stephanie was furthering a plot to give them an evening totally alone together.

It was about nine o'clock when Larry let himself out of the apartment, having appeared with a light raincoat over his arm and thus made it clear he was going. He banged the door on his way out.

Stephanie smiled at Cornelius over the coffee tray she was dealing with. "Alone at last!" she laughed. It was a quotation from a comedy recently popular on the New York stage. But she had forgotten that Cornelius didn't go to the theatre, because he couldn't hear.

"I don't know what your parents would say," he returned, looking troubled.

"Why should they ever know?"

He sipped his coffee, at a loss. Was she saying she would keep it a secret on purpose? And if so, was she saying there would be something important enough to need secrecy?

Until they had finished coffee she chatted about the apartment. It was a wholly masculine place, big, high-ceilinged, with paintings of country scenes on the walls together with posed photographs of his school friends and the Bell family. The armchairs

245

were leather, the furniture rather heavy though handsome. Books and scientific journals were much in evidence, and a special cabinet of maps showing climatic conditions and growing areas throughout the world.

There was a small private laboratory next door, and a study beyond that. She had been shown these when she first arrived. There was, she knew, a set of bedrooms at the far end of the long passage; the manservant had shown her into one so that she could tidy her hair before dinner.

If Cornelius had been a Frenchman, there would have been no problem. But he came from a different moral climate, and was moreover inhibited by the idea that he was unattractive because of his deafness. How was she to let him know she found him desirable?

A pretext came to her. She let her coffee cup slip, so that the remains within it went over her skirt. "Oh," she cried, springing up, "look what I've done!"

"Oh, what a shame!" Cornelius cried. He dabbed at it with his napkin. She stood up. He was stooping, on one knee, dabbing at her skirt. She put out a hand and caught his, stilling his movement.

He looked up and met her gaze. It was full of meaning. He rose to his feet, his eyes on hers all the way. He put his arms around her and drew her close. Then he kissed her as she tilted her head back.

He made no pretence of kissing her gently. The

246

invitation had been too clear. Her response startled him. She wound her arms about him and dragged him closer, moulding her body against his.

For the first time it dawned on him that she was experienced. He had been so caring about her reputation—but she clearly didn't think it important because she had had a lover already. In Paris, where life is seen differently.

They sank into the sofa where she had been sitting and embraced with a growing passion. He pulled away the high-necked top of her gown to kiss the slender neck and the little area of shoulder thus exposed. She pulled his head down, holding his lips against her skin. Her pulses were racing at the touch, at the strong crushing pressure of his arms around her.

He stood up and swept her into his arms. Carrying her lightly, he went along the wide passage. She saw the ornamented ceiling go by overhead as she lay back, submissive and yet eager.

When they reached his room he put her on the bed. Looking down at her he said in a careful, steady tone and with great clarity: "You had better mean this, Stephanie."

She smiled up at him. "I mean it," she said, making the words clear so that he could see them without mistake.

She expected him to be shy and inexperienced, but she was wrong. He undressed her deftly: the stiff boned gown quickly unhooked at the back, the lacings at her small waist, the two silk petticoats that gave the luxurious rustle to her skirts, the fine lawn undergarments edged with broderie anglaise. She was revealed as ivory-skinned, small-boned, with only curves enough to make her feminine. She laughed up at him. "Am I a disappointment?"

His body was superb. She was breathless at the fine muscles, the long hard limbs. He was the handsomest man she had ever gone to bed with. She wanted him so badly that when they came together it was almost too fast—over in a great surge of achievement and pleasure.

By and by he rose, pulled a dressing-gown on, and disappeared. He came back with brandy and two glasses. They sat up in bed, sipping, one arm round the shoulders of each other.

"Is this why we came to Chicago?" he asked her, half-shaking his head in wonderment.

"It's why I came. But not you, I fancy."

"Certainly not. The other young ladies I know would faint at this scene."

"I'm not the fainting sort," she said.

"Why me, Stephanie?"

She leaned forward to brush her lips lightly against his. "I love you," she said.

He set her away from him. He had felt the movement of her lips but couldn't understand the words unless he saw them. "What did you say?"

"I love you."

He knew it was true. She could never have given herself to him as she had, otherwise.

"I don't understand it," he said in a helpless way.

"Oh, you're a fool, my darling!" She threw her arms around him, letting the brandy glass fall from her hand on to the bed. She kissed him passionately on the mouth, the cheeks, the eyes.

He set his glass and hers on the bedside table so that they could make love again. This time they were in no hurry. It was a time of exploration, and of delight. She found him powerful, ardent, yet tender. And silent—his wordlessness gave the experience a magical, dreamlike quality.

When the manservant, Larry, returned around midnight, he found the apartment empty. Mr. Craigallan had clearly taken the young lady back to her hotel, as was only right.

But he made a quick tour of the apartment before clearing the coffee things from the living-room. He found the rumpled bed.

"Well, good for you, boy-o," he said aloud.

He was very fond of Cornelius.

13

THE first few days of his affair with Stephanie were such a wonder to Cornelius that he was incapable of thinking beyond his present happiness. He took her back to New York, but there was no change in their relationship; he went to her studio most evenings to take her to dinner or eat with her, haphazard, at a table cluttered with tubes of paint and sketching equipment.

When either of them had an evening engagement, they met afterwards. Their nights were joyous, richly rewarding. They would lie face to face afterwards, he watching her as her mouth formed the words of endearment he couldn't hear. Their flashing fingers would speak to each other as intimately as they had moved in the exploration of each other's bodies.

By and by Cornelius, brought up to respect the standards of society, began to speak about marriage. Stephanie eluded the topic as often as she could, but in the end he asked her outright, as they were preparing to part in the early morning.

"When do you think we should announce our engagement?" he asked, using his fingers, for engagement was a difficult word to pronounce.

She sighed. "I don't want to get engaged, Neil,"

she said, sitting down and picking up a shoe.

"What?" He knelt in front of her, to make sure he understood what she was saying.

She shook her head, threw down the shoe, and sighed: "I don't want to get engaged." Her hand was emphatic.

He hesitated. "What then? Get married straight away?"

Once more she shook her head.

"But when, Stephanie? When?"

"I don't want to get married, Neil."

He stared at her. It wasn't possible. She wasn't one of the women you coupled with and then walked away from. She was a lady, a girl known to his parents, her parents known to him. They *must* get married.

And then the reason occurred to him. She didn't want to tie herself to someone like him. He looked down.

She seized his hands and made him look at her. "It isn't because of your deafness." And as he flinched, "Well, that's what you were thinking, wasn't it? But it's nothing to do with that. I don't want you to even think it."

He rose from in front of her and went to pick up his jacket, shaking his head in disbelief. She came after him, reached up to put both hands on his shoulders, and turned him.

"I love you, Neil. I never met anyone like you in my life before." She gazed up at him. "Let me try to explain to you. Come, sit down."

They sat side by side on the bed, turned to each other. She said: "You know I take my painting seriously. I've begun to make a bit of a name for myself—just begun." She was thinking of Julius and his rich clients. If she could stretch their interest beyond pseudo-Monets to match their decor, if she could make them look at her portraits, she might be launched. Not to become a vogue, as Julius had said, but as a painter in her own right.

"I don't want to get married yet," she went on, "because I don't want to lose my own name in my husband's—"

He made as if to interrupt, to say, "You could paint under your own name," but she gestured him to silence.

"It's not just that, of course. Newly-weds have to set up house, entertain, go through all the social nonsense—"

"I wouldn't ask you to do that," he protested.

"No, but our parents . . . We could fend them off, I know that, but it would take so much energy. I can't spare the time and effort, Neil, to bother with them. I feel I've just got the door opening for me . . ."

He was about to query her phrase, the door opening, and then understood it. She was speaking figuratively; sometimes when he was lip-reading, people used unexpected turns of speech which made it difficult for him to catch the meaning.

He understood what she meant about the pressure to have the usual kind of wedding. True,

252

his mother would be happy enough to have a less brilliant affair than Ellie-Rose's, because she hated to draw attention to the fact that she had a deaf son. But all the same, there would have to be celebrations, and friends would expect to be invited, and they would have to find a house, and furnish it. Or they could leave all that part to Uncle Julius—he'd love to be given the commission. Yet he guessed she would find even that irksome.

"I've done one or two things recently," she was saying, "that I think are really good. Perhaps before the year is out I'll have enough for a show. That's if I can get a gallery to accept me."

"Oh, surely your parents would pay for a show?"

"But that's not the way, Neil! I want a gallery-owner to show my work because he has faith in it, not because Mama and Papa pay for it!" There was a flash of indignation in her face—the first time he had ever seen any kind of animosity towards himself since they met.

"Just another six months, Neil," she pleaded. And then, "Am I being selfish?"

How could he say yet to that? She had given herself to him generously and completely. Many another man would have been cynically envious of what he had—all the joys of marriage without the pains. She had made no conditions; it was he who now wanted to alter their relationship. He had no right to inflict his conventional moral standards on her. That she loved him was enough.

So he kissed her, and told her he would abide by

253

her wishes, and it ended in making love, so that he was very late for an appointment with a member of a foreign agricultural deputation.

In any case, he told himself later when he had bade farewell to the anxious Italian scientist, it didn't matter. By and by in the nature of things, Stephanie would probably become pregnant and then they would have to get married.

He still had a lot to learn about her. In the first place she was not the kind of girl who would have felt she had to get married in such circumstances. And secondly, she had taken precautions so that the situation never arose.

In Paris she had been part of a movement thought of as very modern, almost revolutionary. They would sit in sidewalk cafes along the Boul' Mich', criticising the world as they saw it, planning a change towards freedom and equality. The revolution always came with much drama and red blood, but none of the blood had anything to do with them.

Among her friends had been medical students, who in the cause of the freedom of woman had explained to her how to avoid the all-too-dismal results of a love affair. Stephanie didn't talk about such things to Cornelius: not yet, he was still too much part of his capitalist environment. But when she had won him over to the cause of the pro-letariat, he would bring his scientific knowledge to the support of their work, and she would be able to discuss with him every aspect of her beliefs, including the freedom to make love and the freedom not to have babies.

She didn't find anything contradictory in the notion of being the mistress of the heir to one of the largest fortunes in America. That was part of her mission: to win over wealthy and influential men to a better understanding of the workers' situation.

She was one of the guests at a small gathering Rob Craigallan arranged for the entertainment of the Italians who had come on an agricultural deputation. Rob had noted at once that something was going on between his elder son and this dark little lightning flash from Paris, though he was far from guessing how far things had gone. To help the romance along, he'd asked Ellie-Rose to put Stephanie's name on the guest list. Ellie-Rose was to play hostess, since Luisa had departed for a season at Long Branch, among the gambling tables.

There were twelve to sit down to table; two Italian scientists, two attractive young women from Cornelius's research office so that the Italians would have something to look at, Cornelius and Stephanie, Rob and Ellie-Rose, Sam Yarwood and his lady friend of the moment, and a Republican Congressman and his wife, Mr. and Mrs. Powell. As usual the food was excellent. When the gentlemen joined the ladies in the great drawing-room, they were mellow with good port and cigars.

The women had been talking music. One of the secretaries sat down at the piano and played some tunes from the latest craze sweeping New York, the cake-walk dance. It was all very informal and relaxed.

When the Philippines came into the conversation, Ellie-Rose should have caught the scent of danger, but she was busy supervising the removal of coffee-cups. When she turned back to pay attention, the argument had already started.

"But you say, don't you, that the Filipinos needed our help because they wanted their freedom from Spain?" Stephanie was saying.

"Certainly," Congressman Powell said, "and that's what they've got."

"Freedom?"

"Indeed."

"But they wanted to become a republic—"

"My dear young lady," the Congressman said, "a nation cannot just become a republic overnight. They have to learn what government is."

"I should have thought they knew that," Stephanie flashed. "They had enough of it from the Spaniards."

"But that was bad government, Stephanie," Rob put in.

"And ours is better?"

"Can you doubt it?" asked Mr. Powell. "We will give them democracy—"

"We will? When?" she asked.

It was well-known that things were going badly in the Philippines. There were some who said it had been a very big mistake for the United States to get involved. There had been a liberation army

256

working in the jungles against the Spaniards, and from all that could be learned it seemed the same army was now fighting the Americans.

A member of the administration had sentimentally called the Filipinos "our little brown brothers" when America first got into the war with Spain. Other terms were now being used. To the tune of the well-known military song, "Tramp, tramp, tramp the boys are marching," the soldiers of the army fighting in the Philippines now sang:

> Damn, damn, damn the Filipino,
> Pock marked khaki-shaded gnome!
> Underneath the starry flag,
> Civilise him with a Krag
> And return us to our own beloved home!

—a Krag being the Krag-Jorgensen rifle recently imported from Denmark.

"I gather Mr. McKinley is busy arranging talks on that point," Ellie-Rose put in. "I saw him and his wife only last Tuesday—the treatment she recently received for thin blood seems to have benefitted her."

"Poor lady," said one of the secretaries, coming to her aid. "She often looks very ill—"

"You didn't answer my question," Stephanie insisted to the Congressman.

"As Mrs. Gracebridge just remarked," the Congressman said, "talks are going on—"

"Between the Republicans and the Democrats!

257

What right have they to decide the fate of the Filipinos?"

"Well, let's say, young lady," he replied, displeased, "the right of being in control."

"Well, now," Sam Yarwood said round his cigar, "I wouldn't exactly say we're in *control* there."

"No, nor likely to be while our troops are there as an army of conquest!"

"There's no intention of making it a conquest. All we want is to get the place quieted down."

"I wish I thought the military understood that," Rob remarked. "They seem pretty heavy-handed, the way they go on—"

"What can you expect, when bandits creep up and attack sleeping men?"

"Oh, you mean it's unfair to attack while they're asleep? Should wake 'em up and say: We're going to attack?" Rob mocked.

"It's nothing to make light of, Craigallan! Our losses have been quite significant—"

"More from yellow-jack than bullets, though," Sam interrupted. "That's if I read the reports aright."

"Our medical mission is doing very good work," Ellie-Rose began in a valiant effort to turn the talk. "I believe they are conducting a long-term experiment—"

"It hadn't better be too long-term," Sam said. "We could have lost the war before they find a treatment."

"And we deserve to," Stephanie cried. "What

258

we're doing is wrong. You sit there, Mr. Yarwood, casually talking about what you gather from reports, but the reality is bitter and tragic to the Filipinos."

"Go on, kitten," Rob urged, grinning. "Give him hell!"

Sam cast an amused glance at him. "It's pretty kind of damn tragic to our boys too, you know, Miss Jouvard. They don't want to be there, fighting in a steamy jungle—"

"So why don't they refuse?"

"Refuse?" Congressman Powell echoed, aghast. "Refuse to fight?" He swallowed hard. "You mean, mutiny?"

"If they hate the war so much, and we have no justice on our side, surely logic ought to tell them to—"

"Now, now," Ellie-Rose intervened, driven at last to bluntness, "I'm sure this is all very dull for our Italian guests. They don't want to listen to a discussion of American politics. Wouldn't it be nice if Signor Aldarotti were to sing us another of those charming folk-songs?"

When the guests had gone, she turned to her father. "Is she always like that?" she inquired.

"Cornelius's girl? No idea. But she lived three years or so on the Left Bank. Pretty Bohemian atmosphere there, I gather."

"Bohemianism is one thing. Wild ideas about mutiny among American troops is another. I notice Cornelius didn't do anything to help."

"Maybe he agrees with her."

"You're joking!"

"I don't know so much. Neil has idealistic notions, you know. It could be that he thinks the United States is wrong to be involved in the Philippines."

"*I* think the United States is wrong to be involved in the Philippines," Ellie-Rose said tartly, "but not from any idealistic notions. I just feel it's wrong to be involved in a war overseas—which is going badly—with an election coming on."

"Oh, there aren't enough voters who think strongly about it to make any problem for McKinley."

"Mm . . ." She had returned to the events of the evening. "Do you think there's a possibility Neil might marry her?"

"I sure hope so. She's a darling."

"A darling?"

"A bit of a spitfire, but a darling. If she fell for Neil, she'd really make a world of difference to his life—bring him out of himself, make him take part."

"In what? A revolution?"

Rob laughed and put his arm around his daughter. "Nobody's going to bring about a revolution in these United States," he said. "Come on, it's time for bed."

Cornelius had driven Stephanie back to his apartment in New York, and they too were thinking of bed. It had now become an accepted fact of

Larry's life, that the master would from time to time bring the young lady home to the apartment off Sixth Avenue. There would be breakfast for two in the morning. Discreet and kindhearted, Larry was scarcely visible on these occasions. He had set the pattern on that first visit to Chicago, a tactful but inconspicuous helper.

"My sister wasn't very pleased with you this evening," Cornelius said as they undressed.

"I'm sorry about that. But there are times when you have to give up politeness in favour of truth."

"What was it all about? I couldn't catch much—you kept turning away to speak so I couldn't see your face."

This might have been an opportunity to speak to him about her ideals. By and by she must explain to him how deeply she felt her commitment to those less fortunate than themselves. But this wasn't the time.

She had been irritated too much by the attitude of the others. Congressman Powell's patronising use of the words "my dear young lady", meaning "Don't talk of things you don't understand", Ellie-Rose's conventional anxiety to preserve calmness, even Rob's cry of approval, "Give him hell, kitten"—she felt that none of them had taken her seriously. She was even unjustly annoyed with Cornelius, because he hadn't come to her aid.

She said: "I was expressing some concern for the people of the Philippines—"

"Yes, I understood it was about the Philippines.

261

What I didn't understand was why you seemed to get so heated?"

"Never mind," she said with a sigh. One day she would explain it all to him. Not now. Now she was being moved by that strong impulse for sexual satisfaction that came from a mixture of emotions—frustration, muted anger, the need for sympathy. She wound her arms round his neck and with her lips against his chest said, "Let's think about ourselves, Neil—not other people."

When she spoke with her lips so near his chest, some vibration of her voice reached him. It was something that had never happened to him before, for no other woman had been so loving and close to him as Stephanie. It was like a powerful spell—when Stephanie lay against his heart, he could almost hear her voice. It always moved him as nothing else in the world had ever done.

He pulled her down and began to kiss her with the strength and power she longed to feel. He forgot to question the events of that evening. The moment had gone by when he might have learned that she took politics very seriously.

Ellie-Rose had been put out by Stephanie's behaviour, but next day regretted her ill-will. "It's because I'm pregnant again," she told herself ruefully. "Being pregnant seems to make me awfully touchy."

To make amends, she decided to visit Stephanie and be especially sweet to her. She had seen the flash of anger in the girl's eyes when she so blatantly told her to be quiet. She discounted the fact that no young lady of breeding should have driven her hostess to the point where she had to do such a thing, and made the trip to New York to visit Stephanie's studio.

She telephoned first to ask if it was convenient for her to call. Stephanie was vexed. She was busy, she would rather not be disturbed. But Ellie-Rose put herself out to sound interested in her work so Stephanie agreed, although she didn't put herself out so far as to buy a cake for five o'clock tea.

Ellie-Rose arrived at mid-afternoon, already regretting the impulse that had brought her here. It was a steamy hot day, airless and grey in the city despite the fact that the sun was shining elsewhere; the smoke from a million chimneys cast a pall over the buildings to keep out the sunlight, and there was no breeze to disperse it.

She knew, naturally, that Stephanie had a good address; Uncle Julius would have seen to that. His clients wouldn't relish visiting an artist in the tumbledown lanes of Greenwich Village, which were beginning to attract the less well-off painters. Even so, she was surprised by the handsome apartment with its great windows pushed open to allow the entry of whatever breeze might blow.

Stephanie, naturally untidy, had made an effort to make the place neat for her visitor. She had the kettle boiling and was able to provide fresh iced tea when Ellie-Rose stated a preference for that.

"New York is really getting unbearable," Ellie-

Rose said, moving her ivory-spoked fan in front of her face. "It's time to go out of town."

"But Washington is little better, surely?"

"It's worse, in fact. No, I mean, right out—up into the hills. Curtis and I have taken a place in the Blue Mountains." She paused. "Shall you be going out of town?"

"I'm not sure." Cornelius hadn't as yet put forward any plan. "I have some work to finish—a client is expecting a landscape that I've got half-finished."

"But couldn't you take that out with you? Or do you have to sit and look at the scene to be able to paint it?"

"Hardly," Stephanie replied with a cynical smile. "Since it's a French woodland scene."

"Oh, I see. You're doing it from memory."

Stephanie could have told her that the place was entirely imaginary, that the whole point was to make it look like a Corot. But that was something she didn't quite want to say to Ellie-Rose. She could joke with Cornelius about the rich people who bought her so-called landscapes, but Ellie-Rose had a more critical view of her. Ellie-Rose might not think it funny.

"Would you like to see it?" she asked, and whisked the dust-sheet off the great canvas she was working on.

Ellie-Rose had already seen some samples of her decorative paintings. Uncle Julius had some on display in the rather handsome premises he now

264

rented on Fifth Avenue. She said one or two complimentary things about the draughtsmanship and the colour—and certainly the colour sense was excellent, though the picture was uninspired in her opinion, an early-nineteenth century landscape without figures.

"Don't you ever do anything just for yourself?" she asked when Stephanie had showed her six or seven other canvasses of a like kind.

Stephanie hesitated. She didn't really like Ellie-Rose. But there had been an olive-branch intended in this visit, and besides, she was Cornelius's sister.

"I have done some portraits," she said slowly.

"Really? May I see them?"

"We-ell . . . I don't want to let anyone look until I can have a proper one-man show. But there is one I think would interest you."

She led Ellie-Rose into another room, intended as a bedroom but used by her to keep things she didn't want Julius Van Huten's clients to see. She picked up a canvas and leaned it against the wall.

It was a painting of Cornelius. Ellie-Rose gave an exclamation of pleasure. "Why, that's marvellous!"

"Do you like it?"

"It's . . . it's so like him! You've caught . . . I don't know how to describe it."

Indeed she didn't. Stephanie had caught the inward Cornelius, the man who seldom showed through the shell of reserve. He was looking out from the canvas with his head tilted, in the way he did when he was watching someone's lips. There was no smile on his face, but the expression conveyed that he had understood what was being said and that it pleased him. There was eagerness, alertness, but no wariness. He was with a friend. No, someone who was more than a friend.

Ellie-Rose looked at the painting and understood that her brother had been looking at the girl he loved while it was being painted. Somehow she also knew that he felt himself beloved.

Her throat seemed to thicken with something like a sob. Could it really be? These two were in love?

"I think it's . . . wonderful," she said. And she meant more than the painting.

Stephanie looked embarrassed, a rare occurrence. Luckily the moment was broken by the loud ringing of Stephanie's telephone.

"Excuse me a minute," she said. "I think this is your Uncle Julius with warning of a forthcoming caller."

When she had gone, Ellie-Rose stood for a long time staring at her brother's portrait. For the first time she noted the strange paint hues that Stephanie had used—much green and brown in the skin tints, and yet there was no feeling of its being unnatural. But was that how it would seem to someone who hadn't immediately been struck by a likeness, as Ellie-Rose had?

Perhaps there would be a painting of someone she didn't know. She stepped to the wall and turned another canvas.

The face that looked back at her was plain,

square-ish, brooding. It took her a moment to realise that this was a woman, not a man—the clue was the quickly-brushed-in dark silk shoulders. All the attention must be on the face: strong, snub-nosed, dark-eyed. Somehow you knew the eyes were short-sighted, and the gaze was led to the chain of her pince-nez, scarcely visible in the darkness from which the face looked out.

It was a passionate face, foreign-looking—Polish, perhaps. Ellie-Rose knew that face but couldn't think who it was. Someone intellectual, some fighter for women's rights. She ought to know the name, but it eluded her.

She heard Stephanie end her telephone conversation so put the canvas back, remembering that the girl had said she didn't want anyone to see her work. She offered a few more complimentary remarks on the portrait of Cornelius then murmured that she ought to take her leave—the evening rush hour would soon be starting and the horses did so hate the noise and uproar. Might she have a mirror so that she could put on her hat again?

Stephanie showed her into her bedroom. Ellie-Rose put her rose-decked straw hat on top of her flat-curled hair and skewered it with a jewelled hat pin. Then she went into the bathroom to run cold water over her wrists, a protection against the heat of the enclosed carriage journey.

Lying on the side of the wash-hand basin was a man's razor case. She looked at it with an amused frown as she dried her hands, then curiosity prompted her to open it. Inside were the two usual long ivory-backed razors.

But then she closed the case with a snap. For on the handle, inlaid in gold were the initials CLC—her brother's initials.

She remembered her father speaking of these razors; he had had the initials put on by Tiffany for a birthday two years ago.

Well, why should it shock her so? Cornelius was a grown man, and fully entitled to have a mistress. Yet she was shocked. She couldn't deny it to herself. To think that it had gone so far . . .

She found it quite difficult to say goodbye adequately. If Stephanie thought her stiff, it couldn't be helped.

All the way back to Craigallan Castle she was deep in thought. Everything she had seen on her visit whirled in her mind. She gave her hat, parasol and purse to Soames, asking: "Is my father at home?"

"Yes, Mrs. Gracebridge. In the drawingroom. He asked for old-fashioned lemonade with ice—shall I bring some for you?"

"Yes, please, Soames."

Rob was lolling on one of the settees with his legs spread out, his stiff collar undone and in his shirt sleeves. He sat up as she came in. "Oh, sorry—I'll go up and change in a minute—"

"No, Papa, don't trouble yourself. It's very hot and you've a right to get comfortable." She dropped

268

into a chair, weary from the heat but from more than the heat.

"Papa, I've just been to pay a visit to Stephanie Jouvard in her studio."

"Really? Thought you were cross with her after last night."

"That's why I went—because I felt I was a bit tactless over her opinions. Put it down to being in 'a certain condition'."

"Yeah," Rob said with a fond grin, "that's an excuse for a lot of things, eh?"

Soames came in with a glass that tinkled with ice. She took it, drank deep, and sighed with pleasure. "Ah, that's good. Really, this climate's unbearable. I'm glad we're off to join Curtis in the hills tomorrow."

"Kind of hot for travelling with the kiddie, Ellie. Don't you think we should put it off for a day or two, to see if the weather cools off a little?"

"Listen, Papa," she said, with a gesture that dismissed the weather, "Stephanie showed me a portrait she's done—of Neil."

"She did? I got a hint she was doing one—about a month ago." He looked at her with interest. "Is it any good?"

"It's good. Too good," she said. "It shows they're awfully in love."

He stared. "Oh, come on, Ellie. You can't tell that from a painting."

"You can if you know Neil. It shows, Papa. He thinks the world of that girl." She hesitated, about

269

to tell him what else she knew. Yet that wasn't her business. She bit her lip and went on, "I realised something as I was on my way home. I sneaked a look at another painting, one that she didn't actually show me. And guess who it was, Papa?"

Rob was looking faintly irritated. "How can I guess who else has sat for her?" he muttered, slumping back into the settee.

"It was Emma Goldman."

That made him sit up again. "Emma Goldman? The radical?"

"Yes."

He frowned, felt in his pocket for a handkerchief, and mopped his brow. "Seems an odd sitter to choose," he said.

"Odd? I think it's outrageous! Everyone knows the woman's a dangerous revolutionary."

"Oh, now . . ." He put his handkerchief away, then decided to take a grip of the situation. Ellie-Rose was getting herself into a state, but that was only due to the baby coming, and it was too hot to be worked up about a thing like that. "You can't say she's dangerous, Ellie. She's one of Mable Lodge's carpet communists—gets up at a soirée like a soprano hired to sing 'Hark Hark the Lark'."

"But do you want us to be mixed up with people of that kind, Papa?"

"Mixed up? How are we mixed up?"

"Well, Stephanie is clearly a friend of hers, and Cornelius is in love with Stephanie, so it could well

270

be you'll end up with a daughter-in-law who's bosom friends with a revolutionary."

"Oh, come, now, daughter. Granted that it looks like being a match between those two—and thank God for it, say I. But that doesn't mean we'll be connected with the radicals from Russia. The fact that Stephanie has painted her portrait doesn't mean she's a friend."

Ellie-Rose shook her head emphatically. "She certainly wasn't commissioned to paint it. Emma Goldman isn't the kind of woman who hires someone for money to paint her. Stephanie did it out of friendship. Perhaps," she added, with afterthought, "from admiration."

"Oh, come on . . ."

"I tell you, if you'd seen it . . . There was admiration in that portrait."

Rob saw that she was in earnest. "Well, so what?" he countered. "You heard last night—she's got these schoolgirlish views about the rights of man and so forth. She's quite likely to admire Goldman if she's heard her speak."

"But she *knows* her, Papa. She's had her to her studio to sit. It's more than just having heard her speak."

"I can understand it, Ellie. I've heard Goldman in full spate, and she is kind of impressive. And—though she's not my type—she has a remarkable face." His attempt to lighten the atmosphere was a flop. His daughter continued to sit in the armchair across from him looking very alarmed. "Forget it, Ellie," he advised. "She's a grown woman and entitled to make friends where she likes. If Cornelius has fallen for her, he'll have to take her friends in his stride. It doesn't mean we have to concern ourselves."

"You mean you don't care if he gets mixed up with anarchists?"

"Oh, anarchists! The whole thing's a joke, love. Wild-eyed theorists, that's all they are. Anyone with any sense knows they're talking nonsense."

"But they preach assassination as one of the means of getting power, don't they? I've read about it—"

"Oh yeah, to scare their listeners into sitting up and taking notice. But put it out of your head, Ellie. It's a joke."

Even the most shrewd of businessmen can make a mistake.

272

14

FEELING unwell because of the heat and the queasiness of early pregnancy, Ellie-Rose retired to her room to have a light supper of consommée and *truite chaudfroid*. She had to remember that tomorrow she must set out for Virginia with her little daughter and her daughter's nurse and her own maid and her father. She regretted now that she had delayed the journey; the weather was punishingly hot.

Left to contemplate eating dinner by himself, Rob became discontented. Cornelius wouldn't be at the Castle tonight. Recently—and quite understandably—he'd spent a lot of time in the city. But tonight as it happened he was taking the Italians out to dinner and then handing them on to someone else to sample the night life.

As yet Gregor was still in college. Rob considered ringing a friend or two, inviting them for a meal and a game of cards, but decided against it. Many of his business acquaintances had left for the seashore or the mountains. Sam Yarwood was in Chicago. Politicos were taken up with the forthcoming election.

He decided after a while to telephone Stephanie. On consideration, what Ellie-Rose had said about that portrait worried him a little; it wouldn't be a bad thing to have a chat. Besides, he shrewdly deduced, Cornelius was busy elsewhere this evening; Stephanie might be at loose ends.

She didn't sound too delighted when she answered the telephone. This seemed to be her day for attention from the Craigallans. As she didn't approve of any of them except Cornelius, their conversation gave her no pleasure.

"I wondered if you were free for dinner?" he ventured.

"What?" She was astonished—and impolitely showed it.

"Don't sound so staggered. I thought you and I ought to get to know each other a little better. Have you an engagement?"

"Tonight?" She was still surprised. She hadn't thought they'd got to the stage of casual dropping-in on each other.

"Well, I happen to know Cornelius is busy," he pointed out.

"Ah. Yes. Well . . ." First Ellie-Rose and now Rob. What could have brought all this on? "I . . . er . . . have an engagement later," she said.

"Okay, then," he said at once, taking that as agreement to the invitation. "Pick you up in about an hour?"

"I . . . well . . . all right."

He hurried upstairs to dress, pleased with himself. The prospect of sharing a dinner table with her was infinitely better than pottering around at home after a solitary meal. Sure, it was hot—but it was worth the discomfort of getting himself up in evening clothes for the pleasure of taking her out.

That gave him pause. He looked at himself in the mirror as he fastened his stiff collar with its gleaming stud. Pleasure? Why should it give him such pleasure to look forward to an evening with Stephanie?

Well, she's a pretty girl, after all, he told himself. And fun—a little spitfire. A man wouldn't be human if he didn't like the thought of her company.

All the same, he thought, "Careful, boy. She's Cornelius's girl."

Stephanie didn't put herself out much to look attractive for him. It was too hot for grand evening dresses and all their accessories. She put on a dress of sprigged lilac voile trimmed with narrow satin bands, and had no idea how virginal and appealing it made her look.

When her doorbell rang she went to answer it. She saw the admiration in his eyes and was flattered. She invited him in for a moment while she gathered up the voile cape that went with the dress and pulled on the necessary white gloves.

"Hey, while I'm here, can I see Neil's portrait?" he begged. "Ellie-Rose told me about it."

She was regretting that she had shown the portrait. She was on the verge of saying, "No, I don't want people to see my work." But then she thought, "Well, after all, he's Neil's father." She went to the storage room for the portrait, brought it out, and set it on a chair so that Rob could study it.

He didn't see in it what Ellie-Rose had seen. He wasn't so attuned to Cornelius's every expression as she was. He saw other things, chiefly about Stephanie.

She could paint. Here was no dabbler. There was strength, individuality, purpose in her work. He was surprised. He'd been thinking of her as a girl—a kitten-girl, almost schoolgirlish. But this was the work of a woman.

"Well, well," he said. "How long have you been painting?"

"Since I was seventeen. Seriously, the last three years."

"How long in this style?"

"About a year."

"Who was your teacher?"

"I had several. Cézanne gave me a lot of help—not in actual teaching but he helped me find my own way."

"Hm." Cézanne was one of the oddest of the odd painters whose work was discussed in the magazines. It seemed to Rob that he recalled something about Cézanne taking part in the Paris Commune during the Franco-Prussian War. That might well account for Stephanie's silly idealism. If a teacher whose work you admired talked to you about the brotherhood of man, of course you'd be impressed.

Rob had reserved a table at the Metropole, thinking that the "Parisian" atmosphere would appeal to her—marble-topped tables, velvet banquettes, and wide windows opening on to the

276

corner of Forty-second Street for the evening air. Even though so many people had left town, the place was well-filled.

What Rob had forgotten, or perhaps not even known, was that Cornelius was taking his visiting scientists on a tour of the cocktail world. It was an all male party, the two Italians, Cornelius, a senior Civil Servant from the Department of Agriculture, and a manufacturer of reaping machines. They were to pause for dinner at the Metropole before Cornelius handed them on to a friend who would take them to Koster and Bial's Music Hall.

As Rob and Stephanie followed the maitre d'hotel to their table, Cornelius finished studying the wine-list and looked up, seeing them. He froze in disbelief. A stab of something hard and cruel went through his guts.

Rob saw him, saw the frozen expression. "By God, the boy's jealous," he thought in dismay.

He let the maitre d'hotel settle them, then excused himself to Stephanie. "Cornelius is over there, I'll just say a word." Stephanie looked about, saw him, and raised a gloved hand in salutation.

Rob threaded his way among the tables to his son's side. "How's it going?" he inquired in a jovial manner, smiling a little exaggeratedly to show bonhomie.

"All right, I think."

"*Meriviglioso! Ché città!*" the Italians cried.

The two other men smiled and added words of approval. They had drunk a lot, were glad to sit down now and eat, but were looking forward to other delights later.

"I was on my own," Rob said to Cornelius, facing him and barely voicing the words aloud, "so I thought I'd telephone to Stephanie to see if she was free."

"Oh yes?"

"Thought we were a bit hard on her last night—that argument, remember? Felt I owed a bit of an apology."

"I see."

It was difficult to tell from that flat tone whether he was convinced or not. His guests claimed his attention. He ordered the wines by pointing at the numbers on the list. Rob waited to say, "She tells me she has an engagement for later."

"Yes," Cornelius said, looking up with a hard gaze, "with me."

"Uh-huh," Rob said. He smiled and nodded. He was trying to say, "I thought as much, of course I'll fade out by that time."

Oh, if only the boy could hear! A tone of voice would be enough to tell him, "I understand. She's your girl." But you couldn't mime all that, and to use sign language would be to bring it out as a factor to be thought about. And it wasn't that. He was simply taking this pretty girl out to dinner because they were both at a loose end.

After a few more moments' chat he went back to Stephanie. The waiter had been fussing over her in his absence, presenting the menu, bringing iced water, replacing the tired flowers with a vase of fresh. Rob sat down with a dismissive jerk of the head. When he was ready to order he summoned him with a little gesture. He didn't enjoy the meal. He had an uneasy feeling that Cornelius's eyes were turned on them often, until at length he came over—duty bound—to pay his respects before leaving.

"They're going on to Koster's," he reported to his father. "I'm off duty now."

"Yeah—glad to be, in this heat, eh?"

Cornelius shrugged. "Enjoyed your meal?" he inquired, the question directed mainly at Stephanie.

She smiled and toyed with the elegant dessert she had ordered. It was too hot to eat. "It's been fun," she said, with just enough enthusiasm. It had been in fact rather tiresome. Rob had not been much of a conversationalist.

He'd meant to draw her out about her student days in Paris and the socialist-minded friends she might have had there. But he couldn't keep his mind on it. After one or two clumsy attempts he'd abandoned the idea. Absurd, in any case, to think there was much in it. Sure, she knew Emma Goldman, had probably met her at Mrs. Lodge's house, but so had a hundred other New Yorkers. Mabel Lodge was one of those idiotic women who fancied herself an intellectual, who took up causes and made herself a nuisance. Anybody could be forgiven for getting caught up in her enthusiasms—

she was probably the one who'd commissioned the portrait of Goldman.

It was more important to take the girl home and get out of her way for the rest of the evening. He cursed himself for not realising she probably had a date with his son. When Cornelius said goodbye and left, Rob ensured that they weren't long in following.

He took her home to Gramercy Park in a hackney. She invited him in at her door, offering a cool drink against the heat of his journey back to Craigallan Castle.

For a moment he was tempted to say yes. But it was better to say goodnight and get going. He took her hand, bowed over it.

And then as he felt the soft fingers through the kid gloves, he suddenly was aware that he wanted her. Nothing paternal or fondly affectionate in it—it was a physical surge of desire that beat in him like furnace heat. He let her hand go rather suddenly. She looked up in surprise. He turned away, for fear she should see it in his eyes. "Goodnight," he said. His voice was rather thick, but he hoped she would think it was weariness.

"Goodnight," she said, and closed her door. She listened to his footsteps descending the staircase. Well, the lecherous old fox! She had felt it, that warmth suddenly enveloping him. He had actually wanted to go to bed with her! And he was old enough to be her father.

She was amused. When Cornelius arrived about

half an hour later she was still letting it bring up the corners of her mouth in ironic consideration.

Cornelius was in an edgy mood. That moment of consternation in the restaurant still loomed in his mind. "What was the idea, going out to dinner with my father?" he demanded.

"Well, why not, Neil? I had nothing better to do."

He wanted to say, "I expect you never to go out with anyone except me." But how could you say that when the other man he was angry about was his own father?

"What made him invite you?"

"I've no idea. Perhaps Ellie-Rose told him about your portrait—she was here this afternoon, so I let her see it."

Ellie-Rose had been here. Somehow that made it seem better. It was as if his family were taking an interest in Stephanie, not just his father.

"You said you had fun," he remarked.

"Oh, I was only being polite. It was a drag, really. He didn't seem to have anything to talk about."

"So you won't be going to dinner with him again?"

"I reckon not." She looked at him. "Neil, you're not jealous?"

"No," he said woodenly. He couldn't betray himself by a tone of voice, as another man might. But she saw his hands were trembling a little, and he was paler than usual.

"But darling, he's an old man!" she cried.

In a way that was how Cornelius had thought of him. Papa, Father, Mr. Craig as Gregor called him: the elder, the controller, the head of the household.

But walking into the Metropole behind Stephanie, he hadn't looked old. Tall, slim, walking with the ease of a thirty-year-old, head erect, russet hair gleaming . . .

"He was just being fatherly," she insisted. She knew it wasn't strictly true; it might have started out that way, but there had been a hint of something different at the end. "Anyhow, it won't happen again because I've better things to do." She went to him and put her arms round his waist. "Haven't I?" she teased, pulling herself close to him.

She understood about jealousy. It was a very Gallic emotion. The way to defuse it was to give immediate proof of constancy. She leaned her body in its soft voile dress against Cornelius, and let herself melt into his arms when he responded.

When he claimed her it was with a savagery that added a new dimension to their lovemaking. In her delight and elation she misread it; she thought he was re-establishing mastery over her.

She had never seen Cornelius angry. Insofar as she knew him he was quiet, wary, controlled in company. She didn't know that in his childhood, before his deafness was diagnosed, there had been scenes of rage and frustration that made him unmanageable. He had learned to control it, that volcanic temper. But it was there, and she was ignorant of it.

That crisis passed without further trouble because Rob was off next day to the mountains with his daughter and granddaughter. Cornelius was expected to meet his father in Chicago in August. The wheat harvest would be in by then and prices would start to move. He played a part in analysing the reports about crop results. The Visible Supply Report from the Department of Agriculture, surveys by the scientific departments of various universities and agricultural colleges, and private sources of information built over the years gave Craigallan Agricultural Products an edge in reading the market.

The recent "war" in Cuba and the Philippines had brought up the price of grain for animal feedstuffs but now Cuba was at peace and although there was still trouble in the Philippines, the market for grain was a buyer's market—with few buyers.

The equation to be considered was this: Should C.A.P. buy on the futures market on the assumption that there would be a big demand for wheat in Europe? Russia, with her usual ineptitude and inefficiency, had somehow managed to have crop failures again.

Also, there was a big demand for animal feedstuffs from the British Army. They were engaged in a war with the Boers in South Africa and needed good feeding to keep their wagon horses and pack animals in condition to pursue the Boer commando groups. Was this going to continue? Or would the pressure being brought by the Europeans upon Britain to end the war actually succeed?

Another factor in the equation was storage. Vast quantities of grain were now in store in the United States. But confidential information had let C.A.P. know that the grain was deteriorating fast. The longer wheat is stored, the greater the danger of infection by fungus and the depredations of rats and mice. One big store facility known to Rob was over-run by rats, so much so that the wheat was about to be condemned. When the dealers in The Pit heard this, it would be sure to start an alarm. How much of that stored grain, which had kept prices depressed for new harvests, would turn out to be useless? The price could well rise, in which case the wheat stored in perfect conditions in C.A.P.'s silos would be more valuable in a week's time than it was today.

It was like a vast conundrum, and the man who could get even close to the right answer could make a fortune. The one who got it a bit wrong could lose his hide. Somewhere in between there was a safety line trodden by most of the dealers. As to the farmers, the men who produced the commodity in which the dealers gambled—they came nowhere.

For Rob Craigallan the pros and cons of the harvest were not so vital as they were to many others. He had built up a vast empire—land, storage facilities, flour mills, agricultural machinery, rail freighting, seeds and soil chemicals—so that the actual price of wheat was merely one factor in his considerations. He was beginning to see that the agricultural industry itself was going into decline, not just wheat, whose price had been falling for twenty years as new farmers opened up new fertile lands in the west. The price of meat was going down, hogs and beef cattle were going for the lowest prices ever in the livestock market because South America was coming into the game and the canning industry made it less important to have fresh meat. Cotton had taken a knock as India and Egypt kept up production while the boll weevil took its toll of the plantations in the United States. Sugar cane was being over-produced now that peace had been brought about in Cuba and other Caribbean islands.

This August Rob had decisions to make. He had to make up his mind whether to diversify out of the agricultural industry into a growth industry. If he decided in favour of the move, he had to decide which industry.

His instinct was taking him towards some experiments going on in the eastern states with steam wagons. He had a feeling that a form of transport that could go on all day and all night—like a steam locomotive but using the roads—would have a big advantage over horse wagons. Sam Yarwood scoffed at the notion: "It's okay having steam engines working the reapers and binders in the fields, Rob, but they just sit there."

"But those steam traction engines can be made to move, Sam. You've seen them yourself—"

"Yeah, yeah, they go at the speed of an iceberg thawing in the Antarctic. Come on, now, Rob. Be sensible. They're never going to get those things to move with the speed and versatility of a horse-drawn cart."

Well, Sam might be right. Certainly the problem of having enough fuel to make a steam wagon viable was not yet solved. Rob was watching experiments with an interested eye. One day some bright young man would walk out of a shed and say: I've solved the problem of having enough fuel to make a horseless wagon work.

So if he didn't diversify yet into steam wagons, he must think where else to put some money. Eighteen months ago a factory at Marion, Ohio, had trundled out a tractor driven by fuel derived from petroleum. President McKinley, interested in everything that happened in his home state, had mentioned it to Rob during a fund-raising dinner. Well, now . . . if a tractor could be driven by petroleum, maybe a wagon could. Perhaps he would look around for an experimenter who was working on that idea. A tankful of petroleum oil was certainly a lot more easy to tack on to a wagon than a trailer carrying coal or wood for a steam engine.

Rob wouldn't divulge all his thinking to the group of men with whom he would consult before they began dealing in The Pit. The chief reason for the conclave in Chicago, at his handsome offices there, would be to determine their attitude to the way trading developed. They had to have a strategy ready to benefit from a bull market or a bear—though a bull market was the least likely thing in the world at the moment, with prices always, always falling.

Cornelius had to plan his summer too. He had an engagement to spend a couple of weeks at Beinn Breagh with the Bells and he generally spent some time with Gregor. They were good friends, had been since the boy was first brought into the family. Then by mid-August he must be in Chicago, to sit below the big revolving fans in the heat of his father's office, studying the sheets of reports from all over the wheat-producing regions of the world.

In the first or second week of September, Craig-allan Agricultural Products would have done what dealing they intended to do for futures in wheat for the coming year. After that, the matter could be left in the capable hands of their brokers, until spring brought a new estimate of the probable harvests.

But Cornelius didn't want to be parted from Stephanie for all that time. "Won't you change your mind and come with me to the Bells?" he urged.

"Darling, I can't," Stephanie said. "Papa and Maman simply insist I go to them in Plymouth for the Fourth."

It didn't occur to Cornelius to think it strange she should obey her parents. For a girl so uncon-ventional, Stephanie had some curbs on her behaviour. She had been brought up to obey Maman and Papa, a habit that had held good through all her later years. Even in Paris, where she had lived very much as she wished, she'd taken care never to offend Tante Jeannine and Oncle Pierre.

These two kindly people hoped very much that their niece wouldn't take a lover. But if she did, they hoped she wouldn't bring it to their attention so that they would have to act. Stephanie perfectly understood these limitations; she lived in their house, came home to sleep in her bedroom each night, and generally behaved like a dutiful niece.

She kept up the same attitude with her parents. Partly it was just to avoid uproar. Partly it was because the allowance she received from them was so generous. She could perhaps have lived on what she was now earning from her work with Julius, but hitherto it had been the money from Papa that made it possible for her to paint. Habit dies hard; she liked to be unworried about money matters, and so she took care not to offend Papa.

Since they brought her home from Paris in the spring, Papa and Maman had been waiting with interest and considerable patience to see whether their daughter would land a rich husband in New York. They knew she had been taken up by the Craigallans; in her letters she mentioned dinners at the lavish home out at Carmansville. They had an inkling that the deaf son, Cornelius, was a friend.

They were not particularly keen for Stephanie to marry a deaf and nearly dumb young man, but if he was very rich that made it better. However, the weeks went by and there was no news of the friendship blossoming into anything more attractive.

So now the Jouvards had moved, as they did every year, to Plymouth, for the month of July. They liked to take part in the Fourth of July celebrations there which, because the town had associations with the very beginnings of the country, were always lavish. They always met the same families on the outskirts of the town where vacation houses were for rent. One of these families had a son as yet unmarried, a Wall Street broker, doing well, about Stephanie's age and a Catholic. The elder Jouvards had decided to do some matchmaking this year. It was time, it really was. She was twenty-three. Soon people would begin to hint that she couldn't catch a man, that she was heading for spinsterhood. Unfair, and untrue . . . Besides, they had a comfortable dowry ready to go with her to a suitable husband. This year was the year when it must be brought to the point.

Stephanie sensed all this, and knew she would be hard put to it to avoid entanglement with the young man. But she also knew she must go. If she didn't, Papa would come and fetch her, and undoubtedly he would learn much about her way of life by questioning the neighbours in Gramercy Park.

God help her if that ever happened. He would lock her up. Every kind of obstacle would be thrown in the way of her continuing to paint. She could, of course, defy Papa—walk out, bang the door, make a living by her brush. Yes, she could do that if she were forced into it. But it was better to go to Plymouth, live through a month of provincial holiday-making, and get away for another holiday on some pretext in August.

She certainly wasn't going to Chicago to join Cornelius in August. Chicago would be awful during the August heat. The smell of the stockyards, she'd heard, was nauseating in hot weather.

"But we can't be parted for two months," Cornelius protested. "Stephanie, we can't!"

In the end they arranged a timetable whereby they saw each other for a few days here and there. Then, they would be back in New York by the beginning of September and everything would be as before.

But not quite. Already the necessity of thinking of separation had made Stephanie feel less involved with Cornelius. Moreover, she had to make a vow inside herself to give up love-making while she was staying with her parents, and one of the ties that bound her to Cornelius was sexual. They were an exciting pair when they were in each other's arms, but when she was apart from him he seemed to become less exciting, less important.

When Cornelius called on the Jouvards in Plymouth, it was quite impossible to arrange a meeting alone with him; his hotel was too busy, her home was out of the question, the difficulties of arranging an assignation were too great. Stolen kisses weren't the same thing at all.

Surrounded by the barriers of her parents' conventions, which she accepted, Stephanie found Cornelius almost an embarrassment. Yet his visit had its uses. Papa and Maman were encouraged to think that, after all, there might be a match that would unite their family with the rich Craigallans; they ceased to urge their daughter into the young broker's arms with so much determination. They even raised less opposition to her plan to return to New York at the end of July, although they predicted she would make herself ill in the heat.

Her excuse was that the Hattan-Prior home was being redecorated and that her landscapes were needed before the owners returned in September. "I've such a lot to do still, Papa," she murmured, sounding hard-worked and conscientious. "Mr. Hattan-Prior has asked for some water scenes, and I don't really do those very well. I think I'll try to get to the lakes for a few days—so don't worry too much about the heat in New York, I'll be on a lake-shore somewhere, getting the colour effects down on canvas."

Papa protested a little, as he felt was required. But secretly he was pleased that his daughter should be doing landscapes for a blue-blood family like the Hattan-Priors.

So Stephanie went to New York to collect her painting things and spend a few days. It was, as predicted, hot and humid. Traffic was generally at a standstill because of the excavations going on for the building of a new form of transport, the "subway". At the corner of Broadway and Fifth Avenue, another great hole was being dug, for the erection of a triangular building intended to be at least twenty storeys high and destined to be called, because of its shape, the Flatiron. Already the newspapers were speaking of it as a "skyscraper".

She wondered why she'd come back to this noisy, steamy, dirty city. And then a series of heavy thunderstorms brought a cleansing flood of water, the tall buildings gleamed in the light, and in the cool of the evening she could look out and see the lights of Manhattan glittering like a formal pattern of sequins against the night sky. Her artist's eye was enchanted. It might be the outward display of the careless use of wealth, it might show that the rich cared nothing for the poor—but it was beautiful.

Her telephone rang. A quick, decisive voice with a hint of an accent said: "Is that you, Stephanie? I wondered if you really would come back."

"I told you I had to, Emma."

"I think there's little you really 'have to' do, my dear. Well, are you coming to the meeting?"

"It's getting late—"

"That's never worried you before. Take a cab all the way."

The truth was, Stephanie didn't much want to travel to the East Side at night to hear a lecture on the wrongs of capitalism. "I'm tired, Emma."

Emma Goldman snorted. "If you had sweated

twelve hours in a garment house, I would believe 'tired' . . . What have you really done today? Tell me truthfully."

"I've been packing my painting things. I'm heading out to Lake Michigan tomorrow."

"So? This is tiring? Putting a few tubes of paint in a box?"

"All right, all right," Stephanie agreed. There were only two ways to end the argument: to put the phone down or to agree. And she didn't want to put the phone down on Emma Goldman, whom she much admired.

The radical speaker very much wanted to see Stephanie at the hall. At the end of her talk a collection would be taken up to help "the cause". Out of embarrassment, Stephanie always contributed as much as she could. Funds were low at the moment; that was why Miss Goldman was telephoning round to all her rich devotees. She had no illusions about Stephanie's dedication to socialism; she was a rich spoiled girl playing at being an intellectual until she settled down to marriage with a suitable young man. But in the meantime, Emma Goldman intended to get as much as she could out of her and the likes of her.

The lecture was good. Emma spoke with fire and flame, her strident voice soaring through the dingy hall. The audience was quite large despite the fact that the night was wet and sultry—her hearers were workers from the neighbourhood, little daunted by bad weather which they had to endure summer and winter while the rich took themselves off to better climes.

Stephanie assuaged her conscience by putting twenty dollars in the wooden box that was presented. She saw the young man sitting next to her put only coins in the box. He was thin and pale; his jacket and trousers were damp, showing that he'd been caught in one of the intense thunder showers. He was shivering as they filed out from the row.

"Wasn't she wonderful?" Stephanie said.

"Oh yes," he replied, with a sudden dreamy smile that surprised her with its beauty. "Oh, she is like a star that flashes across the sky."

"A comet," Stephanie amended.

"Comet—yes. I have wanted a long time to hear her."

"You're from out of town?"

"Alpena, Michigan."

She heard the foreign tinge to his speech. He clearly came from Polish origins; towns in Michigan such as Posen and Alpena were dominated by Polish immigrants. "That's a coincidence," she said, "I'm heading out to Michigan tomorrow."

"You are? To work? I also."

"In a way." She didn't like to admit to him that she was only going to paint. She sensed that this shabbily dressed man would think being a painter was a life of luxury. He looked like one of those to whom Emma Goldman's message was a gospel, giving them hope of a life better than the drudgery they endured.

"Goodnight then, Miss . . . ?"

"Jouvard. Perhaps I'll see you on the train tomorrow?"

"I'll look out for you. My name is Nieman, Fred Nieman."

She went back to her studio half-hoping the strangely handsome young man would come along the train looking for her. He would be in the cheap part of the train, of course. Perhaps it had better be the other way about—she had better go from her private compartment looking for him.

After lunch had been served on the flyer, she took a walk along and found him in the carriage near the locomotive, where the smuts of soot and sparks from the coal could fall on the less-expensive suiting. He looked up bemused when she touched him on the shoulder.

"Oh . . . Miss Jouvard? I didn't really expect to see you."

"How are you getting along?"

"Fine, fine." He showed her the paper from a sandwich he'd brought along for lunch. "I haven't any left to offer you . . ."

She was a little ashamed. She had had a four course meal. Was he so unobservant that he couldn't see by her clothes that she was in the first class part of the train? "You're going home?"

He shook his head and frowned. "Not home."

Clearly he didn't cherish the memory of home. "To Chicago only."

She took the seat beside him and chatted a while with him. He told her, rather unwillingly, that his family had a small farm near Cleveland. He had worked in factories and his father's grocery store. He had helped to lead a strike in the wire mill where he had had a job and as a result had been fired.

Stephanie was impressed. Here was a true member of the proletariat—a worker, a hewer of wood and drawer of water. She had seldom come into contact with them if the truth were told. Her socialism, learned in Paris, was largely theoretical. She questioned Nieman but gradually he grew less willing to talk. She could see he wanted to get back to his book.

"So long," she said as she left him. Then added, to show comradeship, "If you're ever in New York again, look me up." She gave him her address. He smiled, nodded, and said he'd remember.

She wasn't to know that she had done a foolish thing which would affect her future greatly. Although no one could have guessed it, the time would soon come when the name of Fred Nieman would be on everyone's lips in America.

15

MORAG McGARTH had looked forward to Gregor's arrival as she always did. He came looking taller and more filled out; she felt the thrill of pride as he swung up the path to her door and engulfed her in a welcoming hug.

Now Rob, who had accompanied him in the carriage, appeared, and kissed her lightly on the cheek. "How are you? You look so well, Morag!"

"I'm fine, really fine. Dr. Luce says he can find almost nothing wrong with me."

The longer she stayed in the mountains, the more her health seemed to stabilise. She lived a very active life these days, going often into the Springs to visit friends and attend parties. Dr. Luce still advised that she should spend as much time as possible out of doors and avoid smoky atmosphere, enclosed places, and any over-exertion or loss of rest. But otherwise she was a free woman, able to do as she pleased.

For the first few days of his visit Gregor stayed close to home with her. But it was only natural that he should want to go to some of the events arranged in the Springs. Morag encouraged him to do so. She had a horror of being a possessive mother, the kind who wouldn't allow her son to go anywhere without accounting for his movements.

Besides, she had Rob for company. He liked to walk with her in the mountain paths she now knew so well. "Sometimes," he murmured, "I feel I'm back in my boyhood. I knew the mountains around my home in Scotland just as well as you know these, Morag."

"Do you ever want to go back?"

"Never! I think of the place with fondness, but nothing ties me to it now. My mother's dead—there was no one else I cared about."

"No, everyone you love is here, Rob."

He took her arm through his. "That's true. And the one I love most is here beside me."

"Oh, Rob . . ." She was rebuking him. "You know that's not true. You love Ellie-Rose. You even love Gregor more."

"They're my children. Of course I love them. But not in the way I love you, Morag." He stopped, turned her to look at him, and smiled. "You're a bonnie lass, my love."

"Rob! You shouldn't say things like that!"

"Why not? It's true."

"But . . . But . . . All that kind of thing is over."

"Is it?" he remarked.

After a moment they walked on. Sudden new thoughts had come to them.

Morag had been so accustomed to think of herself as a widow, and as an invalid, that the notion of love had left her entirely. As for Rob, he had physical needs which he quenched with the help of pretty young ladies in Chicago or New York. He had a

298

strong sexual urge, which sometimes caused him problems; he was still a little ashamed of the feeling that had surged up in him when he took Stephanie home that night.

Now he felt again that quickening of the pulses which told him he was in the grip of the familiar old flood-tide. And he felt the deep warmth of an old love never extinguished. She was so inexpressibly dear to him—part of his life, part of his inner being.

When he parted from her at the house, he pressed her hand. "I'll come back this evening," he murmured.

"No, Rob . . ." Gregor was going out this evening, to a concert in the town. "I don't think we . . ."

"I'll be here," he said.

They both knew what was going to happen. Morag's heart was already beating thickly at the promise in his words. She had seen in his eyes the quick flaming of desire, and her own words had been a sort of defence. She didn't think of love any more—not that kind of love. She had put it all behind her, its pains and its hectic pleasures.

But after all, she wasn't old. There was a time when she had felt old, when she had been ill, and nothing had mattered except crawling slowly along the path back to life. Now she walked that path, with normal strength and energy. And with that normality came physical longings she thought she had put away for ever.

Desire, long dormant, leaped up in her. When

Rob walked in that evening, she threw herself into his arms with all the old ardour.

"My darling," he whispered, "my only real love . . ."

The stars, so big and bright in the sky above the mountains, shone down. The pine-scented air drifted in at the open windows. Somewhere in the valley an owl called as it floated by on soft, wide wings. The two lovers came together in a happiness greater, perhaps, than any they had ever known. It was almost as if life was giving them their reward for the years of living without each other.

Yet every happiness is shot through with heartaches. They both knew that after these precious few days came to an end, Rob must go on his way to Chicago, where he was needed. His business affairs needed his attention. His empire couldn't be left without its ruler.

"One day, not too far in the future," he told Morag, "I'll hand it all over to Gregor, and then I'll be able to settle here with you—"

"Oh, my dear, don't talk nonsense," she interrupted. "You know you couldn't settle down here. It would irk you worse than a burr under a pack-mule's saddle! You have to be in a whirl of activity. It's what your life has become—and it's become like that because you've enjoyed it."

"But I was younger then, Morag—"

"You're not old now. As to handing it on to Greg . . ." She hesitated. "Is that wise? It could cause a lot of trouble in the family." By "the family" she meant the Craigallans, particularly Luisa.

"You leave all that to me. I'll deal with it so carefully no one will see what I'm up to. That boy's a marvel, Morag. He'll take Craigallan Agricultural into the twentieth century with flags flying!"

Gregor would stay on after his father left for Chicago. It was accepted that as yet he'd play no part in the decisions taken at the harvest dealing in The Pit. When he left Harvard, he would go into the New York office for a year, to familiarise himself with the various branches of the firm, and to learn a little about the Stock Exchange in action. Then perhaps after a year he could move to Chicago, to the main headquarters, and stay for two or three years.

For the moment he was an undergraduate, on vacation in the mountains of Colorado, asked to do nothing except enjoy himself and look after his mother. He was conducting a mild flirtation with one of the pretty young holidaymakers in Colorado Springs, so didn't notice the change in the atmosphere between his mother and Rob. If he had become aware of it he might have been shocked—for young people don't believe that beings over twenty-five have any need for physical love. But he would have come to terms with it. He had already learnt that in this life you have to come to terms with what can't be changed.

His father left for Chicago. Cornelius arrived for a short stay. He seemed much as usual to Gregor—

301

but then Gregor was busy with the pretty little blonde from St. Louis.

If Cornelius had been in the habit of speaking about his feelings, he might have confided that he was restless and unhappy. He was missing Stephanie. She had become such a great part of his existence that when he was away from her he felt as if he had lost a limb. The few days' visit to Plymouth had only aggravated his sense of loss. It had hardly been possible to get her alone, and when he did they didn't have time to speak of anything important.

He was to see her at Ravinia, one of the quiet outposts along the lake north of Chicago. Here the well-to-do sought respite from the city's harsh, money-grabbing rhythms. Here Stephanie would find some quiet spot on the shore where she could paint, and they would be together with no one else to trouble them.

Rob, attuned to other people's emotions after his own time of happiness with Morag, guessed that Cornelius had a girl tucked away somewhere in Chicago. He would hurry away from the day's conferences with an urgency that couldn't be accounted for by anything that the city itself had to offer. Rob didn't dream of prying. His eldest child had his own life to lead. He was a little surprised, though, to find him straying. He had thought Cornelius was devoted to Stephanie Jouvard.

Dealing on the Chicago Board of Trade that fall was in a muddle. During Rob's stay in Colorado, a terrible thing had happened in Europe: King Umberto of Italy had been assassinated by an anarchist. This had thrown Stock Exchanges and commodity markets into an uproar, because everyone was expecting an outbreak of hostilities. Either Austria, the former rulers of Italy, would seize the chance to regain power, or there would be a punitive expedition, or even there would simply be a revolution.

From the end of July to the end of August statesmen made journeys in closed carriages from one capital to another. The commodities market, expecting war of one kind or another, went into a bullish mood; prices rose, dealing became brisk. Armies on the move have to be fed, so feed-grains become important. Armies on the move tend to live off the land and interfere with farming, so future harvests are put in danger, thus reducing the possible supply of wheat.

But it all died away, and the market returned to its bear status.

"What we need," Sam Yarwood said cynically, "is a nice little war somewhere." But the world seemed to be settling down to peace. The British had got the upper hand over the Boers in South Africa, the Russians had compelled the Chinese to give them huge regions of Manchuria by occupying them with a hundred thousand troops. "One good thing," Sam said, studying the news about Russia's actions in his newspapers, "they're so damned inefficient they can't grow enough foodstuffs for themselves, either of them—Chinese or Russians. So we'll do deals for wheat with both, eh, Rob?"

"Yeah," Rob said thoughtfully. After a pause he said, "Sam, I'm going to put some money into automotive trucks."

Sam laid aside his paper to stare at him in concern. "You're crazy!"

"No, I've thought it all over. I've been keeping an eye on the horseless carriage ever since that trial run they did from Paris to Rouen a few years ago—"

"Listen, feller, that was sport, not business. Okay, I'm not against men racing automotive carriages instead of horses, but it's not commercial—"

"That's what you said about the steam reaper—"

"All right, all right, so I was wrong about that. But I stick by what I said—steam traction's got a place, I'm not saying it hasn't, but that's different from expecting a little machine that could only just make it the seventy miles from Paris—"

"Seventy miles is quite a distance, Sam. And they've done better with the engineering since then. This new internal combustion engine—"

"Internal combustion! How can anything 'combust' internally? To burn, you have to have air. If you don't, you get all kinds of trouble. You went to that show in Madison Square Gardens, didn't you? You told me yourself—these little automobiles, as they seem to call them, were banging and sparking all round the hall."

304

"You don't get it, Sam," Rob said. "That show was put on by the National Automobile Club. When people start forming clubs—"

"Aw, come on, there are clubs for preserving the Dutch heritage of Pennsylvania and collecting butterflies—"

"But have you seen the names of the men who support the Automobile Club?" Rob leaned back with his hands behind his head and glanced about the office. "I'm going to put money into developing the automotive truck for transporting agricultural produce, Sam. Think of it—a wagon driven by an internal combustion engine that could travel at, mebbe, forty miles an hour on ordinary roads, taking perishable goods to market in the cities. Wagons like that would be snapped up by the freight companies."

Sam looked unconvinced, but he could see Rob meant it. "Well," he said, "don't put *much* money into it."

For the time being business in Chicago was completed. Craigallan's directors had made their decisions for the fall and winter brokerage on the Board of Trade. It was time to be about their affairs elsewhere.

Rob waited for Gregor to join him on his way east from Colorado. Letters from Morag had told him with amusement that the romance with the pretty little blonde girl had foundered when she had to return with her parents to St. Louis at the end of August. From Gregor's composed manner it was easy to see his heart wasn't exactly broken.

Cornelius had already returned to New York, his part in the deliberations over future trading being finished once he had analysed the information that came to hand during August. Rob was a little surprised that he left Chicago so quickly; generally he stayed on at the laboratories supervising work on seed samples that came in during September. He could only suppose that the girl, whoever she was, whom Cornelius had been seeing in Chicago, had gone cool.

He wished it was possible to have an easy conversation with Cornelius about personal matters like women friends. He was on good terms with his elder son but all the same was inhibited at the idea of saying, "How's your love life?" Ellie-Rose was closest to Cornelius, but it was the kind of thing you couldn't ask a girl to inquire about. Gregor, however, was quite brotherly with him, so Rob had a word with him.

"Cornelius ever mention his girls to you?" he inquired.

"His girls? You mean he has quite a harem?"

"No, what I meant was . . . I had a feeling there was a girl he was seeing this summer."

"Here? In Chicago?"

"Somewhere around. He seemed to have things to do a lot of the time when he might have been at the club with Sam and me, for instance."

"Well, now, sir," Gregor said, "without meaning to give offence—two or three evenings with you and

306

Sam at the club are quite enough, unless you're fascinated by dealing in futures."

Rob grinned. "I know what you mean. Yet it *is* important, Greg. But there are little parties and outings, and Neil hasn't been around for many of them this year. He hasn't mentioned a girl to you?"

Gregor shook his head. "Are you worried about him?"

"Well, look at it this way. He's heading towards thirty. I don't want to see him turn into a quiet old bachelor. And there was a time earlier this year . . ."

"In New York?"

"Ah, he talked about that, did he? Stephanie Jouvard."

"He mentioned her in one or two letters," Gregor remarked. "He said something to the effect that marriage was not in prospect."

"He said that?"

"Something like it."

"What a pity," Rob sighed. "I thought she kind of liked him. And she was a cut above most of the girls he meets, if you know what I mean. Not involved with teaching the deaf, or running homes for them, or even an earnest young lady of the kind he hires to help in the laboratory. She's got . . . sparkle."

"Could be that he's gone back to New York ahead of us so as to see her."

"Could be. But somehow I don't think so. I don't think she wrote to him while he was here."

"How do you know that?"

"Well, he didn't look out for the mailman." Rob knew this to be so, because he himself had been looking out for the mailman, to take letters from Morag.

"Too bad. But he doesn't seem depressed or anything."

"I guess not. I just wish . . . I worry about Neil, you know, son. He feels things a lot deeper than we know."

"Neil's all right," Gregor said, out of his memory of the man who'd befriended him when he came, a stranger, into the Craigallan family. "As to getting married—well, there's time enough for that."

Election fever had the United States in its grip. The President conducted the same dignified campaign as last time, leaving the dramatics to his unquenchable Vice-Presidential running mate. On the sixth of November, William McKinley was re-elected with 292 votes as against his Democratic rival, William Jennings Bryan, who had only 155.

No one could now deny the popularity and authority of McKinley. The people had spoken. There were those who said many Republicans had really voted for Teddy Roosevelt, but no one could prove that. The fact was, McKinley was popular; the ordinary voter identified with him, with his plainness, his ordinariness. To the more energetic, he might seem to lack fire; one of his entourage once said of him that he "seemed to have been buttoned up in childhood and never got unbuttoned." Yet the fiery spirits couldn't have the same controlling, calming influence that the buttoned-up McKinley wielded.

Life in Washington calmed down a little once the Major was confirmed in office. It seemed that even Teddy Roosevelt was sobered by achieving the Vice-Presidency. "I have to be a good boy from now on," he said regretfully to Ellie-Rose at a celebration banquet. "I have to settle down to be a dignified nonentity for four Vice-Presidential years."

Ellie-Rose laughed. "I can't picture it somehow," she replied. "I have a feeling the Almighty will intervene on your behalf."

Her pregnancy was progressing normally; the baby was due towards the end of January, which pleased her, for the New Year would bring the new century, and there was a thrill in thinking her baby would have that as his birthright.

The queasiness and the tendency to weepiness were over. She bloomed with health. When her father asked, rather tentatively, if she felt up to coming to Craigallan Castle over Christmas to hostess some important parties, she had no hesitation in agreeing.

"Do you think you should?" Curtis objected. "It's cutting it pretty fine, isn't it?"

"Oh, darling, I'm not *ill*," she said. "I'm just having a baby. I feel fine."

"Yes, but the journey . . ."

"Oh, travelling by train's so comfortable, Curtis. I'll sleep most of the way, I'm sure. And you can join us before Christmas Day, so we can have a lovely snowy time at the Castle."

Curtis was quite agreeable to joining one or other of the grandparents for Christmas. He couldn't help feeling, however, that his own parents should take precedence, since Ellie-Rose's mother was off gallivanting in Greece. You couldn't call it a real old-fashioned Christmas if one of the grandparents preferred not to be there.

"I don't know whether we ought not to head for Nebraska this year, Ellie . . ."

"We were in Nebraska in May."

"But my folks would love to have us for Christmas—"

"Listen, Curtis, Papa is having some important wheat growers from Australia as guests at one of the dinners. Don't you think it would be to your advantage to meet them?"

Curtis could see it would be a good thing to talk to wheat men over the brandy and cigars at his father-in-law's table. He gave in, after ensuring that Ellie-Rose would consult her doctor before she set off to New York.

She travelled with the usual entourage of nurses and maids and footmen. At New York her father's carriage was waiting for her, together with a wagonette to take the baggage. The Castle looked unfamiliar as she drove up to it; it was a long time since she had seen it, not since Easter. Snow had fallen, making an ermine collar for the castellations and a mantle for the turrets.

310

She settled in and looked over her father's guest lists. It didn't surprise her to see Stephanie Jouvard's name there. Rob had been rather encouraged when, after the fall social season began, Stephanie appeared at gatherings and seemed to be as interested in Cornelius as before.

Why doesn't he ask her? Rob wondered. It didn't occur to him that his son had spoken to Stephanie and been put off. He could have understood if Stephanie had shied away from Cornelius because of his deafness, but that didn't seem to worry her— so she could have no reason for refusing his son's offer of marriage. Cornelius Craigallan would be quite a catch financially. True, he wasn't going to inherit the entire Craigallan empire, as outsiders probably imagined, but he would be a very rich man, and any girl would be out of her mind to say no—given that she had already come to terms with his speech problems.

So Rob took it for granted that his son was too shy to speak of marriage, and furthermore too shy to speak of anything *other* than marriage. His daughter could have given him a more accurate picture of the relationship between these two, but she had too much respect for Cornelius to prattle about his affairs.

At the first evening to which Stephanie was invited, Ellie-Rose felt that matters were as they had been earlier in the year. Yet when she thought of it as she prepared for bed that night, she doubted her own verdict. Her own experience had taught her that an affair seldom remains in the same state; it waxes or it wanes, but it is never merely static. Only marriage, she told herself rather ruefully, is static.

So she was watchful, and on her visiting trips to friends in New York she tried to find out what was known of Stephanie. So far as she could learn, there was no other young man; so far as was known, indeed, there was no young man at all. Hardly anyone seemed to be aware of the relationship between her brother and Stephanie.

"She's an *intellectual*, my dear," Edna Poynder told her. "Apart from the fact that she paints, which makes her bohemian in the first place, she attends meetings in the East Side about politics, of all things!"

"How can you possibly know that, Edna?"

"Well, in kind of a round-about way, I'll admit."

"How foolish of her," Ellie-Rose murmured. "Her rich buyers will desert her if they think she's tied in with revolutionaries."

"I agree with you, Ellie, I do indeed. But I suppose it's all theoretical, really. They're not really going to have a revolution."

"I sincerely hope not," Ellie-Rose said with some dryness.

Another acquaintance provided a titbit which perturbed her more than the political activities when she first heard it. Mrs. Derek Kittinall Jnr had been to Stephanie's studio to look at paintings, but as she arrived met this shabby, thin young man on the stairs.

"A man?" Ellie-Rose echoed, secretly alarmed. She didn't want to think that Cornelius's girl was playing him false.

"Skinny and foreign-looking—another painter, I suppose. Anyhow, one must speak up for the girl's good heart—she gave him some money and told him to buy an overcoat. I heard her with my own ears, Ellie. "Buy yourself a coat, Mr. Nieman—you'll catch pneumonia.""

Ellie-Rose relaxed. It hardly seemed likely Stephanie was in love with a man to whom she played Lady Bountiful and whom she addressed as "Mr. Nieman".

Thus in the social round she learned enough to put her mind a little at rest. Stephanie hadn't found a new love, at least that was certain. Ellie-Rose made no attempt to find out, on her one visit to the studio, whether Cornelius's belongings were still lying about. Nor, in Cornelius's New York apartment, did she look for feminine knick-knacks. All she could do was observe them when they happened to be together at some engagement with her, and from that all she could learn was that Cornelius was deeply committed to Stephanie. Stephanie, being less familiar to her, was less easy to read.

Until one fateful evening in the week of Christmas Day. Gregor had just arrived from Harvard. He had filled out, broadened in the shoulders, deepened in the chest. His hair was cut in the new short style after Teddy Roosevelt, but without Roosevelt's bushy moustache. He dropped home-coming gifts on Ellie-Rose, Gina, and the chief chamber-maid, who adored him. "My, it's nice to be out of school," he sighed as he lounged in one of the deep sofas of the drawing-room.

"Well, don't lie about like that as if there was nothing else to do," Ellie-Rose scolded. "We have twenty-five guests to dinner in half an hour, and I was having heart failure in case you didn't turn up and made my table one short."

"Have I ever failed you, Ellie-Rose?" He pulled himself up from his semi-reclining position. "I will go and put on my monkey suit, tired and weary though I am after a hard ice-hockey game with Princeton and a long, boring journey—"

"My heart bleeds for you. Don't be late—the guests are due any minute now."

Curtis had already arrived. As they dressed for dinner Ellie-Rose made a mental note of the matters she must attend to during the evening. She must make an opportunity for her husband to speak to Mr. Halliwell and Mr. Tewkes, from Brisbane. She must prevent Sam Yarwood from ogling Miss Quigley, who was here with her brother but was an engaged girl. And she must, if possible, keep an eye on Stephanie and Cornelius.

Everything went well. The ladies rose and left the gentlemen to the pleasures of the nuts, fruit, port and havanas. Ellie-Rose tried to have Stephanie beside her in the drawing-room but was too late; Mrs. Tewkes had captured her, to talk about the paintings that had taken Paris by storm earlier in the year: Renoir's *Nude en Soleil* and *La Modiste* by Toulouse-Lautrec.

"And so what do you think, my dear," Mrs. Tewkes was asking in her nasal voice, "about the skin tones? They certainly look weird."

"But you must realise that we're only judging from tinted photographs, Mrs. Tewkes, or lithographs," Stephanie replied. "Until one can actually see the painting for oneself, it's impossible to make a proper estimation of the colours."

"But in any case, Miss Jouvard," insisted Mrs. Tewkes, "do you think it's really necessary, the way these Parisians go on about nakedness?"

"The human body is very beautiful . . ." Stephanie's voice died away. She had just seen a man walk in who justified her words.

She had not noticed him at dinner. Now, for the first time, she saw Gregor McGarth. Her heart seemed to turn over in her breast. Her voice died in her throat. He seemed to fill her vision with his presence. She was aware of nothing, no one else in that moment.

Ellie-Rose, glancing about the room to see if there was space for Cornelius to join Stephanie, saw that look on her face. Stephanie had fallen in love.

16

ELLIE-ROSE meant to do something about what she had seen. That momentary glimpse of naked concupiscence had startled her, alerted her. She sensed in Stephanie, although she didn't know her well, an egotism that would lead the girl to pursue her own desires at almost any cost.

The first thing to do was to make sure the two didn't meet, or at any rate have time to feel the attraction between them. Gregor was as yet quite unaware; he was politely giving his attention to Miss Quigley and her brother. Ellie-Rose quickly sent the maid over to them with coffee and *petits fours*, sent word to the musicians in the room across the hall to strike up so that the young men might feel encouraged to ask the young ladies to dance, informally.

The irresistible lilt of a *landler* had its effect; Gregor offered his arm to Miss Quigley and they went through the open doors into the hall where there was space to sway and twirl. Other couples followed.

Cornelius, unaware that there was music playing, sat in interested conversation with the Australians, watching their lips and nodded from time to time as they described the climatic problems of their home-land.

Ellie-Rose's next move should have been to keep Gregor occupied with social duties, and bring Cornelius to Stephanie's side.

But to be hostess to twenty-five guests is no easy matter even if you have done it many times before. Besides, there were her husband's interests to pursue. He must be rescued from H. H. Bazalgette and taken to speak at leisure with the Australians.

Then she had to send Curtis to invite Mrs. Tewkes to dance, for politeness's sake. And so on, for the next hour. When at last she had a moment to look for her half-brother, he was nowhere to be seen.

Nor was Stephanie.

Ellie-Rose had under-estimated the other girl. Stephanie had danced once or twice with partners but then had gone herself to ask Gregor to dance.

"We haven't been introduced. My name's Stephanie Jouvard."

"Ah, yes. How do you do?" He was looking down into dark, sparkling eyes, a thin face with thin lips, a tiptilted nose—certainly not a beautiful face, but full of life and, at the moment, something more. There was invitation in the eyes, eagerness in the smile.

"I'm Gregor McGarth," he said.

"Gregor?" She was taken aback. She had thought him just a late-arriving guest. "Mr. Craigallan's ward?"

"That's me." The German band was now thumping out a polka. "Can you polk?" he inquired, laughing.

"I think I can remember how to do it." They went out to the flagstoned hall and began a lively circuit to the outmoded music. They hopped and swung to the beat. It was easy for Stephanie to arrange to lose her balance so that she fell against him and he had to catch her in his arms to keep her upright.

She clung to him a moment before he set her back on her feet.

"My God," he said to himself, "she's a 'fast' one!"

In all that happened afterwards Gregor was, if not innocent, at least unwitting. The little he knew about Stephanie came from remarks made in the Craigallan family, and busy in Harvard with his own girls and his studies and his athletics, he had learned little about her. As far as he knew, she was a girl with whom his half-brother had had some kind of relationship earlier in the year. When Gregor asked, as he was entitled to do, whether this was heading towards marriage, he'd been told there was no prospect of that.

Therefore, the girl wasn't the marrying kind. That seemed to be the implication. There were girls around, girls even of good family, who seemed determined to play the field to the fullest extent before their families clipped their wings in a conventional match. Evidently Stephanie Jouvard

318

was one of those, and could look out for herself.

That moment when she clung to him had told him so. Her slender body in its soft silk evening gown had moulded itself against him knowingly. She was no innocent. Hadn't he heard she'd spent two or three years in Paris?

Gregor had more than the usual American male's acquaintance with Paris. Interested in languages, he had made a trip there last year to polish up his accent. He knew that the city was more than the titillating centre of naughtiness that the leering, winking reader of *La Vie Parisienne* imagined. Nevertheless, he had met some very liberal-thinking people there. They didn't allow themselves to be tied down by conventions. The women had a freedom that as yet the more puritanical circles of New York couldn't assimilate. Colette, for example—in Paris she had been accepted as a novelist whose work could speak of love and sex without inhibition. In New York, she caused shocked looks, raised eyebrows.

When Gregor took Stephanie back to the drawing-room at the end of the polka, he already knew something about her—that she was interested in him and wanted him to be conscious of that. He took her to a chair and went to fetch fresh coffee. When he returned Norman Hudson was monopolising her, so he delivered the cup and withdrew. He might do something about it later, he thought.

When the German band had played dance tunes for about an hour, they had instructions to change over to songs and instrumental pieces so that the guests would be encouraged to sit down and listen, or talk. It had been no part of the programme that the evening should turn into an impromptu ball. Casualness was pleasing, but it mustn't be allowed to go too far.

They had instructions to play carols for singing at about eleven. Rob had said, when Ellie-Rose told him of this: "That'll make sure folk start thinking of going home. Nothing's more embarrassing than being asked to stand around and sing hymns."

He spoke with feeling. The President himself loved to have hymn-singing at his evening gatherings, so it had become a rather fashionable thing to do. But many people hated it, especially male guests.

So when the little band struck up Adeste Fideles, those who enjoyed such things began to beat time and sing, and those who found it naive began to think of asking for their coats.

Stephanie Jouvard moved round the back of the group who had decided to stand in the doorway of the music room and sing. She touched Gregor on the elbow. "Is there somewhere we can escape from this noise?" She stood on tiptoe so as to say it close to his ear.

That warm breath so close to his cheek gave him a little *frisson* of physical arousal. He turned to look down at her. His usual faintly ironic expression was strengthened as he smiled at her. "By all means," he said.

Silently they withdrew from the group and melted into the shadows further along the hall. He led her through a door, through a pretty sitting-room, and into the conservatory. The great display of ferns and palms was dark against a less dark sky seen through the glass roof. Clouds were racing there; a strong high wind was blowing. The sound moaned faintly against the panes. Far off, beyond two closed doors, the Christmas music was almost inaudible.

Stephanie had never experienced an instant passion like this before. From the moment she saw Gregor her whole body seemed to be attuned to his. Wherever he went, she was aware of him. An irresistible force had made her cross the room and ask him to dance with her. It had been inevitable that she would let him know she wanted him. She couldn't have prevented herself from clinging to him, urging herself against him as the dance ended. When he left her afterwards she had felt desolate. She had scarcely heard a word Norman Hudson was saying; her whole being was turned towards Gregor, like a flower seeking the sun.

Now when they moved into the warmth of the conservatory the very air seemed to be symbolic of the heat driving through her veins. She turned and melted into his arms, totally, heavy against his strength, so that he had to pull her against him.

She gave a little groan of abandonment. He kissed her, and on his part it was experimental, exploratory. But that couldn't satisfy her. She dragged his head down to her and with something like savagery drank the kiss from his mouth. They staggered, a plant fell from the shelf and crashed on the tiled floor.

He exerted a little effort to push her away and make her stand upright. "Hey, there, let's not get too carried away here," he murmured in a soothing voice. "This isn't the place—"

"No, I know that—but I had to be alone with you—"

She leaned against him, breathless. Her arms were round his neck, loosely, but her fingers were caressing the nape where his thick russet hair was like springing silk strands. He was holding her against him, but there was as yet no intensity in his embrace.

"Don't you want me?" she asked, her voice breaking.

"Of course I do." Did he? Well, why not? "But we can't get carried away now. We'll be missed—people will be leaving soon."

"I don't care about that."

He could tell it was true. She seemed to have totally lost her head. He had never had to deal with a situation like this. Most of the so-called respectable girls with whom he'd made love were only too eager to preserve the conventions. "But I care, for your sake," he said gently.

It was both true and untrue. He didn't want a gossipy guest to talk about them tomorrow. On the other hand, if she were prepared to make a fool of herself, why should he stop her? He found himself wondering how Cornelius had coped with this unbridled urge towards gratification. Cornelius was so reticent and shy . . .

Shy she certainly was not. She was blatant in the manner she showed her physical need. He found himself beginning to want her as she moved her body against his, touched his face with her lips. He dragged her hard against him and kissed her to put himself in control of their relationship, he the conqueror, she the conquered. At once she submitted; she was skilled, she understood why he let savagery show in his reaction. She let the pleasure of the pain flow through her. She wanted to give herself to him completely, now, while they had this moment of first knowing each other.

But though he wanted her Gregor hadn't lost his senses. He forced a distance between them and said, "Well, it can't be here and now. Where and when?"

"Later tonight? I live alone—I have a studio in Gramercy Park."

"Did you come with someone?"

"Yes, the Wayfolds. I'll have to go back with them."

"I'll come afterwards. It'll be about one o'clock."

"I'll be waiting."

One last kiss that sealed the bargain, and they went back through the sitting-room and out to the hall. Everyone was now launched into "Silent Night". No one noticed that they had vanished and come back, least of all Cornelius, who wasn't even with the group of singers since he couldn't hear music and couldn't sing. He was with his father and Curtis in the drawing-room, looking up dates in diaries so as to be helpful to the Australians over showing them around.

Ellie-Rose, who might have seen and understood that slight increase of colour in Stephanie's cheeks, the ruffled appearance of her coiffeur, was busy ensuring that the carriages were being called.

"Not a bad evening," Rob remarked as the last set of wheels crunched down the frozen gravel of the drive. "I was a bit dubious, Ellie, but you chose just the right note with that folksy music."

"Oh, that kind of thing is quite the vogue in Washington, Papa. Mrs. McKinley likes to sing Rock of Ages and so forth."

"Ye Gods," Rob muttered. "Well, what's tomorrow?"

"Tomorrow's the children's party." It would be Gina's first Christmas party; Ellie-Rose wanted it to be a memory forever—the first Christmas tree gleaming and glinting with its candles and silver baubles, the first songs and games of Christmas. At two Gina was unlikely to contribute much to it, but the other little guests would rush about and make a noise. It would end with Father Christmas—Soames the butler—arriving to distribute gifts from his sack at four o'clock. There would even be a sleigh outside the door—no reindeer, but no horses either. Soames had been instructed to say he'd let his animals wander off to graze.

"Nothing in the evening, though."

"Goodness, no, it'll take all evening for me to recover," she said.

"You sure you aren't doing too much, daughter?"

"Not at all," she laughed. "I'm fine, really I am. It's all such fun. Christmas is different when you've got children, somehow."

Curtis was sitting on the foot of the stairs, yawning openly. Ellie-Rose moved to him, put a hand on his shoulder, and as he rose went with him thus up to their room.

"Come and have a nightcap, son," Rob said to Gregor.

"Just a small one, sir. I've had enough to drink for one night."

"Yeah, that port's a bit heavy. I'll have to see Soames about it—there must be a better label. What'll you have?"

"Scotch, plenty of water. Mr. Craig, remember we were talking about Cornelius last time I saw you?"

"Mm?" Rob said, pouring.

"About him getting married. Wasn't it Stephanie Jouvard you had in mind?"

"Why do you ask?" asked Rob, turning to look at him as he handed him his drink.

Gregor sipped before he responded. "She was here tonight. Was that at his suggestion?"

"No, it was my idea. He hasn't mentioned her in a long time but I thought if she was invited they might get together again."

"You mean he hasn't been seeing her?"

"Not particularly. Not that I know of, at least." Rob perched on the end of the big leather sofa. "Why this sudden interest?"

"Well, she's an interesting girl."

"You can say that again." Rob let a pause ensue, while he remembered with some wry amusement how he himself had felt a more than passing interest in her. "Ellie-Rose doesn't seem to care for her much," he went on.

"No?"

"She thinks she's . . . too adventurous."

Gregor let the word hover on the air. Adventurous? Could Ellie-Rose possibly know, have guessed, how sexually liberated the girl was? "How exactly does she mean that?"

"Well, I gather Stephanie's interested in politics—"

"Politics?" Gregor gave a burst of laughter.

"It's true, I think."

"But Ellie's interested in politics—"

"Only because she's married to them," Rob put in with humour. "Stephanie appears to embrace them out of idealism. And if what we hear is true, she's a bit off the beaten track in her views. She's been around with the anarchists."

"Oh, nonsense."

"I expect it is. You know that old fool Mabel Lodge invites them to her place and they all spout about the wrongs of the system and so forth. I think Stephanie's been to evening occasions of that sort."

326

"Nobody takes the anarchists seriously—"

"I'd have agreed with you, Greg, until this last couple of months. But it was an anarchist who killed King Umberto."

"You think Stephanie's going to shoot somebody?" Gregor said, laughing again.

"Of course not. I only meant, some of them are more dangerous than others. I don't think Mabel and her little friends are anything to worry about, but Emma Goldman is a different kettle of fish."

"And Stephanie knows Goldman?"

"Has been to her meetings."

"How could you possibly know that, sir?"

"*I* don't know it. Some friends of Ellie-Rose came up with it. You know those woman-talk sessions—somebody heard it from somebody who happened to tell somebody else."

"Oh, that . . ." Gregor's shrug dismissed the tattle of womenfolk. "To go back to Cornelius . . ."

"What about him?"

"I don't know. I think I was asking if he'd suggested you invite Stephanie—"

"The answer to that is no. If ever you get the chance, Greg, try to sound him out about what he feels on settling down. Gina is great, but she doesn't bear my name, you see."

"I don't foresee myself having that kind of talk with Neil, Mr. Craig."

"No. He doesn't discuss things like that." Rob sighed and finished his drink. "Well, I'm for bed.

Got to get my rest so as to be fit for the children's party."

"You're going to be there?"

"Wouldn't miss it," Rob said, and with a nod and a smile, went out and upstairs.

Gregor sat over the remains of his whisky for a long time. The small sounds of the house died away. The servants had already been dismissed to bed when the last carriage left. At twelve-thirty Gregor went to the hall, pulled on his thick napped overcoat, and unbolted the big front door. Outside the night was very cold. The ground was iron hard, a strong east wind was blowing. He walked fast to the outer lodge, opened the wicket gate and went out. It was a half mile trudge to Carmansville, where he knocked up the livery man to hire a carriage for the drive to the city.

New York was still bright with lights. Never sleeping, it glittered still. Homegoing party guests and theatre audiences crowded the streets. Restaurants were still open, the big hotels exuded warmth and the odour of wine and food.

There were even a few people about in Gramercy Park, but they paid no heed to Gregor as he stepped into the vestibule of Stephanie's apartment block. She had already told him which floor. He went quietly upstairs, taking them three at a time with his long stride.

He pulled the bell pull. Almost at once the door flew open.

She was wearing a loose robe of pale blue lace.

Her hair was unpinned to flow down her back in a thick cascade of curled tresses. Her feet were bare. She held out her arms so that the frilled sleeves fell back to show the soft satiny curve to her elbows.

"I thought you weren't coming," she said, almost on a sob.

"Of course I was coming. I promised, didn't I?"

"Come," she said, pulling at his thick coat. He took it off, tossed it over a chair. Already she was unfastening the dinner jacket. Her urgency made him catch fire. He put an arm about her and almost swept her into the bedroom, where he could see a shaded lamp gleaming over the white of the bedsheets.

Stephanie had never wanted anything more in her whole life than that first moment when they threw themselves together on the cool sheets.

Just before six next morning Gregor returned to Craigallan Castle. The servants were just stirring. He went to his room, slept until eight, then bathed and dressed and had breakfast. Rob was just coming downstairs as Gregor made for the front door.

"Out so early?" he inquired, picking up his morning paper from the hall table.

"I've got things to do," Gregor said. Then he added, as embroidery, "Presents to buy."

"Oh, I see. You'll be here for the children's party?"

"Not my kind of thing, Mr. Craig."

"I daresay not. Well, dinner then?"

"Probably. So long." Out he went. He had

promised Stephanie to be back as soon as he could.

She had been out to the grocery store and the wine shop. Supplies for a day to be devoted exclusively to her new lover. She had made him promise to spend the entire day with her because tomorrow her father was coming to take her home to New Jersey for Christmas. The thought of not seeing Gregor for the whole of that one day was like a knife in her side. When she thought of it, her breath caught in pain. So to give her the strength to live through it, she would have today.

After he came she locked the door and took the telephone off the hook. Nothing must disturb them. They spent the hours exploring each other physically and mentally. Although the tide that had swept her towards him had been pure physical passion, it happened they had much in common. Gregor spoke good French, had visited Paris, knew French literature. Though he knew little of painting he listened with respect to what she said. They had entered almost at once into a world of their own, more precious to her than to him because she was much the more in love, but offering both a new happiness and pleasure.

The day passed too quickly for Stephanie. She dared not look at the clock.

At three-thirty in the afternoon Cornelius was supervising his little entertainments for the children invited to Gina's party. Simple tricks with electricity and chemistry, they caused shrieks of delight. Cornelius, watching a footman play the part of magician, saw the mouths of the little creatures opening in oh's of wonder. He was happy.

At that moment, the girl with whom his entire life was bound up was lying sated momentarily with love, in the arms of his half-brother.

331

17

GREGOR got back to Craigallan Castle in the early hours of Christmas morning. His absence all day had not been noted; Ellie-Rose, the only one who might have thought of it, had been so taken up with the pleasures and responsibilities of entertaining Gina's little friends that Gregor's whereabouts hadn't concerned her.

Exhausted by the noise and energy of the youngsters, she had gone to bed early and slept heavily, as she tended to do while her body was so big and ungainly. When she woke next day, there was Gregor at the breakfast table. If she thought of Stephanie at all, it was to reflect with satisfaction that the girl had mentioned spending Christmas in New Jersey. So all problems were for the moment in abeyance, and she would find a moment before New Year to speak to Gregor, hint that Stephanie belonged to someone else.

Although, it crossed her mind uneasily, how could that be true if Stephanie herself were so ready to let herself feel the attractions of another man?

But it wasn't the immediate problem. For the moment she had to think about Christmas Day, guests to dinner, Gina with a slight temperature after the excitement and over-eating of yesterday. Tomorrow was the servants' ball; the ballroom was given over to them, they invited their friends and families, a huge buffet supper was served, an orchestra was hired—in every way it was like a ball given to friends of the Craigallans except that the clothes of the guests weren't so fine.

Once that was over, there was a respite until the New Year celebrations, then home to Washington. Thank heaven, she thought to herself. Her body was so heavy and wearisome; only another four weeks after her homecoming, then it would be hers again, her old slim self, active and energetic.

The fancy dress ball at New Year was a sumptuous affair, the costumes were lavish. Stephanie had not seen Cornelius in a week or more. She had blocked him out of her mind, not with any conscious effort but simply living in the moment, the enraptured moment of finding and loving Gregor. Cornelius, though he missed her, had not thought it odd that they didn't meet; Christmas was a time when families claimed sons and daughters, so he took it for granted she was with her parents from Christmas Day onwards. He had known she would be at the ball; they would arrange to meet later, for Cornelius never stayed at any event where there was music. He couldn't hear it, couldn't dance; Stephanie understood this and would steal a moment to agree a time when he could come to her at the studio.

But she didn't. On the contrary she seemed to be avoiding him. He couldn't understand it, told himself he was mistaken. Naturally she was much in demand as a dance partner so his only chance of speaking with her was if she sat out. That was not likely to happen until the supper interval. He would single her out then.

At the supper interval Stephanie mixed herself in a group with Gregor and the Yancy family and Lady Barnot from England. Once again, if she had stopped to think about it, she would have told herself she wasn't putting Cornelius out of her mind—it just wasn't convenient to speak to him here.

She had discarded lovers before. It had never been exactly easy, but in Paris men understood that such things happen. They might be jealous, angry, reproachful, but they accepted it. They knew they could move on to someone else when their hearts mended.

Stephanie felt within herself that this wasn't true of Cornelius. He had never been in love before he met her, and probably never would be again. To tell him it was over was a difficult undertaking, and she shied away from it without knowing she was doing so.

Ellie-Rose, her hostess eye roving over the throng and trying to ascertain that everything was going well, saw Gregor and Stephanie dancing together. Her gaze was about to pass on, then she looked again. The two were holding each other in the polite, accepted way: Gregor had Stephanie's right hand held out in his gloved left, and his own right hand was at her waist. Her left hand rested lightly on his shoulder. Her kid glove was peeled back and tucked in at the wrist so that the hand was bare.

As Ellie-Rose's glance lighted on them Stephanie moved her hand from Gregor's shoulder in a quick, gliding gesture to caress the side of his face. Her fingers lingered only a moment there, but the stroking, flickering touch was like a kiss.

Ellie-Rose gave a gasp. From that one movement she knew. They were lovers. They were lovers already, it was too late to prevent. She had been so taken up with her own silly matters that she had almost forgotten she meant to prevent it. "Oh God," she said on an indrawn breath.

Curtis, standing beside her for a breather before his social duties took him to the side of some important matron, glanced at her in alarm. "Anything wrong? Feeling faint?"

"No," she said, but she sat down on the chair behind her and fanned herself with her handkerchief. She did feel a little giddy. The shock had been tremendous. What was she to do now? What *could* she do?

Her protective love for Cornelius welled up. She was angry with Gregor, because he was a whole man, young, handsome, the favourite of his father, without a hearing defect—what right had he, who had everything, to take the one thing that Cornelius had found?

Tears came into her eyes. Curtis, leaning over her to make sure she was all right, saw them glint. "This is all too tiring for you. I knew it would be, in your condition," he scolded. "Come along now, you're going upstairs to bed."

"No, Curtis—I can't, really. The hostess can't—"

"Now, Ellie," he said. It was a tone she knew, his master-of-the-house tone. To argue would only mean raised voices and an unpleasantness. Besides, if she had to go upstairs because she was unwell, expecting a baby, tired out . . . she couldn't take any steps about Gregor and Stephanie. It was out of her hands.

Curtis escorted her up to their room and called her maid. "Get your mistress out of those hot robes," he ordered, "and get her to bed with a little of that bromide the doctor prescribed."

"Yes sir." But Ellie-Rose wouldn't go to bed after he'd gone. She allowed herself to be divested of her costume but wrapped herself in a negligee. She was too worried to sleep.

In the ballroom, Gregor and Stephanie were dancing together for only the second time since they met. "Do you remember the first time, the polka?" he had said to her.

The result was the quick caress with her warm hand against his cheek, which Ellie-Rose had witnessed.

"I remember, darling." She laughed. "Did you think me awfully fast?"

"Yes, I did. Still do. You take my breath away, Stephanie,"

She smiled up at him. "Glad to hear it. A man who's out of breath can't run after other girls."

"But there are other things he can't do, angel."

She saw the wicked glint and closed her eyes slowly to re-open them in a lazy glance of invitation. "When shall we leave?" she asked.

"Soon as possible." He glanced at the ornate clock in its ornate sunburst surround on the wall opposite the door. "Ten after eleven. In another twenty minutes people will begin to say goodnight. We wouldn't be noticed."

Stephanie had come alone in a hackney, and intended to return the same way, but not alone. Although most of the carriages that would call between eleven-thirty and twelve-thirty were private, a line of cab-drivers was waiting outside the main gates in hopes of being summoned after a big event like the Craigallan New Year Ball.

When Gregor took her back to a chair by the window, another partner was waiting to claim her; his name was written in her *carnet*. She floated away in his arms. Over his shoulder she glimpsed Cornelius watching her hungrily.

"I must tell him," she said, almost aloud.

"I beg your pardon?" her partner said.

"Nothing. Have you enjoyed the evening?"

They talked politely until the dance ended. Stephanie looked about for the next man whose name appeared on her card, but he was still escorting a previous partner to her friends. Cornelius appeared at Stephanie's elbow.

"I must talk to you," he said in her ear in his flat voice.

337

Her courage deserted her. "Not now, Neil, please."

"But we have to—"

"Not *now*." She turned to him, remembering he had to see her full face if he was to understand. "Not now."

"Shall we see each other later?"

"No, Cornelius. Not tonight."

He had learned that there were times when a woman could not go to bed with a man no matter how much she might want to. He was too shy on the matter to protest that it was only a short time ago they had been unable to make love. His pale face took on a troubled, disappointed look. "When, Stephanie?"

"I . . . I can't discuss it now. Please, Cornelius—I have a partner for this dance."

He couldn't hear her tone, but her manner was so strange. It was almost as if she were irritated with him.

"Is something wrong?" he asked. Had he done anything to annoy her? Sometimes, because he couldn't hear, he made mistakes in comprehension. But these had been few where Stephanie was concerned. They were so attuned that he caught her every nuance. And if he had indeed done something clumsy or embarrassing, she would tell him; they were so close that she could speak to him of his mistakes, easily, without hurting.

"Nothing. Please, Cornelius—this isn't the time."

He frowned. "What is all this, Stephanie?" he asked, in that strange, level voice of his.

It scared her. There was a grimness about it. For the first time it dawned on her that it wouldn't be a simple thing, to tell Cornelius Craigallan that she had found someone else. Faced with that realisation for the first startling moment, she backed away.

"We'll talk some other time," she blurted out, and fled to take the hand of the man who was to lead her out on to the dance floor.

Cornelius watched them whirl away on the strains of an Ancliffe waltz. As she turned in her partner's arm, he glimpsed her face. It was tense and apprehensive.

He had caused her to look like that. Why? He had only wanted to arrange for them to meet, as they always did, when they were free to do so. After this long parting, more than a week, he had expected her to want to fly to his arms. She was so eager, so easily roused to physical passion by the merest touch. Yet she had almost shuddered away from him.

Cornelius was unskilled in the ways of women, but he had intuition enough to guess that a lover does not feel so great a reluctance unless the love has totally died. The thought, half-formed, seized his brain for a moment and made him stagger. Then it passed and he thought: "Nonsense, it's just that in the middle of a roomful of people she didn't want to have a conversation. I have to remember—it's probably terribly noisy." Yet that scarcely mattered to them, for he could have read her lips if she had spoken to him in a whisper.

A hand slapped him on the back. "Well, Neil, enjoying yourself?" Rob asked jovially, and then remembered the boy couldn't hear him until he turned. He repeated the question, and was greeted with a nod that was almost curt. Well, he was a fool to ask—naturally Cornelius found a dance less fun than anybody else.

Yet when his son moved away from him to take a place by the door, Rob's eyes followed him. There was something wretched about the way he threw himself on the chair and looked at the floor.

Duties as host called him away, however. Guests were beginning to leave. Ellie-Rose reappeared to bid her guests goodnight and a Happy New Year. She had put on a soft evening gown instead of her costume, and looked rather pale but composed. She had decided to find Gregor and have it out with him. It might not be too late for him to withdraw from an affair with Stephanie—if it was simply a sexual attraction on both sides he might be willing to let it stop now.

But she couldn't find Gregor. She stood in the hall accepting congratulations on a wonderful ball and saying farewells, but Gregor didn't appear to join the family in these duties. Cornelius was there, and her eyes rested for a moment on him. He seemed quiet and morose. She edged towards him, put a sisterly hand on his sleeve.

When at last the guests had gone she realised that

340

she had not said goodnight to Stephanie Jouvard, and that Gregor was nowhere to be seen.

Behind her the servants were clearing the ballroom. The usual selection of lost items would be brought to her in the morning: several odd gloves, a tortoise-shell comb, at least one fan, hair ornaments, ear-rings.

"You'll come up straight away?" Curtis demanded, already halfway up the stairs.

"Right away, dear. I'm just doing my usual check."

"Don't be long. You need your rest."

"I had a nap, Curtis. I'm all right."

He nodded and went on. Only Ellie-Rose and Cornelius were left downstairs except for the servants.

"Ellie, is anything wrong with Stephanie?" he asked suddenly.

The question took her breath away, literally. The shock of it made her go pale. Cornelius, always quicker than others to sense unspoken emotions, seized her wrist. "What is it?" he demanded. "What do you know?"

"Nothing, Neil—nothing, truly!"

"She seemed . . . I don't know . . . She didn't even want to talk to me!"

"Oh, Neil, don't think about it now," she urged. "It's late, you're tired—"

"What's that got to do with it?" He let her go, and used his hands in a sudden spate of words that he knew his tongue couldn't keep up with. "I

341

thought she and I understood each other perfectly, but tonight she backed off from me. Almost as if she was afraid. But why should she be afraid of me? Of *me*?"

"Neil, you have to understand, nothing stays the same. People change—"

"Change?" He made a violent gesture with his hands as he repeated the word she had used. "You know Stephanie has changed? How do you know? What do you know?"

"Nothing, Neil, I know nothing—"

"Suspect, then? What is it?"

"It's not my business," she cried, out of an exhaustion of body and spirit. "It's between you and Stephanie!"

"So . . . There is something . . ." He watched his sister, but she made no movement of denial. "Someone?" he continued. "Is that it? Someone else?"

"I don't think we should talk about it," she said, sitting down on a nearby chair. "It's too late to be having this kind of discussion—"

He was at the stairs in two strides.

"What are you going to do, Neil?" she cried, grasping his wrist as he touched the banister.

"I'm going to see her."

"What, now?"

"As soon as I've gotten out of this damn fancy dress." He was gone.

She sat in a haze of apprehension, trying to think what she ought to do. Should she call her father from his room? But what could she say? Neil's going to have a showdown with Stephanie—so what, her father would reply. It's their business.

The trouble was, no one but Ellie-Rose knew how deep it went with Cornelius. And no one else knew who had replaced him.

That brought her to her feet, as if a whip had flicked her. Dear God, if Cornelius went to Stephanie now, ten to one he'd find Gregor there. Where else could Gregor be, having vanished without a word from the ball and all his duties there? As ward to Rob Craigallan, he was expected to stand with the family and see the guests safely into their carriages—but he had not been there.

When Cornelius reappeared in an ordinary suit Ellie-Rose joined him at the foot of the staircase.

"Don't go, Neil."

He shook off her restraining hand. "I'm going."

"Then I'm going with you."

He drew back. "No."

"Yes, I'm going with you." She wanted to be there, to help restrain the anguish he might express, the pain he would feel. She remembered him as a little boy, white as ice with rage and frustrated physical emotion. She couldn't let him go alone to face what might be coming.

"I've ordered a carriage round," he said, as with an impatient shrug he went out. He didn't even help her into the carriage until she had trouble with the step.

They drove in silence. It was difficult to have a conversation with Cornelius when he couldn't see lips clearly or couldn't watch signs. Although there was a little lamp in the carriage its flicker was inadequate for any speech between them.

When they got to Gramercy Park Ellie-Rose made one last attempt. Under the street lamp she faced him. "This is unwise, Neil," she warned. "Please come away."

He shook his head without a word and walked past her. She toiled up the stairs behind him, aghast to find him putting a key in the lock when she reached the landing. "No!" she cried, starting forward.

But he had the door open and was walking in.

There was no light on in the studio, but the bedroom beyond was lit. Through the half open door she heard an exclamation of surprise, unheard by Cornelius. He walked towards the bedroom door.

It was swung wide open. Gregor appeared in the opening, a sheet dragged about him. He had heard the sound of their entrance, thought it was a thief.

He stopped in the doorway, his expression incredulous at sight of Cornelius.

"Neil?" he gasped.

His half-brother pushed past him into the bedroom. Stephanie was just sitting up among the rumpled pillows. She was entirely naked. Her hands flew to her mouth in fright when she saw Cornelius.

Gregor came out to grasp Ellie-Rose's arm.

"What the hell goes on?" he exclaimed. "Is this some kind of joke?"

"Greg, for God's sake," she cried, "come away—get dressed and come home—"

"But what the devil are you doing here?"

Before she could give any explanation there came a cry of rage and pain from Cornelius. He swept round and came into the studio. "You—!" he shouted. It was a wild sound, almost inhuman.

He threw himself towards Gregor. "No!" Ellie-Rose shrieked, and cast herself on him to drag down his upraised fist.

He threw her off as a dog shakes water from its coat. His fist landed against Gregor's chin.

Gregor went down, helpless, unprepared, shocked out of understanding. Cornelius's hands were round his throat. He could scarcely breathe. His own hands were tangled in the sheet he'd caught up as he came from the bed. He made a strangled sound.

Ellie-Rose recovered herself and seized her brother's arms from behind. She pulled with all her strength. "Don't, Neil, don't."

Cornelius couldn't hear. No sound had ever reached him, but now there was a roaring in his ears. His hands tightened round the neck of his enemy.

Gregor, freeing one hand, shoved it with all his strength in Cornelius's face. Cornelius jerked back, lost his hold for a moment, and flung himself sideways to recover.

Ellie-Rose, clinging to his shoulders, was thrown against the big studio table with enormous force. It rocked, some of the clutter slid off, a chair went over.

The chair got in Cornelius's way. He kicked it aside. But his half-brother was no longer where he had fallen at that first blow. He was kneeling beside something on the floor.

As Cornelius's hands grabbed him, Gregor looked up. "Don't be a fool!" he shouted, and flung out an arm.

Momentarily halted, Cornelius followed the gesture.

Ellie-Rose was lying half under the big elmwood table with the chair rolling away from her. There was a great cut on her forehead where it had hit the table corner.

She was unconscious.

18

THE white cloud came and went. Sometimes it was smaller, sometimes larger. It was always associated with pain.

The pain was a constant tide, growing, receding, but never absent. It was important to live with the pain, to appease it and not to allow it to overwhelm completely.

Now there were sounds. Muffled, far away. Voices.

Someone was saying, "That's it, dear. Hold on. We're not going to lose our baby, are we?"

We're not going to lose our baby. Our baby. Curtis was speaking to her? But it was a woman's voice.

"Quietly, now. Quietly. Breathe light. Mrs. Gracebridge, slow down—don't, dear, don't. Back off from it. There, there."

The present tide of agony receded. "Now it's better again, isn't it? Drink this, dear. Try, Mrs. Gracebridge. It will help you."

Liquid was slipped between her lips. Her head fell back against something soft. Did she sleep? The pain seemed to go away for a time.

But it came back. This time Ellie-Rose opened her eyes. The hovering cloud was there again. It moved, came closer. Her eyes focused on it. It was the wings of a white muslin head-dress.

A nurse was bending over her. "Here we are, dear," said the voice. "You can see me now, can't you?"

Ellie-Rose tried to speak, but nothing came out except a faint thread of sound.

"Lie quiet, Mrs. Gracebridge. Don't try to speak. Everything is all right."

Ellie-Rose moistened her lips with a tongue that seemed thick and clumsy.

"Where . . . ?"

"You're in St. Mary's Hospital, dear. You're doing fine. Just keep very still. Another sip of water?" The nurse put a strong arm under her head, held a small glass to her lips. The water tasted odd. Ellie-Rose took a sip or two, swallowed, was laid back on the pillows.

"What . . . ?"

"Now, dear, we must be quiet. Go to sleep, there's a good girl."

Ellie-Rose had been trying to ask, "What happened to my baby?" She couldn't remember what had happened but some deep instinct told her the baby had been threatened. But the words wouldn't come and the thought was too complex to pursue. Instead, she glanced down at her own body under the hospital quilt. She could see the rounded bulk. The baby was still there, she hadn't lost it.

Her eyelids dropped down. She went to sleep.

How long she slept and woke, slept and woke, she

didn't know. Sometimes she was in pain, sometimes not. But as her brain began to function she realised that the pains, though like the onset of labour, were not birth pangs.

With that understanding came a determination to do whatever she was told. The friendly nurse was replaced by another, who spoke less often but who held her hands. When the pains came, she would rise swiftly from her place by the bed and give Ellie-Rose sips of sedative. The pain would recede, quietness would return.

The time came when the barrier of gentle sedation broke. The contractions Ellie-Rose had been befriending, begging them not to harm her baby, were ruthless now. The long quiet wait had been disturbed. The body, losing its rhythm, its sources overtaxed, knew that it must send the child into the world.

Conscious now, Ellie-Rose did all she could to help. Nurses and doctors seemed to bend over her like angels out of a cloud in a Renaissance painting. She obeyed all their commands, desperate to save the baby. But she was as much a slave to her own body at that moment as any opium smoker to the pipe. A red curtain seemed to descend on her. She didn't know where she was any longer.

When at last she opened her eyes again her lids felt supremely heavy, as if she were under water and the ocean weighed on them. She waited. No voice immediately spoke, as on former occasions when she regained consciousness.

It required much thought to roll her head side-ways on the pillow. A nurse sitting on a chair about a foot away immediately rose and took her wrist in her hand.

"How are you feeling, Mrs. Gracebridge?"

"I don't . . . know."

"Your pulse is better."

"Is it?" Once again she accepted a drink from careful hands but this time it was different—she thought it was milk and brandy. The taste almost made her gag. It seemed months, years, since she had swallowed anything so identifiable. For a long moment she lay looking at the ceiling. Then she made a move with her hand, and the nurse leaned over.

"My baby?"

"A boy, Mrs. Gracebridge."

"A boy." She caught the nurse's wrist in her hand and held on to it, but a long moment passed before she could voice the next question. "Is he . . . all right?"

"A month premature, my dear. He's small and delicate. But all right."

Great tears welled up in Ellie-Rose's eyes. They felt as big as the pearls her father had given her on her twenty-first birthday.

"Oh, thank God," she whispered on a note that sobbed. "Thank God."

She slept then, and woke to sleep again, and woke at last to find that she could see the moulding of the ceiling without making a great effort to concentrate.

She turned her head. Wintry daylight was streaming through the centre panes of a lace-curtained window. The sun was shining with that silver light of a January morning in New York. Light reflected off snow somewhere underfoot. The room was bright, yet cosy. The scent of flowers pervaded it.

Her gaze travelled. Banks of flowers—roses, gardenias, stephenotis, carnations, lilies, even some early daffodils and narcissus. Baskets and vases seemed to take up every surface not in use for the sickroom equipment.

She was pleased with the flowers. They were a celebration of her victory. She had given birth to a baby boy. Before his time, he had yet been brought into the world alive and well.

Presently she was brought some beef tea in a feeding cup, then some innocuous milky concoction. Doctors came, beamed at her, took her pulse, her temperature, examined her, soothed and encouraged her, and told her to rest. It was all very exhausting. She went back to sleep.

Perhaps it was another day. She woke and found the light had changed. When she let it be known she was awake, she was given more nourishment in the feeding cup. When she protested that she could drink from a cup, they let her take hold of the feeder, and when it wavered to and fro then fell from her grasp, she had to agree she needed to be given her food from a spout.

She inquired what time it was. Seven in the

morning, they told her. "You've had a lovely sleep. You feel the better for it, don't you?"

"Yes," she agreed, "I feel better." Not strong, not well, but less a stranger to her own senses.

"In that case," said the nurse, "I think we could allow a visitor later on."

"A visitor?" She had to pull her mind about to think of anyone outside this room and her own struggles in it.

"He's been waiting ever so long to get a glimpse of you, Mrs. Gracebridge."

That was a thought. "How long?" she inquired.

"Eight days."

"I've been here for eight days?"

"Indeed you have. You've been a very sick girl, Mrs. Gracebridge."

"Yes, I have." She knew that was true. The pain, the muddle of effort and non-effort, the long battle and then afterwards the loss of herself in a dreamland of weakness . . .

She lay thinking about it. Eight days. How strange. But she felt better and her son was all right.

Presently she was bathed and dressed in one of the nightdresses brought from her home, and then her prettiest bed jacket was draped around her. Her pillows were arranged so that, though she wasn't exactly sitting up, she could see someone standing at the foot of the bed.

"There," said the nurse who had made her presentable. It was the one who kept addressing Ellie-Rose as "we", as if she and the nurse were some indissoluble partnership. "Now we look real pretty. We're ready to face our visitor, aren't we."

"Yes," said Ellie-Rose.

The door opened. A man came in. Almost to her surprise, Ellie-Rose saw that it was Curtis, her husband. Names and faces seemed to have gone away from her during these last few days. No one had existed except herself and the people helping her to save her baby.

"Curtis . . ." she said wonderingly.

"Oh, my darling!" he exclaimed. Tears were on the upper edge of his cheeks. He stumbled forward.

"Now, now," said the nurse, intervening. "We mustn't tire our little girl, must we?"

"No, of course not." He seemed to straighten, and reappeared from behind the nurse looking more in control of himself. He came to the point a little beyond the end of the bed and to one side. "How are you, my darling?"

"I'm fine," she said. She didn't feel exactly fine, but she didn't feel so ill as she had felt yesterday.

"You look so . . . so . . ."

"So well," the nurse put in in a warning voice.

"Yes, you look so well," Curtis said, gulping. He brushed at the tears on his cheeks. "They tell me you put up one hell of a fight for our little boy, dearest."

"Did I? Yes, I suppose I did. Have you seen him?"

"Only from a distance. He's very little, Ellie.

353

They've got him on a cushion in a special nursery—"

"A cushion we use when the baby's premature," the nurse put in. "To keep him safe from any knocks and draughts. He's doing well."

"Does he look like you?"

"He . . . I . . ." Curtis hesitated. How could he tell her the baby was a little crumpled thing like a rose petal not yet fully formed? Very small, lying wrapped in cotton and then in finest lamb's wool, on a big cushion in a kind of box. Screens round him to keep off draughts of the January air. A nurse sitting by him at all times. They fed him, so Curtis had been told, by means of a pipette, tiny drops of diluted milk and glucose. He was holding his own, their baby, but he should still have been inside his mother, not out in the hostile world.

At a nod of permission from the nurse, Curtis went closer to take Ellie-Rose's hand very gently. He had never loved her more. She looked so sick—no colour in her cheeks, her eyes huge in their sockets, flesh all wasted away from her cheekbones, a dressing on her brow where it had been cut and the bruise from the wound colouring the skin up to her beautiful dark blonde hair.

He wanted to fall on his knees by the bedside, cover her hand with kisses, cry out that he adored her. But he had been warned not to exhaust her with emotion. She had been very near death. She needed every vestige of strength for the long

354

journey back from that margin, from which so many never return.

"We're going to call him Curtis," he said. "Little Curt. Gina's got a little brother."

"Gina," echoed Ellie-Rose, remembering. "How is Gina—?"

"She's fine, fine. Missing you, of course. We told her you'd gone to fetch her little brother and she wanted to know why it was taking you such a long time. So we told her it was a far journey."

"A far journey," Ellie-Rose agreed. For no reason at all, tears came into her eyes at the words.

"I think it's time to go now, Mr. Gracebridge," the nurse intervened in a brisk manner. "We must get our rest, you know."

"Of course." Curtis bore Ellie-Rose's hand to his lips for the briefest touch. "I'll be back tomorrow, darling. Get plenty of rest."

He went out on tiptoe, as if any sound he might make with his shoes would harm her. The door closed behind him. "There," said the nurse, "we're going to have a nice little nap after all that excitement, aren't we?"

Ellie-Rose pondered whether it was worth the expense of energy to point out that though she might take a nap, the nurse would not. But while she was still thinking about it, she fell asleep.

When she awoke later she felt an increase in her strength. When soup and cornstarch pudding were brought, she swallowed them almost with appetite. After the meal, which she thought must have been dinner, because it was now dark again, she lay back and rested. She didn't go to sleep at once as she had done recently. She lay awake, her mind moving undirected through her thoughts.

She had been brought here because the baby was coming too soon. There had been a long and careful rearguard action to stop him. There had also been a pain in her head. She put her hand up and felt the dressing on her brow. She had hit her head. She had fallen and hit her head.

Why had she fallen? Where had she been?

But it was too difficult to go down that mysterious path. She let her memory move away. Curtis said their son was all right. Curtis Junior—Curt. Gina wanted to know why it took so long to fetch him. When would she see Gina? Curtis had been allowed to come. Perhaps he could bring Gina soon.

Next day she woke early. Her life was beginning to return to its normal programme. She was brought tea and farina for breakfast, red wine and rice cookie at mid-morning, beef tea, egg souffle and champagne for lunch. Then she was made pretty, and told she was allowed two visitors today.

"Two minutes each," said the nurse. "We mustn't let them tire us."

Curtis came in first, carrying flowers. The nurse relieved him of them and made a great fuss of going out of the room to put them in water. This was to allow husband and wife a moment alone. But she was back before he'd had time to do more than drop

356

a kiss on Ellie-Rose's lips. "You look so much better, dear," he said in a voice full of love and gratitude. "You'll be up and about soon."

"Yes, any day now," agreed the nurse. "But now it's time to make way for our other guest." She showed Curtis out. There was pause, the door re-opened.

Ellie-Rose saw her father come in.

"Papa!" she gasped. It was a shock. She had just got used to the idea that Curtis could visit, and now here was another man walking in. "Papa!" And then a surge of pleasure. "How lovely to see you!"

"How are you, my love?" he said, taking a chair from the side of the room and sitting down at the bedside.

"I'm . . . doing well, I think."

"So I hear. Quite a heroine. Nice little boy you brought us."

"You've seen him?"

"Aye. Small. You know what they used to say in my homeland? 'Guid gear gangs into sma' bulk'—which means good things come in small packages."

Ellie-Rose smiled. Her spirit seemed to lighten. "Did you come with Curtis?"

"In a way. We've both been here, off and on, for days—"

"Now, now, we don't want to dwell on that, do we," the nurse put in in a warning tone.

Rob glanced round at her. Then with a shrug he said, "Do you want anything, Ellie? Shall I tell your maid to bring—"

357

"We don't need any more clothing, thank you," the nurse said. "We don't want to have to worry about things like that."

"We don't want to keep having interruptions either, do we?" Rob said with a sudden note of steel in his voice. "We'll either keep our trap shut or we'll leave the room."

The nurse went pink and bristled, but said nothing.

Ellie-Rose made a sound that was almost a laugh. She felt more herself all at once. More of a person, less of a subject to whom things had been happening. Her mind seemed to start functioning much more alertly. "Did . . . everything go on all right at the Castle?" she began. "I . . . we . . . had parties and things . . . ?"

"Never bother your head about that. We just cancelled."

"*Cancelled*?" That was a thing you never did. Come hell or high water, fire, flood or bankruptcy, you never shut your doors on New York guests once they'd been invited.

She stared at her father. Something very bad must have been wrong with her.

She clutched wildly at a wisp of memory. "Papa? How is . . . How is Gregor?"

Why did she ask that? A picture rushed through her mind. Gregor on the floor. Hands round his neck.

"Papa!"

"He's all right," Rob said, rising to lay a hand on

her shoulder as panic made her try to struggle up. "All right, I tell you. Gregor's fine."

"All right? He wasn't hurt?"

"You were the one that was hurt."

"Mr. Craigallan," the nurse put in in a very angry tone.

"Papa," Ellie-Rose said, "there was something else. I was in Stephanie's studio . . ."

"Yes, you were."

"Cornelius?"

"He's fine," Rob said.

"He's all right?"

"Yes."

"What happened?"

"Nothing. Except that you had a fall."

"I fell. Yes, I remember that."

"Mr. Craigallan," the nurse said, "I think you've stayed long enough."

"No, wait. Papa. I remember now . . . Cornelius and Stephanie . . ."

"Don't worry about it."

"But . . . but . . . Poor Cornelius . . ." Tears of weakness and sorrow came like a flood over her cheeks. It was all coming back.

"Mr. Craigallan, I really must ask you to leave—"

"All right, nurse, I'm going. Just a moment." Rob took his daughter's thin hand in his. "It's all right, Ellie. Don't let it make you sad. Do you hear me? Everything is all right. Just save all your thoughts for yourself, get well as fast as you can for the baby's sake and the sake of your family. Okay?"

"Yes, Papa. Okay." She lay back, feeling the tears run down either side of her temples like a waterfall. Even then one part of her mind was saying, "Don't be a *fool*! Crying over it is a waste of time."

" 'Bye for now, Ellie."

" 'Bye, Papa."

She heard the door close on him. The nurse hurried back and with a soft handkerchief wiped the tears away. "There, there," she murmured, "we don't want to let silly men upset us."

"You don't understand," sobbed Ellie-Rose. "There was such trouble."

Rob found Curtis pacing about outside in the big tiled corridor. "All right?" Curtis demanded, grabbing his sleeve.

"I told her a little. She's broken up over it, I'm afraid. But she asked. I had to tell her."

Curtis sighed. "I suppose so. You couldn't stay away for ever. And once she started thinking about the family she was bound to want to know what happened. Did you tell her Cornelius cleared out?"

"I thought I'd keep that for another time. She's very fond of her brother, you see."

"She asked after him?"

"She asked about Gregor first. Damned if I know why. Generally Cornelius comes first with her."

"You made it plain that—"

"Of course. I said they were both fine. Which, I suppose, is true in a way."

"I don't know," sighed Curtis as they made their way out to the cold early dusk of New York in

January. "All that fuss over a girl like that. I don't even think she's all that attractive."

"You don't?" Rob remembered how he had felt an impulse of desire for her. "Well, she has a certain something—"

"But she's a rabid Red—"

"Oh, men don't talk about things like that when they're in bed with a woman. And I don't know whether it would matter to either of them, if they discussed it."

"It would matter to Gregor," Curtis said. They had reached the porch outside the hospital, where the cab was waiting for them. The horse was stamping in impatience against the cold road surface. "Gregor's a very shrewd fellow. He ought to know it doesn't do you any good in business to have contacts with friends of Emma Goldman."

They got in and fell back on the leather seat. The cabbie clucked at his horse, they moved off. A light powder of snow was beginning to fall. "Damned weather," Rob growled. "I'm almost tempted to follow Luisa out to the Mediterranean, when I see skies like that."

"When Ellie-Rose comes out of hospital she ought to go some place mild and quiet, to convalesce."

"Sure, name it, she can go where you like. Travel might be tiring, though."

"And there's the baby."

"He really is going to be all right?" Rob inquired anxiously.

361

"I guess so. They say he'll make up the weight and everything. I don't think they're just lying to placate us." Curtis frowned. "If I ever get my hands on that man—"

Rob pulled up the collar of his coat against the draught. He sighed. "I don't understand it. Cornelius loves Ellie, you know. They've always been close. He would never hurt her if he hadn't been out of his mind with jealousy."

"He better stay out of my way, that's all," Curtis muttered.

Rob shrugged, made no further reply. After what he'd said to Cornelius, there was almost no chance he and Curtis would ever encounter each other for the foreseeable future.

"I'm going," Cornelius had told Rob. "I've made up my mind. There's nothing for me here any more, and I couldn't face Ellie-Rose now."

At the time Rob had still been furiously angry with him. "So much the better!" he shouted. "Clear out, pack up and go. And don't come back! I never want you at the Castle again, ever! Clear?"

Cornelius was watching him with a strained, closed expression. He could see that his father was speaking in a loud voice because of the strain on the cords of his neck. He could tell he was full of anger because of his face. He could understand the meaning because he could read the lips.

But the emotion didn't really reach him. A barrier of grey stone had been built overnight in Cornelius's world, cutting him off from the others.

362

It was as if he was in a prison with great granite battlements. There was no sound, yet he was accustomed to that. But there was no light, no warmth either. He was cut off from all that made life bearable.

He had lost Stephanie. That in itself was a raw wound, still bleeding on the surface of his soul. She had taken another lover, without even the humanity to break it to him herself. He had found her with the other man.

The other man was his brother. Gregor. He had tried to kill Gregor. The mark of Cain was on him, he had tried to kill his brother. He was an outcast.

Worse than all that, he had hurt Ellie-Rose. The dear, loving sister who had cared when almost no one else did, who had learned his language so as to laugh and play with him as a child—his arms had thrown her across the room.

She nearly died, nearly lost her baby. Cornelius lived in dread and despair all the time she struggled to survive. He stationed his manservant by the telephone in his apartment so that the moment there was news, Larry would tell him. At first there had been nothing: Ellie-Rose was very ill, that was all he could learn. Then Larry turned from the receiver with word that the baby was coming. Two days of soul-killing anxiety followed, the answer to enquiry always the same: "The baby hasn't yet been born."

At last it was over. The baby born, the mother still alive. Both weak, but both still in this world.

For the first time since he left Craigallan Castle on the night of the ball, Cornelius fell into bed and slept.

His father came to his apartment to see him. "You've heard?" he asked.

"She'll be all right."

"No thanks to you."

Cornelius bowed his head and said nothing.

Rob touched him on the shoulder, so that he looked up. "You understand that if she had died I'd have seen you were prosecuted for manslaughter?"

"I would have deserved it."

"She's survived, and the last thing I want is to distress her any further. So I'll let the matter drop. But understand me, Cornelius—from now on you're no son of mine."

"I understand."

"You don't protest that it was Gregor's fault?"

Cornelius shook his head. "I realise now that he didn't know. His face . . . He was utterly astonished to see me. He didn't know. She didn't tell him."

"That little selfish bitch," Rob said through gritted teeth. "I wish Luisa had never met her. She's nothing but trouble."

"It's not her fault." Cornelius hesitated, trying to explain to his father that Stephanie was as she was, never intending harm but too self-centred to see she caused it.

But it was too subtle and complex for him to put into words and if he used sign language it somehow made him seem to be begging for pity because of his deafness. And that didn't come into it.

Stephanie had loved him as he was. Whatever might have changed, that remained true. She had loved and wanted him. It was in her nature to change, and when she saw Gregor she had seen someone she wanted more than Cornelius. That was all there was to it.

That violent temper which had been the bane of his childhood had erupted like a volcano. When he looked back he couldn't recall what had happened.

He had seen Gregor's face, its blank amazement, its unpreparedness. Yet it hadn't registered. His one thought had been, "I am betrayed!" His one aim had been to kill the man. He remembered nothing of what he had actually done.

Consciousness only came back as Gregor threw out an arm and seemed to be shouting at him about something across the room. A moment's hesitation had come to Cornelius, a moment's pause lifting the veil of rage.

When he turned, Cornelius saw his sister lying under the table. A chair, which he must have thrown, was rocking across her body. There was a gaping cut on her forehead, from which blood was pulsing out.

Although he couldn't hear her, Stephanie was screaming, shriek after shriek of hysterical protest.

He was thrust aside. Gregor leapt to Ellie-Rose's side. He leaned down, listened to her heart. He jumped up, whirled to Stephanie's telephone, dialled, spoke quickly. He was the only one who could act. He alone could summon help by telephone—Cornelius was deaf and couldn't use it, Stephanie was distraught. Almost as an afterthought he took Stephanie by the shoulders, shook her, and pushed her into a chair.

A moment later he was in the bedroom. Cornelius, dazed, went after him. Gregor was dressing. He saw him look past him. "Someone at the door," Gregor said. "Neighbours, probably."

Cornelius stared at him. He couldn't catch up with what was happening. His mind seemed to have frozen.

Gregor was in shirt and trousers now. He passed Cornelius in the doorway, pulling on his jacket. In a moment he turned back and took his half-brother by the shoulders.

He looked him in the face. "Cornelius," he said, "you'd better get out of here. The way you look, it's a give-away. Clear out."

"But Ellie—"

"I'll say she fell."

"Is she dead?"

"No. I've called an ambulance. I'm going to pacify the neighbours and then I'm going to telephone to Mr. Craig. You better not be here when he arrives."

"But . . . but . . ."

"Get out, Neil," Gregor said.

"I tried to kill you."

Gregor put one hand to his neck. He gave a

crooked smile. "You had cause, I gather," he said. "Get going."

He pulled Cornelius with him to the door of the studio. When he opened it, a man and a woman in dressing gowns were anxiously hovering there on the landing. "What's going on?" they wanted to know. "All that racket . . ."

"There's been an accident. My sister had a fall." With one arm behind him, Gregor was urging Cornelius out of the studio. "My brother's going for a doctor."

"Is it serious?" the woman asked. "Shall I—"

"No, it needs an expert. *Go on*, Neil."

Dazed, lost, Cornelius gave in to the urging of that arm at his back. He pushed between the two neighbours and went down the stairs. At the corner he saw a cab. He flagged it, gave the address of his New York apartment. Larry heard him stumble in and came hurrying in his nightshirt to find out what was wrong. The manservant stood by helplessly while Cornelius was sick as a dog in the bathroom. When he tried to put him to bed, Cornelius shoved him off.

Then the vigil. Now it was over. Cornelius knew his sister had not died at his hands, nor lost her child.

But there was nothing for him now. All that had made life desirable was gone.

For several hours after Ellie-Rose was declared safe, Cornelius seriously thought about suicide. He felt he didn't deserve to live. What was there to live for anyhow?

But in the end he remembered what his father had said. It would distress Ellie-Rose to have him prosecuted. How much the more if he took his own life? No, that wasn't the way.

But it was a life he had no use for any longer. He couldn't go back to the old ways, before he had met Stephanie. That door had been closed when he was told his father never wanted to see him again.

For two days after he knew Ellie-Rose was safe, he went out for walks and came home, sat in his armchair and thought, and never said a word to Larry except "Yes" and "No".

Then he said: "Pack a bag."

"A bag? Overnight bag, sir?"

"That will do."

"Am I coming with you, sir?"

"No." A pause. "I'm going away, Larry. You're discharged."

"Discharged? You're going away for good?"

Cornelius nodded. "Just a minute." He took out his pocket book, changed his mind, and produced his cheque book. "A year's pay," he said.

"Oh no—sir—that's not necessary—"

But Cornelius's head was bent over the cheque book. He couldn't hear. He tore out the cheque and gave it to Larry.

"That's in return for good service," he said.

"But Mr. Craigallan—sir—what's happened?" All through his vigil over the telephone Larry had been unable to make sense of any of it. Miss Ellie-Rose was ill—but in what way did that make the master to blame?

"Never mind. Pack a bag. A shirt and a razor. I don't want much."

Larry did as he was bid. Baffled and alarmed, he handed the valise to Cornelius. "The apartment, sir—"

"Go to my father. Tell him to dispose of it."

"Sir—"

"Yes?"

"I . . . wish you'd reconsider. It can't be as bad as this."

Cornelius looked at him, and actually smiled—a weary, lost smile. "Goodbye," he said. "Thanks for everything, Larry."

He caught the next train to Washington. The next thing his father knew, he had volunteered for service with the scientific team about to sail out to the Philippines to deal with the problems of that unhappy land. He had pulled strings through friends in the Department of Agriculture. "What does it matter if I'm deaf?" he demanded. "I'm only going to talk to plants."

So they accepted him. He sailed at the end of the week that Rob was allowed his first visit to Ellie-Rose.

19

GREGOR had done his best to minimise what had happened. Certain facts couldn't be altered, so he had admitted those to his father. He and Stephanie had been in her apartment: Cornelius had arrived with Ellie-Rose: there had been a quarrel; in the uproar—which had to be mentioned because it had brought out the neighbours—Ellie-Rose had had a bad fall.

"A fall?" Rob snarled. "The doctors tell me she has a great bruise across her belly and a three-inch gash on her forehead! What do you mean, a fall?"

"Well, she . . . got in the way. She got knocked over."

"Got in the way of what, for God's sake?"

"I told you, there was an argument—"

Rob gave a hard glare at Gregor's bruised face, the marks on his neck, now dark red and due to turn purple later, the marks where Cornelius's hands had squeezed at his life's breath.

"I'll get to the bottom of this, boy," he said. "Don't think I won't. But first things first—we've got to be sure Ellie-Rose is going to live."

Gregor had gone back to the studio to try to clear up as best he could. Stephanie was still crouched in a weeping huddle on the chair where he had put her. The woman neighbour was hovering over her.

"She doesn't seem to hear me," she said helplessly.

"Never mind. Leave her to me."

He had his hands full then, and for the next few days. It was a good excuse for staying out of his father's way. Rob telephoned; Gregor said he couldn't talk on the telephone, couldn't come out to see him. "Don't come, Father. Stephanie's really sick."

Rob slammed down the receiver on him. Cornelius had departed, so it was impossible to question him. Nor could he subject his daughter to an inquisition, not while she lay so pale and debilitated in a sickroom after nearly losing her life.

The news of Cornelius's going was kept from Ellie-Rose for a few days after it was known. Rob felt it would set her back in her slow recovery. He and Curtis were her only visitors at first; both men tried to soothe her, keeping back anything that might worry or alarm.

One of her anxieties was that Gregor really had been harmed. She would have nightmares, waking in a sweat-bathed nightgown from the vision of her brother's strong hands fixed on Gregor's throat. Finally the doctor took Rob aside.

"This man she calls out about in her sleep—Gregor?"

"He's my ward."

"She's very concerned about him."

"I've told her he's all right, dammit!"

"But the problem is, she's intelligent—she senses things are being kept from her for her own good.

371

About the baby, for instance. She keeps demanding to see him, because she guesses how delicate he is. We can let her have a glimpse of him tomorrow, to set her mind at rest. But as to this other matter . . . ?"

"Well," growled Rob, "she can see Gregor too. Nothing simpler."

Gregor had always been a little wary of Ellie-Rose. She had never been hostile in her manner, but he sensed she had been kind out of a sense of duty. As a result, he had been guarded in his attitude towards her. He had seen her as a pretty, intelligent, ambitious young woman, rather hard in her outlook.

But when he came into her sickroom, the only emotion he felt was pity.

She had been very ill. There was only a shadow of the real Ellie-Rose here, despite the pretty bedjacket of rose-pink crepe-de-chine and the pink velvet ribbon tying back her hair. She was half-reclining on lace-edged pillows. Her cheeks were nearly as white as the fine lawn surface.

Like most men, Gregor wasn't at his best in a sickroom. Even so, his habitual air of self-possession didn't desert him.

"So you decided not to leave us, after all," he said as he took the chair by the bed. "For a while there, at the studio, I thought you were gone."

"The studio," she repeated. Her eyes fastened on his. "They don't tell me things, Gregor. What happened there? After I was knocked out?"

372

"I called an ambulance and then telephoned to Mr. Craig. You were here within ten minutes."

"And Cornelius?"

"He was numbed. I shoved him out the door, told him to keep clear. The neighbours were coming out—I told them you'd had a fall."

"The police weren't involved?"

"No."

"You didn't make a complaint against Cornelius?"

"What do you take me for, Ellie?" he said in reproach. "The poor guy didn't know what he was doing."

"Yes."

"Besides, think of the scandal. It wouldn't do the family any good to have this kind of thing get out."

"No." She was silent for a moment then ventured, "So Cornelius isn't under arrest?"

"Of course not."

"Why doesn't he come to see me then?"

"He's . . . gone away."

"Papa said that. 'Cleared out'. What does it mean, Greg?"

"He's gone away, that's all."

"But where? Greg, he needs me now. He's . . . he's got no one else now. Unless, that is, Stephanie . . . ?"

Gregor shook his head.

"She's still with you?"

"Yes." He gave it a moment's swift thought then said: "You know the kind of girl she is, Ellie. She's

373

ruled by her senses. All she feels for Cornelius now is revulsion."

"Poor Neil," mourned Ellie, "poor Neil. Tell him to come and see me, Greg. Tell him I want to see him."

"I can't do that, Ellie."

"Why not?" Immediate alarm flamed in her eyes. She threw out a hand to clutch at Gregor. "Something's wrong. You haven't been telling me the truth! You've none of you been telling me! When a person's ill you think they're stupid too, but I know, I know—something has happened to my brother!"

Her voice was rising in a crescendo of weak hysteria. He pressed her hand hard and said: "Quiet down, Ellie, or you'll have that cheery nurse bursting in and sending me away."

"But you don't tell me the *truth—*"

"I'll tell you. But you must promise to be still. Promise? Just listen to what I have to tell you and take it easy. Do you promise?"

The fearful anxiety died out of her expression. "It's bad, then?"

"Not so bad. When Mr. Craig told you Neil had gone, it was true. It's where he's gone that's depressing."

"Where? Where?"

"I'll tell you about it the way we learned of it. Your father got a letter from a United States naval vessel which had sailed from San Francisco. Cornelius said he felt it would be wrong just to disappear without letting us know—it might add to our anxieties. He's joined a government research team headed for the Philippines."

When he stopped speaking he watched her anxiously. If possible, she became even paler. She closed her eyes. There was a silence. Then she looked at him.

"There's fighting in the Philippines," she whispered between pale lips.

"That's so, Ellie, but a research team won't be involved. It'll be based in one of the towns—"

"But don't we read in the papers that the insurgents raid the towns—"

"Ellie, if and when they do, they're after food and ammunition, not scientists. Neil is as safe as houses—"

"Don't Gregor. Not you too. Don't talk to me as if I were a fool, just because I'm sick. Cornelius has gone to a very dangerous place."

"We-ell . . . It's more dangerous than New York or Chicago, I guess."

"But how could it happen?" she flared suddenly. "How could he be accepted? A deaf man is no use to them—"

"They didn't find that out, so far as we can tell. Neil got his old friend Pete Sumikiss to put his name forward, and on paper Neil's qualifications are first-rate. There was no medical for the research team. So by just keeping quiet and watching the lips if he had to take part in talk, I suppose he bluffed his way on board the ship. For all we know, they still haven't found out he's deaf. I don't know how much they'd have to consult each other until they start work. If Neil just stuck to his cabin and appeared morose, they'd leave him be. By the time they catch him out, it won't matter. I mean, Ellie, you don't have to be able to hear and speak clearly to know all about plant disease."

She moved her head against the pile of pillows. It was a gesture of impatience. "What is he doing it for?" she exclaimed. "What use is he there?"

"Oh, he can do a good job. You know the Taft Commission is trying to get into action, building roads and harbours in the Philippines. The idea is to show that we're serious in wanting to bring good government to the natives—well, I don't have to tell you, you must have heard it discussed to death in Washington. Mr. Craig made some enquiries—it seems the Department of Agriculture has been given a brief to examine the plants of the islands to see if there are possibilities for money crops other than hemp and sugar cane."

"But Neil isn't a botanist—"

"No, but they've got problems out there with diseases of the rice plant, and what they call maize—I gather that's Indian corn. Blight and black fungus disease and all kinds of stuff. It seems Neil already had correspondence with some old guy in Manila—Senor Doncilo de Gados, or some such name. But Neil actually does know something about the situation out there. So you see . . ."

Gregor spread his hands, as if to say, There's logic in it after all.

"But . . . but . . . Gregor, he'll be so *alone*. Only a few other Americans who even speak the same language. Neil can't learn a foreign language, you know. It would take him almost a lifetime to classify the mouth positions of any language other than English . . ."

"But they'll have things in common, Ellie. Scientists are a funny breed. They'll come to terms with his speech defects."

"How many in the team?"

"Nine, as I hear it. Of course they're subject to military authority, but I imagine the brass will leave them alone to get on with their own projects."

"I hope they turn him right around and send him home when he gets there!"

"He won't come home, Ellie. If they send him back on the next boat, and land him forcibly on American soil, he'll stay away from Craigallan Castle."

"He could come to me! I would always have a welcome—"

"Now, be sensible, Ellie. Your husband's never going to have Cornelius in the house, not after what happened."

"But it was an *accident*—"

"We know that. But the fact is, Mr. Craig and Curtis blame Cornelius for dragging you into the affair in the first place. Then that wild temper scares them. Those people next door to the

377

studio—they've said they heard a few things. I think it's been a hell of a shock to Curtis. He didn't believe Cornelius was capable of an outburst like that." Gregor shook his head. "He doesn't know the half of it!"

"You don't know him. None of you know him as I do." Ellie-Rose felt that old protective urge towards her brother. She looked at Gregor almost with enmity. "I suppose you're more than ever fixed as the favourite son, now that Cornelius has been pushed out into the wilderness."

"Jacob and Esau, eh? I haven't done any harm to Cornelius, Ellie. I don't *wish* him any harm. I think the poor guy was out of his mind when he attacked me and he's paying for it now in more ways than one. He's welcome to come home as far as I'm concerned. I don't see any point in holding a grudge against him. Facts are facts, though. Your husband and Mr. Craig have got it in for Cornelius at the moment. The Philippines isn't far enough—they wish he'd gone to Outer Mongolia."

What he said was true, and yet there was a sort of rueful humour in it that, despite herself, made Ellie-Rose smile. And moreover he had been the bearer of good tidings. Deep inside herself she'd been afraid her brother had done away with himself. All the soothing and shifting that had gone on each time she mentioned his name had frightened her. Now at last, from her half-brother, she heard the facts. She felt gratitude to him.

378

She held out her hand. "Thank you for telling me, Greg."

"I'm going to get stick from Mr. Craig over it."

"No. You did a good thing. I've been sick with worry."

"And now you feel better?"

"Yes, much better."

"That's good. Take care, then, Ellie-Rose. I'll come back for another visit in a couple of days."

"Do that. Goodbye, Gregor."

When he had gone she lay in thought for a long time. She was less unhappy about Cornelius now, but she was still worried. The Philippines! It was riddled with corruption, full of bandits and armed thugs, infested with poisonous snakes and insects, and was so unhealthy that more troops were shipped home with malaria and yellow-fever than with wounds from the fighting.

Not given to prayer, Ellie-Rose found words forming in her mind: Dear God, Look after my brother.

When Gregor told Rob he'd given Ellie-Rose news of Cornelius, the result was an outburst of anger such as he'd never seen before.

"What the hell d'you think you're up to? I never want that boy's name mentioned to her again, so long as I live! Do you hear me?"

Gregor was too taken aback to reply. He had expected to be scolded, but not this shout of rage.

"It must have upset her tremendously. What were you thinking of, to blurt it all out?"

"I didn't blurt it, sir. She was getting in a state over him and I thought it best to tell her what we knew." He paused. "Doesn't it occur to you that she thought he'd committed suicide?"

"What?"

"She thought we were keeping it from her. I just felt it didn't do any good to feed her more soothing syrup."

"Nobody asked you to make decisions for this family! Who the hell do you think you are?"

Gregor didn't let his anger show. "I'm the guy who was there, remember?" he remarked, very cool and quiet.

They were in Rob's study at the Castle. Rob threw himself back in his leather chair to stare at his son. "Yes, by God, and let's get to the bottom of that," he said. "We've all been so concentrated on Ellie and whether we were going to lose her, we never got to the facts. What were you doing in Stephanie's studio in the middle of the night?"

"Having an argument that got out of hand."

"Don't play games with me, boy. Had that hot little bitch taken up with you?"

"Mr. Craig, let's not use terms like that—"

"She's picked up with you, that's it—while she was still going with Cornelius!" Rob rose to his feet, to be on a level with his son, who was standing in a half-leaning posture against his desk. He stared into his face. "That's it, isn't it? She was running with both of you!"

Gregor pulled himself upright and moved away

from that hard stare. His own thoughts had been along those lines though not couched in those terms. There was no point in acting moral indignation.

"You have to understand I didn't know about Cornelius," he began. "I was totally astounded when he walked in—"

"Walked in! And where were you at the time?"

"I certainly wasn't admiring the paintings. Listen, Mr. Craig, it couldn't have been worse. Cornelius was within his rights to want to skin me alive. If I'd known that he was involved, of course—"

"You'd have steered clear? Yes, I give you that much intelligence. You wouldn't have mixed with a woman who'd two-time your own brother—"

"It's no use throwing terms like 'two-timing' at her. I don't think Stephanie intended that. She meant to speak to Cornelius, only she hadn't nerved herself to it—"

"Oh, she meant to speak to him, did she? Decent of her. Is that how she views her life? Off with the old love, on with the new?"

Gregor sighed. "I'm not defending her outlook. Though, in fact, it's quite common. I know a lot of fellows in college who live their lives under just those rules."

"But that's men—for women it's different."

"That's the problem. Stephanie doesn't think it should be different. She thinks she should be free to love whom she pleases. And the time she spent in

Paris on the Left Bank has demonstrated to her that she can do just that."

"I don't know how you can justify—"

"I'm not justifying. I'm explaining."

Rob considered him. "You don't seem wrought up with loving concern for her, all the same."

"Mr. Craig, I think we both know I'm not the kind to lose my head over her. I . . . I feel a commitment to her, because in fact she's pretty much come to pieces over what's happened—"

"Has she! Well, that's only fair. Everybody else has taken their lumps. It's only right she should get some."

Gregor made no reply to that. He alone had seen the condition of hysterical collapse that had followed the episode in her studio. He had gone with Ellie-Rose to St. Mary's, where he had at once been banished while the medical staff took over. There Rob and Curtis had joined him in the waiting room, rightly bewildered and full of anxiety. Gregor had made himself scarce as soon as they appeared, and since then had tried to steer clear of them both.

"She's had a nervous breakdown. If you want her to suffer she's suffering."

"A nervous breakdown," Rob sneered. "Tears and noisy lamentations—"

"It's more that that. Her hand shakes so much she can't hold a paint brush. She can't eat, she can't sleep. She cries a lot, sits in a corner looking into nothingness."

"Guilty conscience. Serves her dam' well right."

"Father, don't be shortsighted. If this goes on, she's going to have to get treatment."

"Let her go back to her parents in Schenechtedy or wherever the hell it is—"

"And have all this come out? Is that what you want?"

Rob was brought up short. "We-ell . . ."

"How do you think it's going to sound to Mr. and Mrs. Jouvard when Stephanie sits weeping over what she saw, going over and over it in her mind?"

"What exactly did she see?"

Gregor moved a pace or two about the rather sombre room. The afternoon light was insufficient to brighten the heavy wooden panelling. He eyed his father for a moment, wondering how best to handle this. He needed Rob's help, was prepared to give information in return for it. After a rapid survey of the situation he made his decision.

"All right, Mr. Craig," he said. "I'll lay it on the line for you. She and I were in bed when Cornelius walked in using a key. I haven't been able to find out how long Stephanie and Cornelius were paired up—she just isn't able to talk about it. But he certainly thought he had a right to walk in there in the middle of the night, and he certainly was shattered when he saw me." Gregor put a hand to his throat. It still hurt inside, though the bruises had faded. "Not to put too fine a point on it, he tried to kill me."

"What?"

"Now hold on—we're not talking about this so as to work up a rage about it. We're trying to understand what Stephanie would come out with in her present state, if her parents got to her. What she saw was one man trying to strangle another. She went straight into hysterics. I don't know if she understands that I'm still alive and well. Sometimes she knows me, sometimes she doesn't. Then there was Ellie-Rose. Stephanie saw Ellie-Rose knocked sprawling. There was blood everywhere—you know how a scalp wound bleeds."

"By God, Gregor—"

"He didn't mean it. Keep a hold on that, sir. Neil didn't mean it. He'd rather cut off his right hand than harm Ellie-Rose. He didn't even see her, until I somehow got through to him for a minute. But from where Stephanie was standing, Ellie-Rose was bleeding, and not moving. She was carried away on a stretcher. Stephanie doesn't really know what happened to her. I can't make her believe Ellie-Rose is okay. I can't get through to her."

Rob let the words sink in for a long moment. He got up, opened the box on his desk, and applied himself to cutting and lighting a cigar. "The way you tell this, she's pretty well gone out of her senses," he said.

"That about sums it up."

"And so what then?"

"I have to get back to college, sir. But I can't leave her. If it were measles or an attack of the grippe, I'd take her home to her parents. But as things are, that's out of the question. So I need a doctor. But I don't know anything about doctors."

"Hm." Rob blew smoke out into the air. "Well," he mused, "I'll say one thing for you, Greg. You keep your head."

"I try to."

"So you want me to find a brain doctor for your girl, eh?"

Gregor made no voiced reply to that.

"Not what you thought you were getting into, is it?"

"It certainly isn't. All the same, I can't just walk away. Apart from the scandal that might erupt, I owe her."

"You owe her? For getting you tangled up in a mess like this? Your own brother's mistress?"

"Don't let's try to explain it," Gregor said. He still recalled the intoxication of the senses that Stephanie had brought him. Different, deeper than anything he had felt with other women. She had given herself to him in a way that was totally different. If for nothing else, he owed her for that— the experience of the complete merging of one being in another.

"Right then. I'll find you a doctor. Someone who can be discreet, of course—"

"Listen, Mr. Craig, I'm not asking for some old hack who'd get rid of a baby for her. This is serious. She could lose her reason." That scared Gregor. He couldn't be responsible for another person losing contact with the world. He had to get her made

385

better or it would haunt him for the rest of his life. Before he could walk away from her, she had to be made sane again.

"Of course, I understand that. When I say discreet, I mean someone who won't call in her parents—"

"I don't think a doctor will call in anyone against the patient's wishes. It's like between a priest and a penitent—completely confidential."

"I believe you're right. Well, that simplifies things. I'll inquire around, and be in touch later today. You're staying at her place?"

Gregor nodded. "I try not to leave her more than necessary. I'm going back there now."

He found her as he had left her, huddled in a chair, arms grasped about herself, head tilted over on her shoulder, eyes fixed on nothingness. She spent hours like this. Now and again she would start up and become frantically busy.

"I can't sit around like this any more! I've got things to do!"

Then she would bustle about in the little kitchen, in a flurry of activity until her attention faded. She would dwindle to a standstill, wondering why she was there, at a loss.

Gregor made some tea and toast, coaxed her to eat. She was becoming painfully thin because she ate so little.

About four o'clock her telephone rang. It was Rob. "I'm with a Dr. Zeichman," he said. "We'll be with you in about twenty minutes, Greg, if it's all right to come straight over."

"Yes, the sooner the better."

He was waiting almost by the door when they came. Stephanie was hanging on to his arm, in one of her moods when she wouldn't let him go as far as even a step away. Dr. Zeichman proved to be a middle-aged man of medium height, with sparse dark hair and a lined face. He was dressed in the regulation doctor's suit of dark cloth, with a high collar and a stiff silk cravat. In his hand he carried the regulation black bag.

"This is the patient?" he said in a voice with a faint German accent. He stepped forward to take Stephanie's hand. She drew back. "It's all right, my dear," he went on, gentle and comforting. "I just wanted to say how-do-you-do."

"How do you do?" Stephanie said, looking at him in surprise.

"My name is Zeichman. What's yours?"

"Jouvard. Stephanie Jouvard."

"Ah, good. Stephanie, suppose we sit down and have a little talk while your friends make us a cup of coffee."

"Oh, no, that wouldn't be polite—to let them—"

"They'll be happy to." He raised his eyebrows at Gregor, who made a sound of agreement and drew his father into the kitchen.

"Zeichman?" he queried. "Is he a nerve doctor?"

"He's one of these doctors who follow the Viennese guy—"

"Freud?"

"That's the one. I talked to Dr. Glindall about our problem—"

"You didn't tell him everything—"

"No, of course not, just that we had this young friend who'd lost a few buttons. He recommended Zeichman. Seems he's highly thought of."

"But this man Freud—have you read anything about him? It's a load of rubbish—"

"No, Greg, it seems there's something to it. I'm not saying I understand it, but Glindall seemed to have faith in it." Glindall was the doctor who came to the Castle when there was anything wrong with the staff there. A good, steady, unambitious family doctor, who made a good living without putting himself out too much yet liked to read about all the new treatments.

Gregor made coffee and took it out to them. As far as he could see, the doctor was simply sitting looking at Stephanie, who was not speaking. A silence like a strong thread seemed to bind the two of them. The rattle of the coffee cups was an intrusion. Zeichman glanced up, shook his head, and jerked it as a signal that Gregor should leave them. He did so, relieved not to be asked any questions or made to play any part.

"I think we ought to clear out for a bit," he said to Rob when he rejoined him. "We can go out on the landing."

"I notice you don't invite me into the bedroom."

"We can go there if you want. But it's a mess.

Nothing's been tidied up for days. Come on, let's get out." They moved quietly across the studio and out of the door. For the first time in days, Stephanie didn't cry out in protest as Gregor closed the door.

By and by Dr. Zeichman opened it and came out to join them. "She is suffering from a quite severe depression brought on by trauma, perhaps recent, but not fundamentally caused by that. She is quite ill."

"Could you put that into English?" Gregor said in a sceptical tone.

"She has had a very bad shock, which has made her very depressed, very sad. But there is more, of course. Something in her life has been growing into a great anxiety, and she has used this recent shock to make a turning point, a running away."

"What that amounts to is that she's lost her grip on life."

"Quite so. Unless she receives treatment, it may grow much worse."

"What kind of treatment?"

"I have asked her if she will confide herself to me for a time. A month or two, perhaps more. She has agreed."

"Agreed?" Gregor said in astonishment. "In a few minutes, she's agreed to let you take control of her life?"

"She wanted to. Subconsciously she has been waiting for someone to say 'Leave it all to me—I will see to it all'."

"See to it all? What all?"

"That is what we have to discover, my young friend. She has many problems, I have no doubt. She will tell them to me. And in doing so, she will solve them."

"And you say this will take a month or two?"

"Perhaps more."

Gregor cast an agonised glance at his father. He was supposed to be in college. Although he would, if necessary, miss this semester, it would interrupt his studies—and exams were looming.

"My suggestion is that she should come into my clinic. I have a place in Brooklyn."

"Oh, I don't know . . ."

"She has agreed to come," Zeichman said with quiet authority. "She wants to. She knows she must have help."

Gregor looked at his father. "Do you go along with this?" he asked.

"Well, son, I don't know anything about it. All I can tell you is, Dr. Glindall thought Zeichman was the right kind of doctor. And I've got confidence in Glindall."

"So what happens now?" Greg asked.

"I have asked her to come with me to Oakgrove, my private nursing home. It would reassure her if you came with us, and saw her settled in."

Gregor sighed. "Very well."

The clinic was a rather handsome old house in the not-yet large suburb of Brooklyn. Inside it was quiet, rather elegant, not too antiseptic. Stephanie was shown up to a room to which Gregor accompanied her.

"You had better leave now," Zeichman said.

"No, don't go," she cried, suddenly throwing her arms round him. "What am I doing here, Greg? What's going on?"

"You've come to be looked after for a bit, Stephanie, to have a rest."

"But I don't know this place!"

"No, but you'll like it here." Would she? He could only hope so.

She sank down on the side of the bed. "Will you be here?"

"I have to go back to Harvard, Stephanie. You know that."

"Oh . . . Yes . . . I'll come and see you."

Gregor looked at Zeichman. Zeichman nodded, as if to say, Go along with that. "All right, Stephanie, when you feel up to it you can come and see me."

"Soon?"

"As soon as you feel fit."

She nodded, and looked down. For the moment she seemed to have lost interest in the conversation.

As Gregor was shown downstairs he bethought himself of Stephanie's parents. They would wonder what on earth had happened to her if they didn't hear from her, or happened to call at her studio.

"Shall I write to her parents, or will you?" he asked.

"Just as you like."

"It would be best coming from you. I don't really

391

understand what it is you say is wrong with her. Could you write them a reassuring letter explaining that she felt she needed help for her nerves?"

"Of course. I'm quite accustomed to dealing with anxious relatives. A great many people have the idea that we psychologists are charlatans, Mr. Craigallan."

Gregor noticed the mistake in his name but didn't correct it. Absolved from responsibility, Gregor closed up the Gramercy Park studio and went back to Harvard.

20

STEPHANIE'S parents hastened to the clinic in Brooklyn on receipt of Dr. Zeichman's letter. They found their daughter quiet, looking sad, thin and listless. She didn't seem very ill, merely what they would have called "run down".

The way the story came over to them, Stephanie had been deep in a romance with the son of Rob Craigallan. They took this to be Cornelius, whom they'd met. Cornelius, from what they supposed were patriotic motives, had gone out to the Philippines. For the moment Stephanie was upset, naturally so.

They were a little surprised to find that Rob Craigallan was picking up the tab for Stephanie's treatment, and had it been some other kind of clinic they might have had alarmed suspicions—of a baby disposed of, which they as good Catholics could not have brooked. But this was a very respectable establishment for the treatment of nervous diseases. Dr. Zeichman, about whom they'd made inquiries, was highly thought of.

The Jouvards' conclusion was that the Craigallans felt a responsibility to Stephanie because Cornelius had walked out on her. Young men were apt to get high-flown, patriotic notions. Perhaps they'd had a lovers' tiff and he'd marched out in a huff, just to show her. They thanked Rob for his kindness but insisted on taking over the charge of their daughter.

She made good progress. By Easter she seemed herself again. They whisked her home for a convalescence, tactfully not prying into her emotions and avoiding the name of Cornelius. They couldn't help noticing that no letters came for her from the Philippines. She received few letters, in fact.

None at all from Gregor. As far as he was concerned, it was over. He had known her for something like a month—from just before Christmas until the last week of January. It had been a disastrous month. Seductive and ardent as she was, she spelled trouble. He might have fallen quite deeply in love with her if he had known her longer, but thank heaven the disasters had struck early in their acquaintance.

He took it somewhat for granted that the same would be true of Stephanie. He was surprised to get a telephone call from her at his rooms in Boston.

Gregor lived on campus, but for his leisure times and weekends he had a pleasant set of rooms in an old part of Boston. His father actually owned the building, had bought it many years ago for some old relative. The district wasn't fashionable, being too near the waterfront and rather far from the area where the great new buildings were going up.

Gregor liked to get away from his fellow-students at times. They were decent enough, but sometimes they struck him as jejune, and sometimes as over-boisterous. Here in Hull Street he could be quiet; no dorm neighbours could surge in with silly practical jokes, no anxious scholar could corner him for an explanation of the theory of investment flow. He had books, a phonographic machine of the latest kind, a few paintings he had bought. He would go out rowing in the early morning, eat in some good, quiet restaurant, spend his evening at a theatre or a concert. He invited no one there. Few people knew of this retreat.

So when his telephone rang one day in late May, and the operator's cheerful tone announced "Long distance!", he expected some emergency call from his father. He braced himself. The news of Ellie-Rose had continued good, but anxiety was always under the surface for the baby boy.

"Hello? Gregor?"

He recognised the voice at once. His heart sank. "Stephanie?"

"Gregor, why haven't you written or come to see me? I've been waiting and waiting to hear from you!"

"What a surprise," he said. "How are you, Stephanie?"

"I'm quite all right," she said. Her tone was hurt and reproachful. "You said you'd come and see me, but you never did."

"Well, I had to get back in school—"

"But that was at New Year. I thought for sure you'd come during the Easter vacation, but you didn't."

"I had to go to Colorado to see my mother. I *should* have gone after Christmas but . . . well . . ."

"And you couldn't take one single day off from your classes to come and see me?"

"I . . . er . . . I heard your parents had taken you home. It wouldn't have been very good to visit you at home."

"But you did want to?" she cut in, eager and quick.

He cursed himself for the mistake. "It seemed best just to let it go, Stephanie."

"I understand. It wasn't convenient then. But it's different now, Greg. I'm back in New York."

"Back in the studio?" he asked, staggered. He would have thought she would never go back there, after the scene that had wrecked her mind.

"Of course. It's where the buyers can find me. They know my address."

"You're painting again?"

"I'm trying. Dr. Zeichman says it's good for me. Greg, when can you come?"

He hedged at once. "I've got exams, Stephanie."

"Oh, exams!"

"They're important. I can't flunk them or I'll—"

"You're not the kind to flunk exams, Greg."

"Well, I can't do poorly, if you want to be exact. My teachers expect me to do well. I need to give my mind to them."

"When will they be over?"

"By June."

"But that's such a long time, darling." She

396

exaggerated the vowel in the word long, to show how she felt. "Can't you come for just one night?"

"No, it can't be done." Inwardly he was groaning. She couldn't really imagine they would pick up just where they left off? He went on, to forestall her protests, "How did you get this telephone number, Stephanie?"

"I asked the operator."

"But how did you know this address?"

"I searched your pockets one night when you were here." She laughed, a teasing little sound. "You were fast asleep, and I got up to get a drink, and saw your jacket, and I just wanted to know all about you. So I took everything out of your pockets, looked in your diary, saw the address on a letter you were carrying."

He said nothing.

"You're not angry?" she asked, in sudden panic. "I only wanted to know you through and through, Greg. And it's a good thing, isn't it—otherwise how would I have got to speak to you today?"

He was in a cold rage at the revelation, but he knew better than to say so. "It doesn't matter, Stephanie. It's all in the past, anyhow."

"Yes, everything that might spoil things for us is in the past. Now we can be everything to each other without barriers."

"I don't think so, Stephanie."

"What do you mean? Everything is all right now. I'm well again, and Cornelius . . . Cornelius has gone . . ."

397

"Yes, he's gone, but everything isn't all right between us. It never was. The whole thing was a mistake—"

"Don't say that! I love you, Greg!"

"No, you've just made too much of a simple infatuation—"

"How can you! How can you!" He could hear her sobbing. "I knew when you didn't come that you were thinking things like that. You blame me. Well, I wasn't to blame. I didn't mean any of that to happen—that fight with Cornelius—it wasn't my fault."

"Did I say it was?" he replied, with a glance up at the ceiling of his room, as if asking help from the Almighty. "I haven't accused you. I just say it was a mistake. We have to face it."

"No! You love me and I love you. You mustn't let silly conventions of right and wrong come between us! What happened about Cornelius was just a blunder. But it makes no difference to the—"

"It makes a difference to me, Stephanie," he said, with complete firmness. "I'm not going to go on with this conversation. I'm going to put the phone down."

"No! Don't, Greg! Don't shut me out—"

"Goodbye, Stephanie." He replaced the receiver on the hook, then stood looking at the instrument. After a moment's thought he took it up again and called the operator. "If there are any more telephone calls from New York, would you please find out who is calling before you put them through? I'd like to know before I take the call."

"Certainly, sir. My pleasure."

But she didn't telephone again. He wasn't sure whether that was good or bad. He went back to Harvard that Sunday night a little apprehensive about Stephanie. Had he set her back by refusing to go along with her view of their relationship? She had sounded normal enough, although perhaps a bit tense. But the tenseness was only to be expected if she was trying to re-establish a love affair that had gone wrong.

Classes and lectures took up his time for the next four days. He looked out at the sparkling water of the Charles River as his cab took him over the Harvard Bridge again, and thought that he'd be up at dawn tomorrow, and out in his shell for some good strong sculling on that calm surface.

When he walked into the downstairs hall of his apartment building, the old man who got the basement rooms for nothing in return for some janitorial duties was mopping the tiled floor. He looked up with a knowing smile. "Evening, Mr. McGarth, sir."

"Evening, Mr. Boyle."

"Nice weekend comin' up."

"I think so."

"You'll enjoy it, sir, I'm sure."

"Why . . . yes, I think I will." Gregor was halfway up to the first floor landing by this time. He said to himself, "The old boy's half-tipsy again," and put his key in the lock of his apartment.

The door swung open before the key could turn. Stephanie was standing in the doorway.

"Darling!" she cried, and cast herself upon him.

She hugged him close and covered the side of his face with kisses. Gregor, encumbered with a small valise and an armful of books, was at a loss. She pulled him inside, pushed the door shut. The books went cascading all over the floor.

"Darling," she gasped again, winding her arms round his neck and pulling herself close to him. "Oh, if you knew how I've *longed* for this."

"Stephanie." He disengaged her arms and held her off by the elbows. "What the devil are you doing here?"

"I came to talk to you. I knew it was no use trying to explain over the telephone."

"How did you get in?"

"That nice Mr. Boyle let me in with his key."

So that explained the roguish twinkle and the knowing tone of voice. "He had no right to do that."

"Oh, rubbish! I told him you'd be glad to see me and he let me in. It's very comfortable here, Gregor—you look after yourself well."

"How long have you been here?" he demanded, for his glance about his living-room showed him the clutter he associated with her studio in New York.

"I arrived on Monday. I knew after our telephone talk that I had to come in person so I just packed a bag next day and came. But I thought you lived here, Greg. I'd no idea I'd have to spend three days all alone."

He had let go of her during the conversation. Now he strode to the door of his bedroom. Her clothes were everywhere—petticoats slung over the back of a chair, nightgown on the rumpled bed, robe on a hook on the back of the door.

An impulse of sheer indignation made him wheel on her. "Who the hell gave you the right to move in here?" he exclaimed. It was like a violation. This was his own place, where he could be himself without reference to the wishes of others.

"Oh, darling," she pouted. She had made up her mind that she would ride out his annoyance. She had taken him by surprise and probably put out his arrangements for the weekend, but once they'd had this important talk, everything would be all right. She came up to him and took hold of one of his arms with her two hands. She leaned against his chest. "My darling, I knew I shouldn't have come without asking you if it was all right, but I had to speak to you. And it was useless trying to do that over the telephone. It's such an unfriendly instrument, isn't it, the telephone."

"Now listen," he said, disengaging himself. "This has got to stop. I want you to understand right now that we have nothing to talk about. The past is—"

"The past is where the present comes from," she put in quickly. "Dr. Zeichman says that. And it's true, of course. Our past was linked, Gregor. You can't cut that link just by saying it never happened."

"I'm not saying that. I'm saying it was based on a huge misunderstanding."

"But that's been cleared up now!" she said triumphantly. "Everything is plain sailing from now on—"

"Plain sailing? Ellie-Rose spends six months under doctor's orders, her baby is still not a hundred per cent fit, my brother is off in some tropical hell-hole making amends for his outburst of fury, and you say it's plain sailing?"

"Dr. Zeichman says we have to accept the black things, not try to turn them white. I was wrong, I admit that, Gregor. I should have had the strength of mind to tell you about Neil. But at that time I was less stable than I am now. I was afraid I'd lose you if you knew . . . about Neil. So—"

"Damn right you'd have lost me. And did," Gregor retorted. "You lost me the minute that poor beggar walked in that studio, his face scarred with the pain you'd inflicted. My God!" Gregor swung away from her. "I'll never forget it," he ended in a muffled voice.

"We don't have to forget it," Stephanie said, coming round to tug at his elbow. "Dr. Zeichman says—"

"Don't tell me what Dr. Zeichman says," Gregor interrupted. "I've no faith in all that psychological mumbo-jumbo. The way I look at it, we're human beings, not automatons. We have to take

402

responsibility for what we do. And we're responsible for the things that happened because we drove Cornelius out of his mind with jealousy—"

"That's true, that's true, absolutely," she agreed, eagerness in her voice and look. "I don't deny that. What I'm saying is, we don't have to keep reproaching ourselves. We build on the good, we live with the bad. We go ahead into the future. And our future doesn't have to be permanently shadowed—"

"We have no future. Hear me? There's nothing for us any more."

"But why?" she cried, falling back. The eagerness died out, replaced by perplexity. "We love each other—"

"We don't. I don't love you, Stephanie."

"You do, you do!"

"No."

"But . . . those nights we spent together—"

"Yes, those nights. I'm grateful for them." He sighed. "I'm not saying I might not have had a deep involvement with you, Stephanie. You were different from any other girl I ever met. But it went horribly wrong. You can say what you like about facing all that and putting it behind us, but it changed things for me."

Stephanie hadn't expected rejection. She had been convinced that once she saw Gregor—once they were face to face—everything would be all right. She had had long sessions with Dr. Zeichman, talking out all her fears, so that in the end she had become convinced all you had to do was talk, put things into words, and the nightmare ended.

Gregor's inflexibility wounded her. It was based on a fact she hadn't let herself consider: he had fallen out of love with her.

She moved slowly across the room as if drugged, to sink down on a chair. Her dark glossy hair gleamed in the early evening sun streaming through the window.

After a moment she turned to look at him. "Is it because I was sick? Did I scare you, because I had a breakdown?"

"Oh, for God's sake!" He sounded merely irritated at the question. But all the same she had hit a nerve. He couldn't forget how she'd looked then—thin, unkempt, haunted.

"I'm well again, Greg," she said. "Look at me—don't I look well?"

That was true. She had regained the lost weight, her skin was shining with a glow of physical health. Although she was dressed in her usual casual style, she was fresh and pretty.

"You look fine," he said. "It's nothing to do with your health—"

"Then you're punishing me—is that it? For causing you so much trouble?"

"Don't be childish. I'm not in the business of meting out punishment." He needed to say to her, "You don't attract me any more." If she drove him far enough, he would say it. But all he wanted was

404

to end the conversation, to get rid of her and be at peace.

To his dismay her eyes filled with tears. They sparkled for a moment on the rim, then toppled over to gleam on her dark lashes and trickle on to her cheeks. She didn't cry out. She simply sat looking at him in desolation, with the tears rolling down her cheeks.

"Now, don't, Stephanie," he burst out. "Don't cry."

He'd never seen her cry before. There was something despairing about it. If she had made an outcry, loud sobs and complaints, she would have had something less tragic in her air. But as he watched her it seemed as if she was the epitome of desolation.

Afterwards he knew he made his big mistake in going to her side. Physical contact was what Stephanie needed to re-establish her hold on him. When he put his arm about her in a clumsy attempt to comfort her, she instinctively seized her chance.

She turned and buried her face against his chest. Still without words, but with shuddering breaths that told of her tears, she wept for a time while he murmured soothing things into her ear. "There there. Don't cry. You have to be brave."

She put her arms round his neck and clung to him. She didn't protest, "I can't be brave. I love you." She simply held him, lying close against him, warm and helpless in his arms.

After a time she raised her head and moved her

cheek against his. If he had had the willpower to
jerk away, that would have been the end. But he
didn't want to hurt her feelings, so he smiled and let
it happen. Then she was pressing her lips to his,
and opening them to let her tongue touch his
mouth, while her hands caressed the nape of his
neck in a way that she remembered was exciting to
him.

He felt his own response, and a momentary
warning signal flickered. But she had turned on the
chair and leaned heavily so that he swayed,
dragging her down with him. They were on the
floor, in each other's arms. He had her body on top
of him, heavy, touching him at every point of sexual
arousal. He rolled her so that she was under him
and began to kiss her with the sudden need to bring
her to the same state of physical urgency as himself.

She was as eager as he. She tore at her own
clothes so that he could come to her. Months had
gone by since they made love, and her physical
appetite had always been strong. She gasped with
longing as he took her. Nothing else mattered—not
the earthiness of their love-making, the animal
energy they used, the surroundings. In fact, these
things added to the excitement that swept them
away.

Besides the climax of physical satisfaction, she
had another triumph. She had brought it about by
pure instinct. By this single act he bound himself to
her again. Her hold on him was re-established.

"Damn," he said to himself as he tied his tie later,

preparatory to taking her out to the Slaters' party, which he had been invited to. He stared at himself in the mirror. "Mr. Craig said you keep your head. He should see you now."

On thinking it over, his plan was to let her stay a couple of days and then get rid of her by staying on campus, working with his language teachers. She'd get bored on her own. By and by she'd go back to New York. If he showed her that his way of life here was bound up with learning, that he had no time for playing the lover—she'd go back to New York.

He misjudged her tenacity. She appeared in Harvard, asking for him in hall. The porter came up to his room with the announcement of her presence. "Young lady, asking after you, sir— expected to see you in Boston but you didn't turn up and she's worried."

His room-mate raised his eyebrows. "What's this, McGarth? Your secret light o'love? I always knew you had a ribbon or two put away."

"I'll come," Gregor said. He ran down the stairs three at a time to find, as he expected, Stephanie looking demure and anxious in the vestibule.

"What the hell are you doing here?" he demanded in a low voice. "Do you want to throw away your reputation?"

"I don't care about that, darling," she said in her normal voice, seizing his hand. "I was so worried about you! When you didn't come—"

The dean of the college, coming in to check on

attendance, paused in his step. "Good afternoon, Mr. McGarth. Anything wrong?"

"Not a thing, sir. May I present Miss Jouvard, a friend of the family?" He said to Stephanie, with a flicker of his lids, "This is the dean."

"How do you do?" the dean said, glancing about for her escort or chaperone.

"Mama is looking at the church, sir," she said, with a little bow. "She'll be along in a moment. She promised Mr. McGarth's mother to look in on him."

"Very good of her. Well, McGarth, mustn't tarry. Work to do." He swept on, leaving it a question whether the remarks about tarrying and work were to be applied to himself or Gregor.

"Get out of here," Gregor said. "You can't come walking into a men's college!"

"I wouldn't embarrass you for the world," she said, looking up at him with an expression of loving solicitude. "Shall I see you in Hull Street this evening?"

"Not this evening, Stephanie. I have to attend a fraternity meeting."

"You could come afterwards."

He shook his head. "Those things go on," he told her.

"But you could slip away."

"No, I don't think so."

"Tomorrow, then? You're coming to Boston for the weekend?"

"I'm going to work out with the rowing eight—"

"Greg, now marvellous! I'll come and cheer you from the bank."

He gazed at her. She met his eyes. There was an unspoken argument between them. He sighed. "Very well, I'll be with you tomorrow evening about six."

"I'll have a nice meal ready, Greg," she replied at once, clapping her hands. "Some wine—"

"No, don't do that. I don't like to cook there. I always eat out."

"Whatever you say, darling," she agreed, giving in on small things.

He knew he was trapped. If he didn't join her in Boston with at least some show of regularity, she'd come to the college. He wasn't sure whether she knew how outrageous it was of her to appear on campus like this. True, men had their womenfolk to see them, but they didn't come calling at the dormitories except on special occasions when the inmates expected them and put on their best behaviour. Otherwise, a Mama or sister was likely to see a young man in a state of considerable undress, or even drunk and disgusting. Women just didn't come on campus. She surely knew that?

He explained it to her when he got to his apartment on Friday evening. She was immediately contrite. "I'm sorry, I didn't know. But I got so worried, not seeing you or hearing from you."

"But you knew I only use this place inter-mittently."

"Mr. Boyle says you come most weekends and sometimes during the week."

Damn Mr. Boyle. "I'm really tied up in college, Stephanie. I've a paper on trade to do, and a *viva voce* in languages coming up."

"On what?"

"French literature—"

"Oh, I can help you with that!" she cried. "After all, I was educated in a French-speaking convent—"

"Yes, I know, Stephanie, but this is to be a discussion on the plays of Corneille—"

"I know them! I played the part of Chimène in a production we put on, us senior girls—"

"But I've got to study and talk about Médée and Polyeucte—"

"Oh, we studied Polyeucte! That's the one about the saint, isn't it—just right for a convent! Oh yes, I know it well. Greg, I can really *help* you."

It turned out to be true. In the four days before his *viva* on Wednesday morning, she took him back and forth through the works of Corneille, with the book of the play in her hand or Guizot's *Corneille et son Temps*. The result was that he came through with flying colours in an encounter he had been dreading, for he had no real interest in Corneille.

"Very pleasing," Professor Lesueur said to him in dismissing him. "I had no idea you were so attuned to the work of this school. It's good to find an economics student who sees something in language beyond an instrument of trade."

410

"Thank you, sir," Gregor said. But it was Stephanie he had to thank.

It would have been grudging not to tell her how much he owed her. He went home to Snow Street that evening with a bottle of fine wine to celebrate. She was delighted on his behalf; they drank the wine, laughed and talked. It was all as it used to be when he first met her. They went to bed that night to make love without any need for seduction techniques from Stephanie.

She stayed until the end of the term then travelled home to New York with him. She then had to go to see her parents, who thought she'd been staying with a woman friend in Boston. Arrangements had to be discussed about the family's summer. Mrs. Jouvard insisted that Stephanie must come to Plymouth as usual—it was more important than ever this year, since she had been ill and the sea air would do her good. Moreover, still no letter from Cornelius Craigallan. That romance had apparently died the death. And Stephanie was twenty-four. Mrs. Jouvard herself had been married with a five year old daughter at that age.

Stephanie had never wanted to confide in her mother about Cornelius, and was unable to do so about Gregor. Mrs. Jouvard was aware of the common gossip about Gregor's birth, and was apt to be sharp about it. "Everyone knows men have these little encumbrances, but is it necessary to flourish them as Rob Craigallan does?"

"Now, now, Maman," said Mr. Jouvard, "he's a

very agreeable young man and I rather fancy Craig-allan intends to do something handsome by him."

"Maybe. But I shall never issue any invitations to that young man. One must preserve *some* standards."

So all through the long month of August Stephanie didn't see Gregor. She didn't even receive letters from him. She had told him not to write. "But I'll write to you," she said, "every day!" The letters hurried to him on the great fast trains to Denver and on to Colorado Springs. After the first six or seven, he began to put them by unopened. They were always the same: *I love you, I miss you, think of me, miss me.*

He didn't miss her. Not in the least. When he was parted from her his good sense told him he could live very easily without her. There was something claustrophobic in the way she clung to him, emphasising her need of him at every point.

He was glad to have an excuse to write to her at last and say he wouldn't be returning to New York immediately from Colorado Springs. "Curtis and Ellie-Rose are in the entourage of the President, going via Cleveland to Buffalo for the Pan-American Exposition, and have asked me to join them there. They're to be on the special train, which gets to Buffalo on September 5th. Mr. Craig-allan will be there too. It's the kind of occasion I can hardly miss out on, so I shan't be in town until mid-September at earliest, and perhaps later."

Gregor kept under-estimating Stephanie. Longing to see him, she found this letter awaiting her when she got to her studio at the end of August. She didn't even bother to unpack. She sent for a cab to take her to the station, then told her kindly neighbour, who had come out to welcome her home, that she was off to Buffalo.

She was about to take part in the tragedy of the decade.

21

ALTHOUGH the process had taken a long time, Ellie-Rose had made a good recovery. Little Curt still seemed fretful and delicate, always needing careful attention, but he was gaining weight and had become a pretty, fair-skinned baby with a will of his own.

In this first year of the President's new term, Curtis had been kept busy. The Democratic opposition shrieked against the mishandling of the Philippines question; "Disgraceful to buy as a colony a people we promised to set free!" they chorused. And in fact many members of the Republican party were uneasy about American colonialism. For so long the United States had heaped infamy on European powers who took over great regions of the earth without reference to the wishes of the population—yet here was their own government doing the same thing.

The general public, however, seemed inclined to forgive the President for buying them a colony. They feted him during a long tour of the South. They grieved and watched with him while his wife Ida fought against death in the home of H. T. Scott in San Francisco. They rejoiced when she recovered.

Wherever McKinley went he was received with

414

cheers and shouts of "Long live the President!" If, now and again, someone in the crowd shouted "Good old Teddy!" McKinley tried not to notice.

But the Vice-President's ambitions were no secret. He was looking towards 1904, the next Presidential election, when he would be a candidate. This made life hard for the President's personal aides, for those who wanted favours were sometimes inclined to play both ends against the middle. Matters weren't improved when McKinley issued a press statement stating categorically that he wouldn't seek a third term. He was more or less handing the future patronage of the Republican party to Theodore Roosevelt.

"Why did he do it?" groaned Curtis to his wife. "We *tried* to stop him."

"What does it matter, Curtis? It only means you'll have fewer men dragging at your coat sleeve."

"But why did he have to do it so soon?" he cried. "Why make a statement like that in the first year of a four-year-term?"

She looked at him, and she knew what he really meant was: Why didn't he give me time to make some headway with Roosevelt before announcing his plans? For of course when McKinley went, his personal aides were likely to go with him. Curtis could then stand for the Senate if he wished, and would probably get in without trouble. But having spent four years in the corridors of the White

House, he didn't like the idea of being put outside with the other nobodies.

At the end of August the close advisers of the President were summoned to his private residence in Canton Ohio to settle the details of his trip to the Pan-American Exposition.

They were now beginning to be worried by an aspect of life that had not seemed too important before. During the election campaign, a spate of crank letters had begun, threatening the President's life. Some of them were clearly by lunatics, but one or two gave reasons for the proposed murder: "You've enslaved the people of Cuba! You've oppressed the workers! You've killed Freedom Fighters in the Philippines!"

"I tell you," Cortelyou said to Curtis, "I'm the one who opens them, and they're scary!"

At first Curtis had shared the President's opinion that it was all a fuss about nothing. But a member of the Secret Service, Ralph Redfern, came up with a report that alarmed them all. An operative called Moretti had managed to penetrate an anarchist group in Paterson New Jersey, the feared headquarters of the anarchist movement in America. The report listed people who were to be assassinated as a demonstration of anarchist power: Empress Elizabeth of Austria, King Umberto of Italy, the Czar of Russia, Queen Victoria of England, the President of the United States, and the German Kaiser.

What made this list so frightening was its date. It

had been made by Moretti in 1898. Since then Empress Elizabeth and King Umberto had been assassinated. There had been two or three attempts on Queen Victoria's life, although the most famous was by a madman.

Mark Hanna sat long hours with Curtis and John Wilkie of the Secret Service trying to concoct measures to protect the President that the President would permit. "Who'd want to shoot me?" he would retort when Hanna begged him not to walk without escort in the crowds.

"An anarchist, that's who!" raged Hanna.

"Nonsense," said the Major, taking his portly figure off to show itself to the friends on his Canton doorstep.

"Why are you so worried about it?" Ellie-Rose asked Curtis at dinner the evening before they left Canton for Cleveland on the Presidential train. There was an atmosphere about the Presidential group quite different from usual. They seemed genuinely worried. "You've got enough security around him, haven't you?"

"Oh yes. Oh, we've got it in hand. We're not really worried, except for this tendency of the Major's to jink away from his escort and chat with voters."

"Well, he's not likely to do that in Buffalo," she comforted. "It's a big state occasion—he's got to stick to protocol."

"That's right." He finished his coffee and rose.

"Well, honey, if you don't mind, I'll get down to the House."

By early evening the next day, the Presidential Special was winding its way between the steel mills and grain elevators of Buffalo's lake-front. At Terrace Station a special welcome had been arranged. A gun crew of the Coast Artillery began a twenty-one gun salute.

The cannon boomed. The glass in the President's train shattered to cascade in upon the travellers. The train stopped with a shuddering jolt. The cannons roared again. More glass.

"Damnation!" shouted George Cortelyou. He ran to the observation platform to signal to the Artillery captain to stop, but the smoke from the explosions hid him from view. Boom! went the guns. The visitors to the train, scared at the splintering and clattering of window glass, began to cry out.

"It's all right," Curtis soothed, although he had no more idea than anyone else what was happening. "It's quite all right."

More glass fell around the train, this time from the offices surrounding the station. The crowd on the platform had retreated in confusion. The band, previously playing Souza, had stopped. Police and military were running about in alarmed bewilderment. Some of the public, cut by flying glass, were keeling over with blood running from wounds.

"Anarchists! They've bombed the train!"

Who raised the cry can never be known. The

crowd, now panicky, turned on a tall man of middle-European complexion standing by the track. Rough hands were laid on him.

Rob Craigallan, brushing splinters from his frock coat, looked out and saw the wave of people grabbing the by-stander. One look at the man's frightened, aghast expression was enough to tell him he was innocent. Rob leaned out of the broken window. "Friends! Friends! Don't do anything rash!"

"An anarchist—!"

"There's been no attack." Boom! went the guns. "Dynamite would have blown the train to smithereens. It's the guns—don't you hear them?"

One more round was fired before the Artillery captain received the order—later he realised he didn't know whence it came and should have ignored it. He ceased fire. The crowd in the station calmed down. The man they had seized turned out to be a draper from Albany. Glass was swept away, the injured were taken up and tended. But rumour ran among the citizens for a long time afterwards, a rumour that the Russian anarchists had made an attempt on the President. Only the newspapers coming on the streets an hour later were able to settle the matter with their amused account of Captain Leonard Wisser's salute.

The passengers on the train brushed themselves down. Mrs. McKinley was given a restorative by the McKinley's private physician, Dr. Rixey.

Trainmaster Charlesworth gave the signal; the train lurched on.

The station for the Pan-American Exposition was Amherst, a short distance down the line. Because of the fears expressed by the Secret Service, a special search was to be allowed on the premises while the President's arrival was in progress.

The station had been specially decorated for the duration of the Exposition. It was painted a rich purple, strung with bunting and electric lights. A huge crowd had gathered. Stephanie Jouvard, waiting to see Gregor step down from the Presidential train and greet him, regretted her decision now. In this throng she'd never get near him. She resigned herself to remaining anonymous for the time being. The President was staying with the Milburns at their mansion on Delaware Avenue but she had ascertained that his entourage were booked in at the Buffalo Grand Hotel. Mr. Craigallan and Gregor were sure to be staying there.

Her attention was caught by a commotion to her left. Someone had attempted to come through the gate in the railing and onto the platform, but a station guard had seized him.

The man twisted under the guard's hand as he raised his club. There was a yell of "Stop him!" as he ran. For one moment Stephanie thought she knew the man. It looked almost like Mr. Nieman, that friend of Emma Goldman. Then the band struck up. All attention turned to the train.

Out stepped the President to raise his hand in

420

greeting at the welcome from the crowd. His wife followed, looking pale and fragile. After inaudible speeches of welcome the couple entered a smart victoria, for a short tour of the sights: the Electric Tower, three hundred and eighty-nine feet high with its gilded statue of the Goddess of Light, the Esplanade, the Court of Fountains, the Temple of Music . . .

The crowd lining the Exposition causeway melted away. Those who had made a welcoming party at the station had already left. Stephanie took the electric train from Amherst to the centre of town, where Main Street blazed with red, white and blue in strings of lights. The Buffalo Grand, host to the officials of the Presidential party, had the American flag draped along its canopy, with a picture of McKinley at centre under the American eagle.

"Mr. Craigallan's suite?" she inquired at the desk, as if it was a certainty there would be one. She was proved right.

"Suite four-two-one."

"Where may I telephone through to it?"

"In the cubicle to the right, ma'am."

She was put through with efficiency by a lady operator. Gregor's voice said, "Suite four-two-one?"

"Greg?"

A pause. "Stephanie?"

"Darling, how wonderful to hear your voice!"

"Where are you speaking from, Stephanie?"

"I'm downstairs in the lobby! Shall I come up, Greg?"

"No!" The last thing he wanted was for his father to meet Stephanie again. Rob had never forgiven Stephanie's part in the near-tragedy of January. There would be an ugly scene if she came to the suite.

"Are you staying in the hotel?" he asked, apprehensive.

"I couldn't get in—it's all booked up with officials and posh people. I'm at the Delaware, opposite City Hall."

"I'll come and see you there," Gregor said.

"Shall I book a table for dinner?"

"Stephanie," he groaned, "have some sense. I've got to go to a banquet given by the city fathers. I might not have a free hour until some time tomorrow afternoon, after the visit to the Exposition buildings."

"Goodness, Gregor, you don't really want to waste time visiting the Exposition tomorrow?"

"Don't you understand, I have to! We're going to follow in the President's path. We're in his party. I'm not here to please myself, Stephanie."

"Come tonight, Greg. After your banquet."

"Can't be done."

"Please, Gregor! It's been so long since I saw you!"

"I can't. I explained in my letter. This is a political and business trip. Mr. Craig expects me to pull my weight. I have to go to this function tonight

422

and stay with the Presidential party tomorrow until after the lunch."

She tried everything she could think of to change his mind—reproaches, coaxing, promises of pleasure. He only said, "I can't. It's not possible."

"Tomorrow evening, then?"

He had an engagement with Mark Hanna and a quartet of businessmen to discuss Cuban investment.

"The day after?"

"That's the President's picnic at Niagara. We have to be there."

It ended with Stephanie begging him to promise to see her later that day, the sixth. Privately she decided to be near him, to go to Niagara too. But aloud she merely said, "Friday evening, Greg?"

"All right," he said, because there was nothing else to say. He put back the receiver. His father called from the bathroom, "Was that anyone important?"

"No, just someone from the Chamber of Commerce verifying tonight." He sighed. "Confound the girl," he thought. "It's got to end. It's like being in shackles."

Next day seemed to justify all Secretary Cortelyou's misgivings about security. President's Day at the Exposition was utter chaos. There were two policemen with a rope barrier to keep the pressure off the pathway the President would take. Other than that, nothing.

No one realised that during the events of that day,

a man with a revolver in his pocket had come face to face with the President. He didn't take the revolver out, he didn't shoot. And the reason?

President McKinley was talking to another man, his host John Milburn. Both were in silk hats, frock coats, and stiff collars. The man with the revolver had no idea which of them was the President. He didn't want to shoot the wrong man. So he turned away.

For the rest of that day William McKinley moved about the Exposition. After dark, the celebrated Mr. Pain put on one of his firework displays, witnessed by the President and his wife from a boat on Park Lake. A huge crowd shared the spectacle with him, then slowly dispersed.

Friday the 6th September was the day of the President's trip to see the Falls. As The Buffalo Commercial expressed it: "Yesterday, the nation's chief executive viewed the masterpiece of the creative genius of the nineteenth century; today he is viewing the triumph of nature's handicraft . . ."

Bidding had been keen among the local dignitaries to be in the Presidential picnic party but the party could only number one hundred and four. To make up for this it had been arranged that there would be a Presidential Reception at four o'clock, in the Temple of Music on the Exposition grounds. This was open to all. You only need queue in line and eventually you would shake the hand of the President of the United States.

Curtis and Ellie-Rose did not go to Niagara but

instead were at the Temple of Music supervising the last decorative details—two potted bay trees, draped flags, tables with palms and other fronds to make a background of greenery to the President's person. The line of citizens was to come in one side and, guided by a baize draped barrier, walk along an aisle, pause to shake hands, and then go out at the other side of the room. Certain dignitaries and officials would flank the President but would stand a little behind him.

Stephanie had gone to Niagara that day to be near Gregor, but had had no chance to reach him. Frustrated and sulky, she went back to Buffalo and the Exposition. She saw the queue forming to shake hands with McKinley, and it struck her as a fine ironic gesture to join it, move up with them into the presence, and thus to see Gregor and his father.

George Cortelyou and his colleagues had insisted that there should be no repetition today of yesterday's chaos. The guard on the President was increased, and the method of filtering people in and out was excellent. But one great change was allowed. So that McKinley could be given the names of citizens by his aide, John Milburn, his Secret Service bodyguard had to give up his place. In a quiet line of well-dressed people filing into the Temple of Music he foresaw no dangers.

The reception began at four o'clock promptly. William McKinley was on the dais, smiling and affable. Organ music filled the room. Ellie-Rose, who hated organ music, shivered a little even in the heat.

"Dr. Clinton Colgrave," whispered Milburn.

"How do you do?" murmured McKinley, shaking hands.

"Justice Alfred Spring," Cortelyou reminded.

"How do you do, Judge," said McKinley.

The first ten or twelve were such minor luminaries. Then came five or six ladies, in their best gowns and hats, new gloves on their hands, new shoes on their aching feet. Stephanie was soon in the Temple. McKinley smiled at her and said, "How do you do, my dear?"

Stephanie gave him a slight curtsey, just to be different, then moved on. But she didn't go out. She took up a place on the edge of the background group, and when Agent Foster was about to edge her away said imperiously, "I'm with the Gracebridges."

"Sorry, ma'am," Foster began. But at that moment he was called away by the entrance of a dark, Italianate man.

Most of the nightmares about anarchists featured Italians. It was known that Italy was one of the hotbeds of revolution, so any Mediterranean type approaching the President without warning caused alarm. However, a brief face-to-face examination by Foster showed this newcomer to be innocuous. He was passed on to greet his President and Stephanie, with a secret smile of triumph, edged round the group and wormed her way to stand next to Gregor.

"Hello," she murmured. "You didn't expect to see me so soon, did you?"

"You're nothing if not inventive," Gregor said, with a shrug. He was longing for this day to end. It had bored him nearly out of his mind so far.

A young, neatly dressed man with a bandaged hand was next in line to shake hands. McKinley, seeing the handkerchief over the hand, paused before making any move, to see if the man would extend the bandaged hand or his left.

The bandage vanished. In its place was a revolver. Flame leapt from it. A barking shot rang out.

The President jerked, fell forward. A second shot sent him backward. A detective sprang forward to break his fall. Milburn and Cortelyou supported him as he was lowered to the floor.

Foster leapt on the gunman. "You bastard!" he snarled, and felled him with a blow.

Everyone else was transfixed. In the stunned silence, the President's voice was heard. "Be careful about my wife," he murmured. "Don't tell her . . ."

"Sir, sir!" gasped Cortelyou.

Foster was pounding the assailant with both fists. Guards had rushed in and were flailing at him with clubs and rifle butts. The panting, snarling sound of their fury filled the salon.

"Go easy on him, boys," said a voice. It was McKinley.

Startled and ashamed, they drew back. The

battered, bloodstained features were visible as the gunman collapsed on his side.

"Oh my God, it's . . . it's Mr. Nieman," exclaimed Stephanie.

The world whirled about her. She began to give at the knees. Gregor put an arm round her and herded her out by the exit she should have taken ten minutes ago. There he let her collapse into a chair, unnoticed in the turmoil that was now rising as the news was passed from mouth to mouth.

"The President's been shot! The President's been shot!"

It took Major William McKinley eight days to die.

22

WHEN Stephanie recovered enough to move on and Gregor supported her out into the fresh air, he found the news was already abroad. Police were clearing a space so that the automobile ambulance from the emergency hospital of the Exposition could come close in to the Temple of Music.

People were crowding in. Because Gregor was taking Stephanie in the opposite direction, everyone disregarded them. By good luck he found a hackney standing on the Causeway.

"Say bud," said the driver as he helped Stephanie in, "what goes on?"

"The President's been hurt," he said.

"Hurt? Had a fall?"

"I couldn't say," Gregor replied, "please drive on. This lady is ill."

At the Delaware Hotel he found a bellboy to help to get her to her room. A chambermaid was summoned. Stephanie was put to bed. She had resisted none of his acts. But when he went in to see her after she had been put between the sheets, she grasped his hand suddenly. "I didn't do it, did I?" she gasped. "I didn't hurt him?"

"No, no, of course not."

"I never meant to hurt him," she said, and began to weep.

Gregor asked for the hotel doctor to come to her. He arrived in about twenty minutes, pince-nez gleaming above a round, pink face. "Yes, yes, dear me, hysteria," he said. "I'll just mix her a bromide."

Gregor stayed until she went to sleep. Then the chambermaid was liberally tipped to sit with her until she went off duty at midnight. "Oh, she'll sleep through the night," the doctor said briskly, "no problem."

But there was a problem. When the gunman's face was disclosed, Stephanie had recognised him. And now she had cried, "I didn't mean to hurt him." What the hell did it mean?

Gregor headed for the Buffalo Grand. It was by then about eight in the evening. The President was in the little hospital at the north-east corner of the Exposition. A dozen doctors had rushed there to offer their services. The President's wife had been informed of the attack and had borne the news without fainting. No statement had as yet been issued by the hospital but it was clear McKinley wasn't dead. The attacker was at Police Headquarters, where a great crowd was milling round threatening to pull him out and lynch him.

Gregor groaned over the report. As he went up in the elevator to his suite his eye skimmed the front page for further details. He was caught by a name. "Our reporter at police headquarters tells us that two facts have been elicited from the man brought here from the scene of the dastardly act. He claims he is an anarchist. His name is Fred Nieman."

Gregor folded the paper convulsively and put it into the trash can by the elevator. When he reached the door of the suite, it stood open. His father sat at a table, speaking into the telephone. The table was spread with late editions of the newspapers.

"Greg," his father called as he was about to cross the sitting-room to his bedroom, "hold on." Into the phone he said, "Just a minute, we can do it." He put down the receiver, came to Gregor's room as he took off his jacket and undid his tie.

"This is a hell of a note, isn't it! Did you see it?"

"I was in the room, just as you were," Gregor said, avoiding a direct answer.

"Yes, but I had my head turned away talking to Parrett! Listen, Greg, can you go out to the Milburns' house and fetch Ellie-Rose here? She went to help break the news to Mrs. McKinley, but she's just telephoned to say she feels pretty much in the way now. Could you grab a hackney cab and fetch her home?"

"Of course." He put on his jacket again.

"I'd go myself, but Mark Hanna's coming in from Cleveland. They say he's pretty cut up. You know how he idolised the Major. They've asked me to meet him off the train."

"What about Curtis?"

"Oh, God, Curtis! He's at the hospital with George Cortelyou, trying to sort out the muddle.

431

He telephoned about an hour ago. Doctors everywhere, reporters in every niche, the public standing in rows on the doorstep—he can't leave. He had a hard enough time getting to a phone. You're the only one available to bring Ellie back. She's exhausted, by the sound of it."

Gregor nodded and went out, retying his tie. On his way through the hotel lobby he passed groups reading the newspapers, talking in angry tones. "I hope they string him up! Protect him? He doesn't deserve it!"

At the gates of the Milburn house his cab was stopped by soldiers posted as guards.

At the door, Ellie-Rose was waiting. That morning she had put on a walking dress of glossy striped cotton trimmed with a long jabot from neck to waist of fine white lace. On her head had been a straw toque piled high with cornflowers to match the blue of the stripes. She had looked like a fashion plate.

Now her hat was gone, who remembered where? The fine lace was stained and drooping. Above it, her face was white and strained.

He got out, under the watchful eye of a private with a rifle, to help her in. She collapsed on the seat, her head almost lolling.

"Oh, Greg," she whispered as the carriage moved away, "it's been so *awful*."

"I'll bet. How is Mrs. McKinley?"

"She's resting on a sofa. They're expecting the President any moment."

"*Here?*"

"Yes, from what we can gather they've removed the bullets and it's a question of nursing now. They couldn't keep him at that little emergency hospital—"

"But a private house? Wouldn't he be better off in a big hospital?"

"That's not *my* decision, thank God." She leaned into the corner of the cab. "My lord, I'm tired. All I want is to get to bed and sleep for a week."

"I believe you."

They drove in silence for a few minutes. Delaware Avenue was now being roped off in preparation for the passage of the ambulance carrying the President. Policemen and soldiers were at points along the sidewalk. Gregor saw them with a sinking heart. Tension was in the air. And Stephanie . . . Stephanie seemed to be somehow involved in what had happened.

As if thinking about her had put her into Ellie-Rose's thoughts, his half-sister murmured, "Didn't I see Stephanie with you at the reception?"

"Yes. She came in with the line, and then stayed."

"She did? What was the point of that?"

"Ellie-Rose, can I talk to you about her? It's serious."

"What about her?" she asked, sitting up straight to look at him.

"Have you seen a paper?"

"No, there hasn't been an opportunity—"

"They've put a name to the gunman. Fred Nieman."

"Nieman?" Ellie-Rose repeated. "Nieman? I've heard that name."

"Ellie, when the guard stepped back and you could see the man on the floor . . . Stephanie said his name."

"She what?"

"She said, 'My God, it's Mr. Nieman.' "

Ellie-Rose closed her eyes and wrinkled her brow. "That's where I heard it. Somebody said . . . Last year, was it? . . . they'd seen a Mr. Nieman at Stephanie's studio."

"That's the man the police are holding, Ellie."

"She . . . she knows the man who shot the President?"

"It was a shock to her. She almost passed out. I got her to her hotel and had her put to bed. But, Ellie . . . She said, 'I didn't mean to hurt him'."

"Hurt him? Who? The President?"

"I don't know. I don't know what she meant. I wish to God I did."

The cab was slowing down in front of the Buffalo Grand Hotel. "What are you going to do?" Ellie-Rose asked as she leaned forward to get out.

He made no reply until he had paid off the cabbie and joined her in the doorway. "Should I do something?" he asked.

"Well, shouldn't you? She recognised the man who shot the President."

"I can't believe she has anything to do with all

this." He glanced around at the groups in the hotel lobby, the queue at the news kiosk.

"You should inform the authorities."

"The police? It would destroy her to have the police cross-questioning her."

"But if she's involved—?"

"I can't believe it, Ellie. She knows the man, yes. But there's no violence in Stephanie."

"I'm too tired to think any more now. Let's sleep on it, shall we?" Ellie-Rose said.

Once Ellie-Rose was in bed, she had expected that exhaustion would send her straight into unconsciousness, but pictures whirled in her mind. The scenes in the Milburn house when Mrs. McKinley heard the news. The wan faces of the Milburn family. The crowd in the Temple of Music's reception salon. Gregor with Stephanie at his elbow. The flash of the gun.

Then, more clearly than she had heard them in the real event, McKinley's words: "Don't be hard on him, boys."

She shivered. The echo of those powerful words could be heard behind them. "Father forgive them . . ."

Could it be so? Had William McKinley, whom she had often belittled, been a great spirit? A true Christian?

Tears, which she had not shed hitherto, welled up in her eyes. She could have called back every unkind word she had ever said of him. It made her own life seem shallow and trivial. She knew she was incapable of a sentiment like that.

Presently she slept, to wake about five in the morning when Curtis came in. She sat up. "How is he?"

"Holding his own," he said, dragging off his frock coat. "God, I'm bushed! We've sent out nearly two hundred telegrams."

"Is the Vice-President coming?"

"On his way. He better behave himself! There's many a man who remembers the things he's said against the Major."

"Is he going to be all right, Curtis?"

"The doctors seem to think so. Things are calming down. Now I'm going to have a bath and a shave, then I have to get down to the Exposition— the police are taking statements from witnesses who saw the attack. Order me some breakfast, will you, honey?"

"Shall I be needed to give a statement? As an eye witness?"

"I don't think so, dear. I'll speak for the two of us."

"Very well." While he bathed she had breakfast brought up, and all the morning papers. Curtis reappeared, looking pale but refreshed. He ate quickly, kissed her, and vanished again. Ellie-Rose rang suite four-two-one.

"Gregor?"

"Is that you, Ellie-Rose?"

"Have you seen the morning papers, Greg?"

The headlines announced: "I Am An Anarchist, States Attacker. Claims Emma Goldman Inspiration." The report below extended the headline; the arrested man had confessed to his crime, had outlined three attempts before his successful attack, and added, "I am a disciple of Emma Goldman. Her words set me on fire."

"I've seen it," Gregor replied in a weary voice.

"We'd better have a talk," she returned. "Can you come down to my room?"

A few minutes later Gregor tapped on her door. She opened to him, gesturing to the breakfast table. "Have you eaten yet?"

"I'm not hungry. I'll have some coffee."

"Did you check yet on Stephanie Jouvard?"

"I rang about six. Apparently she woke half the hotel during the night screaming and crying, so the hotel doctor dosed her with another bromide and she's asleep again."

Ellie-Rose poured coffee, handed it to him, then watched him sip. "We've got to do something. You see in the paper—this madman says he was inspired by Emma Goldman. And, Gregor, Stephanie is a friend of Emma Goldman's."

"It doesn't necessarily mean anything, Ellie. She may just—"

"Look," Ellie-Rose broke in. "I'm not saying Stephanie had anything to do with the attempted assassination. But I do say she's a sympathiser with these wrong-headed people—"

"Guilt by association. Is that it?"

She hesitated. "I don't say she's guilty. But I think she may have helped bring this about by her support—"

"She doesn't support murder, Ellie-Rose. No one is less likely to help in a plot to harm people."

"How can you possibly know? You met her around Christmas and parted from her a month later—"

"That's not so, Ellie. She lived with me in Boston from mid-June until the end of July."

"*What?*"

"I know her as well as anybody can, I think." He sighed. "If you want my honest opinion, I think she's a self-centred, insecure, nervy character. If she has been friendly with anarchists, she's the *least* likely they'd choose to impart any secrets to. She's too unreliable."

"Greg, what were you thinking of, to pick up with her again?" Ellie-Rose cried in rebuke.

"It wasn't so much that *I* picked up with *her*." He gave a wry smile. "She turned up on my doorstep. I couldn't get rid of her. I made one or two attempts but she—well, she's like the Old Man of the Sea. She doesn't shake off very easily."

His half-sister remembered the look of dazed enchantment she'd witnessed on Stephanie's face the first time she had seen Gregor. At that moment Ellie-Rose had guessed it was serious. How serious, she couldn't possibly have imagined.

"Well, you only have to read the newspapers to realise the police are on the track of Goldman and all her friends. Anyone who's been connected with her is going to be put under the microscope."

"If they grill Stephanie, she'll confess to anything they suggest. She's in a state of shock. I thought . . . when I heard the doctor on the line this morning . . . Perhaps I ought to get her back to Dr. Zeichman's clinic."

"You mean, hide her there?"

He gave a little laugh. "You're no fool, Ellie. No, not quite. If they get her name from anywhere and track her down, it would be up to Dr. Zeichman to say whether or not she's fit to undergo interrogation."

"I see."

"I can't move her without your agreement. If you feel you must go to the police, then to have moved Stephanie would look like an admission that she's somehow involved." He tilted his head, trying out the sound of the words. "Fleeing the scene of the crime."

"I don't know, Gregor . . ." She got up from the table and paced to the window. The sun was shining down on Main Street but with less harshness than the last few days. Outside it was cooler, with little clouds gathering.

"I'd have to see her for myself," she said at last over her shoulder. "She might be pulling the wool over your eyes."

"Easier to hoodwink a man than a woman? All right. Meet me in the lobby at ten-fifteen and we'll go together."

439

Ellie-Rose put on a thick braided cotton costume with the new high *gigot* sleeves and a matching hat of brown straw. She had a feeling that she was donning semi-mourning—one couldn't wear bright plumage while the President was so ill.

Downstairs she spied Gregor's tall figure in a suit with a short jacket and a smart bowler. As he offered her his arm she was aware of admiring glances from both sexes.

At the Delaware Hotel, which was within walking distance, Dr. Crumwin was awaiting them. Gregor had telephoned ahead. The doctor hurried forward, looking relieved at seeing a woman participant in this crisis. "The management is becoming very concerned," he remarked as he took them up in the elevator. "Miss Jouvard is being something of a trouble to them. Unaccompanied young ladies are not easy to handle."

"How does she seem?" Ellie-Rose inquired, with some hauteur. She was vexed that the doctor seemed more concerned about the hotel than his patient.

"Oh, she's quiet at the moment. But last night! She seemed to be having a nightmare. She ran out in the corridor in her night attire. Quite unseemly!" He led the way along the corridor, to tap on a door. A uniformed chambermaid opened to them. "How is she, Lilian?"

"Just waking up, sir."

Consciousness came back into Stephanie's eyes. "Oh!" she cried. "I remember! At the reception—!"

440

She flung up her hands as if to ward off a blow. "Oh, no! I didn't want that!"

"Now, Stephanie, don't upset yourself—"

"Don't! Don't!" she shrank down among the bedcovers. Then as if a film had spread over her features, they went calm. "Nothing to do with me," she muttered, and stared unseeing at the ceiling.

The doctor shook his head. "Tut-tut," he said. "Her nerves are in a very bad state."

"Could we have a few words?" Gregor said, and taking him by the elbow, led him to the window. "The fact is, Miss Jouvard was undergoing treatment at a clinic for nervous disorders. Would it be your view that she ought to return there?"

"She should go home, that's my opinion."

"Is she fit to travel?"

"We-ell . . ." Gregor watched him. He was torn between his duty as a physician and as a hotel employee. "If she had a nurse with her . . . ?"

"Perhaps you could arrange for one? Or, better still—if Mrs. Gracebridge and I were to accompany her?"

"Oh, that would be best. If she were with people she knew."

"Let me talk it over with Mrs. Gracebridge." He took Ellie-Rose aside and put the project to her. "I know it's a lot to ask, Ellie, but it's better not to have a stranger brought in. Who knows what she may come out with?"

Ellie-Rose thought it over quickly. "All right," she said, "I'll help you. The way things are, Curtis

441

is so busy I shouldn't see anything of him for the next day or two. I'll leave him a note saying I've gone to Craigallan Castle so as to leave him free for action here."

"I'll find out about trains and see if I can book a compartment on the Pullman. I'd better telephone Zeichman first, to make sure he'll take her."

"In the meantime I'll pack her things. You'll settle the hotel bill?"

"Of course. When do you think we can leave?"

"Say in a couple of hours? If there's a train, we can be on it in time for lunch on board."

Dr. Zeichman was expecting them at the clinic. As Stephanie stepped down he took her hand to say gently, "My dear, I told you you ought not to leave me."

She gave herself unresisting into his care. He took her up to her room then returned to hear the background from Gregor. "Ah," he murmured, "I knew she was interested in these political theories, but she has talked more of personal difficulties to me."

"From what you said, in greeting," Ellie-Rose ventured, "it sounded as if you didn't think she was one hundred per cent cured when she left?"

"None of us are a hundred per cent, Mrs. Gracebridge."

She smiled in reply. "Perhaps not. What I meant was, why did you let her go if you felt she wasn't cured?"

"How could I prevent her? This is not a prison. She had talked her problems through with me and assured me she had come to terms with her difficulties. I wasn't so sure, but what could I do if she wished to withdraw from analysis?"

"She seems very . . . overcome," Ellie-Rose said. "I admit I am worried in case she really has some responsibility for what happened to Mr. McKinley."

Zeichman shook his head. "Not at all."

"You think not?"

"I am certain of it."

"Then why was she in particular so affected? I mean, we were all shocked, doctor."

Zeichman's quiet explanation of how he saw Stephanie's illness left Ellie-Rose thoughtful and Gregor sceptical.

"Hysteria can cause the most extraordinary confusion in the mind of the patient," Zeichman concluded. "The fact that she was not connected to the President's death, that she has done nothing wrong in the physical world is not important. In the mental world, she feels guilty. To avoid her guilt she goes into hysteria or depression."

"And you can help her?" Ellie-Rose asked.

"I can do my best."

Gregor wrote that evening to Stephanie's parents, explaining that he happened to be in Buffalo when she was taken ill and had therefore brought her to Dr. Zeichman's clinic where she had received previous treatment. They replied immediately thanking him for his Christian act. "Stephanie suffers from delicate nerves, it appears," Mr.

443

Jouvard wrote. "We feel that this recurring illness means she is not really suited to living alone. In November the family is removing to Quebec, where we have relatives and where we intend to retire. If ever you are in that part of the world, we would be honoured by a visit."

Gregor smiled over the letter, which had been sent on to Harvard by Ellie-Rose from its first stop at Craigallan Castle. He had not the slightest intention of ever going near Quebec or any other place where Stephanie might be living. It was time for both of them to be free of one another.

23

ELLIE-ROSE found her mother in residence at Craigallan Castle, avid to hear all the news from Buffalo. "You mean you were actually in the room when the shots were fired?" cried Luisa. "My dear, how thrilling! I mean, how shocking too, but after all—to be present at a moment like that!"

Ellie-Rose found her hunger for gore very repellent. She murmured that she had seen and heard very little. She couldn't bring herself to discuss with her mother the words she had heard, "Go easy on him, boys." She knew Luisa's reaction would be either, "Good gracious, what a silly thing to say! When the man had half-killed him!" Or "How noble and Christian! Oh, how suitable for the leader of this great country!"

The fact that they had been real words, uttered by a pain-racked man after a confrontation that might have meant instant death, would not occur to Luisa. She saw them as something written by a dramatist for the great stage of world events. But for Ellie-Rose they were real, and they didn't lose their effect even as the days passed.

On Wednesday, Curtis asked Ellie-Rose to return to Buffalo.

He wasn't in the hotel when she got there. A note was propped on the writing bureau. "The doctors

445

are worried in some way. I have a feeling you may be needed at the Milburn house. I'll telephone you if it becomes urgent, so stay around the hotel."

That could only mean that the President's life was in danger. After four or five days of reassurance, so totally believed that even the close friends and advisers had left Buffalo to go about their own concerns, the patient had taken a turn for the worse.

Curtis came back to the hotel that evening. He looked worn out with fatigue. "There's some talk of the wound being infected deep inside," he said. "I don't understand the jargon. Mrs. McKinley was in tears when she came out of the sickroom this afternoon. Ellie-Rose, I believe they're preparing her for the news he isn't going to make it."

"You can't mean it—"

"It looks that way."

"But all those famous doctors?"

"It's to do with the attempts to get the second bullet out. The first one was easy, it practically fell out. The second went deep into his body, I think into the wall of the stomach. And the Major's gone to fat a lot recently—they just dared not probe in there."

"Curtis, if he dies . . . That man will be a murderer."

"That's why they haven't charged him yet. The police are waiting to know whether the charge should be assault or murder."

The following day he rang from the Milburn

446

house to ask her to come as soon as she could. The ladies of the household were now very distressed and exhausted. The First Lady needed constant companionship of a kind that only those who knew her could provide.

On Friday the 13th, a great storm broke over Buffalo. A constant stream of visitors hurried to the Milburn mansion on Delaware Avenue, summoned back by urgent telegrams to all corners of the country. The Vice-President could not be reached; he had gone on a climbing expedition in a remote area near Lake Champlain. The President's relations were grouped in the sickroom, his wife sat by his bedside for an hour but was then led away by gentle hands when he appeared to sleep.

"Tell her," Dr. Mynter whispered to Ellie-Rose, "that the President will not awaken in this life."

But it was some hours before he left this world. The bulletin was issued at half-past two in the morning of the 14th. The President had ceased to breathe at fifteen minutes past two.

The world seemed hushed around the Presidential party. Yet almost at once preparations had to begin, for the funeral, for the handing over of office to the Vice-President, for the removal of the personal belongings of McKinley from the White House. There was a funeral procession of sombre dignity to show the grief of Buffalo, then the coffin was put aboard a special train for Washington. Ellie-Rose had expected to go on it, to accompany Mrs. McKinley, but by this time the widow was so bowed down with grief that comradeship was useless; she sat huddled in the train with her niece and her maid for attendance, knowing nothing of her whereabouts.

Ellie-Rose returned to the Buffalo Grand after watching the train steam out. She took off her black hat and gloves, called the floor waiter for a tray of coffee. It was still only a little past nine in the morning. Curtis had gone back to the Milburns to help clear up the mass of paperwork that had piled up there during the President's illness.

She was finishing her first cup of coffee and wondering whether to ring through to her father's suite when the telephone sounded. It was the desk. "Mrs. Gracebridge, there is a gentleman here, a Mr. Kendall, asking to see you."

"Kendall? Do I know him?"

"No, Mrs. Gracebridge. He is from the office of the Erie County Bar Association."

"The Bar Association?" She was puzzled. "He wishes to see my husband, I believe."

There was a pause, as if the receiver was being handed over. Then a deep, slow voice said: "Mrs. Gracebridge? Thaddeus Kendall here. Mrs. Gracebridge, I came hoping to speak with both you and your husband but the clerk tells me Mr. Gracebridge is not in the hotel."

"That is so."

"Might I ask you to spare me a few minutes of your time? It's important."

"But on what matter, Mr. Kendall? I don't think

either my husband or I expected to be contacted by the Bar Association.''

"If I could come up to your suite—"

"That would hardly be suitable."

"Then could you spare me a few minutes in the lounge? I promise not to keep you. I know you're probably very busy."

"What is it about, Mr. Kendall?"

"I'll explain when I see you. Ten minutes time? I'll be at the desk." The phone was put down before she could say that she didn't feel in the mood for encounters with strange lawyers. Irritated that good manners would now force her to go to see him, she put on her hat again, picked up her gloves and purse, and went down to the lobby.

A tall, rather thin man was standing by the desk. As the elevator gate opened he came towards her at once. "Mrs. Gracebridge," he said, taking off his black homburg.

"You already know me, sir?"

"I've seen your picture in the papers, going in and out of the Milburn house."

"I see. What can this be about, Mr. Kendall?"

"May we go into the lounge and find a quiet corner? I won't detain you if you are occupied."

He already had his hand under her elbow, urging her towards the palm-decked lounge of the hotel. It was relatively empty at this hour of the morning, with only a few businessmen leafing through the papers prior to going out on moneymaking matters. He led her to a nook by a window, through which the sable drapings on the buildings could be seen.

She sat in one of the big armchairs. He perched on the arm of another opposite her. He had something of the air of a long-legged secretary-bird in his black suit.

"I'll come straight to the point," he said. "The President's attacker, Fred Nieman, alias Leon Czolgosz, has been arraigned and will come to trial presently. Since he has no legal representative, the judge has asked the Erie Bar to appoint two attorneys."

"But how can this concern me, Mr. Kendall?"

"Only indirectly, of course. You were present in the salon when the attack took place?"

"Yes, I was."

"I have undertaken the task of questioning as many eye witnesses as possible, on behalf of the defence—"

"Defence? What defence can there possibly be?" she broke in. "The man shot the President. Scores of people saw him do it."

"Nevertheless, when he comes to trial he must have a defence—"

"How can that be? He has confessed—the newspapers quoted his very words! He *must* plead guilty."

"That plea is impermissible in New York State, ma'am," Kendall replied. His wide thin mouth quirked in apologetic amusement. "It may seem a paradox, when a man wants to throw away his life, that the state insists he defend it."

"Is that really true?"

"Yes, it is. That being so, I have been ordered by the Bar Association to furnish what facts I can to the two learned judges—"

"They seem very high-powered men for this short task—"

"High-powered, ma'am?" He hesitated. "They are of course very respected men. But it's many years since either of them examined a witness or addressed the bench. They have been retired for some time now, after long and distinguished careers. To my mind it would have been better to give the work to a younger pair—"

"You would have liked to be one of them yourself?" she put in with angry rebuke. "What are you after? Notoriety?"

"No, ma'am. Justice."

The quiet word dropped into the divide of indignation she had opened up between them. She sat silent for a moment. Then she said, "Naturally, I want justice too. But the man is guilty. I was there, don't forget. I saw him fire the shots."

"Exactly. Can you tell me, Mrs. Gracebridge, what was his appearance at the time? Did he seem calm, determined? Or excited? Out of control?"

"Ah, I see! You want to say he did it as the result of some brainstorm, is that it? But the newspapers say he is part of a great anarchist plot—"

He was shaking his head. "Not so, Mrs. Gracebridge. There may be a plot—God knows there does seem design in the deaths or the attempts against

451

the lives of European heads of state. But so far as Czolgosz is concerned, he's a loner. Not a word in his confession speaks of conspiracy.''

"What else would you expect, sir? Isn't it part of their dogma that they should give no aid to the authorities, hold their silence under questioning, and take their chance to make a speech about the wrongs of the system when sentenced? Everyone expects Czolgosz to do that.''

"Then I think they'll be disappointed, ma'am. So far as I can tell, Leon Czolgosz is a poor sick young man who has drifted more and more into a fantasy world in the last couple of years.''

"You've talked to him?"

"No, that isn't permitted. But I've been allowed to speak to the detectives guarding him.''

"I can hardly believe they speak well of him!"

"Quite so," Thaddeus Kendall agreed with a faint smile. "Yet even they cannot report that he is a ranting revolutionary, or a 'hard' assassin. From what I can hear, he is a not very intelligent, shy, dreamy man.''

"But not insane," Ellie-Rose pointed out.

"Who is to say what is sane and what is not? What kind of man steps up to an elderly gentleman he doesn't know and, instead of shaking the hand held out to him, shoots him in the stomach?"

"A dangerous man, Mr. Kendall. One best taken out of society.''

"That could be done without sending him to the

electric chair, ma'am. If he was judged insane, he could be put in an asylum."

"And that is what you're trying to achieve?" she asked. "By going about, speaking to those who saw the crime?"

"There's no other method of getting up a defence, as far as I can see."

"You're wasting your time, Mr. Kendall."

He sighed. "That's how it looks. Most people have me thrown out when I explain the purpose of my visit. I thank you for bearing with me this far."

"This far and no further," she said, shaking her head at him. "I've no wish to help save Czolgosz from the death sentence."

Thaddeus Kendall studied her. He saw a pale, tired face under the black hat of mourning, but the eyes were clear and alive, the red lips were responsive. She hadn't closed herself up in an armour of steely revenge against the murderer. There might be hope of some help from her.

"Mrs. Gracebridge," he ventured, "you were in the salon at the time. Weren't there some words uttered by the President?"

He saw that she flinched visibly. Like others, she had been deeply affected by McKinley's attempt to stop the blows raining on his assailant.

"I don't ask you to equal that," he went on, in a low, quiet tone, "for to 'go easy on him' is not what the law requires. But if the man is mad, he has the right to be tried under that section of our law. His life wouldn't be forfeit."

"But is it a life worth saving?" Ellie-Rose cried, clenching her fists in revulsion.

Thaddeus leaned forward and took one of her gloved hands in his. "Who can say?" he inquired. "I'm not a religious man myself, Mrs. Gracebridge. But I've read of lives that seem utterly derelict, changing and becoming of value. Who knows what Leon Czolgosz might become if he were allowed the time to regain his mental balance and work for the good of society?"

She sat for a long moment, looking into his thin, earnest features and feeling the pressure of his hand on hers through her glove. Then she withdrew from him.

"I will tell you what I can," she said, very calm and exact. "The man came in at the front of the line. He had a handkerchief over his right hand, as if he had bandaged it after a cut. The President waited to see whether he would hold out that hand or his left. The hand with the bandage moved to point straight at the Major, there was an explosion and the handkerchief fluttered to the floor with smoke billowing through it."

"You were looking at the handkerchief then? Not the man?"

"They were part and parcel of the same tableau. It was like a series of photographs such as one sees in a stereopticon. The handkerchief fluttered to the floor. The gun barked again. The President fell back."

"And Czolgosz?"

"He was knocked to the ground by the guards."

"There was a violent struggle?"

Ellie-Rose shook her head. "Not that I recall. Certainly it was a violent scene, but there was no *struggle*. Czolgosz simply lay there, huddled under the blows." She met Thaddeus's eyes squarely. "That was why the President called out," she said. "To stop the men killing him while he lay there unresisting."

"Did he get to his feet? Did he attempt to escape?"

"No, he was still lying there when we were shepherded out of the room. I didn't see his face at that time. It was turned away from me."

"But when he first came in—you saw his face then?"

"Yes."

"Was it contorted? Enraged? What?"

"Neither of those." She thought about it. "He was entirely unremarkable. A youngish man with untidy fair hair. He might have been a clerk or a storekeeper. There was nothing about him to catch the attention until the gun exploded."

"I see. Thank you."

"I'm afraid it's no help to you, Mr. Kendall," she said, rising.

"I'm afraid not. But I'll add it to my notes and present them to the judges, Lewis and Titus." He sighed as he too rose to escort her to the lobby.

She gave him a half smile. "From your manner I

455

gather you think Mr. Lewis and Mr. Titus will do little good."

"Between you and me, ma'am, they don't want the job at all. I don't blame 'em. It's a thankless task. But the United States owes it to its own traditions to put up the best defence it can, even for a man like Czolgosz."

"You may be right," Ellie-Rose said, with a little shake of the head. "But with ideals like that, you must find life hard as a lawyer. Are you in business on your own?"

"No, ma'am, I'm part of the firm of Howham, Granning, Bower and Bard. A junior partner."

"Here in Buffalo?"

"No, my firm's office is in New York City. But the Erie Bar Association asked me to come to Buffalo on this matter."

"Why you, particulary? I understand they might want an outside opinion, but why you?"

"As you just said, with ideals like that . . . I'm somewhat known for espousing lost causes. Well, Mrs. Gracebridge, I sure thank you for your patience with me. Perhaps we'll meet again some time, in happier circumstances."

"Perhaps we will," she agreed.

It hardly seemed likely. Events moved on with their own inexorable force. She and her husband returned to Washington next day, from which city they followed the trial of Leon Czolgosz through the newspaper reports. It wasn't a lengthy affair. It began on September 23rd and ended next day with a unanimous verdict of guilty after the jury had retired for only half an hour. So far as Ellie-Rose could tell from the printed account, no use at all had been made of any evidence gathered by Thaddeus Kendall. Two days later sentence was pronounced. It was at this point the public expected the tirade about anarchist principles. None came. Leon Czolgosz, asked if there was anything he wished to say, spoke a few broken sentences.

"My family, they had nothing to do with it. I want to say I was alone and had no one else. No one else but me."

White-haired George Titus prompted him to continue.

"I never told nothing to nobody. I never thought of that."

His delivery was so inaudible that Titus had to repeat everything he said. The mumbled phrases fell far short of the dramatic speech the press had been waiting for.

Reading the report, Ellie-Rose heard in her mind the description of the murderer from Thaddeus Kendall: "a not very intelligent, shy, dreamy man." How utterly absurd that this nonentity should have ended the life of the Chief Executive of the United States!

Her mind was set at rest over Stephanie's part in a supposed plot. She could understand why Stephanie had helped Czolgosz. He was the kind of shy, ineffectual type who would appeal to the protective instinct in a woman. As she recalled,

Stephanie had given him money and urged him to buy an overcoat. That was probably the limit of her association with the man. Once and for all she dismissed from her thoughts the idea that Stephanie had done anything wrong in regard to the death of McKinley.

With the onset of the fall, Washington carefully resumed its usual activities. The new President had been installed—President Theodore Roosevelt. Life changed at the White House. Instead of a lethargic elderly man with an ailing wife there was a vigorous forty-two year old athlete. He had retained McKinley's cabinet members but there was a fresh breeze beginning to blow.

"He's got a lot of snap in him," Curtis admitted, pulling at his new moustache. It was a pseudo-Roosevelt moustache. "He's got the goodwill of the nation but has to keep it. Teddy understands that. He's a showman."

"Curtis, I have to set out for New York in a day or two. Now that we're in official mourning, my plans for Papa's entertaining will have to be revised," Ellie-Rose said. "I thought I'd set off on Thursday. Is that all right with you?"

"Sure. When do you want to have me at the Castle?"

"Can you make it on Saturday for the weekend?"

"No, I'm too busy. I don't think I can make it until the following Thursday."

"All right, dear. I'll tell Papa."

Rob was glad to see her when she stepped down

from the new Duryea horseless carriage which had been sent to meet her train. He hugged her heartily. "How did you like the ride?" he asked.

"It was fun, Papa. But everyone stared at us!"

"Let 'em stare! In ten years time there will be more gasoline cars than horses on the streets of New York."

"Oh, come, Papa!" She tucked her arm through his and walked with him indoors, while the maids and footmen collected up her children, and her luggage. "Well, what's the plan for today?"

"We'll have an early dinner and settle down with these guest lists, shall we? If we're not going to give a grand ball or even a dance, we've a lot of people to entertain quietly between now and Christmas."

"The mourning's made a big difference to entertaining. In Washington quite a lot of people have used restaurants, so as to avoid showing their houses lit and decked for company."

"I'll take some of the fellows to the Waldorf, of course. But I should like to have as many here as we can. Quiet dinner parties are okay, I gather, and genteel amusements such as pianists and contraltos."

"Papa," she laughed. "Don't make fun. It was a terrible tragedy."

"Going dull and insipid isn't going to make it less," he retorted. Then added, in her ear, "Now we've got Teddy, who's to say it was such a tragedy?"

She shook her head at him.

After dinner they settled in his study to re-organise all the plans for pre-Christmas parties. It was necessary to keep the old die-hards of the Republican party feeling that they still wielded power, yet already Ellie-Rose could sense a difference in her father's guest list.

"We want a few young men with some ideas outside close-dealing and Tammany Hall," he murmured. "Quay and Pratt are losing their influence."

"If you say so, Papa. Whom shall I invite instead?"

"We'll have Lusinski, Gower, and Mrs. Dorf."

"Mrs. Dorf?" She was a well-known worker for the betterment of the garment industry on the East Side. "She's a trade union organiser, isn't she?"

"Don't sound so shocked. She's human. A bit of a bore, but it's a good idea to know what she's up to."

"Who else?"

They wrestled with it for a time, then Rob threw down his pencil. "Look, my pet, I leave it to you. Those are the main guests. Just fill up the spaces with the requisite number of bodies, eh? But let's try to keep them on the fair side of fifty years, and with some ideas in their heads. If we're going to have to deal with Teddy for the next few years, we'll need to know as much as he does about the country's new organisations."

They put the list away and went to bed. Next morning, sitting in her boudoir leafing through her address book for possible New York guests, she saw

460

noted down a name that caught her attention with a jolt.

A tall, black clad, long-legged figure came into her memory, two hazel eyes in a thin face.

She ran her fore-finger along the line. "Thaddeus Kendall of Howham, Granning, Bower and Bard." No office address. She shrugged and turned the page. She listed a few other names, studied them.

She couldn't invite Thaddeus Kendall. She didn't have his office address. She added more names to her dinner list, crossed some out, inserted others.

Why should she invite Thaddeus Kendall? She'd only met him once, when they had been quite at cross purposes.

By and by she rang the bell. When Soames appeared she said: "Bring me the New York Directory, will you, Soames?"

461

24

GERTRUDE DORF, fat, forty and formidable, surged across the drawing-room to greet him as he came through the Tiffany glass doors. "Tad Kendall! What are you doing here? I didn't know you were a friend of the high-toned Craigallans?"

"I could say the same of you," he said, shaking hands with cordiality. "What are you doing in this den of capitalism?"

"Ah . . . well . . . I ran a campaign at spring's end, to get funds for a holiday home for my girls." Gertie Dorf's girls were the garment-workers. "I was kind of surprised to get a big cheque from Mr. Craigallan."

"Conscience money?" Tad suggested.

"Well, so long as his conscience directs it at me, I'm not going to question it."

Tad expected to be seated next to Gertrude Dorf, and so it proved.

"There's been enough spent on this meal to keep a worker's family in food for a month," Gertie grumbled to him.

"To say nothing of all the food we didn't eat."

"What happens to the left-overs, do you reckon?"

"I suppose it goes to the servants' hall."

"How would it be if I asked our host to let me

have it for distribution among my girls?"

Tad laughed. "Don't do it, Gertie. Servants too are workers—they wouldn't like it if you took the *sole bonne femme* from their mouths."

"That's true. Say, Tad, can you catch me a few more of those little sugar things? I never had them before."

"Candied rose leaves, I think," he said, and went in search of the silver dish in which they'd been offered.

As he found it on a side-table, Ellie-Rose came to him. "Can I help you, Mr. Kendall? Are you looking for a cigar?"

"No, for these." He held up the dish. "Gertie has a sweet tooth."

Ellie-Rose beckoned a maid and sent her with the dish. With a touch of her hand she detained Tad. "I read the reports of the Czolgosz trial with attention," she said. "I didn't see any mention of your work."

"None of it was used."

"It was generally accepted that the man was sane."

He nodded. "It depends what you mean by sane, of course. But it's too late now to argue over it."

"You speak with less regret than I expected?"

"I see no point in regretting what can't be remedied. Czolgosz is dead." To change the subject, which was still painful to him if truth were told, he said, "I didn't have the pleasure of meeting

463

your husband in Buffalo, and I believe he isn't here tonight either?"

"He joins us in a day or two. Duties keep him in Washington."

"I was surprised and flattered you remembered me enough to invite me, Mrs. Gracebridge."

"Oh, I remembered you." They looked at each other for a moment. She went on rather quickly, "You already knew some of the other guests?"

"Oh, yes, Gertie, of course, and Cyrus Morpurgo, and the Reverend Chitty. I defended a parishioner of Mr. Chitty's last year on a charge of breaking and entering."

"Did you win?"

"Of course. Otherwise I shouldn't have mentioned it to you."

They laughed and Ellie-Rose moved on to see to her other guests. But when the entertainment was about to begin, she made sure she took a seat on one of the sofas alongside Tad Kendall.

The diversion was a recitation by an actor from the cast of *The Moth and the Flame*. Ellie-Rose, uncertain what to provide, had left the choice of words to him, so Francis Wilson treated them to the poems of Longfellow and then some patriotic lines about the war, still continuing in the Philippines. The last poem ended:

> Though we die on foreign soil, lads,
> Never let our courage lag;
> **Ever strike in freedom's name, lads,**

For our country and our flag.

It was sentimental rubbish, but Wilson brought it forth with so much emotion and conviction that Ellie-Rose's eyes filled with tears as she remembered Cornelius. When the reciter had taken his bow and been escorted away by Soames, Ellie-Rose found herself being observed by the penetrating hazel eye of Tad Kendall.

"You found that affecting?" he asked.

"You must think me a fool! It's so jingoistic . . . But I have a brother out in the Philippines."

"Is that so? I had no idea of it. He's not in one of the dangerous theatres of war, I hope?"

"I don't really know . . ."

He looked puzzled. "You don't hear from him?"

She wished him at the other end of the earth, although until this moment she'd wanted to get to know him better. "We . . . er . . . there was a family disagreement," she mumbled, colouring at her admission.

"I'm sorry. I didn't mean to intrude."

"It's not your fault. It was I who mentioned Cornelius." Suddenly she wanted to talk about it to someone who wasn't a member of the family, with family attitudes already entrenched. "He packed up and left without letting us know he was going to do it," she said. "He only wrote afterwards—when he was at San Francisco waiting to sail. Since then, nothing."

"Have you written to him?"

465

She shook her head. "It's not considered right that we should be in touch."

"Who, may I ask, dictates what is right or wrong for you?"

Her colour deepened even more. She had no idea how it changed her appearance to Tad—from an assured, elegant woman to a confused girl.

"You don't understand. It would take a long time to explain the situation. But there is a good reason why both my father and my husband are very angry with Cornelius and don't want me to contact him."

"It doesn't appear to be a very good reason to *you*," he remarked. "If it makes you unhappy, why do you let yourself be bound by it?"

Gertie Dorf ploughed up to them at that moment. "Well, so there you are, Tad! I think it's about that time, for me. I came to say goodnight, Mrs. Gracebridge, and thank you for a very pleasant evening."

"I hope you've enjoyed it," Ellie-Rose said with hostess politeness and not unwilling to have her conversation with Tad interrupted.

"Sure did. I love that Longfellow. 'Thou too, O Ship of State. Sail on, O Union Strong and Great . . .' "

"You liked the patriotic verses?" Ellie-Rose asked in surprise.

"Why not? Second generation American, like you, Mrs. Gracebridge." But Mrs. Dorf's broad smile took the sting out of this barb. "Say, could I get you to buy tickets for a concert? In aid of my convalescent home."

"Why not?" agreed Ellie-Rose. Then to Tad, "Perhaps your wife would like to be enlisted, Mr. Kendall."

"I'm not married, Mrs. Gracebridge."

"Say, would you like to come down my end of town? See how the other half lives?" Gertie surged on.

"Hold on now, Gertie, your crusading zeal's carrying you away. Mrs. Gracebridge—"

"Ellie-Rose," Gertie said. "Her name's Ellie-Rose. Let's not be stuffy."

"Ellie-Rose may not want to get tangled in your trade union work."

"I'd like to," Ellie-Rose said, "I really would, Gertie. But my husband will be here in a day or two, and I'll be tied up. Could it be soon?"

"Day after tomorrow?"

"No, I've an engagement for that evening, I'm afraid."

"What about during the day?" Tad put in. "Are you free Thursday for lunch? I could offer you a decent meal at my club."

"Are ladies allowed in?" Ellie-Rose inquired, with recollections of some hide-bound institutions her father belonged to.

"On Thursdays, yes. Whether they'll let Gertie in is another matter."

Other guests were now beginning to take their departure, so she quickly made a note of Tad's club and the time of the lunch. Afterwards, when the servants were clearing up, her father said to her:

"You enjoyed yourself more than you expected to, didn't you!"

"It was pleasant enough, Papa."

"Saw you having a good giggle with Gertie Dorf. She's a great old gal, isn't she?"

"Mr. Kendall is nice too. Did you talk to him?"

"Yes, quite a long chat. He's bright."

"Perhaps you could put some work his way, Papa?"

"How's that again?"

"I thought you had things he might do—"

"He's a criminal lawyer, Ellie! I've no need of a criminal lawyer."

"Of course. So he is." She was amazed at her own muddle-headedness. She was also a little disappointed to find she could do nothing to further Tad's career. The disappointment, when she came to examine it, troubled her.

She was too interested in Tad Kendall. She decided she would tell Soames to ring his office next day and cancel the engagement to lunch with him.

But then she told herself as she sat at breakfast in her boudoir that it would be unfair to do so. She'd promised Gertie Dorf she would come. Tad was different from the other men she met—not self-seeking, not politically ambitious. Money and position seemed to have no meaning for him. He moved easily between the under-privileged of New York's East Side and the conservative legal society of the law firms without embarrassment.

468

She saw him twice more before she left for Washington with Curtis. On the second occasion Mrs. Dorf, who had acted the part of unconscious chaperone, excused herself on the grounds that she had a negotiation to attend. For another fifteen minutes Ellie-Rose and Tad continued to discuss the proposed concert, but then the conversation was turned by a question from him.

"Did you ever do anything about that problem? Over your brother?"

"No."

He gave a little shrug.

"You think I'm a coward for doing nothing."

"Wouldn't it be nice to write to him for Christmas?"

"But . . . if he replies . . ."

"You'd want him to reply, surely."

"If my husband saw the letter, he'd be furious."

"I see. I'm sorry, I shouldn't interfere."

She found herself telling him the whole story of the dreadful events of January. He heard her out almost in silence, then sighed. "Poor devil," he said.

"But you do see why my menfolk are strongly against making any move towards him."

"I can understand their being angry with him. But anger's a wasteful emotion, Ellie-Rose. And I never knew anything good come out of unforgiving."

"But I'm not angry with Neil. I never was. And if

there was anything to forgive on my part, I've forgiven."

"Then why don't you write and tell him so?"

She sat without speaking, then smiled slowly. "You're always on the side of the underdog."

"Once again, forgive me. It's not my affair. It just occurred to me that probably everybody else in Manila will be having mail this Christmas—except your brother Cornelius."

That stayed with her. After she got back to Washington she thought about it, then wrote to Cornelius, asking him to reply, assuring him that she felt no ill-will towards him, begging him to take care of himself. It was too late now for the letter to reach him for Christmas, because she had hesitated a long time with the echo of Tad's words haunting her. But she hoped it would cheer Cornelius's New Year.

The Christmas visit this year was to Nebraska. It seemed long and tedious. Now that she had to listen once more to Curtis with his local supporters talking smalltown politics, she was irritated. Curtis had never been idealistic, had always been a career politician, but now it seemed so blatant. Had it always been so, and she simply hadn't noticed it until Tad Kendall's way of life opened her eyes to it?

She returned to New York for the charity concert organised by Gertie Dorf. Gertie greeted her warmly, led her to a seat of honour. Several of the artistes appearing were doing so as a favour to Ellie-

Rose. The success of the event was assured through her efforts, and the money from tickets was substantial.

When the applause had died away, Gertie insisted on offering a little celebration in a restaurant near the concert hall. The place was inexpensive but pleasant; there was a little orchestra of Hungarians, with a romantic violinist. Taking it into his head that Ellie-Rose and Tad were husband and wife, the violinist came to their side and played a sentimental gypsy love song, *When the Summer Night is Young*. Gertie beat time to the music, smiling with pleasure.

It was only afterwards that Ellie-Rose realised she had put her hand into Tad's during the serenade.

He escorted her to the permanent suite her father kept at the Waldorf; it was too far to go home to Carmansville at this late hour. He took her key from her and opened the room door, then stood by to say goodnight.

"Thank you for coming to the concert," he said. "It meant a lot to Gertie."

"I . . . enjoyed it."

"Yes, it was good, wasn't it? Thanks to you, mostly. It was your friends who topped the bill. It was very generous of you to take the trouble."

"Generous? Oh, Tad, I—"

"What?"

She looked at him. "I only did it so as to have an excuse to see you," she said.

He made no reply. They stood in the doorway,

with the silent corridor stretching away on either side, and beyond that the hotel and the impersonal world of New York.

Tad took a step that brought him to her side. He put an arm about her. Then, holding her so that her high-piled hair brushed his cheek, he walked into the suite with her.

25

THEIR love affair was like a mountain stream in spate, sometimes checked by snags and boulders but always resuming its rushing flow in the end. Sometimes Ellie-Rose couldn't get away to see him, for she had always to invent some excuse that would stand up under examination.

She wasn't only Curtis's wife and the mother of her children, she was a hostess for Curtis in Washington and a helper in his career. She couldn't just back out of all that. Just because she'd fallen in love with someone else was no reason to make Curtis suffer.

She had no idea as yet how deep this affair would go. She'd never had a lover since her marriage, although she knew other wives who had—and it had always appalled her to think of the lies and subterfuges they had to invent. Now she found herself doing just that. She despised herself, but she couldn't see any other course. Except, if she was honest, to end the alliance.

But she couldn't do that. Not yet. She knew in the end it would die away—extra-marital escapades always did. Yet, even as she said that to herself, she sensed that it wasn't true. This wasn't just an escapade.

When she married, Ellie-Rose knew what she

473

wanted out of that state. She had had two lovers, the first a young innocent like herself when she was eighteen, the other an experienced roué when she was a debutante in New York society. The second, Beecher Troughton, had taught her to understand physical desire, so that before she married Curtis she had studied him and decided he would make a good partner in that respect. It had been a conscious decision.

Their love-making had always been a pleasure. Perhaps Curtis got more from it than Ellie-Rose, since he was the more deeply in love, but nevertheless Ellie-Rose had found it rewarding.

But with Tad it was different. It wasn't just a time of physical delight, it was a fusing of body and spirit such as she'd never experienced before. At last she had found what she had always been seeking, a different dimension, a significance, a reason for giving herself up to the wishes of another. She found that she wanted to be unselfish, to give without asking for a return—and yet she was rewarded a thousand times more richly than ever before.

"I've fallen in love," she told her mirror. "For the very first time, I'm in love!" She was twenty-seven years old, sophisticated, worldly-wise—and for the first time in her life the merest touch could make her bones melt, the slightest murmur could make her pulses race.

She was like a young girl, helpless in the grip of her longing when she was with him. When he

474

whispered that she was beautiful, that he wanted her, she would pull that slender body down upon her with arms that trembled for need of him.

For Tad it was the same. That first night, he had known he was lost for ever. Ellie-Rose Gracebridge had caught at his heart from the first. When he looked at her he saw the attractive, elegant woman others saw, but something else as well—a lonesomeness, a vulnerability, that made him feel protective towards her. The tears that had sparkled on those long lashes when she spoke of her brother were like diamond knives piercing his heart. He wanted to help her.

Help her? What an absurd notion! She was rich, daughter of one of the most powerful men in the United States, a grain tycoon who held in his hands the life-giving store of whole populations. She was the wife of a man close to the President, a man spoken of as having a promising future. What could he do that would be of help to such as Ellie-Rose Gracebridge?

He could let her talk about her brother. It seemed the topic was taboo in her family. It was through her unhappy confidences about Cornelius that he got to know her. He was of some use to her—she told him she had written as a result of things he had said, and although she hadn't had a reply as yet her mind was more at ease. She had taken the first step towards a reconciliation.

Perhaps after that he should have withdrawn

from the friendship. But, he said to himself, what's the harm? She need never know how I feel.

When she said, almost in so many words, that she loved him, his fate was sealed. He had never imagined himself embarking on a clandestine affair with a married woman but so it was—and he didn't care about the morality of it. They loved one another. It was too soon as yet to know what might come of it.

They met in New York, mostly. It was possible for Ellie-Rose to provide good reasons for the trip to the city. If the gap until her next visit seemed long, Tad would go to Washington. It was easier for her to get away there, because Curtis would be tied up at the White House for a whole day at a time. The problem there was that they had to be very, very discreet. It was a city of gossip, thriving on titbits of malice. One mistake on Ellie-Rose's part, and some enemy might learn something to be used against Curtis.

Tad found it distasteful to be stealing around like a thief. "I don't think I can do this again," he told Ellie-Rose as they lay in each other's arms in the small hotel where he had a room. "It cheapens everything, Ellie."

"I know, darling. I feel the same way. But what's the alternative? It's another three weeks until I can make it to New York."

"And then when the hot weather comes you'll be off somewhere unapproachable."

She buried her head in his chest, avoiding a reply.

476

"What happens in July, Ellie? Do you go to Nebraska?"

"We generally go to Mount Morris in Virginia—miles from anywhere." She snuggled against him. "Don't let's talk about it, Tad."

Enticed by her warmth and sweetness, he said no more. But it was between them now. In a few more weeks, they would have to part for the whole of the summer. He didn't know how he would endure it.

Next time they met he had a plan. "Didn't you say you were born on a farm near Albany?" he asked. "Could you invent a reason for visiting in that area?"

She hesitated. "Mama has a house in Saratoga Springs."

"Ellie, could you go and visit her?"

"But . . . I never do that, Tad. She and I don't really get on."

"But it would be reasonable to do it, wouldn't it? What about the grandchildren? Doesn't she like to see them from time to time?"

"Not really. She doesn't care for young children much—they muss up her gowns."

Tad sighed. She sounded the kind of woman he wouldn't care to visit, himself. He couldn't ask Ellie-Rose to endure that, just for a few stolen moments with him. But it was the only way for them to meet during the long summer months.

Luisa was always pleased when she was installed for her term as mistress of Craigallan Castle. Everything there seemed more than usually agreeable.

Ellie-Rose's children were more entertaining—little Gina was a small person in her own right now, and though Curtis Junior was still rather delicate, he was quiet and undemanding.

"You know, Rob, I really believe motherhood is having a good effect on Ellie," Luisa remarked to him over an ample breakfast one morning.

"Glad to hear it. In what way?"

"Don't you think she looks very well these days? A sort of glow about her."

"I've noticed that." He smiled to himself. He never pried, but very little escaped him. And it struck him that when Ellie-Rose was at Craigallan Castle, she had more engagements of a personal nature than she used to. In days gone by Ellie-Rose would have concentrated on cultivating people who could be useful to Curtis; these days she seemed to foregather with the earnest and worthy rather than the powerful, or else she would disappear on some small errand of her own.

He hadn't as yet identified the man in the case. Nor did he wish to. The less he knew, the better. He didn't want to feel involved in a secret kept from Curtis, whom on the whole he liked. But nor did he want to spoil anything for Ellie-Rose. Rob had known happiness from love outside marriage and would never censure it as other, more conventional men did.

His relationship with Morag was precious to him, the more so because he could see her so rarely. She must stay in the mountains for her health's sake, whereas he was needed here, there and everywhere by the calls of his business. But the knowledge that Morag was always there, gentle, welcoming, tranquil yet eager—that was one of the mainstays of his life. He understood what his daughter was feeling, and held his peace.

When Ellie-Rose began to put out feelers about staying with Luisa in Saratoga Springs, Rob soon guessed the reason. He watched his wife falling in with it, flattered and pleased that her daughter should mention the idea. One word from him could have put a stop to it.

But why should he meddle? So long as the thing was managed discreetly, he would say nothing.

"It's really settled, then?" Tad cried when Ellie-Rose told him. "I can hardly believe it!"

"We'll be able to see each other every day. Mama likes to go out to visit the casino with friends in the evenings. I'll be able to get out of most of the engagements—she doesn't really care whether I accompany her."

The next thing was to arrange where they would meet. Tad decided to put up at the Hunting Lodge Inn on the lake, three miles out of the town. He could drive in to meet Ellie-Rose and take her out to the Inn.

When Ellie-Rose made the journey from Washington to Saratoga Springs she banished any sense of guilt from her heart. No one would suffer by what she was doing. Her children were in the goods hands of their nurse, Curtis had business

479

with the heads of the Republican organisers over the forthcoming convention. Her mother would have her company for the greater part of each day if she wanted it. All that would happen was that she would take some time to herself, to be with the man she loved.

It was extraordinary how little she and Luisa had to say to each other. Luisa liked to boast about her foreign travels, but she could seldom answer any questions if one chose to take an interest. About family matters, she had little to say. She would inquire after Curtis and the children, but didn't want to hear many details. She had scant interest in Rob's doings, didn't want to hear about Gregor, and as for Cornelius—it hadn't surprised her to hear he had attacked Gregor in an uncontrollable rage because she always felt Cornelius was odd, and if he had gone abroad so much the better. He had never been a son she could be proud of. If he could manage to die on foreign service, *then* she could be proud of him.

They had five o'clock tea together, two women in light-coloured holiday dresses on the porch of the wooden house with the scent of late May flowers drifting to them from the crowded garden. Ellie-Rose let her mind wander, to the evening that was to come when she would be in Tad's arms.

They were rising to go indoors and dress for dinner when a telegraph boy came hurrying in at the garden gate. "Mrs. Gracebridge?" he inquired, touching his cap.

480

"That's me," Ellie-Rose said, her heart giving a lurch. Something had happened to the children!

He gave her the envelope. She tore it open and found it was a short message from her father. "Please telephone me—very urgent."

She hurried to the Springs Hotel to put through a call. She heard her father's voice, echoing a little in his study at the Castle.

"Papa, what is it? What does the telegram mean?"

She heard him sigh. "Daughter, I hate to do this to you. But can you come back to New York? I've just had a notification—Cornelius has gone missing in the Philippines."

26

WHEN Cornelius arrived in Manila, he had just missed the best part of the year's weather. Towards the beginning of March the thermometer starts to climb in the Philippines. Some of the research team were inclined to complain, but conditions on board ship had been so airless and cramped that they were all glad to be ashore, no matter if it was hot.

Cornelius had had few problems with his deafness on the ship. He had kept out of the way of most of his colleagues until they were a day out at sea. Then he went to the senior scientist, James A. Barnaway.

"Sir, I have something to tell you," he began, giving intense care to his pronunciation and his intonation. Intonation was always his problem; he never himself heard the sounds he made, and only the work he had done as a child with Alexander Graham Bell's teachers had given him the ability to judge from his own formations what sound he was making.

Barnaway, who had assumed the strange flat tone of his colleague was due to a bad cold, nodded encouragingly and waved him to a seat on the edge of his bunk. The cabin was too cluttered to allow more than one chair.

"Sir, I have to confess to you that I am totally deaf."

"Eh?" said Barnaway. And then, "Hard of hearing, you mean?"

"No, sir, totally deaf."

"But that can't be," Barnaway replied, irritated at such inexactitude in a scientist. "You can hear what I'm saying, otherwise how are we having this conversation?"

"By lip-reading, sir. Doesn't always work. It happens you speak with movement of the lips, but some keep teeth gritted all the time and I can't understand."

This was the longest speech Barnaway had heard from Cornelius and it now occurred to him that it was oddly intoned and that some of the words were only approximate to their usual pronunciation.

"Is this a joke, Craigallan?" he inquired, worried. He thought he had left undergraduate jokes behind him when he left his teaching post to undertake his work in the Philippines.

"People make jokes about it, doctor, but it's never seemed funny to me."

"Let's get this straight. You can't hear what I'm saying?"

Cornelius shook his head.

"Now hold on. Let's test this. I'll turn my back and say something, and then you tell me if you know what it was—"

"Sir, I shouldn't bother. If it were a joke I'd just pretend not to have heard you, shouldn't I? But in

483

fact I have no hearing. You'll see the truth of it as the voyage goes on."

"But . . . Craigallan! What's the meaning of this? What use are you going to be on a scientific expedition if you can't hear?"

"Sir, hearing has no part in what I do. I collect specimens of damaged crop plants and try to ascertain what's the cause. I analyse and categorise productivity of plants. I try to find remedies for diseases of plants."

It was this last speech that convinced Barnaway that Cornelius was in earnest. The way he brought out the longer words, particularly "productivity", was quite odd. He said it as if it was a word he used often, but it didn't sound right at all.

"You've been like this all your life?"

Cornelius nodded.

Barnaway stared at him. He had never before met a man with such a handicap. True, one's elderly relatives became deaf; Barnaway himself was beginning to be, at forty, a little hard of hearing in his left ear. But either there were few totally deaf people in the world, or they hid away out of sight.

Cornelius's qualifications paraded before Dr. Barnaway's inner eye. They had been very impressive. Barnaway had had no choice in the selection of the research team—that had been done by the government. But he had been given the right to cast his eye over the list and say if there was anyone who would be less than useful in the project. Of the nine men, Cornelius had been one of the most useful—on paper.

But in real life? Could a deaf man pull his weight? Yet why not? He had got himself thus far in life. In fact, Barnaway's scientific interest was roused. He had never seen a man with no hearing at work in competition with the rest of the world. He was interested to see how Cornelius made out. Moreover, how was he to get rid of him? There was no stop until they reached Manila. If by that time Cornelius Craigallan had shown himself to be a nuisance rather than an asset, he'd send him back to the States on the next available boat.

He kept Cornelius with him for the next half hour, talking with him. He found that there were problems. If he turned away so that Cornelius didn't see his lips clearly, the conversation came to an end. He also learned that it became less difficult to follow his speech once you got used to the tone of his voice and the difficulties he had with certain sounds. Short words with simple consonants Cornelius could produce quite well. Compound consonants troubled him. Long words sometimes ceased to be voiced as he came to the end of them—it had to do with knowing how to organise the breathing to keep the sound going.

It was all intensely interesting. When Barnaway dismissed his young colleague, he was favourably disposed towards him. He decided to tell the other members of the team to accept Cornelius's defect with matter-of-factness if not with enthusiasm, and see how the work went once they were on station.

The other men were varied in their reaction. One or two were amazed, one or two were amused, others were irritated at having to deal with someone who, they were sure, wouldn't pull his weight. Because their leader, Dr. Barnaway, told them to put up with it, they obeyed. But by the time their four weeks' voyage to Manila had ended, they had largely forgotten Cornelius had anything wrong with him.

The city of Manila proved a revelation. Most of the newcomers had expected a sort of jungle outpost, although the crew of the ship had insisted they'd find a handsome centre of society. It was a beautiful place. Above the red earth and lush green vegetation, the white and pale pink buildings towered—cathedrals, palaces, battlements, fortifications . . .

It was marred somewhat by the fact that many of the public buildings were taken over for billeting troops. There was also a canvas city on the outskirts. But these were the inevitable corollaries of the war still going on.

The baggage of the scientists and the new military officials was carried to their lodgings by a team of little white-clad youths. Throughout Cornelius's stay in Manila he was always amazed at the unending supply of these youngsters, all keen and active, with undying energy no matter how hot it became.

The noise in the streets was strident. Most of the

newcomers ended up with a headache. Cornelius couldn't hear it and so was unaffected. His first view of his new home was pleasing to him.

But problems began to crowd in, not only for Cornelius. It had been widely supposed that an acquaintance with the Spanish language would see them through the communications difficulty, but this proved to be quite untrue. Spanish was, in the first place, a hated language, the language of the oppressor. Moreover, only a small proportion spoke it. The official class, the professionals in careers such as administration, medicine, and teaching— these were the Spanish speakers. But the information needed by the research team was quite different.

They were here at the behest of the American government to find ways of increasing the income of the Philippine population. They needed to know what cattle they had, what other domestic animals, what products they used for their homes, their farms, their tools. They wanted to inquire about health, childbirth, sanitation. They were hoping to compile information about soil components, cultivation methods, farm life in general. They wanted to be shown the jungle paths, the river transport, the fish, the birds, the butterflies and insects.

It took the Spanish speakers in the group three days to discover that the main language in the Philippines was Tagalog, not Spanish. The only way to communicate with the peasant population and the jungle dwellers was through Tagalog, or some other dialect which had first to be translated into Tagalog.

To everyone's surprise, Cornelius got on better than any of them. He used sign language to the natives and they, taken aback at first, would quickly copy his movements. The complex sign language used in the United States was too fast for them but they themselves used signs, and were quick to understand meanings.

And then, by watching carefully how they shaped their lips, as he always did, Cornelius learned a few words of Tagalog. He didn't have problems, as the others did, with thinking first in English and trying to translate. Cornelius thought in word shapes, not sounds. He adapted to this new situation quite quickly.

"If you're not careful we'll be taking you around as interpreter," Dr. Barnaway joked. "It's a pity you've work of your own to do."

Cornelius grinned. "In my view, the work I'm doing is a lot more important than making a statistical survey of river transport. People have got to eat before they start moving about."

"How true." The food was one of the problems in Manila. Most of the Americans had suffered from stomach upsets. Hygiene was bad; dysentery and cholera were common. Yellow fever had laid low many of the soldiers in the canvas camp outside the city.

Another danger the American research teams had

to combat was guerrilla attack. The leader of the main Filipino army, Aguinaldo, had been seized and exiled to Hong Kong in the previous year. But many Filipinos continued to resist American occupation. They had hoped, by helping the Americans conquer the Spaniards, to obtain self-government. Now they found themselves taken over by the supposedly friendly army alongside whom they had fought. They had been furious at the proclamation of conquest published after the conclusion of the peace treaty with Spain.

The late President McKinley had been so ignorant of the situation in the Philippines that he had actually imagined they were heathen. To a group of Methodist ministers who visited him in the White House, he had said: "I prayed Almighty God for guidance . . . and one night late it came to me . . . there was nothing left for us to do but take them all, and to educate the Filipinos, and uplift them and civilise them and Christianise them . . ." He was apparently unaware that eighty per cent of Filipinos were Catholic.

Being Christian didn't, alas, make the Filipinos kind-hearted as fighters. They were clever, hard-hitting, and ruthless. They had good reason to hate the Americans. Most of the military men had no experience of dealing with other cultures. They were tactless and often downright rude. The tendency to drown their sorrows in drink made them quarrelsome and sometimes dangerous.

Finding that the "niggers" whom they despised

489

were contemptuous of them made the American forces feel beleagured. Outside the towns, where they had complete control, there was a strong tendency to be trigger happy.

This didn't help the work of the peaceful forces who came to improve the country. They were tarred with the same brush as the military, or else were resented for poking their noses in where they weren't asked. So the American government had decided to investigate rice production in Luzon? Who asked the American government to do any such thing?

Cornelius was less aware of this feeling than his colleagues. He wasn't able to tune in to conversation, so he failed to catch the dozens of anecdotes about the recalcitrance, the waywardness, the absolute wrongheadedness of the local population. He dealt with the people as he found them—sulky sometimes perhaps, but on the whole not unhelpful once he'd established communications. The fact that he approached the Filipinos in a totally different way was an unwitting advantage to him.

In his work, Cornelius found forgetfulness of the events in Stephanie's studio. They began to fade from his mind and his heart. When something recalled the incident to him, he still blamed himself totally, but it wasn't a continual ache any more. As his first Christmas in Manila drew on, he began to think he would one day have difficulty in summoning up a picture of Stephanie in his mind.

He had loved her and the scar would always be there—but a scar is a wound healed.

In his investigations he had begun to understand that the best cultivators of rice on the main island, Luzon, were a people known as Igorrotes who lived in the central and northern mountains. As he inquired about rice culture, the Filipinos kept saying with a sage nod, "You should see the rice terraces of the Igorrotes!"

To be able to view these areas, Cornelius would have to make an overland journey beyond what was known as the Safe Zone. Manila and some thirty miles around it constituted a Safe Zone, as did the confines of some other towns. But the great central plain of Luzon and its mountains were infiltrated by bands of guerrillas—bandits, as the military governor preferred to call them—who might strike anywhere.

Cornelius applied for permission to make the trip to Nueva Viscaya Province. It was rejected at once. He applied again, and then again. His three applications went through the chief of the scientific mission, Dr. Barnaway, who was summoned to the office of an irate colonel of security.

"Look here, doctor, you ought to know better than to waste my time with crackpot demands like this!"

"Er . . . Crackpot?" Barnaway echoed. "Seems to me entirely reasonable."

"You must be joking! Allow civilians out of the Safe Zone? Certainly not."

"But, Colonel, plants don't grow neatly inside the Safe Zone. If this report is to have any validity, it must include information from outer areas of Luzon."

"Not while I'm in command!"

"Hm," said Barnaway. "The Philippine Commissioners aren't going to like *that*."

The colonel, sweltering gently in his high buttoned tunic, frowned at the doctor. "How's that again?"

"Well, sir, you know we're here at the request of the Commission, to provide the Department of Agriculture with information for planned improvement of the economy. Mr. Craigallan's part is to forewarn about possible plant diseases. He has done all he can in the regions permissible to visit, but if he is to give a reasonable survey of the cultivation of rice he must go further afield."

"But Nueva Viscaya is the territory of the Igorrotes!"

"Yes, sir, he knows that."

"But the Igorrotes are savages! It's a risk I can't take," Colonel Manders said tersely. "The application is refused, and don't let me hear any more of it."

Barnaway, dismissed, still didn't get up out of his chair. "Well, now," he said, "I wouldn't be at all surprised if Mr. Craigallan set out without permission if you keep refusing him."

"What?" The colonel bounded up, red with anger.

"His instructions—our instructions, sir—from the Commissioners—are to make whatever investigations we may deem necessary to provide information for the furtherance of the Philippine economy under the guidance of the United States." That was verbatim from his letter of appointment, and the words had an effect on the colonel.

"See here," he began, his high colour receding, "the fellows who wrote that for you in Washington don't know the conditions—"

"The Commissioners have been here, sir. They know at least something."

"But that was before the army—"

"Began to make rules and regulations to control civilians. Exactly." Dr. Barnaway had a surprising bite when necessary. "It's this way, Colonel Manders. Mr. Craigallan needs to go to look at the Igorrotes and you're being obstructive."

"I can't let him go blundering out there alone!"

"Then send an escort with him."

"An escort? How many troops do you think I have at my disposal? I haven't men to spare to escort Craigallan on this crackpot trip."

"Well, then, he must go on his own. I'll write an advice to that effect and have it cabled to—"

"No, no, don't do that," Colonel Manders said, throwing himself back into his chair and gazing over his desk at the doctor. "All right. If Mr. Craigallan can be ready to leave in four days time, there's a patrol going out to visit the province. He can go along. But mind, they can't hang about for him.

He's got to travel with them and not be a nuisance."

"I'm sure you'll find he's no trouble, Colonel," Barnaway said, and took his leave, pleased with at least one victory over the stultifying military rule of Luzon.

No concessions were made to Cornelius and his servant Angel on the patrol; they must either keep up or be left behind. But Cornelius had done some travelling on the island, and knew how to sit the little fast-trotting pony without discomfort. He knew that Lieutenant Freeman was punishing him for insisting on this trip; he knew he was regarded as a nuisance.

Soon they began to climb. The mountains were beautiful, with great valleys and meadows that reminded Cornelius of the scenes around Morag McGarth's house in Colorado. The air here was crisp and cool. Grass grew knee high from a rich soil, black whereas the coastal plain was red. Within a day's journey they were at an elevation of five thousand feet, and villages became rare. Pines and firs grew in great dark groves. When they descended again towards a valley, dense jungle vegetation would clothe the slopes below the conifer line.

The first night they stayed in an Agalo village, welcomed by the mayor with ceremony. Spanish influence was everywhere—in the architecture of the main building and in the entertainment provided after supper, a concert by the village band.

Cornelius sat through this with politeness, although not a note was audible to him.

Next day brought them to the verge of Igorrote territory. Scouts were sent out by the lieutenant, but whether this was because he expected attack from the headhunters or from guerrilla parties, Cornelius couldn't make out. They had no trouble, and rode into the upland village at nightfall to the welcoming grins of a group of very scantily clad natives.

The arrival of the American army patrol was greeted with great excitement. The chief of the village arrived, the *datu*, clad in a skirt of soft cotton and a cape of pineapple fibre. He had a spear with a handle of palm, but Cornelius noted that it wasn't carved in any grand manner. In fact, the general appearance was quite primitive. He began to doubt that the rice cultivation would be anything out-standing—a people that had so little personal adornment and decoration were unlikely to have any agricultural knowledge.

Next day proved him wrong. The chief took him on a tour of the rice terraces. This village alone had terraces able to produce three crops a year, with a huge surplus which they traded to other tribes on the coast. The crop went downriver by canoe and pirogue and then by larger boats on the more open waters.

The terraces were on the mountain above the village, not visible to the casual traveller because of the trees on the lower slopes. They were cut like giant steps into the sides of the steep mountain canyons to a height of three thousand feet and more, following the contour of the canyon wall for as much as a half-mile in some cases.

All day Cornelius walked among the terraces, knee deep in the dark brown water. He was able to ask questions by gesture, and though at first he received a reply in a torrent of dialect, he was able by headshaking and continual use of his hands to convince them to do likewise.

He spent that night taking notes. Next day the patrol went on, leaving him for the time being. He inspected the irrigation system, which consisted of diverting the mountain streams by means of stone walls and bamboo channels. He asked for and was given specimens of plants. They were healthy, grain buds already forming well, several seeds feeling plump to the touch. The return on each seed planted was exceptional. Considering that these terraces were in continual use—he could find no plan of rotation—the yield was extraordinary.

Late that day he discovered how it was done. The chief, deciding he was a friend to be trusted, showed him the fertilising system. The streamlet which was to take water from its source to a lower level was led through a pile of manure, decayed vegetables, loam, ashes and alluvial soil, all of this carted to the spot in exact quantities and replenished as it was washed off.

"Thus," wrote Cornelius in his notes, "these so-called ignorant people have solved a problem which our own farmers have not yet even begun to address—they irrigate and fertilise their crops in one operation without waste, whereas the American farmer laboriously spreads fertiliser, often chemical, so that it is later washed off by the application of mechanical water supplies or rain."

In the normal course of events Cornelius would have made a note in his personal diary to write to his father about this idea, but, since he had been warned to keep away, he closed his notebook and put it in his travel pack.

He spent a week with the Igorrotes before the soldiers came back. They had established a guard post on one of the mountain slopes with a detachment of eight men; this was to keep a lookout for activity by the guerrillas. Now they would make their way back to Manila by a different route, to show the flag over as much territory as possible and glean information.

Their first night out from the Igorrotes village they failed to reach their objective, a small settlement of Moros. It meant sleeping under canvas. Cornelius wasn't displeased; he and Angel put up the tent, then after supper—wild pig shot by the military hunter—he settled down with his microscope to look at some preliminary slides he had prepared.

The light from his tent was clearly visible to the guerrilla sent out to scout the camp. The cookfire leapt up as the men threw more logs on it for the night watch. The scout counted. When he went back to his leader he reported that the patrol, already watched as it took its way north, was depleted by about ten.

"Good," said Rinaldo. "We can take them, I think."

Going into the camp, they had surprise on their side. But once the alarm was raised there was a brief, fierce skirmish. It ended with the death of half the patrol, including the lieutenant. The others were taken prisoner.

Rinaldo, having seen them tied up securely, stood looking at the shadow cast on the wall of the tent on the far side of the clearing. The man in it must be either very brave, or dead. He appeared to be leaning over a small table, looking through a piece of equipment. He was so still, it was obvious he had died from a shot through the canvas.

But no—his hand moved, he seemed to be adjusting a screw at the side of his equipment.

Extraordinary . . . Why hadn't he run out at the attack? Why had he taken no part in the fighting? Why hadn't he made his escape?

Rinaldo walked to the tent, raised the flap, and went in.

"Senor," he said.

No response.

"Senor." Louder.

Still no response.

"This is impertinence!" said the guerrilla commander. "Senor, turn around or I will shoot you!"

The figure at the microscope neither turned nor spoke.

Rinaldo crossed the space between them in one soft stride of his bare feet. Cornelius felt something cold and hard pressed against the nape of his neck. For one bewildered moment he misjudged the sensation, thought it was the sting of an insect. He threw up a hand to slap it. His hand was grasped in a small, hard fist. The pressure on the nape of his neck increased.

He recognised what it was—the barrel of a pistol.

27

THE news was slow to reach the United States.

It wasn't until twenty-one days after the patrol had set out that any anxiety began to be felt about Lieutenant Freeman's party.

The search party moved fast, covering Freeman's mapped route but without pausing for any side forays. They were back in eight days. They had found no trace.

At that point the information was relayed to Washington by cable. Lieutenant James Freeman and his patrol had gone missing in the Province of Nueva Viscaya with one civilian European and one civilian Filipino.

A telegram was dispatched to the scientist's next of kin.

Ellie-Rose arrived at the Castle the same evening as the phone call from her father. He handed her the official telegram form: *Regret to inform you Cornelius Craigallan missing with military patrol in Nueva Viscaya Province. Search has been instituted. Deepest sympathy meanwhile.* It was signed with the name of an unknown colonel in Washington.

"Have you found out anything?" she asked at once, handing it back.

"They either don't know or won't tell," he

500

replied, his curtness a mirror-image of his feelings.

"We could get someone to inquire for us."

"I contacted a couple of men. But what I want, Ellie, is for you to telephone Curtis and ask him for a word from the President. I want those blockheads at Army H.Q. in Manila to understand they've got to move their butt! I want my boy back."

There was so much anxiety and affection in his tone that she went to him and put her arms about him. It was rare to see Rob without his defences. He let her hold him for a moment and then hugged her hard. "I feel it's all my fault," he whispered. "He never would have gone out there if I hadn't been so mad at him."

"Don't blame yourself," she said. "That's all in the past."

"But I shouldn't have let it go on," he said. "I should have gotten over it. I should have . . . written to say I didn't feel like that any more." She felt him sigh. "All those months out there in that damned sweaty hell-hole, and not a line from any of us."

"I wrote, Papa, around Christmas. It seemed wrong for the family to be so at odds."

"What did he reply? Can I see the letter?"

"I didn't hear," she said. "I begged him to write, but he didn't."

"Do you think Curtis will hold back from asking the President, on account of how he feels?" Rob asked.

"Oh, no, of course not, Papa! Everything's different now!"

"You think he got over his resentment?"

She hesitated. She couldn't bring herself to claim that much. She had seen her husband looking at little Curt, with the knowledge behind his anxious smile that, but for Cornelius Craigallan, his son would have been born well and strong.

"I don't think he'd want Neil to stay lost in the Philippine jungle," she said. If he felt like that, she'd argue him out of it. She knew how to handle Curtis.

But although Curtis came around and made the request, President Roosevelt proved unwilling to interfere. "See, Gracebridge, it's like this. Our fellows out there have a hard row to hoe, and putting pressure on them won't help. They're doing all they can. I don't want them to risk any more lives in the search just because the President's aide has a relative missing."

"Sir, I wouldn't ask you to do more than just express an interest—"

"But that's not necessary, boy. The President is interested in the safety and wellbeing of all the people—the army knows that. Just let them get on with it in their own way, Gracebridge. I know the army. They'll find him if he's still alive. Convey my sympathy to your lady wife, won't you, and tell her I'm thinking about that brave brother of hers."

"So you see," Curtis reported to his wife and father-in-law, "he's playing it on the 'no favourites' basis, because of course there are other men missing. It wouldn't look good in the newspapers if a reporter smoked it out that the President had interested himself in one man above the ordinary soldiers."

"Why, that stuffed shirt!" Rob cried. "That's the last penny the Republican Party gets out of me! All that money to help get them in, and what the hell good are they when you need them?"

"I think, to be honest," Curtis said, "even Roosevelt couldn't do much to improve the effort out there." Curtis wasn't exactly glad that Cornelius had gone missing, but he wasn't displeased that the President had taken this stand. Curtis didn't really care one way or the other about the safe delivery of his brother-in-law. It was only because his wife was so upset that he'd made the move, and now he had done it, that was his duty fulfilled. Let Cornelius Craigallan stand or fall by the ordinary rules of life, like the other men out in the Philippines. For once, money and influence couldn't help.

To add to Ellie-Rose's distress, she had her first quarrel with Tad. Before she rushed away from Saratoga Springs at her father's summons, she rang Tad at the Hunter's Inn. But he had left the hotel to meet her in the centre of town. He hung around a long while, returned to the hotel three hours later furiously angry, and got a garbled version of the message she'd left: "Mrs. Gracebridge had to return to New York unexpectedly, will be in touch."

"She'll be in touch, will she!" he said grimly to himself. He had never been so angry. It was more than a week later that at last each understood what the other had been doing.

Reconciliation, of course, is sweet. They forced an opportunity to be together but it was only for half an hour, just long enough to kiss and talk and reassure each other. Their plan to see something of each other had gone wrong and it was difficult to arrange anything else with the emergency about Cornelius taking up Ellie-Rose's emotional energy.

The weeks went by. It became clear it wasn't going to be easy to learn the fate of Lieutenant Freeman's party. For the children's sake Ellie-Rose was persuaded to go to the house at Morris Mount while Curtis remained in Washington.

Then there was news. She rushed back to confer with her father. En route she sent a wire to Tad from a railway telegraph office: *In Washington for the next few days. Come to the usual place. I will telephone.*

When she snatched an evening to be with Tad at his Washington hotel she explained that a microscope had been found in a shop in a small town to the north of the central plain of Luzon. The shopkeeper said he had taken it in exchange for provisions. He was arrested, taken from Dagupan to Manila, and there cross-questioned. The consensus of opinion was that he was an innocent who had taken the microscope in hopes of selling it eventually at a profit.

"Are they out of their minds?" Gregor exclaimed when he heard this view at a conference in Ellie-Rose's drawing-room. "Sell a microscope at the back of beyond, in a tin shack where the natives go? To whom would he sell it?"

"God knows," Rob said. "You think he was in league with the guerrillas, then?"

Gregor had graduated at the head of his class out of Harvard. He and Rob were on their way to Chicago for the Board of Trade dealing in the year's harvest, which was just coming in. For the second year running, Rob didn't have the benefit of Cornelius's analysis of the scientific information on the crop and the prospects for the planting season. Last year he had told himself resentfully that he could manage all right without the boy, but this year he missed him so acutely that it was an almost physical ache. Gregor would do his best, he knew, but Gregor's speciality was economics and languages, not agriculture. When Rob turned over the papers detailing the agricultural information, it was Cornelius's croaking voice he wanted to hear, not Gregor's.

Gregor thought over the news that had just reached them. "This guy Modisto," he mused. "He takes a high-class scientific instrument from a customer in exchange for coffee, sugar, dried beans and tobacco . . . Did he take it because he thought it was a good bargain, or was he forced to?"

His father thought it over. "Well, if he's any good as a storekeeper he ought to have known it was a bad bargain. Nobody in Dagupan is likely to need a microscope."

"You said it. So I think he was forced to take it."

"Yes, but . . ."

"I think it's a message! I think it's to tell us Cornelius is still alive." Gregor ran a hand through his dark auburn hair. "The guerrillas gave it to the storekeeper knowing that by and by the search party would come across it." He paused. "Don't you think it means they want us to contact them?"

"But why?"

Ellie-Rose looked perplexed. The two men stared at each other. Then in unison they made the reply that experience on the one hand and intelligent deduction on the other seemed to dictate.

"Money."

Rob made the trip to the War Department to speak to the military authorities. They didn't want to hear the word ransom. "If once we start giving in to these sons of bitches, no one is safe," Colonel Velmer insisted. "We have trouble enough keeping the Safe Zone intact. Once we let it be known we're prepared to buy back prisoners, the *insurrectos* will snatch anybody they can get hold of—not just soldiers, but civilian Americans and Filipinos."

"Then it's up to you to keep the civilians safe," Rob returned. "What the hell were you up to, letting my son go out with a stingy guard of twenty men?"

506

"Sir, we have problems with keeping our patrols up to strength. There's a lot of sickness among our men. Let me tell you, I have it on good authority that Mr. Craigallan was warned not to go on this trip. If he insisted, then it was up to him to take the risks involved."

"All right, he did that. But now there's a chance to get him back, maybe. Are you telling me you aren't going to take it?"

"No, sir."

"But there may be some of your own men with him. Don't you want them back?"

"Of course we do! But they're soldiers. They know we can't pay ransoms."

"Maybe you can't, Colonel. But there's no law stops me from doing it."

"Mr. Craigallan, you are forbidden to do any such thing. No one on our staff will act as your agent. You'll get no help anywhere through American channels. Am I clear?"

Rob glared at him, got up, crammed his hat on his head, and stormed out.

"Damn fool," he snarled to Gregor afterwards. "Sat there spouting noble sentiments. It's not *his* son that's missing!"

Gregor shrugged. "He's only obeying orders. You can see their point, sir. It sure makes life hard for them if guerrillas should sneak into the Safe Zone and make off with an official or a civil servant."

"I'm not concerned with what *might* happen. I'm

concerned with what's already gone by—the fact that my son's gone missing. Damn it, they're not even investigating to find out whether they could get in touch with someone through that microscope business. They're treating it as a 'search-and-recover' operation, purely military."

"Well, that's sure to fail," Gregor said. "If we read that message aright, the guerrillas are far too clever to let the American patrols catch them. The only way to get in touch is by diplomacy."

"But how, if we can't get anyone to act for us on that basis?"

"There must be someone," Gregor said. "Curtis must know someone who's on the Philippines Commission."

Curtis, of course, did, and inquired if there was the chance of an intervention through any of their agents. He met with resistance, because the Commission could only function in the Philippines if they had the support of the military. Moreover, Curtis didn't push very hard. He wasn't a hundred per cent behind his wife's relations on this. The President had told him he wanted Cornelius treated like any soldier who had gone missing, and to be too insistent was going against his expressed wish.

"You can understand it," Tad said to Ellie-Rose when she expressed these fears to him. "It's a very delicate situation. Don't be hard on him, Ellie."

"It's just that I feel he isn't . . ."

"What?"

"I was going to say, 'honest'." She coloured.

"But I'm the last person to complain about that, aren't I?"

Curtis had expressed himself with some force to Gregor, who—he imagined—shared his views. "I don't give a damn if he comes home or not," he had said. "All I want is for Ellie to stop grieving about him."

After Curtis had left the Washington house for his office, Gregor went in search of his father and Ellie-Rose. Rob was in her boudoir, sharing breakfast with her and little Gina. Grandfather Craigallan played with his little granddaughter until it was time for her to be taken away and put into her coat and bonnet for her walk.

When they were alone, Gregor cleared his throat. "I gave this business of Cornelius a lot of thought last night," he began, "and I've come to the conclusion that the only way we'll get anything done is for somebody to go out there and act independently of the military authorities."

Rob nodded. "Who do you suggest?" he inquired, his mind ranging over the staff at Craigallan Agricultural Products and the finance office.

"Me."

"You?"

"Oh, no, Gregor!" Ellie-Rose cried.

"Why not me? I know all the ins and outs of what's happened, you know you can trust me, and I speak Spanish."

"Greg, don't go," Ellie-Rose begged. "It's so dangerous—"

"Spanish!" exclaimed Rob. "A fat lot of use that'll be! They all talk gibberish, from what I hear!"

"It's better than nothing," Gregor insisted. "If we were to send Mitchell, for instance, from the Chicago office—he's a bright guy but he could only act through an English-speaking Spanish interpreter who speaks the native dialect. At least I don't have to have a Spanish interpreter—I'd be one stage nearer a first hand meeting."

"No, Greg, please don't," Ellie-Rose said. "You know nothing about the Philippines—"

"I know men who want to make money," he cut in. "And that's what I think these *insurrectos* are after." He turned to his father. "Look at it this way, sir. If ever we did get a message, somebody would have to dicker with them. Who would you trust more than me?"

There was a long pause.

"He's right, Ellie-Rose," Rob said.

"But . . . but . . . we might lose him too!"

"I don't think so."

"They won't let you," she said. "They won't let any member of the Craigallan family interfere in the search—"

"Who's going to know I'm connected?" Gregor asked in a rather crisp tone. "My name isn't even the same."

Ellie-Rose looked at him, eyes wide.

"For the first time," he added, "it seems an actual advantage."

"But why should you do this? Why should you put yourself in danger, perhaps—"

"Because I feel it's all my fault in the first place. The poor guy wouldn't have gone out there if it hadn't been for me."

"Ellie," her father said, "let's not make a big argument of it. Greg's right. Someone has to go out there and take personal charge—"

"And soon, otherwise it may be too late," Gregor put in.

"Right. We'd better get moving on it."

"And the first thing," Gregor added, "is to make arrangements for a large sum of money to be available. This isn't going to be a cheap undertaking. I hear bribery is the rule rather than the exception out there, but expectations have gone up since American money came into the area."

"Leave it to me. You'd better have gold, hadn't you?"

The campaign to find and rescue Cornelius was under way. Action of any kind was a relief. But Rob Craigallan couldn't help feeling that the lives of his children had been cast in stony places indeed—one son missing in a wild foreign place, the other off into danger to find him, and a daughter beginning to see faults in her marriage.

28

ARRANGEMENTS were made by cable to Hong Kong for gold coins to be available to Gregor in Manila. The voyage from Hong Kong to the Philippines was only two or three days, so the Chinese merchant was waiting on the docks at Manila when Gregor disembarked after his month-long journey from Los Angeles.

"Sir?" he addressed him with quiet certainty. "Mr. McGarth? My name is Thomas Kuan. Mr. Craigallan sent word to be here to meet you."

"Well, Mr. Kuan, I believe you have something for me?"

"Indeed yes, sir, in safe keeping in the strong room of my uncle's house. Would you care for me to bring the package to you at your hotel?"

"Not for the moment, thank you. How do I get to the hotel?"

"I have a carriage waiting, Mr. McGarth."

A sudden thundery downpour made them scurry under a porter's umbrella for the carriage in the road outside the harbour buildings. Despite the umbrella, Gregor was very wet when he climbed in. "Does it often rain like this?" he asked, looking out at the steel lines of moisture falling from the clouds.

"Rainy season ends about November, sir. You

should have chosen a better time to visit than the end of September."

As Gregor was here unofficially, in the guise of a young American businessman looking for likely investments in this new domain, he didn't have to present letters of introduction or credentials to anyone. He had thought, while on the boat, of the best way to begin his inquiries, and had come to the conclusion that the family of Angel, Cornelius's servant, was the obvious place.

Gregor was surprised when he met the parents; they seemed to him scarcely old enough to have a son out at work, but in the next few days he realised that Filipinos had to begin earning as soon as they could and that Angel, always imagined to be about thirty, was in fact fourteen years old.

Angel's father, Mario, answered eagerly when Gregor asked what had been done to find Angel. He spoke Spanish with a strange accent.

"Senor, after the finding of the microscope I went to the soldiers to say that if they would let it be known to the guerillas they were interested in buying other items of equipment, they would hear more, for sure. This they did, but when news came that a small cabinet with drawers of dried plants was for sale, they refused to offer any money and no more was heard of the cabinet."

"The idiots!" Gregor cried.

"*Si*, senor, idiots. What could I do? I have no money, as you can see." Mario gestured at the bare, clean interior of his living-room. "I did what I

513

could, but there was no response. They knew I could not pay anything."

"But it's possible to get in touch?" Gregor asked.

"Not now, I believe. For a time there was the possibility. The *insurrectos* were hoping for a reaction, for money. But time has gone by since then and they have not made any sound, so I think they are not so near as they were."

"If you were to inherit a large sum of money and wanted to pay ransom for Angel, Senor Relojo, how would you go about it?"

Mario was about to reply, but his wife laid a warning hand on his arm. Mario stopped with the words on the tip of his tongue.

Gregor looked at Senora Relogo. "There is a way?" he queried.

"We have heard of a way, but whether it is possible or not, we cannot tell."

"Senora, this possibility—could money bring it into the world of existence?"

"Not in the first place, senor. What we have heard is little to do with money."

"Tell me what you know. I promise I will do all I can to bring your son back to you."

Once again Mario was about to speak, and once again his wife prevented him with a gentle touch.

"Senor," she said, "there is little to tell. It is better if we speak to a certain person, to find out whether or not we have permission to take you to a place where you will meet someone."

"Someone of importance?"

514

"Until now, we have not thought so. But now there is a reason to think differently. My husband will come to speak with you in a day or two . . ."

Gregor sent a cable home: *Arrived safely, met our agent. Inquiries started, further moves soon.*

Mario came to see him on the evening of the second day. The gentle tap at the room door announced his arrival. He came in, looking flushed with excitement.

"Senor, I am empowered to take you to someone who may help find Angel and your friend, Mr. Craigallan. We have to make a journey. When can you start?"

"Immediately! Where are we going?"

"To Nueva Viscaya, senor. I will take you to meet someone, at a special place. After that, much depends on what you arrange between you."

"Should I take money, Mario?"

Mario hesitated. "It is always dangerous to carry money outside the Safe Zone, senor. There are many brigands and thieves. But . . . yes . . . in the end money will be needed."

"Very well. When can we set out?"

"At dawn tomorrow, Senor McGarth."

When he had gone, Gregor set out for the house of Thomas Kuan's uncle, in the Chinatown section of Manila known as Binondo. He was greeted with respect. The uncle, who spoke English less well than Thomas, retired into an inner room, to return after some minutes with a shallow wooden box. When he opened it, gold coins of various nations were to be seen, to the value of ten thousand dollars. Gregor had thought this sum quite insufficient, but now he understood Thomas Kuan's recommendation had been well-judged—Mario had been stunned at a five-dollar advance for travel supplies.

"You need the money, so that means there is a development?" Thomas inquired.

"Yes, but I'm sworn to secrecy. I've sent a cable to New York explaining I'm off on the trail. Thomas, if I'm not back in two weeks, raise the alarm."

"If it is possible, send back word before then. Two weeks is a long time for a man outside the Safe Zone, Mr. McGarth." It was impossible to know from Thomas Kuan's expression whether he approved of what was happening or not.

Next morning Gregor was waiting at the appointed place. It was surprisingly cold. The air was very moist, so that he could see his breath. The moisture dripped from the narra trees planted for shade along the sidewalks. There were occasional passers-by. A cart loaded with vegetables came in from the outskirts of the city, headed for the market square.

A padding of hooves on the dirt road announced the arrival of Mario with the ponies. He came into sight through the mist, riding one stalwart little horse and leading two, one a packhorse and the other saddled. Gregor, in the clothes he had bought since arriving in Manila, mounted and fell in

516

behind Mario. They went out of Manila at a walk.

Mario avoided the "gate" of the Safe Zone. Instead he made for a sort of no-man's-land, an area which existed for about thirty miles around the capital and which, during the fighting between the American and Philippine armies, had been burned, looted, rebuilt and burned again. Between the wrecked *barrios* paths wandered which had once been the communications between the villages. It was impossible for the U.S. army to post a sentinel at every crossroads; by selecting the right paths, Mario led Gregor out of the so-called Safe Zone.

They headed off to the east. Rain streamed down like a waterfall. Drenched and heavy with the weight of his own sweat and the money, Gregor's clothes felt like a mountain he was carrying.

But soon they were making better progress. Untiring, the ponies trudged between the dense walls of forest on either side. It was impossible to see where they were going on this track, for the trees closed in and beyond the trees was the thick rain cloud. But they were climbing; Gregor could feel it in the incline of the saddle and a slight drop in temperature.

At nightfall they came out on the edge of a hilly valley. It was just possible to make out in the poor light the shape of buildings. "A village?" Gregor asked, drawing rein.

"*Si*, senor—or what is left of it. Come, ride on."

"But it's going to be dark in a minute—"

"No matter, we shall be met." And almost as

soon as he said the words lanterns could be seen heading towards them across the valley.

On the journey Gregor had tried to find out where they were going. Mario had refused to tell him. "I promised my wife not to name any names to you, because if we are captured by the *insurrectos*, the less you know the better."

"This man we're going to see isn't an *insurrecto*, then?"

Mario turned to him with a secretive smile. "No, senor, not at all."

Men came, calling out questions. A password was demanded and given. Hands were laid on the bridles, the horses were led along a well defined path. As far as Gregor could make out, the villagers were Filipinos, in the usual white jacket and trousers. Nothing military about their appearance. They led the travellers in the wake of the lantern-bearers.

"Dismount, senor," Gregor was urged when the party had gone under a ruined arch into a paved courtyard. He obeyed. He was in a quadrangle bounded on three sides by high stone walls, with a round pool in the centre where a fountain had once played. The fourth side of the quadrangle consisted of a stone building, two storeys high, impossible to make out with any certainty in the flickering light of the four or five lanterns.

"What is this place?" he demanded of Mario. He had an awful feeling he was being ushered into a prison where he too could be held for ransom.

"This used to be the Hacienda San Isidro," said Mario. "I used to work here before it was burned out. Then I had to go to Manila as a refugee and take work in the cigar factory for the sake of my children. They left us nothing here, you see."

"They? Who?"

"The guerrillas."

"Then the people here are not supporters of the guerrillas?"

"Oh, no, senor," said Mario with a short laugh. "Quite the reverse. Please go in."

A fire was burning in the big room into which he was shown. "Please, senor, drink some coffee. I will unload your baggage."

"And then what?"

"Then when you are refreshed you will meet my former employer, the owner of the estate. If you are to get help in finding your friend Senor Craigallan, it is from my chief you will receive it."

"I see." So this was was the headquarters of another of the factions of which he had heard so much in Manila, in the talk among the residents of the Hotel del Oriente.

For the moment there was no way of knowing which band had their home in this ruin. Gregor sat down, pulled off his boots, stretched out his legs, wriggled his toes in appreciation. A boy about twelve years old came in with a pot of coffee and a cracked cup. He poured the coffee. "Your pleasure, senor," he said politely, and withdrew.

While Gregor was sipping the black, bitter brew,

519

Mario appeared with a pair of shoes and a dry shirt. "Here, senor. Please to change. I will bring water so you can wash."

"Thank you." It was curious. Mario seemed to be asking him to make himself presentable, as if he were going to present him to royalty. He finished the coffee, washed in the tin bowl brought to him by Mario, changed out of his damp shirt and put on the spare shoes.

"Dinner will be served presently, senor," Mario informed him.

"Dinner!"

"It will not be much, but we hope you will enjoy it."

"Thank you, Mario. I didn't expect hospitality like this." Indeed not. He had thought they might put up in the house of some villager for the night or, at worst, camp out in a cave or a quickly made shelter. To have a roof—no matter how damaged—over his head and a hot meal was more than he had dreamed of.

He was standing by the fire, staring into its flickering embers, when he heard the door open. A slight figure entered the great room. In the weak light of the one lantern he could make out the usual white jacket and trousers—a Filipino?

"Good evening, Senor McGarth. Welcome. *Mi casa e su casa*."

The first words were in English, the last sentence in Spanish. But it was the voice that shocked Gregor like a touch of ice against his cheeks.

It was light and sweet, and young. It was a girl's voice.

Mario's "chief" was a woman.

29

"MY family was a natural target," Francesca Rios y Sagasta explained to Gregor over dinner. "I look back and I see now that my father was careless of the welfare of the peons. But that was the way of Spanish estate-owners in those days. When the revolution broke out, our estate was attacked, the house was burned and wrecked, the livestock was run off, the workers either joined the revolutionary army or went into hiding."

"And your family, senorita? Did they go into hiding?"

"My parents were murdered by the *revolucionarios*. My brother was in school in Manila. I, as it happened, was in the church at confession. The priest hid me before he too was killed."

"Senorita . . . Perhaps you'd rather not talk of it," Gregor said in pity.

"No, I wish you to understand why I am helping you against the guerrillas. Since I was thirteen, I have been living in hiding with our former farm-hands. My brother was killed two years ago, fighting on the side of the Americanos against the Filipinos. I made my way back to our home intending to rebuild it, under the American government. But there has been no peace, the various bands of *ladrones*, the bandits, have come back and robbed and looted every time we repair or re-stock. This house has been attacked seven times. The first time was when my parents were killed and it was abandoned. Then the *insurrectos* took it as a headquarters. Then they moved on, after they were driven out by a band of *absolutos*. The last five attacks have been by bands of marauders looking for food and ammunition."

"But this is no kind of life for a woman, senorita," Gregor protested. "Why don't you make your way to Manila, where there is some safety?"

"In the end, that is what I must do. But first," she said, with a fierce smile, "I must kill the man who murdered my parents."

He studied her across the scratched table. The white suit she wore was threadbare and mended. Her black hair was tied back with a strip of white cotton. Her face was thin, partly due to malnutrition, but it looked as if she was the kind of woman who would always be tense and fine-boned. Her mouth was too large, wide and red-lipped. Her eyes were deep set, fringed with great dark lashes.

Judging by the history she had told him, she was about nineteen years old. She looked both younger and older. Her eyes were watchful and adult. Her figure was slender and immature. She was no beauty, yet her face was one that would linger in the memory. Her voice was one of her greatest assets, light and clear, like a Colorado bluebird.

523

"Mario Relojo's parents worked here," she went on, sipping the boiled water which was the only drink to accompany the meal. "They too were killed in the first attack. He tried to make a living in the valley but it proved impossible—no sooner did he grow a little food than a band of guerrillas would appear to take it. But after he went to Manila he kept in touch, and so when his son went missing with your friend Senor Craigallan, he appealed to me to help find him—or the body, if that is all that is left. Mario would wish to have a proper burial, you see." She was businesslike about it.

"Do you think he is dead?" Gregor asked with a sinking heart.

"No, probably not. I think it is almost certain that Senor Craigallan is alive, because Rinaldo has made two gestures calling attention to him."

"Rinaldo?"

"Rinaldo Lucena, the guerrilla leader who holds him prisoner. He was a lieutenant of Aguinaldo, the former President, and refused to surrender when Aguinaldo proclaimed a peace." She smiled thinly. "He has learned to be clever, but he has always been ruthless. It was he who killed my mother and father."

"I see." He did indeed. This was why he had been brought here, to provide a reason for Francesca Rios to get in touch with the brigand Rinaldo. He was a pawn in her game of revenge. But, if it brought him close to Cornelius and obtained his release, he didn't mind.

"What are we going to do, senorita?" he asked.

"We will let it be known that you are here, that you have brought money. You have brought money?"

"Of course."

"Rinaldo will send word to arrange a meeting. I cannot say where that will take place. He will not come here, for he knows we now defend the *hacienda* and there are armed men. He may choose a place halfway between here and his latest stronghold. He may send a guide to take us there."

"You are coming with me?"

"Certainly! You cannot travel into Rinaldo's territory with only Mario for guide. In fact, Mario wouldn't go. No, we must travel with an armed escort—"

"I don't want trouble!" Gregor cut in. "All I want is to get Cornelius back."

"You can only negotiate with Rinaldo from strength," Francesca replied with vehemence. "Believe me, I know him."

"Very well. How long is it likely to be before we move?"

"Two days, perhaps three. Oh, don't worry, Rinaldo probably knew you were on your way from the moment you left Manila and certainly since you entered the foothills. He will be expecting a message. As soon as he gets it he will send us word."

"And in the meantime?"

"You stay here, Senor Gregorio. There is

nowhere else where you would be safe. Now the gossip has started, everyone will guess you have brought money to buy back the Americano, so you are not safe outside my territory."

"Your territory?" He smiled as he said it. It seemed so paradoxical, that this slip of a girl was a leader of a resistance group.

"Don't laugh, senor. I have held this estate against attack for more than two years. I am a thorn in Rinaldo's side. A thorn doesn't have to be big to be painful."

She rose. The boy came in at a call from her. "Show Senor Gregorio to his sleeping place," she commanded. And to Gregor, "I regret we cannot offer a comfortable bed. The roof fell in after the first fire and we have not been able to repair it, so there are only corners where it can be dry and warm—except for this room. And for reasons of dignity I like to keep this room as the grand salon, the meeting place. You understand?"

"Of course. I'm grateful for your hospitality."

His blanket had been spread in a sort of shed built on to the back of the wrecked building. There were four or five other men there, playing cards on their bedrolls. They seemed to be Filipino or *mestizo*. It occurred to Gregor that Francesca must be a very strong character or a very resourceful leader to be able, as a Spaniard, to elicit loyalty from the former peons of the estate.

He slept deeply, exhausted by the journey and the events of the day.

During the two-day wait for a messenger, Francesca seemed to feel it incumbent upon her to act as hostess. She conducted him around the valley, at first on foot to see the vegetable gardens and orchards and livestock, and then on horseback to look at the views.

"It is quite safe," she explained, "so long as we stay within the area guarded by lookouts. They will warn us if any strangers are approaching and then, senor, we ride very fast for the house—understand?"

"I understand." He rode at her side for a moment in silence, then said, "How long do you intend to live like this—under siege?"

"Who knows? That is in the hands of God."

"Don't you feel you're . . . wasting your life?"

"No, Gregorio, I have my purpose. Once that is accomplished . . . well, then it is time to think of what to do with my life, if I still have it."

"Revenge? Is that what fills your world?"

"You don't understand," she replied. She rode on, erect and stiff-backed on the little mountain horse.

It occurred to Gregor that he was the last person to preach at her for her wish to be revenged. He himself had been motivated by just that spirit when he accepted his father's plans to send him to university and groom him to take over the business empire of Craigallan Agricultural Products. But somehow the idea of revenge had faded. Luisa had been the chief object of his resentment, but she was seldom in his field of vision these days. He had wanted to hurt her by supplanting Cornelius, but her lack of concern for Cornelius when he went missing was demonstration enough that she couldn't be hurt that way.

Why should Gregor want to hurt her? She was a silly, fat, middle-aged lady. And her son was now a prisoner in guerrilla hands in a mountain fastness in Luzon—if she couldn't be hurt by that, nothing could touch her.

Rinaldo's messenger came on a Sunday, when the members of Francesca's band were attending church service.

The sound of a shrill whistle broke through the ragged singing. Everyone stopped short. Heads turned. A villager ran to the door of the ruined chapel to look out. "Lopez signals a rider is coming," he said over his shoulder.

"A stranger?"

"Si, senorita."

"This is he," Francesca said to Gregor. "Come, we receive him in the salon. He probably knows the rest of the house is uninhabitable, but it will impress him nevertheless. Rinaldo has no home as good as this."

The messenger was shown in some twenty minutes later. He bowed politely. "Senorita Rios? Greeting from Rinaldo."

"Welcome to my house. Will you have coffee?"

"Nothing stronger?"

"I regret."

"Coffee, then." They made small talk until the coffee was brought. Then, as he gulped it down, he said with a nonchalant smile, "It may be that Rinaldo has something you are interested in."

"I? I am not interested in anything of Rinaldo's."

"The Americano, then," he said, turning with a bow to Gregor. "You did not come to Benguet Mountains to see the sights, I fancy, senor."

"Not quite. Tell me, what does Rinaldo have that might interest me?"

"Not what, but who, senor."

"It is a man, then?"

"Si, senor."

"But what man? That is the question. I am not interested in a stranger."

"This man is an Americano."

"So are many others who have gone missing. Tell me something of this one that will make it certain he is the one I seek."

The man hesitated, as if pondering whether to come out with a description without hedging any more. He made up his mind. "He is a deaf man, senor."

"Ah."

"This is the one you came for?"

"It could be." Gregor glanced at Francesca, asking her to take over. He didn't know what should come next.

"Rinaldo wishes to hand this Americano over to Senor Gregorio?" she inquired.

"For a little something, senorita," he said,

rubbing his thumb and forefinger together to indicate money.

"How much?"

"That remains to be decided."

Francesca shrugged. "When can we talk of this with Rinaldo?"

"Tomorrow? If you set out with me now, we can be at Rinaldo's present headquarters by tomorrow evening."

Francesca glanced at Gregor.

"One moment," he said. "I don't wish to travel without knowing what lies at the end of it. The Americano is there, with Rinaldo?"

"Si, senor."

"Also Angel, his servant?"

"Si."

"And both will be released if Rinaldo and I come to an agreement?"

"Once the money is paid—yes."

"Take him outside," Francesca said to her men. "The senor and I have to talk." When he had gone she said to Gregor, "I think it is a genuine contact. Did you notice how thin he looked? Rinaldo needs money to buy food—there is nothing now to be stolen in this area. So he wants money from you."

"How much should I take?"

"Take? Are you mad? You must leave the money here, in safekeeping! Then when you have argued with Rinaldo and made a bargain, a place must be arranged, in neutral territory, where the senor can

530

be exchanged for the gold." She added, with a little frown, "If it proves necessary to pay it."

"Francesca! I don't want any double-dealing. I want Cornelius back safe and sound, that's all."

"Of course."

He had to be content with that. But he wasn't certain she had such a simple aim.

They set out within the hour, Rinaldo's man in the lead. On either side of him rode two men from Francesca's group, behind him four more, and then Francesca and Gregor. The rearguard consisted of twelve riders. All were armed, including Francesca herself; she wore a belt with a pistol, and seemed perfectly at ease with its weight against her slender body.

As night was approaching they came to a fast-flowing stream with a village on its bank.

"We camp here overnight," said their guide.

"Very well." They all dismounted, unsaddled, let the ponies find some cogon grass shoots. The villagers came out, looking frightened, to offer the hospitality of their houses, built of pina and bamboo on stilts to keep them out of the wet.

Francesca spoke briefly to her men. From what happened he understood she was appointing guards. Food was brought, which Gregor scrupulously paid for; these people seemed so poor that to take anything from them even in the sacred name of hospitality would be unjust.

Gregor, Francesca and the guide had been invited up into the house of the *presidente*, or mayor. It was

531

a spacious cabin divided into three rooms, each of which opened off the other, but also onto a balcony which ran around the outside. Windows there were none; there were openings, fitted with woven reeds on battens, but kept closed because it was night. In the daytime the shutters would be removed to allow light in.

"How much further?" Gregor inquired of their leader.

"Not far, senor. By tomorrow evening."

"We aren't halfway yet, you mean."

"Oh, perhaps, perhaps." The man didn't wish to commit himself to any hard facts.

Giving up the attempt at conversation, Gregor lay down in the corner allotted to him. Rinaldo's man was on the opposite side of the room. Francesca had been given a share of the *presidente*'s sleeping quarters, the *presidente* himself having gone to sleep with a relative.

Quiet fell over the village. All that could be heard was the rushing of the stream outside, the call of some night animal. Gregor fell asleep, to be woken in the middle of the night by a tremendous thunderstorm. The rain beat down on the woven palm leaf room of the cabin, finding its way between the fronds here and there. The lightning could be seen even through the closed shutters.

Gregor was on his elbow, staring at the shutters, when all at once they were gone. In their place was a rectangle lighter than the room. Lightning flickered. He saw a man's head and shoulders. With a warning cry Gregor reached for the pistol under his pillow. Before his hand closed on it, the man had scrambled through and was on him. They wrestled, threshing about in the dark.

A moment later he felt a blow to the head. His brain crashed against the inside of his skull.

He was only unconscious for a few moments. When he opened his eyes he was still lying on his bed rushes but the guide sent by Rinaldo was standing over him with a rifle. The man who had climbed through from outside was lounging by the door of the room, holding up a lantern.

"What . . . what's the meaning of this?" Gregor demanded, although his tongue didn't seem to be quite in his control as yet.

"Oh, we felt it would be better if we had a little reception committee waiting for you here," said the guide.

"And the senorita?" he gasped, making as if to get up.

"We have her too," was the reply. "Now, let us just make sure you won't get away while we go back to our rest." His hands were jerked behind his back, where they were tied with strong hemp cord. "There, senor. I hope you won't be too uncomfortable. It's only until the morning."

"But I shan't be able to ride with my hands like this—"

"Oh, we haven't far to go. Not far at all. Sleep well, senor."

They went out, taking the light with them.

Gregor sat in the darkness, leaning against the bamboo wall and cursing himself.

They had ridden straight into an ambush. Now Rinaldo had another prisoner for ransom, and Francesca, his sworn enemy, at his mercy.

30

WHEN they set off at dawn the sun was first of all visible in a clear sky. But as its heat warmed the earth, vapour rose, so that they picked their way through an eddying mist along the bank of the stream. They travelled east accompanied by a band of Rinaldo's men.

Of Francesca's escort none were to be seen. Gregor asked her in a low voice, "Do you think they killed them all?"

She shook her head. "They would be boasting of it if they had. And they would be leading the spare horses." She nodded towards the rear of the column of twenty men. Only two horses were being led.

Gregor could only hope the rest had escaped. He would have liked to know if Mario had been one of those. It seemed too tragic if Mario had come with him into the mountains to try to get back his son, only to lose his own life in the process.

After six hours of slow progress over the mountain terrain and through dense forests of ebony, dao and molave trees, the man at the head of the column held up his hand. They stopped. He rode on alone. They could hear shouts of greeting, and then there was a signal to proceed.

In a few more minutes they came into a clearing where three or four huts had been constructed.

Some little groups of foresters had lived here, perhaps. They were gone now. In their place was an armed band of Filipinos in the usual semi-military garb—white trousers and jacket, belt with a gun or a dagger, bandalero, straw hat sidebrimmed and stuck about with scraps of cloth torn from uniforms of dead men.

"Well, senor, we are here," said the guide, and hauled him off his mount. He was shoved ahead into the middle hut, where at a bamboo table Rinaldo Lucena was sitting at his ease.

"Welcome," he said. "Senor McGarth, who comes with money to buy back the other Americano."

"He hasn't got the money with him," said his henchman quickly in Tagalog. "We searched his baggage and as you can see, it's not on his person."

Rinaldo frowned. "It must be at the *hacienda*, then. Too bad. But I always intended to raze that house to the ground one day, anyhow." He added to Gregor in Spanish, "How much did you leave at the home of Senorita Rios?"

"Nothing," Gregor said. "Do you think I'd be such a fool as to bring money with me into bandit territory?"

"I am not a bandit, senor. I am a fighter for Filipino freedom. Where is the money and how much?"

"There isn't any."

Rinaldo shrugged thin shoulders. "You will tell me," he said. "And if you do not, I will find it when

536

I pull the last stone from the Casa Rios." He signed to an *insurrecto*, who pushed Gregor before him out of the room and across the compound.

The door of another hut, guarded by an armed man, was pushed open. Gregor was thrust inside, his hands were untied, and the door was closed and barred.

As he stood rubbing his cramped arms to get the circulation going, his eyes became accustomed to the gloom inside the hut. A babble of American voices broke out. He saw seven men in the room. Five were in the remains of army uniforms, one was in stained and soiled white, the other was wearing a suit of grey cotton drill.

"Who are you? What're you doing here? Are you from a search party? Where are you from—Manila?"

Gregor made no response to the tirade of questions. He was staring at the man who stood silent on the far side of the hut. He was staring at Gregor in disbelief.

"Neil!" cried Gregor, holding out his hand.

As if sleepwalking, Cornelius came forward to greet him. He didn't attempt to take the hand held out to him, he was too astounded. After a long moment a slow, wry smile tilted the corners of his mouth.

"Well," he said in his flat, slow way, "I take it this means you've forgiven me for trying to kill you."

They laughed, hugged each other, slapped each

other on the back. For the moment the fact was disregarded that Gregor was a prisoner too. The other men stood round, gaping, firing questions, totally at a loss.

When at last the first elation of finding him alive had faded, Gregor set about exchanging information with Cornelius. He explained his own presence, was given a résumé of what happened at the time of capture.

"They killed the rest of us," the soldiers told him, sighing and looking away. "We just got took unawares."

"I know how you feel," Gregor said. "It happened to me last night."

"We're in a fix," said the corporal who, it proved, was the senior man now remaining. "None of us speaks the native lingo except Angel here, but he can only turn it into Spanish. We're not so hot on that neither. So mostly he tells it to Neil here, by sort of miming, and Neil gives it to us in English. But it's a slow process and we don't know what's going on. Do the authorities know we're here?"

"I'm afraid not. They've been searching, but I think they're nowhere near getting on the track. I only got this far by contacting a resistance group—whom the military would probably disapprove of, if they knew of it."

"It's a hell of a note," said the corporal. "We can only suppose Rinaldo has some hopes of getting something for us, otherwise he'd have killed us off weeks ago."

538

Gregor didn't tell them that the authorities had no intention of paying a ransom in money or in kind to get them released—even if they ever came to be aware they were still alive.

"What happens now?" Corporal Grimes asked.

Gregor shrugged. "That remains to be seen. Rinaldo intends to go after the money I left in a safe place, and if he gets it I suppose he either asks for another ransom for all of us or . . ."

"Or it's the end. He sure wanted someone to come and offer something. He sent Neil's equipment piece by piece to be shown to shopkeepers or the *presidentes* of the villages."

They looked thin and unwell. Poor food, uncertainty, heat, discomfort and sickness had taken their toll. Cornelius's face was yellowed with the after-effects of fever. He had lost a lot of weight. His one-time servant, Angel, had become scarcely more than a shadow.

"What do we do now?" Gregor asked.

"Do? We don't 'do' anything. We just exist from day to day, in a perpetual fog about what's going on, sir," the corporal replied. He stood angrily, "At last somebody's come to show they're still looking for us—and it has to be a civilian!"

"Yeah, this lousy army," growled a private.

For about an hour they talked, bringing each other up to date. Then the door was opened and Gregor was urged out at the point of a rifle. Rinaldo was waiting for him in his quarters. "Now, senor," he said, "save us all much time and pain, and tell me where the money is hidden at the hacienda."

"There is no money," Gregor said. "Didn't Senorita Rios tell you that?"

"But she is lying, and so are you. You would not have made this dangerous journey without the money to buy the freedom of the Americano."

"I have more sense than to bring money in cash with me," Gregor insisted. The gold coins were in fact at the bottom of the well of the hacienda in an oilskin pouch, waiting to be brought up by the small servant boy who had gone down in the bucket to put them there. "Tell me, Rinaldo, what has happened to Senorita Rios?"

"Nothing—as yet. But if you don't tell me what I want to know, I can't guarantee she will remain unharmed."

"You mean you would hurt a woman?" Gregor said with heavy contempt.

Rinaldo was stung, as he had intended. The thin, almost childlike face flamed with anger. "She is my enemy," he said. "She and all her family! Her accursed father worked my father to death! And now *she*—she stands in my way, keeps me from having what I need! I would be happy to kill her at once, senor!"

"But you won't, so long as you imagine she knows where the money is hidden."

"If, as you tell me, there is no money, why shouldn't I kill her at once?"

"Because that would be foolish. She has a value—"

"To whom, in God's name? She is a Spaniard." He spat at the word.

"She has a value to *me*," Gregor said, "and though I have brought no money with me, I have much money in Manila. There is a Chinese merchant there, waiting to hear from me. In return for the safe delivery of all your prisoners I will pay you well."

"Indeed?" Rinaldo had recovered himself, and now sat back in his chair, lighting a thin cigarillo. "How much?"

"What sum are you asking?"

The guerrilla leader thought about it. "A hundred American dollars for each of the American soldiers—they are of little value. Two hundred dollars for the servant Angel—the Americano seems fond of him. One thousand dollars for the American, two thousand dollars for Francesca Rios, three thousand for yourself, for you are clearly a rich man." He had been keeping a rough tally on his fingers as he spoke. "That comes to six thousand seven hundred dollars, no? Let's call it seven thousand."

"That's too much," Gregor said, automatically beginning to bargain. "I haven't got seven thousand dollars."

"Come, senor, you have much more than seven thousand dollars—"

"Not in Manila. At home in New York I have a house and a business, which would fetch more perhaps, but it would take a long time to turn them into cash."

"How much have you got in Manila?"

"Nothing. But the merchant can arrange to make funds available—up to a certain limit."

"What limit?"

"Five thousand dollars."

"You lie! You have more money than that in your American bank—"

"You don't understand banking, Rinaldo. It isn't easy to get hold of cash. I can have five thousand dollars made available within two weeks."

"Two weeks?"

"A few days to get the message to my merchant friend, who is waiting to hear from me. A week while he cables Hong Kong for funds and receives the go-ahead. A few days to bring a message back to you. Two weeks."

They argued for an hour, then Gregor was dragged back to prison. The others questioned him eagerly. "I think it's going to be all right," he said. "At least, he's going to wait until he hears whether or not I can raise money in Manila to ransom all of us."

"You sure he won't trick you and get the money without releasing us?"

"That's a chance we have to take. But he's greedy. I think he's going to fall for it."

He was proved correct. Late that evening Rinaldo sent for him to say he would agree to send a message to Manila through his contacts, but only if the price was raised to six thousand dollars. After enough protest to make it look genuine, Gregor agreed.

He had already ascertained that Rinaldo couldn't read or write, but knew better than to put anything into the message that would endanger them, because Rinaldo probably had friends in Manila who could read and who would look through the letter before it was passed on. He simply wrote to Thomas Kuan that he had found Mr. Craigallan along with the others, that he himself was now in the same hands, and that for the sum of six thousand dollars their freedom could be bought. "Choose a town or village in Nueva Viscaya Province where the money can be handed over in exchange for our persons," he ended. He hoped that sentence wouldn't be deleted before Thomas Kuan received it. He had faith in Kuan; he was shrewd and calm, would understand that care was needed to ensure their deliverance.

The messenger left at once with the letter safely stowed in a leather satchel. He rode off into another downpour, so it was to be hoped he didn't drown or get washed away before reaching Manila.

Next day Gregor asked to see Francesca. She was brought out of the third hut, where the womenfolk of the guerrillas had their quarters. She looked pale and tired, her clothes were mud-stained, but she was unhurt.

When she heard what Gregor had done, she

smiled. "It may be possible," she said. "But Rinaldo will never release me alive."

Gregor could think of nothing to say to that. The hatred he had heard in the Filipino leader's voice was proof that she was right.

Four days later, soon after daybreak, the men were allowed out as usual for fifteen minutes exercise and ablutions. They were allowed to wash but not to shave; no one had had a razor since his capture, with the result that the soldiers and Cornelius had fine beards. Gregor had five days stubble which was nearly driving him insane with its itchiness.

He had washed and was walking about the clearing under the watchful eyes of the armed guards when Angel sidled up to him. "My father is here," he said in a low voice.

Angel's Spanish wasn't good. For a moment Gregor thought the boy had chosen his words incorrectly, but when he said, "Your father?" Angel nodded.

"The man on the rock is my father."

Gregor checked his involuntary movement. He had been about to turn round for a look. He knew the place Angel meant; a guard sat there looking out beyond the trees to the upward slope of the mountains.

"Has he come alone, do you think?"

"Oh, no," Angel said, still low but with vehemence. "They tracked us here after the ambush. I think it means a rescue attack."

544

"When?"

"While it is still misty."

The mist was rising as usual from the drenched earth. The men were already being herded back towards the ladder of the prison hut.

"If only we could tell the others not to go in!" said Angel. "But it's too late."

Gregor looked about. His half-brother was being tapped on the shoulder. He had been looking at a plant growing by a stone in the compound.

Inspiration struck Gregor. He waved at Cornelius, who was straightening.

Gregor hadn't used sign language for two years, yet it sprang back to his fingers. "Laugh at what I'm saying as if it was a big joke," he signed, and laughed uproariously, clapping Angel on the shoulder.

For a moment Cornelius looked bewildered. Then he too laughed, while signing, "What's going on?"

"A rescue, we think. The man on the rock is not a guard, but Angel's father. Stop the others from going inside."

Cornelius nodded and grinned. He shouldered his way among the soldiers, grabbing at them. He began to tell them the news, and a moment of terror struck Gregor for fear his voice would come out loud and undisciplined as it sometimes did, because he himself couldn't hear it. Then remembrance came to him—the guards couldn't speak English anyway.

He saw the men check and turn towards Cornelius. One was stupid enough to wheel and stare at the sentry on the rock, but another grabbed him by the shirt and pulled him away, as if to start a fight.

The armed guards, finding their little flock had turned in the wrong direction, began barking orders in Tagalog and prodding with their rifle barrels. For a moment, in the surge of hope they felt, they almost fell upon them in advance of the attack.

But then there came an ear-piercing shriek from the sentry on the rock. Everyone wheeled towards him. He appeared to pitch out of sight behind his rock. His colleagues gave a cry of alarm and ran to see what had happened.

At that moment there was a fusillade of shots from the other side of the clearing. The guards who had run forward were mown down. The prisoners threw themselves down flat.

Chaos fell on the camp. Men came running out of the commander's hut, women came out of the women's quarters. Cries and commands echoed against the rocks of the mountain. In a moment or two Rinaldo's men were returning the fire.

The soldiers inched forward and grabbed the weapons of the fallen guards. Crouching and running, they headed for cover. Cornelius, who could hear nothing, rolled over and let himself slide into the space under a hut, so as not to be a hindrance. Gregor crawled forward on his belly to the hut where Francesca was held captive.

As he was a few yards away he saw, out of the trees on the edge of the clearing, the figure of Rinaldo running through the mist. He was drawing his pistol as he came. Gregor thought he was about to join the fight but then it seemed as if he checked, saw that it was lost, and made up his mind. He threw himself up the ladder of the women's hut.

He was going to kill Francesca.

Gregor got up and ran. He launched himself in an upward sprawl and caught Rinaldo's ankles. He heaved, the guerrilla leader lost his grip on the ladder and fell over the side. In a moment he was up, reaching for the pistol he had dropped. Gregor clawed at him. They rolled on the muddy earth and stones.

Gregor was much the bigger and stronger of the two. But Rinaldo was powered by fury. He fought like a tiger. His hand found a stone, raised it to bang it into Gregor's face.

But suddenly the stone tumbled from his hand. He collapsed on top of Gregor. With the breath knocked out of him, Gregor lay still for a moment. Then he discovered something moist and warm was trickling on to his chest. He pushed the guerrilla leader off and sat up. There was blood on his shirt. But it was Rinaldo's blood.

Standing about two feet away was Cornelius, with Rinaldo's pistol in his hand.

Later, Francesca shook Cornelius's hand. "I would have preferred to kill him myself," she admitted, "but I am content that he is dead."

"I'm a bit more than content," Gregor put in. "I'm damned glad. You saved my life, I think, Neil."

Cornelius gave him a thoughtful glance. "I nearly took it, once." he said. "Can we call it quits now?"

They saddled the horses and left the place immediately. Francesca's band had come in full strength and killed all Rinaldo's men, but the women had been allowed to run off and would unfailingly bring reinforcements. "We were in another camp about two weeks ago," Corporal Grimes said, "and there was a whole heap more of them there. We better not hang around."

It was decided to disperse. Rinaldo's henchmen would attack the *hacienda*, and in such strength that it would be impossible to hold it—the more so as they probably would hear from the women that there might be money hidden there.

"Where shall you go?" Gregor said to Francesca.

"To Manila with you, if I may. And then to Spain. I have uncles and aunts there."

Spain? thought Gregor. He couldn't believe she would ever fit into the life of a formal Spanish household after her years in hiding from the *insurrectos*. But there was time, on the way to Manila, enough to talk her into changing her mind.

31

ROB made the trip to Seattle to welcome back his two sons from their sojourn in the Philippines. There was quite a welcoming committee on the quayside when the *Prince of Peking*, a steam packet, put in after an uneventful voyage.

Ellie-Rose would have liked to be there too, but little Curtis was unwell again. She felt she ought not to leave him. She had even given up a rendezvous with Tad so as not to quit his bedside.

"You have to make a decision," Tad had said last time they were together. "We can't go on like this. You have to tell Curtis you're leaving him."

"I can't do that, Tad. Not now."

"Why not? It's time to do it."

"No, not while the baby's sick and Neil is on his way home, safe and sound."

Tad groaned inwardly. Whenever he tried to make her a decision about their future, there was always some excuse.

As she sat by the baby's cot, watching him tossing in fever, Ellie-Rose thought yet again of the choice to be made. She loved Tad, with a depth and fervour she had not thought herself capable of. But in order to be able to marry him and be with him for ever, she had to get a divorce.

A divorce would wreck Curtis's chances of political success. No divorced man could ever win a seat in the Senate, even if he were the innocent party in the divorce. She knew it was useless to suggest the idea to Curtis. He would reject it utterly.

The alternative was simply to leave him, to live with Tad without the bonds of marriage. She wanted to do this with a desperate longing. But it meant she had to leave her children behind. She couldn't take them with her to live with a man who was not their father.

Two weeks ago she might have thought she had the strength to do it. But now little Curt was sick with what might turn out to be scarlatina, and the mere thought of not being with him when he needed her tore her heart in two.

Her little girl, Gina, was less dependent on her. But Curt always wanted her when he was sick or restless. Ever since he was born, ahead of time, he had been delicate and difficult. She had a special feeling for Curt that made it impossible ever to abandon him to someone else to bring up.

Yet it was wrong to expect Tad to go on like this, snatching only moments of happiness here and there. It was selfish of her to take so much and give so little. Gertie Dorf, who knew the situation, had said to her in her blunt way: "That's a good man going to waste, Ellie-Rose. If you don't want him, get out of the way for someone who will."

If only it was as easy as that!

Christmas would soon be here. She might have seen Tad when she was in New York with her father, but the baby wouldn't be well enough to travel. In any case, her father was in Seattle greeting Cornelius and Gregor. Gregor intended to go from there to his mother's house in Colorado Springs over Christmas. Cornelius and Rob would come to Washington to be with Ellie-Rose.

But Tad, whom she longed to see, was far away.

Little Curt, in the grip of a fever nightmare, cried in fear. She picked him up, cuddled his head against her shoulder, and walked the nursery speaking soothingly to him. "There, there, my lamb, there, my angel, don't cry, don't cry. Mama's here. Mama's here."

As she murmured the words they sounded like a knell in her ears. Mama's here. It was the answer to all her self-examination. She couldn't leave Curt while he was still so small and ailing. She would have to try to explain to Tad how impossible it was. But she wouldn't see him for weeks yet—not until after the beginning of the year.

Perhaps not even then, for she ought to go to Lincoln Nebraska with Curtis once her little boy was better and could be left. The Republican big-wheels had agreed that Curtis could contest the Senate seat due to be left vacant on the retirement of Senator Wisley. Once Theodore Roosevelt stood for election in his own right and won his own way to the White House, he would feel entitled to build his own cabinet, choose his own aides. So far he had been happy to leave things as McKinley had left them, but Curtis sensed that in a new term of office, Roosevelt would dispense with him.

Now it was agreed that, when that happened, he could stand as Republican candidate in Nebraska. It meant he would have to lay the groundwork for a campaign there. He would need Ellie-Rose to help. There was no way she could invent excuses to absent herself from Lincoln when Curtis needed her there.

Not without telling him openly about Tad.

Sometimes she was tempted to do that. She felt that she so much belonged to Tad that it was wrong to let Curtis touch her. She had been reduced to all kinds of subterfuges to avoid sleeping with him. In a way little Curt's sickness gave her excuse; he so often needed her in the night. Curtis would say, "What the dickens do we pay nursemaids for?" But she would reply that the baby always settled more easily if she went to him. And it was true.

But she couldn't refuse him her help with his career. A man campaigning for office needed his wife's presence—otherwise people began to wonder what was wrong. She would have to throw herself into a round of hand-shaking, speeches, letter-signing, smiling and bowing. There was no escape from it.

She had changed greatly. When she first married Curtis she would have been delighted with the idea of helping campaign for the Senate. The idea of being a Senator's wife would have enthralled her.

Now she saw it as one more link in the fetters she had forged upon herself. Her husband, his career, the children she had borne him . . . all these dragged her back when she longed to throw herself into a new life with Tad.

Next day Curt seemed better. Ellie-Rose left the nurserymaid to sit with him and had some sleep, the first unbroken hours since he fell sick. When she woke it was to find a wire from her father: "With you by Thursday. Much to tell. Gregor has taken Miss Rios to see his mother, must mean something. Neil sends love."

Suddenly she longed for her father—his sturdy good sense, his realistic outlook. She would ask for his advice.

"Why, how pale you look!" was his greeting when he arrived. "You and your brother are a pair!"

Cornelius hugged her eagerly. "Thought I'd never see you again, Ellie," he croaked.

"It sounds as if it was a near thing," she said, and then remembering it was no use sobbing into his neck, pushed him away to say clearly, "I missed you, Neil! Don't ever go away again!"

"Not to the Philippines," he assured her. "Nobody writes to me there—except you, Ellie. Your letter was waiting for me when I got back to Manila at last. Thank you . . ."

Curtis was pleased with the attention the affair had had from the press. It all helped to keep him in the public eye—brother-in-law of the man who had got the better of Filipino bandits, and rescued five American soldiers to boot. It allowed Curtis to speak with authority on Philippine problems—not that he knew anything about them, but he had to have an opinion, and having had a brother-in-law out there made him seem well-informed.

"You reckon there are good business opportunities out there, Cornelius?" he inquired.

"Oh, not bad. But the United States isn't much interested in rice-producing. Fruits—good prospects with fruit. Canning might be big." He turned to his father. "You ought to get some research on liquid feed for crops, to be added to the irrigation system. I saw that out there. Savages, so-called. Been doing it for generations."

"Who could do the research?" Rob asked.

"Might ask George Washington Carver at his Tuskagee college. They have to study irrigation down there."

"Yeah," Rob said thoughtfully. But his mind was elsewhere. He was watching his daughter. Though she had been truly delighted to see Cornelius, there was a shadow of trouble behind those fine blue-grey eyes.

"Is the baby okay?" he asked later, in a pause in the talk.

"He's coming along well," Curtis replied. "Ellie-Rose fretted over him—the doctor thought he had something serious. But it's clearing up fine. Isn't it, honey?"

"Yes, fine," she agreed.

That evening, after dinner, Rob and Cornelius were about to leave for their hotel. Rob lingered a moment to say, "Can I come and see you tomorrow?"

"Of course."

"Alone, Ellie."

She looked startled, but recovered enough to smile and hug him goodnight for Curtis's benefit. In his ear she said, "About eleven in the morning?"

He found her in the drawing-room awaiting him. He kissed her then said without preamble, "Why are you so unhappy, my dear?"

"Does it show?"

"To me it does." He took her hand and went on: "You're not thinking of doing anything foolish, are you, Ellie?"

"I don't know what to do!" she burst out. "I feel so . . . dishonest! Like I don't belong to Curtis any more, yet I go on pretending I do!"

He pressed her hand in his own and sat studying her in silence for a moment. "Do you think you'd be happy if you left Curtis?" he asked. "Could you build a new life for yourself on the ruins of his?"

"No! Yet how can I go on with this never-ending lie?"

"This fellow Tad Kendall . . . what does he say?"

"Oh, he wants me to go to him—to live with him as his wife and never mind the gossip."

"That's out of the question, of course. If you left him, Curtis could go into the backyard and blow his brains out."

"Papa!" It was a gasp of horror.

"That hadn't occurred to you? He loves you, Ellie. He really loves you."

"But not . . . not as much as that . . ."

"What would he have to live for if you left him? His life would be in ruins, his career finished before it was properly begun, his children without a mother . . . I know he seems to have a one-track mind about politics, dear, but that's only on the surface. He couldn't survive if you broke up his marriage."

"Don't say that to me," she pleaded. "I can't bear any more guilt. I . . . I'm almost sinking under it already."

"But if it makes you so unhappy, why don't you end it?"

"I can't," she moaned, "I *can't*! I love Tad. I didn't know what it was like until I met him."

"So now you know," her father said sadly. "And much good it has done you. Believe me, Ellie-Rose, I feel for you with all my heart. Like you, I didn't find out until too late what love really meant."

"Tell me what to do," she begged. "I don't know what to do, Papa!"

He put his arm about her and held her near. He had always had a special feeling for his daughter but he had never loved her so deeply as he did at that moment. He understood about love; it had taken him a long time but Morag had shown him its importance. Compared with Ellie-Rose, he was lucky. There was no one with claims on him, so that

556

he was free to go to Morag whenever he could arrange it, without any feelings of guilt that they were lovers. He even felt he wouldn't have made a secret of it, except that he didn't want to cause any upsets with Morag's friends in Colorado. It was important that Morag should live a happy life.

And it was equally important that Ellie-Rose shouldn't do anything irrevocable. But he knew there was nothing he could say that would help her. It wasn't words that were needed, it was deeds.

Christmas came with all its warmth and charm. Cornelius kept going out to breathe the cold, frosty air—"You don't know how great it is, until you've had to make do with tropical fog," he said.

He and his father returned to New York in the first week of the New Year. After the first day or so of catching up with correspondence, Rob Craig-allan took out the telephone directory for New York City and looked up the firm of Howard, Granning, Bower and Bard. When he had asked for the number and been put through, he requested to speak to Thaddeus Kendall. "This is Robert Craig-allan," he said. "We have met."

"Oh . . . yes . . . I remember, Mr. Craigallan. You invited me to dinner."

"Yes," was the dry response. "I wonder if I did a good thing?"

"I beg your pardon?"

"I'd like to have a chat with you, if you can spare me an hour or so. Could you come to my club?"

"What is this about, Mr. Craigallan?"

557

"I'll tell you when I see you."

He could hear Tad hesitate.

"It's important," he urged.

"Very well."

Tad walked in looking perplexed and rather wary. Rob greeted him, asked what he would drink, and waved at a waiter to bring it.

"Well now, Mr. Kendall," he said, "I hear you are a very good criminal lawyer."

"Thank you. I didn't know you had an interest in criminal law?"

"I haven't. But I have a friend with a very good law practice in San Francisco, Mr. Kendall, who is looking for a clever young man like you to take in as his partner."

"What?" Tad stared at him in astonishment.

"It's a big chance," Rob went on. "San Francisco is a boom city. The climate is famous."

"I don't want to go to San Francisco," Tad said, half smiling. "I'm an East Coast man."

"I'm sure you'd find the West Coast rewarding. Life is so much simpler there."

The waiter came, placed the drinks before them. Tad sipped his bourbon and water in silence. Rob's last words hovered in the air.

"Did Ellie-Rose ask you to speak to me?" Tad asked.

"Of course not! But I was with her over Christmas, Mr. Kendall, and there is a girl being torn to pieces by what's going on in her heart."

Tad nodded. "I know that. But nothing is solved by running away."

"Don't be a fool. Most battles end when one side or the other runs away. And this battle has to end, Kendall, or it will destroy her."

"It can be ended if she'll leave her husband—"

"Why, it would just be at its beginning! Curtis won't let her go without a struggle. You haven't met him?"

"No. Thank God."

"Exactly. It's easier to wreck a man's life when you don't have to look at him while you do it."

"Mr. Craigallan," Kendall said, making as if to get up, "I don't need you to tell me it's a hell of a mess—"

"Sit down, man! I'm not telling you it's a hell of a mess. I'm showing you how to finish it."

"The job in San Francisco does exist?"

"It will, if you want it."

"I don't take bribes, Craigallan."

"Oh, hell, don't be so bloody high-minded! I don't care whether you take bribes or vote Democrat—just clear out of New York and let my girl pull her life together again. If you don't, something bad will happen. She'll blurt it all out to Curtis—God knows how she hasn't up till now."

"So much the better if she did—"

"Rubbish! You're unhappy and she's unhappy, but nothing's helped by making Curtis unhappy."

"But once he knows, we can start discussing how to make a break—"

"Curtis won't let her go. Make your mind up to that. It would end with Ellie-Rose agreeing to try again for his sake and the children's, and being forgiven—and that would be terrible. Ellie-Rose can't be forgiven. She's a girl who's always had a lot of pride. She couldn't endure being the fallen woman."

"But that's not how it's going to go—she's going to leave him—"

"No. I assure you, she won't leave him. She's got a sick little boy to consider. She can't just go. You have two choices—either you go on as you are now, and risk a breakdown for Ellie due to her sense of guilt, or you clear out. You are the one who has freedom of action, don't you understand that? You hold the key. Turn it and walk out."

Tad sat back in his leather armchair, shaking his head from side to side. "I can't, Mr. Craigallan. I love Ellie-Rose."

Rob studied him, and his face took on a sad, kind expression. "I know you do, son. I can see it. That's why I think you'll have the strength to go away."

"You over-estimate my strength of character."

"I don't think so. From all I've heard, you're a man who has a lot of heart. You fight for the underdog. Well, in this case my daughter's the underdog. Rich, married to an up-and-coming young man, two lovely children, more money than she needs . . . Yet she's suffering. You're the only one who can end that suffering."

"But it would wound her terribly if I just walked out on her!"

Rob sighed. "Don't you think I know that? Do you imagine I enjoy the idea of what she'll go through? She's my girl, Kendall. I watched her grow up. That's why I believe she's got the strength to pick herself up and go on once you've left. She'll tell herself that her little boy needs her, that Curtis and the little girl need her—she's still got something to live for after all. But if she has to end it by making a choice between you and her family, I don't think she can ever make it." He paused. "I saw a girl having a nervous breakdown a couple of years ago, Kendall. I think she was less well balanced to begin with than Ellie-Rose, but it was a terrible thing. I don't want to see my daughter in that state. And that's the way she's heading."

"You're wrong. Ellie-Rose is strong. She's strong enough to make her own decisions."

"Do you want to take that risk?"

Tad jumped to his feet. "There's no point in discussing it. I see what *you* want—you think the conventions ought to be observed, the rules obeyed—"

"Conventions?" Rob looked up at him, standing tall and indignant, and almost laughed. "Conventions? When everyone knows I've got a bastard son at my side? And a wife I keep sending off to travel abroad because I can't stand her? Come on, Kendall. Don't try to skip out of it by putting me in the wrong."

561

Tad gave a little bow. "I think we've said all we need to say to each other, Mr. Craigallan. Good evening to you."

When he had gone Rob finished his drink then called for another. Afterwards he went to join Cornelius for dinner. His son said to him, "Why do you look as if you've just run a hundred miles?"

"Old age, boy," Rob said.

He was fifty-one years old. He felt about a hundred.

Gregor was in Colorado trying to persuade Francesca Rios that snow was a good thing and that it would melt in the spring, giving place to a carpet of wild flowers.

"I don't think I can live in a country where it becomes so cold," she objected. "Surely it must be bad for one?"

"Not as bad as steamy heat. You'll like it when you get used to it—won't she, Mother?"

Morag smiled. "I don't know. I never got used to the climate on the Great Plains. It always seemed inimical to me. But I certainly think the snow here is lovely." She paused. "Besides, there are parts of the United States where it doesn't snow at all."

"How can that be?"

"It's such a big country. The weather's different from place to place." She winked at her son. "You could always spend the winter in Florida, Francesca."

"Florida. That's a long way away, isn't it?"

"Clear the other side of the country," Gregor

told her. "We'll go there and have a look, if you like."

Francesca shook her head. "It isn't proper, to travel with you without a chaperone." For a girl who had been so self-reliant, she was strangely conventional.

"True, true," said Gregor. "What we'll do, we'll get Ellie-Rose to come out and pick you up, and then we'll all go to Florida for a vacation. It would do the little boy a world of good, I expect. What do you think, Mother?"

"I don't know," Morag replied. "In his last letter, your father said Ellie-Rose was very unhappy."

"About what?" he asked, surprised. She had always struck him as being one who could soar above ordinary troubles, his half-sister.

"I don't know what about. Little Curt, perhaps. But as to going with you to Florida, that's impossible. She has to go to Nebraska with Curtis—campaigning."

"Lord, what a thought! Campaigning," he explained to Francesca, "not about war, you know—it's politics."

"But," his mother went on, tapping his knee for attention, "if you really want to go to Florida to show it to Francesca, I'll go with you if you like." The idea of travel appealed to her. She and Nellie had been stay-at-homes too long. And if it would help Gregor court this lovely girl, it would be doubly rewarding.

563

"Mrs. McGarth!" Francesca cried. "You would do this?"

"I don't see why not. It's not the ideal climate for me, but it isn't a big city or an industrial zone. And it wouldn't be for ever—you'd be heading for New York in a month or two, wouldn't you, son?"

"Have to," he agreed. "Mr. Craig is being very tolerant at the moment because of our Philippines adventures, but the time will come when he'll expect some work out of me. All the same, a month in Florida wouldn't be bad. Shall we do it, Francesca?"

"I would like it," she said, smiling her bright smile. "But I don't promise to stay in the United States because Florida is warmer than Colorado."

"Let's give it a try," he said. "Who knows? You might change your mind."

When Morag wrote to him of their plan, Rob decided to join them in Florida. He wanted to get to know Francesca who, he suspected, might become his daughter-in-law. From what he already knew of her, she was a great improvement on Stephanie Jouvard, with whom he had feared Gregor might be saddled. She was less pretty, less fashionable, but there was a strength and steadfastness he had admired.

En route south, he stopped in at Ellie-Rose's home for a day. He found her very calm and quiet.

"My love," he said to her at breakfast after Curtis had left for his office, "do you remember what we talked about last time I was here?"

564

She nodded.

"Did you come to a decision?"

She picked up the coffee pot to refill his cup. "The decision was taken out of my hands," she said. "Tad wrote that he had been offered the chance to go to England to make a study of their criminal courts. He left a week ago."

He was watching the hand that held the coffee pot. It trembled, but not too much.

"Did he say when he'll be coming back?"

"A year, he said. A whole year, Papa."

"That gives you time to think it all out," he said. "So that when you see him again—"

"He says we're not going to meet again. He says it had to end." She gave a little, weary shrug. "Why didn't he ask me what I felt?"

"Would you have told him to go?"

"Of course not!"

"That's why he didn't tell you, Ellie. Because he decided it was no good going on the way things were."

"It's as if he didn't care!" she cried. "As if he felt it had become one great big bore!"

He was about to say, "You're wrong." But perhaps it was better not to contradict. If she could feel anger and resentment, it might drive out the hurt.

The door opened and the nursemaid ushered in the four-year-old Gina, all done up in velour bonnet and buttoned boots for a walk.

"Mama! Mama! Curt took my china doll and

broke it! Mama, she's got a crack cross her nose!"

"Oh dear," Ellie-Rose said, "what a tragedy!" She made space on her lap as the little girl clambered up. "We'll get it mended, darling."

"Can things that have broke badly be mended?" Gina inquired looking up at her with anxiety.

"I think so, Gina," Ellie-Rose said. "I think so." Over her daughter's bonneted head her eyes met her father's. Tears glinted for a moment, but were blinked away. Rob watched her with tenderness. Things that have been badly broken can be mended. Even hearts. Yes, even hearts.

THE END

This book is published under the
auspices of the
ULVERSCROFT FOUNDATION,
a registered charity, whose primary object is to
assist those who experience difficulty in reading
print of normal size.

In response to approaches from the medical world,
the Foundation is also helping to purchase the
latest, most sophisticated medical equipment
desperately needed by major eye hospitals for the
diagnosis and treatment of eye diseases.

If you would like to know more about the
ULVERSCROFT FOUNDATION,
and how you can help to further its work,
please write for details to:

THE ULVERSCROFT FOUNDATION
The Green, Bradgate Road
Anstey
Leicestershire
England

GUIDE
TO THE COLOUR CODING
OF
ULVERSCROFT BOOKS

Many of our readers have written to us expressing their appreciation for the way in which our colour coding has assisted them in selecting the Ulverscroft books of their choice. To remind everyone of our colour coding— this is as follows:

BLACK COVERS
Mysteries

★

BLUE COVERS
Romances

★

RED COVERS
Adventure Suspense and General Fiction

★

ORANGE COVERS
Westerns

★

GREEN COVERS
Non-Fiction

FICTION TITLES
in the
Ulverscroft Large Print Series

We hope this Large Print edition gives you the pleasure and enjoyment we ourselves experienced in its publication.

There are now more than 1,600 titles available in this ULVERSCROFT Large Print Series. Ask to see a Selection at your nearest library.

The Publisher will be delighted to send you, free of charge, upon request a complete and up-to-date list of all titles available.

Ulverscroft Large Print Books Ltd.
The Green, Bradgate Road
Anstey
Leicestershire
England

325 LPM.

9774